Blessed and Cursed Alike

Kiarna Boyd

© 2023 Blessed and Cursed Alike Tenth Anniversary Edition
(Original edition 2013)
By Kiarna Boyd
Cover design by Chris Smith.
Additional graphics by James Rogers.

ISBN: 978-1-958669-99-0

Published by Piscataqua Press, Portsmouth, NH

Author's Note for the 2023 edition:
The 2023 anniversary publication provided an opportunity to fix typos in the original. While working to update the manuscript, I decided to make minor changes to the text to align it with the world the story is set in. No major retcons occurred during the update.

For David, who listened to the first one thousand and one nights.

Book 1

The Luck Thieves

THE DISPATCHER'S BARITONE VOICE cut over the motorcycle courier's headset. "90-32, pickup at 28 Duncan Ave, Suite 6, second floor. Going to 207 Victory Square."

"On it." With a sharp nod, the courier snapped her helmet's faceplate fully down before accelerating. She narrowed her eyes at a van changing into the lane in front of her motorcycle.

"Use Fisher Tunnel to Parker to avoid the parade."

"I can take the Straight."

"Zade, use Fisher Tunnel to Parker. S&P have the Straight closed for the parade."

Dipping the bars low, the woman swung around the corner of Green and State, and zipped into the narrow opening behind a bus to take a fast right onto Duncan.

The bike's back tire swept to a stop in a gutter full of autumn leaves and trash as the courier clicked the kickstand down, rocked the motorcycle, angled the front tire, and dismounted. She cracked her faceplate an inch and ran up the wide brick steps to 28 Duncan.

Inside the lobby, she waited for the employees to empty out of the arriving elevator before stepping in and pressing the button for the second floor.

Unlinking the waist strap on her messenger bag, the courier swung the bag around her hip and ripped the clasps apart. She pulled out the recording device and squeezed through the doors as they opened to the second floor.

"Pickup for 207 Victory Square."

The receptionist scowled at the dirty wet bootprints the courier left on the rug as he placed his thumb on the silver plate of her device. He shoved a shiny orange packet across to her, then picked up the phone. The sound of his conversation followed her as she returned to the elevator. Zade secured her bag back into place as the doors closed.

On the ground floor, she jogged through the lobby and pounded down the steps to her motorcycle. She toggled the start switch and hit the ignition as she mounted and clicked up the kickstand. The front tire bit through the muck to grip the pavement as the machine lunged forward.

"Dis, I'm on it to 207 Victory Square." The courier checked her mirror as she changed lanes.

"Confirmed."

A sedan cut her off. She swayed to avoid colliding and rolled open the throttle, the acceleration pulling her machine upright. Her boot shot out as she passed, slamming into the car and leaving a dent. The squeal of tires and the bleat of a car horn rang out behind her.

As the traffic light changed from green to yellow at the intersection of Callaen and Jasper, the courier careened into an opening between a taxi and a delivery truck.

The dispatcher's voice cut in over the courier's headset. "You're not taking the tunnel."

"No, I'm taking the Straight."

"It's closed to traffic."

"I heard you the first time."

She braked hard to avoid a woman and three children who walked into the intersection against the signal. She fishtailed, her bootheel scraping the road surface on Ruby Avenue. One of the children screamed as the motorcycle shot off, sending a cascade of water toward the family.

As she turned onto the Straight, she dodged taxis and wove through openings between vehicles. A truck's horn blared as she passed on the centerline and the passengers of an inbound bus pointed as she skated alongside. Five car lengths ahead, the lane of traffic turned to follow the detour indicated by a blinking sign.

The blue and red lights of two S&P cruisers strobed at the road junction. From Market Square, the front of the Victory Parade curved around the corner, pipes wailing over the drums and spectators flooding around the parked cruisers.

Cutting behind the detour sign, she rode up onto the sidewalk around the cruisers. Dancers spilled onto the Straight, their turquoise silk flags dipping and whirling, blocking her way.

The courier made a hard right onto River Avenue and parked in a tow zone in front of the Market Underground Station. She removed her helmet. With an irritated gesture, the courier scrubbed her gloved fingers into her faded blue hair and surveyed the bushes on the far side of the sidewalk. "Shake it to make it!" Addressing the three shadows uncurling from the sides of the walkway, she waved two fingers at her eyes and then at her motorcycle. "Keep S&P off it for twenty. No stealing."

Slamming her helmet onto the bars, she sprinted for the station, her headset crackling as she jumped down the stairs.

"90-32, status."

"On it, dispatch."

"Your helmet cam is off."

"Taking the U."

"You're not going to make delivery in time."

"Have a little faith, dispatch."

3

She sprinted across the mustard-colored platform of Market Station as a train was beginning to close its doors. An older man with a newspaper tucked under his arm held open the door for the courier as she squeezed through the gap. She grinned at him as the subway car started down the tracks.

❧ ❦ ⑨ ⓿ ❧

On the top floor of the Pierce Tower, a gray-eyed woman frowned out her office window at the parade spectators filling Victory Square below. Her hand clenched around the newspaper she held tightly rolled in her left hand, the skin tightening over the knuckles. "You promised if we had to, we would do this together. You should be here with me to do this, Ty."

She dropped the newspaper next to an antique sea chest and reached for a sheet of paper emblazoned with the Pierce family crest. The metallic trill of the phone caused her to look up sharply.

Carrying it over to the window, she lifted the handset from the cradle. "I gave you clear instructions not to disturb me, Nash." Her brow furrowed as she listened to the caller's response. "Another one? Where did S&P discover the body?" She turned, looking out the window to gaze down at the white marble Seat of Victory in the square. Her expression hardened again as she watched boisterous performers scale the monument. "I see. No, you were correct to inform me immediately. Send for my car, I will be done here shortly."

Her eyes were unfocused as she lowered the receiver away from her ear. "It must be done. Even now, they are moving against us." A dial tone emanated from the neglected phone as she turned and stared at the red plastic packet on her desk.

□ ♍ ♏ ♋ ■

Zade bounded out of the train at Victory Station and pushed her way through the slow-moving crowd up the escalators and through the station's main exit into Victory Square. She slipped in front of a line of costumed spectators and vaulted over a barrier. Using her elbows, she pressed through a crowd of people in animal masks, making her way toward the building rising directly behind the center of the square. The knot of bodies became denser, forcing Zade to move toward the base of the steps leading up to the Seat of Victory.

The troupe on the monument gave a howling cheer as Zade slammed through the crowd and raced up the steps onto the marble seat. A sword flashed from below and she stumbled away, rolling off the seat onto her knees. A young man dressed as a colonial sailor seized her arm and she shoved him in the chest, tearing free of his grip.

She fought the rest of the way through the crowd, then fell against the barrier on the other side of the square. Looking up at the Pierce Tower, she ran toward the entrance. The building's security guard held the glass door open as she sprinted for the reception desk in the center of the lobby.

The receptionist gave the courier a look of annoyance. "We expected this to arrive ten minutes ago."

"You may have noticed, there's a parade outside."

"It's still late." The woman put her thumb on the device the courier held out.

The courier put away the recorder and stalked across the lobby.

The security guard opened the door for her. "It was a good try coming through that crowd."

"Thanks."

The man's gaze followed her down the steps.

"90-32, you're done for the night." The radio whispered in her ear. "Zade, go around to Trellis."

The courier stopped and stared at the dancing crowd in the square. "Why?"

"30-84 is going to pick you up."

"I can make it back to the U, Dis."

5

"Otter is already waiting for you on Trellis."

"Thanks." Zade went around the corner of the building.

She found Otter waiting at the curb, astride his motorcycle. He pushed his faceplate up and winked at her from behind his glasses. "Where did you leave your bike?"

"At Market U."

"Where's your helmet?"

"With my bike."

"Mother. I'm not riding you around the city without a helmet."

"S&P's not going to stop you, they're all babysitting the parade. I'll put my goggles on."

"Why the hell did you leave your bike there? It's probably been towed or stolen by now."

"I needed to use the train to make delivery."

"That's the craziest thing I've ever heard!" Otter laughed. Zade punched him in the arm and got up behind him. He slapped his faceplate down and released the clutch. Zade gripped the motorcycle under her thighs as they took off.

At the entrance to Market Station, he parked next to Zade's motorcycle and raised an eyebrow at the child hunched on the back of it. The grimy pre-adolescent wore garbage bags over her clothes and stared balefully at the couriers. Two other children watched from the bushes as Zade dismounted.

She grabbed a handful of candy from her messenger bag, tossed it toward them, and pulled out a folded bill from the hip pocket of her rain trousers. The child on the back of her bike kept her eyes on the money while the other two scrambled to collect the sweets.

Zade looked down at her bars. "Where's my helmet?"

"Weren't no helmet. Kept the bike safe, like you said." The girl jumped onto the sidewalk and glared at her.

"Liar. There was when you perched. You lost it, you lost the pay."

The child shook her head, sending her matted braids bouncing. She squinted at her waiting comrades on the railing, where they sat gleefully eating bars of chocolate. There was a brief rummaging under their adult-sized trench coats and the missing item was thrown back to the girl. A fast exchange reversed ownership of the money and the helmet, and all three children sprinted into the Station, laughing.

"You're lucky the rats didn't strip the bike." Otter nodded at the station entrance.

"I know where they sleep." Zade checked the inside of her helmet before putting it on. "Are you done working now?"

"Hell yes. I've been running since eight."

"Where do you feel like going?"

"You buying the first round?"

"Yeah."

"Crossing, then." Otter walked his bike onto the road and glided into an opening between a truck and a taxi.

Zade snapped her faceplate down and slipped into the stream of traffic behind the taxi. "Dis, are you free to come down and have a drink with us?"

"Not tonight."

"You always say that." She caught up with Otter and fell into a staggered position behind his motorcycle.

"I have an errand to run and it's going to start raining again."

Zade glanced at her left-hand mirror. "It's always raining."

"It didn't rain for five days last month."

"You're not made out of sugar. You won't melt."

"I'm not walking home in the rain or sleeping here if I miss the last train."

Zade rode down the centerline as a car merged onto the Straight from High Street Extension. "I'm going to stop asking you."

"That would probably be for the best."

Bright white and red lights flashed as an ambulance came silently abreast. Zade watched the street lights skim the ambulance's windshield.

"I'm out Monday and Tuesday next week."

"So, you will be taking four days off in a row instead of your usual three this month."

"Is that a problem?"

"No problem, 90-32."

Zade followed Otter into the Fashion District, cruising down the neon downtown strip on the centerline. Larger vehicles slowed to a crawl as drivers searched for parking and taxis trawled for fares.

The motorcyclists pulled into a fenced-in parking lot at the end of a long line of motorcycles. Otter took off his helmet and finger-combed his short black hair back into place. Zade shoved her riding gloves into her helmet and stripped off her rain gear, revealing her company number on the back of her jacket. She wadded up her gear and shoved it into the hardcase on the back of her bike.

Otter handed Zade a disposable towel packet and checked his face in his side mirror. "I don't know about you, but I feel like I've ridden through every puddle in the city today." Using a corner of the wet cloth, he removed a patch of dirt under his eye.

"Huffing truck exhaust all day will do that." Zade rubbed her towel around her neck and face before using it to clean both hands. Tossing the used towel into the trash, she grabbed him by the arm and headed for the club's back entrance. "Come on, let's go chase some skirts."

❧◌❂⑨❶◌❧

In the crammed dispatcher's booth above the garage of Uptown Deliveries, Dis lifted his heavy-framed glasses and pinched the bridge of his nose, then rubbed the raised white scar on the side of his face. Settling his glasses back into place, he scanned the green text on the job-queue monitor with his good right eye, his left hidden behind a blacked-out lens.

The other screen in front of him automatically cycled through a series of monochromatic images from the couriers' helmet feeds. A third monitor stacked above scrolled the amber text of a traffic incident log.

The dispatcher watched the minute hand tick around the cheerful moon of the mantle clock taped to a monitor. He swiveled his chair as footsteps rang on the steel stairs leading up to the booth.

A tall woman opened the door, panting as she hung onto the knob. Her voice trembled as she caught her breath. "Sorry ... parade ... traffic."

"Late is late." Dis reached for his cane. The side of his leg brace rasped against a metal drawer as he stood up. He hefted his messenger bag over his shoulder. "The board's up to date. 11-44 and 11-20 are still running deliveries, but they should be done any second now."

"Okay. See you at seven?" The night dispatcher hung her jacket on the back of the door and wiped the sweat off her cheek.

"Please have the forecast ready for me on time." Dis walked past her, stepping onto the stairs.

"Right. Sorry about being ..." She dropped her gaze as she walked over to the desk and picked up the headset.

"Stay out of the cabinets, Frankie."

Frankie's eyes darted from the black lens in his glasses to focus on the clear one. "See you tomorrow."

On the sidewalk in front of the motorcycle depot, two older men carrying umbrellas and briefcases averted their eyes from the dispatcher's leg brace. Dis paused and leaned against the side of the open garage bay, waiting for them to pass. Heading in the direction of Claremont Station, he settled the strap of his messenger bag over his chest.

Inside the Underground station entrance, Dis rode the escalator down to the turnstiles, crossing the platform to the outbound side. Fetid air boomed from the tunnels, inverting the handbills stapled to the pillars. A train squealed into the station and disgorged people in colonial-era costumes. The revelers pushed by the commuters on the platform and swarmed up the stairs.

9

Dis got on the train and took one of the seats marked with a handicapped sign. He studied the graffiti drawn on the window across the aisle. An elderly woman sitting under it watched him. He gave her a polite smile as their eyes met. Flustered, she looked away. He removed a journal from his bag and sketched a copy of the symbol.

At Hospital Station, he glanced up as a fresh wave of commuters boarded the train. When a woman with a toddler and infant clung to the overhead strap, Dis rose and offered her his seat. She accepted with a sigh of relief and started to sing a lullaby to her restless children. Dis exited the train at Point Station, waving at the Underground employee by the turnstiles. The escalator was out of order. Dis climbed the stairs to ground level, pausing every few steps with his hand on the railing. He removed a wide-brimmed black hat and telescoping cane from his messenger bag and stepped out into a downpour, navigating around scraps of litter in the feral streams.

Against the exterior wall of the station, a makeshift shrine was set up in a wooden crate. Dis lifted the plastic draped over it to examine the photographs and newspaper obituaries taped to the wall. He bent to place a candy bar between glass pillar candles and a rain-soaked rag doll. He ran a finger over the brown yarn of the doll's hair. "Travel well, little one."

Three blocks down Center Street, under the faded awning of Myln's Market, he shook the rain off his hat. A bell sounded as he entered the overcrowded storefront and picked up a tattered shopping basket. He browsed the collection of leafy greens and wizened oranges, then examined a box of sugar-powdered donuts. At the counter, he unloaded the contents of his basket and added a handful of candy from a side display.

"You forgot your milk?" The grocer tapped prices into the register.

Dis slipped two bills across the counter. "I have to finish what I bought yesterday."

"Your mother always bought it fresh." With a pained expression, the balding man packed the purchases into a brown paper sack.

"Tomorrow I'll buy more milk."

"So you say."

Dis folded the top of the sack down. The corners of his mouth twitched as he turned to leave. "Goodnight."

"Goodnight, cousin."

Dis stepped out of the market. A streetlight sputtered and went dark with an audible pop. An argument between a mother and a young child broke out in an apartment on the second story. Dis crossed the street and headed down the block. Pausing, he tucked a folded bill into the outstretched tin can of a person crouched in a doorway.

At the last brownstone on the street, Dis balanced his sack on an iron railing to fish out his keys. Pushing open the front door, he slipped a hand in along the wall and clicked on the stained-glass hallway light. A cat harnessed into a cart to support her truncated rear legs wheeled toward him, howling.

"I'm sorry. I didn't intend to be late."

The yowling changed to rough-throated purrs as Dis picked up the cat. He placed his cane in an antique wooden holder containing several other walking sticks and limped down the hallway. He wrinkled his nose as the cat lovingly bashed the brown fur of her mask into his chin. "Time to brush your teeth again, Stinky."

He set her down on the kitchen floor, and she raced for her food dish, her wheels squeaking on the linoleum.

The cat trilled and yelled up at him as he opened a can of food. Once she was happily chomping and purring, he set his gear onto the back of a sun-faded kitchen chair and took a can of beer out of the refrigerator. Supporting himself on the back of the chair and the walls, he made his way into the living room.

Dis eased himself into a wing-backed armchair. Sitting in the dark, he stared at the vintage acoustic guitar hanging above the mantel. Stinky wheeled in and yowled at his feet. He lifted her up onto the velvet couch cushion and smiled as she curled up to groom her chest. Reaching over to a corner table between the chair and the couch, he turned on the lamp and picked up a book.

▽↗◢

When the clock on the mantel announced midnight, he closed the book and set it back on the table. He lifted the sleeping cat off the couch, turned off the light, and slowly walked up the stairs to the second-floor bedroom. Stinky licked his fingers as he unfastened the straps on her harness. She fell back asleep as soon as he settled her on the second pillow on his bed.

Leaving the medicine cabinet door open, Dis washed his face in the bathroom across the hall. His jaw muscles flexed as he picked up his glasses and began rinsing the two different lenses. Putting the frames back on, he closed the cabinet and used the mirror to inspect his stubble.

Returning to the bedroom, he sat on the side of the bed to remove his leg brace. He took off his boots, stripped down to his boxers, and ran his hands along the thick keloid scars segmenting the skin of his left thigh. After placing his discarded clothing in a neat stack by his boots, he climbed into bed next to the snoring cat and set his glasses on the nightstand. Massaging the bridge of his nose, Dis stared at the ceiling as the house's old wood creaked over the faint sound of lapping waves.

▽↗◢

The cat opened an eye and trilled as her owner swung his legs out from under the covers.

"Go back to sleep."

Dis pulled on a robe and went downstairs, holding onto the banister. Maneuvering through the dark kitchen, he snapped open the deadbolt on the back door and opened it, letting the cool autumn air sweep through the house.

He gripped the back of the cast iron patio furniture as he threaded his way to the stone path leading into the garden and down to the wooden boat dock. The mist reflected the orange glare of the skyline and muffled the noise of street traffic as the Mam River hidden underneath carried the city's trash out to sea.

Reaching the end of the dock, Dis hung his robe on a post and slipped off his boxers. With a fluid motion, he dropped his head and rolled forward, slipping into the water. He surfaced a few minutes later in the middle of the river, pushed the hair out of his eyes, and turned to float on his back, looking up at the sky.

CHEERY MUSIC FROM A RADIO alarm clock filled Otter's bedroom. A sunbeam coming through the single window inched across an assortment of feathers, pebbles, glass bottles, and cheap gaudy toys neatly arranged on long shelves on the wall next to his bed.

He slapped at the clock and retreated under the covers. After a few moments, the radio snapped back on, filling the bedroom with news of the day. The courier reached out and turned it off, then picked up a carved stone lying next to his glasses on the nightstand. Putting the nub of the lozenge-shaped stone in the center of his left palm, Otter clenched the carving in his fist for a moment. Then, using his thumb and index finger, he balanced the end of the stone on the surface of the nightstand, twisted his fingers, and released it. He yawned and lay in bed, watching it spin.

□ ♍ ♏ ♋ ■

In a nameless alley off Callean Avenue, a child dropped into a pile of garbage bags from the fire escape above. A restaurant vent belched out bacon-scented vapor and the child's stomach rumbled in response. She peeked out of the alleyway, hiding behind a dumpster, and watched as a taxi pulled up to the restaurant and a man in a suit got out. She stared at his wallet as he paid the fare. "Ribbons and curls, everything for the girls." The man stiffened and glanced at the opening of the alley, and she shrank back against the dumpster.

He turned and quickly walked toward the restaurant's entrance. A fifty fell out of his coat pocket and floated to the ground. The girl dashed out of her hiding spot to snag it and kept running without missing a step.

At the corner of Exchange Street, she hopped into a basement entranceway. She smoothed the bill and squealed with delight, burying her mouth into the crook of her elbow. "Wait until Kady sees this."

Stashing the money in the layers of her clothes, she ran down the street. Turning down Line Alley, she scaled a dumpster, jumped up onto the bottom rung of a fire escape, climbed to the rooftop, and continued to run. She hauled her slight weight up the nub of a gargoyle's face and pivoted her legs onto the next window. Running over the roof of Marion's Flowers, she eyed the next building and sprang across the gap.

The sun broke through the clouds, glinting off of a patch of repaired copper flashing, momentarily blinding the girl. She flinched mid-jump, her fingertips falling short of the gutter. Flailing wildly, she fell four stories and struck the top of a metal dumpster, bounced off, and hit the bottom of the alley, dashing her skull against the pavement. As a bloody halo formed around her head, the girl's eyes reflected the widening patch of blue sky above.

□ ♍ ♏ ♋ ■

In Pierce Park, a jogger checked his watch, running along a gravel path to the central fountain. He circled the marble seashells, counting his circuits in a wheezing half-muttered breath. He returned the way he came, bouncing on his toes and puffing as a man with a stroller passed in the other direction.

On the steps of his townhouse on Exchange Street, he stopped to inspect the urns of ornamental flowers flanking his front door. Inside, he marched to the bathroom to undress, folding his sweat-stained jogging suit neatly before depositing it into the hamper. He flipped a non-slip mat onto the shower floor and squared it to the drain.

The man scrubbed at his armpits, alternating a hand on the slate surface of the stall. He portioned out a dollop of shampoo and scrubbed his few remaining hairs. He rinsed his entire body, turned off the faucet, and reached for a towel. The shower curtain came down with a tear as the man, with a look of agonized surprise, collapsed over the lip of the stall. His pulse stopped.

□ ♍ ♏ ♋ ■

The carving on Otter's bedside table wobbled and toppled over, landing with the nub pointing away from him. He groaned, flipping back the covers. "But I don't want to go to work."

Walking into the kitchen, he glowered at the sink overflowing with dishes. He hoisted a precarious assortment out and carried it down the apartment's narrow hallway to his roommate's bedroom.

"I warned you." Otter kicked open the door, pulled back the covers on the empty bed, dropped the dishes, yanked the covers back into place, and headed to the bathroom.

▽ ↗ ◢

Frowning, Otter peeled a traffic violation sticker off the cargo box mounted on the back of his motorcycle. He hit the bike's ignition button and opened the choke, leaning down to listen to the resulting rumble. A pack of joggers gave him dirty looks as he revved the throttle, closed the choke, and adjusted the idle. Yawning inside his helmet, he mounted his bike and joined the flow of traffic

16

on Grant Street. Turning onto the Southern Promenade, he smiled as the sparkling water of the harbor appeared on his right.

At the end of the Promenade, he took a left onto Watt Street. A variety of motorcycles formed a long line at the western end of a brick walkway lined with shops and restaurants. At the end of the outdoor mall, shoppers and tourists filtered around recessed circular stone benches, gawking at the motorcycle couriers occupying the seats. Otter walked his bike backward into the row and glanced at the other couriers lounging around the fountain in the center of the benches. The courier yawned, cracked open his faceplate, and turned on the helmet mike. "Dispatch, 30-84 at the Pit."

"Nothing yet, 30-84."

Otter approached a group of riders gathered around a pristine sport bike. He waved to a younger man slouched in a new mustard and navy livery jacket near the motorcycle. "This Tiver yours? That's a sweet machine."

Moving curly black hair out of his eyes, the younger man stood up from the granite hitching post he was leaning on.

A courier in the same livery appeared with a tray of coffee and held up a hand to greet Otter. "That's Avery, I'm teaching him the routes." With a roguish grin, the courier gave her charge a cup of coffee.

"You'll be fine if Boon's showing you the roads." Otter nodded as Boon held out the tray to him.

A courier in a black leather jacket snagged a cup from Boon's tray. "Avery?" She squinted at him, wrinkling the black and pink cosmetics around her eyes. "What, do you keep fucking birds?"

"You're thinking of an aviary." Boon bounced her hip against the other woman's.

She snorted. "Wouldn't surprise me if the rich boy had a thing for shitbirds. Snotball."

Otter gestured at Avery's jacket and walked around the man's motorcycle. "Lucky number you're sporting."

17

"It's okay." Avery took a step closer to his machine, watching the other man inspect the engine.

"I'm Otter, the trashmouth is Kitty, and those rock stars over there …" Otter waved a hand indicating the other men looking at Avery's motorcycle. "The beefy one is Quiet and the pretty fucker is Mo, they're in Black Dust. You in a band too?"

"No." Avery frowned as Kitty tried his bike's clutch lever.

"Neither am I, but everything's still all about bikes, bands, and brethren." Otter grinned up from the side of the lemon-yellow motorcycle as more couriers converged on the machine. "I didn't know YC was springing for Tivers. Maybe I should jump ship."

The young man's gaze dropped to the pavement. "It's mine."

Kitty sat on the hitching post, twirling her pink and black hair with her fingers. "If this assmonkey doesn't dump by end of the week, I'll buy everyone a round."

"Shut your fucking noise hole." Otter scowled at her, rubbing the silver amulet hanging on his jacket's zipper pull.

She gave him a filthy look and stalked down into the benches, away from the bikes.

Boon watched her walk away. "She's got dumping on the brain because her two-year anniversary is coming up." She nudged Otter with her boot. "You've got the record at what, ten years, old timer?"

Rising to his feet, Otter scrunched up his face and mimicked an old man's voice. "Back in the day, we had to share one channel to only one dispatcher and had to eat our horses in the winter."

Dis's amused voice cut over Otter's radio. "30-84, pickup 3011 Hoyt Street, Suite 6."

Otter gave Avery a thumbs up as he ran to his bike. "Keep the rubber side down and the shiny side up."

"I know." Avery looked away.

Otter started his engine and kicked his bike into gear. "Dispatch, 30-84 on it."

≈⊱⋐⑨❶⋑≈

Daylight poured through the skylights set above the atrium on the top floor of the Pierce Tower. Mercy Pierce walked out of the corridor and along the inner wall. Her gaze swept over the panoramic view of the city beyond the exhibit cases.

Her high-heeled shoes clicked across the black marble. Navigating through the private museum occupying the majority of the Pierce Tower's top floor, she focused straight ahead. She passed a small fountain as it quietly cycled a silver curtain of water into a rectangular reflecting pool.

A fierce look of concentration settled onto her features as she walked between a case containing antique glass floats and another displaying animal skeletons. Slipping her right hand into the inner pocket of her tailored jacket, she removed a brass key. Air whispered around the edges of the glass as she unlocked and opened a case.

Leaving the key in the door, she put on white cotton gloves and reached in, sliding her hands under an animal skin displayed on the glass shelf. Carefully, she lifted the length of sleek fur out of the case. Its coloration rippled, shifting from black to gold.

Furrowing her brow, the woman held the preserved sealskin away from her body. She carried it slowly through the circle of display cases to the corridor beyond the elevator. As she walked, the black ends of the skin hung down, blending into the shadow cast on the wall behind her.

≈⊱⋐⑨❶⋑≈

When Otter returned to the Pit, he exaggerated falling into Quiet's outstretched arms. Laughing, the short, stocky man shook his head and pushed the other courier back onto his feet.

"If Dis makes me run another package right now, I'll burst." Otter hung his helmet off the side of his motorcycle and started trotting away.

Quiet peeled his bag's fasteners apart and took out a book. "Dispatch, this is 11-46, covering for 30-84. Otter's off to piss and too scared of you to say so himself." He flipped to a dog-eared page.

"You're a gem." Otter crossed to the other side of the mall and stuck his head into the Blue Lotus. He called out to a curvaceous woman with shoulder-length blonde hair as she refilled a jar of herbs in the back. "You open yet, Mala?"

Mala's bracelets rang as she waved him into the store. "For you, always." She smiled at him and resumed unwrapping votive candleholders.

"Just need to use the …" Otter headed toward the bathroom.

When Otter returned, he inspected the shelves of spiritual supplies and merchandise with his hands clasped behind his back. Passing by a long shelf of glass jars, he knelt down in front of one of the jewelry display cases. "Is this a new shipment?"

"Last week. Want me to take them out for you?" The shopkeeper set a candleholder aside and came over to assist him.

Otter averted his eyes from Mala's ample cleavage as she bent down to retrieve the velvet-lined jewelry tray.

"These are amulets and talismans from Grava."

Otter pointed at an enameled silver medallion. "What's this one?"

"That would be Saint Yolutz, I believe. Protector of sex workers." Mala winked playfully.

He lifted up his glasses to examine the piece. "You're making that up."

"Never. Did you see the reproductions from the Ornish Museum? Jeniel got them in last week." Mala sifted through the contents of the tray and presented

20

him with a segmented silver fish pendant.

Otter jiggled the piece and grinned, watching each scaled section wriggle freely. The faceted glass eyes of the fish sparkled as it moved.

Mala wiggled another one. "The Ornish used them for luck and fertility."

"Is that legit, or more horseshit you made up?"

"Cross my heart, you can go up to the museum and read about them in the exhibit hall on Ornish customs. Or you can ask your dispatcher. Jeniel says he's the local expert."

Otter wriggled the fish again. "How much?"

"For you, ten."

"If I didn't know better, I'd say you were trying to seduce me with that price."

The blonde's smile widened. "If you were a certain lucky female courier, it would be free."

Otter dug out his wallet. "You really should just ask her out. She likes you."

"Zade likes everyone."

"I'm fairly certain she doesn't like Mat."

"I feel bad for him. He's got the worst luck." Mala shook her head as she rang up his purchase.

Otter put the pendant into his pocket. "Seems like it. His bike got stolen again."

From a door set behind the counter, a woman carrying an armload of embroidered silks entered the shop. Her brown hair hung loose, cascading down her back to her waist. "Good morning." She navigated around the display tables toward the front window. Sequins and tiny mirrors glinted from the fabric in her arms as she stepped up into the sunlit alcove.

Otter slipped his wallet back into his pocket and started toward the display window. "Good Morning, Jeniel. Can I help you carry anything?"

"I'm all set, thank you." The shop owner began to take down the fringed drapes hanging in the display window. A shaft of sunlight glittered on the gold-flecked rouge she wore. "Did you need help with anything specific today?"

"I'm good. Mala helped me out."

Pausing in her work, Jeniel looked up. "Which piece?"

Mala came around to assist her employer. "A silver luck fish."

"That's specifically for luck in love." Jeniel handed a corner of a gauzy cloth to Mala and then looked back at her customer. "We're going to start offering classes on protection spells next week. We finally found time now that the store's been open for a few months."

Otter scrunched up his nose. "I'm not into the wand-waving or chanting bits. Sorry, ladies, I have to get back before my dispatcher sends out a search crew."

"Be safe out there." Mala smiled as she removed an inscribed cedar box from the display.

Otter latched the door and walked back toward the Pit. Three couriers in blue and yellow sat lounging on granite benches facing the fountain, while a dozen more in black stood drinking coffee around the parked motorcycles. Slapping one of the riders on the arm, Otter went around to the side of his bike and unlocked the seat.

Moving aside a crow's feather, Otter shuffled a miniature statue of the Holy Mother around and placed the fish pendant between a frog squeeze toy and a vial of flowers preserved in alcohol.

 ⁓⳨⑨❶⳩

A whirlwind scattered old newspapers down Pioneer Street, carrying with it the smell of the sea. Outside of her apartment, Zade wiped the rain spatter from her motorcycle's seat and stripped crumpled wet paper off its foot pegs. She pulled on a neck warmer, started her bike, and merged into traffic. The morning commuter traffic slowed alongside Post Office Square, and she wove around the larger vehicles. At the intersection of Pioneer and Market Streets, she took a left. The light changed to red above the descending ramp to Fisher Tunnel and she settled on her heels, zipping up her black leather jacket.

To her right, orange hazard tape flapped across the alley between the barbershop and the florist. She looked up at the red light and then glanced at the wooden board adorned with a few daisies and burning pillar candles in the alleyway. Her gaze settled on a fresh spray paint tag and she winced.

Zade put on her signal and edged her way to the curb. She took out a package of caramel corn, tore it open, and hurled the contents into the alley, sending a rat scurrying. She crammed the empty package into her bag and swung her bike back into the line of moving cars.

She veered around an enormous pothole and glided into the mouth of Fisher Tunnel. The last beads of rainwater disappeared from her helmet as she checked her left side mirror and changed into the commuter lane. She watched in her rearview mirror as the driver of a sedan behind her turned around to grab something in the back seat. Zade cranked open her throttle, accelerating out of the lane.

She avoided a line of cars merging in from a ramp by riding the centerline, darting between a bakery van and a commuter bus. She grinned at the horns blaring in her wake as she emerged from the tunnel, water sloshing off the High Street overpass drenching her. She pressed up on her pegs, leaning into the curve as she circled up into the city's gray morning light, shedding water.

Zade waited behind a taxi as pedestrians surged out of Claremont Station. A woman dropped her briefcase while fumbling for her umbrella, her papers spilling into the road. The taxi driver laid on his horn impatiently while the woman scrambled to collect her belongings. When traffic began moving again, Zade swerved to avoid the pedestrian's unclaimed papers.

A shopping cart loaded high with bottles rattled out into the intersection at Pierce and Trellis as Zade drove through. Two barefoot, grimy boys raced after it, banging on cars on their way across the road. One of them clambered up onto the hood of a parked car in pursuit of the cart. In her mirror, Zade watched them recapture their prize and wrestle it up onto the sidewalk.

The traffic was light on Pierce Street. A courier in yellow and blue took up a staggered position behind Zade. The light changed to yellow, then red. Both motorcycles stopped and Zade raised her left hand into the air, flashing her fingers. She watched in her side mirror as the other courier repeated the gesture in response. The light was still red when Zade launched across the intersection, cutting off a limo. The other rider zipped around the floundering vehicle, chasing the courier in black.

Zade swung around the rotary at the mouth of Water Avenue and hopped the double yellow to slide into Sterling. "Ribbons and curls." Her competitor gained another car's length. At the next intersection, she faked a lane change and braked hard, putting her heel down to assist a 90-degree turn toward a set of granite hitching posts.

Her front tire bounced over the curb. She lifted herself up, half-standing on the pegs as she sailed through the posts. While she maneuvered over the cobblestones, a man stepping out of a store entrance jumped back, shouting as the motorcycle whipped by. Zade watched in her mirror as her pursuer braked hard, swinging the motorcycle sideways on the other side of the posts.

Grinning, Zade settled back on her seat as she returned to the pavement. She drove a short distance and parked in a row of motorcycles at the end of the Pit. Her competitor came in from the left and walked her bike in backward, parking beside her.

Boon slapped open her faceplate. "That was insane, even for you." She punched Zade in the arm. "S&P are going to arrest you and lock your ass up one of these days, stunt girl."

"Dis would spring me." Zade dismounted and started in the direction of the coffee vendor's cart.

"Good morning!" Otter intercepted her and extended a tray of cups. "Who won today?"

"The mental patient." Boon reached out to take one of the cups.

Zade laughed and turned on her helmet mike. "Dispatch, 90-32 at the Pit."

"Congratulations, 90-32."

Zade winced and accepted a cup of coffee.

Otter set the empty tray under his heel. "Did you do anything fun yesterday?"

"I accidentally dyed my bathroom blue redoing my hair. Anything interesting happen here?" Zade poked at Otter with her boot.

He pointed dramatically at Boon. "Boon got herself a double."

Turning, Zade poked her friend in the shoulder. "You did? Why didn't you say so?"

Boon shrugged and crossed her arms on her motorcycle's bars. "It was an easy one. Just a red hot from Custom House Hotel to the Hinterlands." She dangled her cup in her gloved fingertips. "Patty knows I'm trying to sock a bit away to cover the tour."

Zade sipped her coffee. "How much does it cost to go on tour? For what, six weeks?"

The other woman sighed and sat back on her bike. "A grand for eight weeks over there, and another for round trip for us and all our equipment. That's in steerage."

With his hand outstretched, Otter made a sweeping gesture. "Fame! Fortune! See the Continent! Come home with a shit ton of dirty laundry!"

"Got that right." Boon scowled.

"When you guys leaving?" Zade hooked her fingers under her neck warmer, stretching the fabric away from her skin.

"Two weeks, if Ju can get his shifts covered."

"Aw, we're going to have to go dancing before that."

Boon shoved her beverage at Otter and waved at Zade. "22-77 on it, Patty." The courier snapped her visor down and walked her bike out of the row.

"90-32, curbside pickup at 39 Trellis Ave going to the Court House. ID only on delivery. Listed as white hot. Repeat, white hot."

"On it." Zade dropped her cup into Otter's other hand and smacked her faceplate down. "Dispatch, any jams?" She started up her bike and sailed out of her parking spot.

"Usual on the standard routes. No known issues."

Zade skimmed around the nose of a truck backing into a loading zone on Glory Avenue. "Time, dispatch."

"Fifteen on the clock."

Midway down Cook Avenue, a taxi slammed on its brakes. Zade did the same, bringing her left foot down as an anchor. She cleared the corner and gunned it on the inside of the one-way road connecting onto Pierce Street. From there she threaded her way along the eastern edge of Victory Square. She sped by a dented station wagon lurching out of the Pierce Hotel parking lot on her right.

The vehicle stalled and its driver got out to lift the hood amid a cacophony of angry shouts and horns. An oncoming truck veered into her lane and Zade squeezed between a parked car on the right and the car in front of her, startling the station wagon's owner as she grazed by him.

A left put her onto Trellis and she spotted the red folder being waved outside of the pickup location. The man holding it ran up to her as she pulled her thumbprint recorder out.

"It's vital you get this to the Court House as soon as possible. Deliver it to Ms. Bridgewell only." He pressed the packet into her hand and jammed his thumb down on the device.

Zade shoved the folder in her bag and watched in her mirror as a parcel delivery truck crossed lanes and cut out in front of a white van. She cracked the throttle and jumped her bike into the opening the van created. She took a left on Parker against the light and opened it up on High Street.

"Time."

"Five and thirty."

Zade flattened herself along the tank and raced down the double centerline. The roundabout at Manson and High appeared up ahead and she swayed the bike low to the right, cutting in front of a tourist bus to continue on High Street. Taking the right onto Market, Zade grinned at the shrill screams behind her as the bus driver opened the vehicle doors to swear at her. She opened her throttle and leaned heavily to the right, counter-steering to the left onto Pioneer Street.

The sidewalk outside the Court House was swarming with reporters. Uniformed officers held them at bay, preventing them from entering the steel and glass facade of the new entrance.

The courier wrinkled her nose as she looked at the crowd. "Dispatch, S&P know I'm on a hot for the court?"

"Your bike's safe."

Zade left the engine running as she dismounted and elbowed her way up the steps, unsnapping her bag in the process. She opened her faceplate. "Delivery for Bridgewell!"

"Out of the way! Let the courier through!" One of the officers pushed reporters back as Zade ran up the stairs.

"Bridgewell! Bridgewell!" Zade elbowed her way through the crowd.

"Here! Here!" A short woman in round glasses appeared from behind an officer and thrust a photo card at Zade as the courier held out the packet.

A camera flash went off in the courier's eyes and she growled.

"Bridgewell, do you have anything to say about Judge Frazer taking over the hearing after Judge Marcy's unexplained death? How will it affect the prosecution's case against Thayer?" A reporter shoved a recorder over Zade's shoulder.

Zade kicked her right boot backward into the man and pushed the packet at Bridgewell.

"No comment. No comment." Bridgewell clutched the packet to her chest and fled into the building.

"Time?" Zade ducked under an arm of a reporter.

"Delivery recorded by live feed with two minutes left on the clock. Congratulations, 90-32, that's a triple."

The courier whooped on her way back down the steps. "Triple! You didn't say anything about a triple!"

"If I had, you would have ridden down the sidewalk. Again."

Zade laughed and rocked her bike off its kickstand.

▽↗◢

The gold-capped spires of St. Anna's Cathedral were lost under a veil of low thunderclouds. Zade watched the sisters trim the ivy threatening to overrun the gated churchyard. A young novice sweeping the cuttings into a wheelbarrow smiled at the passing motorcyclist.

The Market Square clock tolled seven when Zade turned the corner off Duncan and went down Market. When she parked in the fenced-in lot behind Maddy's, a cheer went up from the other couriers standing near the entrance and a few clapped her on the back as she walked in. She slapped hands with Quiet on her way into the bar.

"A triple, first thing!" Boon slapped Zade's palm and draped her arm over Zade's shoulders, herding her to one of the tables in the back of the bar.

Another courier kicked a chair out, and Zade dropped into it, smiling. A waiter came over and looked at her expectantly, hand outstretched.

Zade slapped his palm. "A round for the house, Roy. On me."

Another cheer went up and more couriers dragged chairs over to the table.

"Keys." Roy insisted, his hand still outstretched.

Zade sighed and dropped her motorcycle keys into his palm.

Boon laughed. "We'll go dancing to celebrate. Burn some of your crazy off."

"I need a drink to wind down a bit."

Boon handed her beer over to Zade. "I hear you. I'm wired on adrenaline and caffeine all day, and can't sleep unless I fuck or drink myself into oblivion." She grinned.

"I can't believe you got a fucking triple." A courier in a black jacket staggered up to the table, glaring at Zade.

"Well, thanks, Mat." Zade shot a look at Boon and gulped a mouthful of her friend's beer.

"Why did Dis give you the white hot? He never gives me a hot." The courier's beer sloshed onto the floor as he swayed.

"I don't know, Mat, why don't you ask him? You've still got your earpiece in." Zade drained half the beer and handed the glass back to Boon, nodding. "Thanks, mine should be here any second."

Mat swore and tore his headset off, stuffing it into his jacket pocket.

"Sit down, Matty, you're making me nervous." Boon waved toward an empty chair at the other end of the table.

"Not my fault the fucking street trash stole my bike." He sank into the offered seat. "Why is he always on my ass? Last week he sent me home early." The man's hair, striped blonde and black, fell into his eyes as he stared at the floor.

Roy came back with a tray of drinks. He narrowed his eyes at Mat.

"Oh, come on now. You know your dispatcher's got a thing about us riding when we're wasted. He *disapproves*." Boon winked at Zade.

Zade grinned as Roy handed her a pint. "Disappointed!"

Boon raised her own glass. "Disdainful!"

"Disgruntled!" A courier at another table raised his glass.

"Disgusted!"

"Displeased!"

Mat slammed his beer on the table. "He's fucking jealous is what he is. Fucking jealous and mean because he's fucking crippled and can't ride anymore."

Zade closed her eyes. "Shut up, Mat."

Boon shot Mat a warning look.

"Or what? You'll make me?" Mat half stood out of his chair. "You have the hots for him now? You suddenly sucking cock?"

Zade started out of her chair. Boon put a restraining hand on her shoulder.

"Oh for heaven's sake, shut your noise hole. You'll sour the luck." A jovial woman pushed Mat back into his chair. She blew a kiss at Zade with a chubby hand while winking at Boon.

"Patty!" Boon stood up and was immediately squeezed into the older woman's spotted fake fur lapels.

"Hello, kittens. I thought I'd come down and have a drink with you. Though 90-32 here stole my thunder buying the first round for the house. Just the first, mind you." She raked her long enameled nails through Zade's blue hair and pinched Boon's cheek.

Another cheer went up, and people shuffled seats to make room for the dispatcher.

"I vote for relocating to somewhere with a dance floor." Boon rocked her chair back on two legs.

"The Crossing or Ella's?" Locking eyes with Boon, Zade gestured at Roy.

"The Crossing. They have a decent martini there." Patty played with a lock of Boon's hair as the waiter handed Zade the tab. "Saves us going over to The Point."

Zade gave Roy a couple of bills. He returned with change and her keys. She pushed the money back at him and his lips twitched into a brief smile.

"Meet you there?" Zade pulled her leather back on, avoiding Mat's gaze.

"Oh no, I'm not letting you out of my sight. We're taking a cab." Patty linked her arms into Boon's and Zade's.

"Who else is coming? Bets, Mustard? Avery? Ox? Kitty-Cat, you're coming with us." Boon waved impatiently.

Zade scanned the bar. "Where's Otter?"

Boon groaned, starting toward the exit. "Ju mentioned something about a house meeting."

"Somebody forgot to do the dishes again? Why aren't you there defending him?"

"Not my house." Boon held open the door for Patty.

Zade gave her a reprimanding look. "You could help keep things mellow between them."

"Hey, he's a grown man with his own life. Doesn't need me to protect him from his roommates. Besides, do you have any idea how nasty it is to get into your man's bed and get a dirty fork in the ass?"

"Can't say I do!" Zade laughed as Patty flagged down a taxi.

"We can take a few more. 62-91, you come sit here next to me. Now 90-32, tell us about your triple." Patty got into the taxi and Avery, Zade, and Boon climbed in after her.

"Zade, you met Avery yet? 90-32, meet 62-91. Clink, you've met Avery, yeah? 80-15, this is 62-91." Boon made the introductions as Clink, a slender courier with a shaved head, climbed into her lap.

"Nice to meet you." Avery reached across Patty to shake Zade's hand. His eyes stayed on her face as he withdrew his hand.

"How long have you been with YC?" She asked.

"YC?"

"Your company," Zade offered.

"This is my first week." The new courier looked at her. "Sorry, I still don't know all the terms. What's a triple?"

She gave him a wry smile. "Customers pay extra for priority treatment and how fast we need to get it there. The dispatchers decide if it's a red or white hot and pick one of us to run against the clock. If we don't make it in time, the customer doesn't pay. For in-town runs, the bonus is usually double our daily pay. We get triple if they decide it's insanely hard. That's one of the reasons they keep track of our times on regular routes, so they can pick who's the best bet when a hot comes in."

Patty smoothed a lock of Avery's curly black hair behind his ear. "He's been making good times. I'll give him a hot any day now."

Boon hooted and Avery glanced at the floor. Clink reached over and pinched

Avery's cheek. Avery kept his eyes down and pushed Clink's hand away.

Clink looked at Zade. "Hey, what's up with you working all day after a triple? How many you run today?"

"Twenty. Packages came in. I ran it like every other day."

"When you get tired of working for YC you can come work for me. I won't give anyone more than fifteen jobs in a day. I know how to treat my people." Patty squeezed Zade's knee.

"Fucking hell, I couldn't work for your dispatcher. I don't know how you put up with his shit." With a disdainful expression, Clink flipped a hand up.

"You shouldn't listen to Mat. Dis isn't that bad, he only gets pissed when people are being stupid. Mat's always getting trashed and forgetting to lock his bike's forks when he parks somewhere sketchy." Zade leaned back. "Besides, I like wearing OC's black. YC's colors are too flashy."

Clink made a dismissive sound. "No way, he thinks he's better than we are, that's why he never comes out with us."

"Maybe he's got a strict sweetheart at home." Zade shrugged.

"He used to run deliveries for YC, didn't he? Your dispatcher?" Avery leaned forward.

"Yeah, that was before my time." She shifted to look out the window. A man was walking his dog on the sidewalk. The white and black terrier's legs moved in a blur of motion while his owner tried to keep up.

Resting her head against the window, Zade watched the skyline sink behind them as the taxi came up onto the Riverway.

Patty sighed. "Let's not talk about such sad old things. Tell me how you're doing. Any problems learning the routes from Boon?"

"No. No problems." Avery shook his head.

"She's a good one to learn from." Patty leaned against Zade's back to face Boon. "I wish you weren't going on tour."

"You know the drill, Patty." Boon grinned and shrugged. "Bikes, bands, and brethren."

"You could play more in town, though. I could pull some strings and get you more gigs at The Crossing."

"Play too much in the same venue and the fans get sick of you. Best to spread it around and build up anticipation. Plus you can't beat being booked on the Continent for two months."

"Hey, when are you playing next around here?" Clink asked.

"Tour's kickoff show is at the Crossing a week from next Friday. The Crash Girls are opening for us."

"We're here," Zade announced as the Crossing's neon sign appeared over the hood of the taxi. She opened the door and everyone climbed out onto the sidewalk.

"You alright?" Boon looked at her over the top of the car door.

Zade shrugged. "Yeah."

Boon studied her friend's expression. "He's new, doesn't know what not to ask about. Don't be mad, he's okay."

"It's fine, not like I know anything to tell him anyway." Zade shut the taxi door and handed a wad of cash through the front passenger window to the driver.

"Is it bothering you that your dispatcher didn't come out to celebrate your triple?"

"He never comes out, you know that." Zade dropped her arm around Boon's neck. "Come on, we shouldn't leave the babies alone with Patty."

"Clink?"

"No, the new guy. Patty will sell his ass for a martini." Zade laughed as Boon shoved her toward the queue of people waiting outside the club.

The bouncer waved them to the front of the line, to the complaints of a woman in a cocktail dress and floor-length fur coat.

The man clipped the velvet barrier line back to the pole behind the couriers and crossed his arms while addressing the irate woman. "I don't give a shit who you are, but if you don't zip it, you're never getting in."

"Thanks." Zade smiled at him.

"No worries, ladies."

"I love that he calls us that. No one else would call us ladies." Boon poked Zade as they handed their jackets to the coat check attendant.

"That's probably why he does it." Zade craned her head to scan the dance floor. She swayed on her heels as indistinguishable silhouettes writhed under the oscillating house lights. A new bass line rumbled through the venue's speakers as she descended into the crowd.

"We've lost her." Boon sank into the booth next to Clink. More couriers joined them and Boon nudged Clink to move over.

"Where'd she go?" Avery leaned over.

Boon pointed at the center of the dance floor, then lifted her hand to flag a waitress. "I need to drink more before I try and keep up with her."

Patty sighed exaggeratedly as Avery went over to the railing and scanned the dancers. "Another poor man headed for disappointment."

"Too bad, he can cry on my shoulder." Clink licked his lips in Avery's direction.

"As long as it's not mine." Boon laughed as the waitress came over.

∾Ↄ⑨❶∾

The spindly branches of the saplings outside Market Station shook in the autumn wind. Dis collected a bright red maple leaf from the sidewalk, twirled the stem between his fingers and released it, letting it drift back onto the wet sidewalk.

He crossed the street to move out of the way of a group of Sisters of St. Anna. Continuing down Market, he crossed again and opened the door to Marion's Flowers. The humid air of the shop rushed out, carrying with it the lush fragrance of warmer climates.

He emerged a few minutes later, carrying a bouquet of roses. Coming down the steps, he caught sight of a child leaving something in the nearby alleyway.

The boy froze, then took off running. Dis separated out one of the roses and left it with the other offerings at the shrine next to the flower shop.

Inside Market Station, a group of teenagers stared at him on their way up the escalator. A girl with feathers tied into her hair whispered to her friends as they passed him and a boy in patch-covered pajamas blew him a kiss as the rest of the group bolted up the remaining steps, laughing.

An older couple on the train made space for him to sit and the woman nodded approvingly at the bouquet he carried. Her husband's gaze lingered on Dis's left leg, and Dis flipped the edge of his coat over it. He took out his journal and wrote down the location of the shrine by the flower shop.

Exiting the subway at Victory Station, he crossed the square and started down Pierce Street. He watched a limousine glide to the main entrance of the Pierce Hotel and the doorman assist a woman in an evening gown onto the sidewalk. A strobe of camera flashes accompanied her arrival while S&P officers held back reporters.

As the woman posed for her picture, she noticed Dis across the street. She blew a kiss and languidly waved to him. The reporters whipped around, searching for the target of her affections. Dis ducked his head and resumed his course.

Conversations of evening shoppers and couples echoed from the cobblestones of Pier Alley. A woman apologized after she bumped into Dis, wobbling on her stiletto heels. The bell of the East Church tolled the hour as he entered the brick archway of the wine emporium.

From her desk at the rear of the wine racks, an older woman glanced up as he entered. "Good evening, Mr. Mthdys. I was just thinking of you. I received a case of Constalia from the Continent for a special order." With her eyes twinkling in genuine delight, the proprietor extended her hand as she rose to greet him.

Dis gently shook it and smiled. "Good evening, Ms. Siry. I was hoping for a bottle of Rasedale tonight."

"I do have a few bottles. However, if your heart isn't set on one, I saved a bottle of Elegard Estate out of the last case for you."

"That was very thoughtful, thank you."

Siry inclined her head and walked with him to the rack of wine behind her desk. "Black currant overtones with bright notes of vanilla and whiskey, followed by a smoky, full fruit finish. An excellent dessert wine." She offered him the bottle to inspect.

Dis nodded as he handed it back to her. "Perfect."

"Excellent. I do hope you enjoy it. Eighty-five, please." The woman glanced at the flowers under his arm. "Shall I gift wrap it?"

"No, thank you."

She slipped the bottle into a sleeve of tissue and set it into a bag. "There. Are you certain you do not want any of the Constalia?" She gestured at a bottle on the shelf behind the counter.

As he glanced at the liquor bottle's ornate label, his smile faded. "I am. Thank you." He turned to leave. "Have a good night."

"Good night."

He flipped up his collar against the sea breeze and crossed the deserted street at the end of the alley. The ocean waves slapped through the wooden slats of the pier as he passed a bronze statue of a fisherman crusted with bird droppings. The pigeons abandoned their roost as Dis hooked his cane onto the back of the bench at the end of the pier. He haphazardly scattered the roses into the water and crumpled the plastic into his pocket. Cooing, the birds landed at the man's feet, watching him sit down.

Uncorking the wine, he poured it over the slats, listening to it splatter into the water below. He drank the remainder as the wind sang across the mouth of the bottle and lights rocked in the harbor. Producing a slip of paper from his inner suit pocket, Dis wedged it into the empty bottle and pressed the cork back into place. He stood in silence for a moment before hurling the wine bottle in an arc over the water.

Taking out a bundle wrapped in green silk, he unwound the fabric and removed a deck of cards. He shuffled multiple times, cut the deck into thirds, and reassembled it. He placed three cards face down, side by side, and placed the rest on the bench. Looking at the uniform back of the cards, he changed the order before flipping them over one at a time.

♑︎♍︎♏︎♋︎■

An elderly woman in a long lambskin coat stepped into the Shining Star Bookstore and began browsing the cases of magical paraphernalia. Noting her arrival, the bookstore owner gestured at his assistant to take over his post at the counter and approached the woman. They spoke together in hushed tones and then he guided her into a private consultation room. He sat her in a high-backed antique chair at a circular table draped in silk. After lowering the lights and dropping a heavy curtain across the room's entrance, he took the opposite seat. He closed his eyes and began uttering drawn-out phrases, then shifted into a crooning, wordless song. The woman gripped the table, the silk bunching in her hands as gauzy draperies swirled and lifted from the walls.

♑︎♍︎♏︎♋︎■

On the 53 bus, a young man sleepily watched the lights of the bridge trace a blue web over the Mam. As he started to doze against his window, his water bottle fell out of his grip, waking him. Searching for the bottle, he met the gaze of a well-dressed man behind him. The man held out the lost bottle. Fingertips touched as the container was returned. Shy smiles and polite phrases stretched into conversation.

As the bus crossed the bridge over the river, the young man laughed with his new acquaintance. Lit from behind by the bridge lights, he appeared to be surrounded by a halo of blue light. The other man fell silent, watching him.

□ ♍ ♏ ♋ ■

Dis wrapped the deck of cards and put them back into his coat. As he left the pier, the pigeons scattered, jostling for position on the bronze fisherman. He crossed the street, pausing as a retirement party spilled out onto the cobblestones outside of The Schooner Restaurant in Pier Alley. The men and women congratulated their former business partner in loud voices as Dis circumvented the group and headed into the golden warmth of the restaurant.

BOON POKED ZADE. "I think you're a lifer, like Otter. You're going to be running packages until you're as old as Mother Ida."

Zade laughed and shoved her friend, causing her to bounce off the brick wall. "We can't all be rock stars, rock star."

Boon sang out a swooping note and dropped her arm around Zade's neck. "I wish you knew what it was like being up on stage. Best high. It's better ... than getting. A. Fucking. Triple." She poked her friend to punctuate each word.

"Next you're going to be telling me it's better than the best lay you've ever had."

"It's better than the worst one. I will say that."

Laughing, they crossed Market Street. The Market Square Clock tolled once as the two of them entered Pierce Park near the playground.

Boon herded Zade toward the playground's swing sets. "We need to find you a pretty girl to spend all your hard-earned cash on."

They walked around the metal hobbyhorses. Boon pushed one, sending it rocking on its coiled spring. Zade watched her friend drop onto one of the swings and begin to move back and forth, gaining greater height with each pass.

"I seem to spend it just fine already on a bunch of them." Zade plunked down in the next swing and walked backward, pulling the suspension chains taut.

The supports creaked and groaned as the two of them flew back and forth. Zade extended her legs, using her hips to get a larger arc, while Boon dropped her legs to complete a shorter arc more quickly. After a few minutes, the women evened out, swinging side by side in the cool night air.

"You could come with us. To the Continent."

"And what, carry your shit?" Grinning, Zade kicked out at Boon, sending both swings sideways.

"That and do security for us." Boon dragged the toes of her boots through the worn dip under her seat. "I know you've never been over. I'm sure you could get the time off."

"Yeah, probably." Zade began to pump her legs again, swinging higher as Boon came to a stop.

Boon watched her friend accelerate, forcing the swing set's metal beam to bow under her momentum. The entire set squealed and shuddered. Boon laughed as Zade pitched out of the seat at the apex of the arc, flew over the hobbyhorses, and landed in a tumbling roll at the foot of the slides.

"You're nuts. You know that, right?" Boon walked over as Zade stood up. "Sometimes I think you're seriously trying to get your ass killed."

Zade shrugged. "I just don't let worrying about staying alive get in the way of things."

"I don't want to come home from touring and have to write a sappy song about my dead best friend."

"Make Ju write it, like all your other good songs."

"Hey!" Boon shoved her. "You said 'Star River City' was your favorite!"

"I thought he wrote that one?" Cracking a grin, Zade shoved her back. "I'm just fucking with you."

"In that case, I'll write 'The Ballad of Stunt Girl' when you die at a ripe old age of sixty from boredom. We should go get our bikes before Roy locks up for the night."

Zade nodded as her friend started jogging backward out of the playground.

"Wanna race?" Boon spun around and bolted down the path with Zade in pursuit.

▽↗◢

The high wooden doors of the Market Square warehouse creaked apart. The cart workers yawned as they shuffled out of the morning sun. The electric lights overhead pinged and snapped on, casting cold light over the hundreds of carts inside.

A short man stifled a yawn as he grabbed the handles of a scraped and battered cart. The padlocks rattled against the wood as he hauled the cart toward the exit.

"You out playing a show last night, Ju?" An older woman with a heavy accent looked down her nose at him as he approached the warehouse doors. "You will not be napping instead of selling? I think today will be a bad day for you."

"No show last night."

She clucked her tongue at him and turned her attention to the next person in the line. "You remember to refold all of the t-shirts on your cart today, Maggy?"

Ju kept his eyes on the hill rising up in front of him. The wheels of his cart bounced over the cobblestones.

Next to him, a cart worker wearing his hair in thick braids swore as the street began to incline steeply. "I hate this fucking hill. I hate this fucking job. I hate my fucking life." He threw a mournful look at Ju.

"Five more minutes, and it's done." Ju dug the toes of his sneakers into a space between the cobblestones and hauled his cart five more feet up the slope.

"Yeah, you're right. Still, I'd rather be in bed. You know?"

A brief smile flickered over Ju's face and he nodded, tightening his grip on his cart. His companion's eyes darted away, following a retail clerk crossing the street in front of them. Ju ducked his head and watched his feet again as the sound of shuddering wood and swearing filled the morning air.

When they entered Market Square, he angled his cart to the left. The street began to level off and the cobblestones changed to asphalt. Letting go of the left handle of his cart, he held up a hand to the other man as they separated. Switching his grip, Ju walked backward, following alongside the curbside gutter until the shadow of the Custom House fell across him.

He maneuvered into position next to the wide stairs leading up into the building. He retrieved two pairs of wooden blocks and wedged them under the cart's wheels, unlocked the padlocks, rolled up the cover and lashed it to the underside of the frame. Then he set about organizing the displays of sunglasses, hats, and souvenirs.

Ju unhooked a folding chair from under the cart and set it up in the corner between the cart and the stairs into Custom House. He angled the high fabric-backed chair and sat down, picking at the callouses on his palm and watching the early morning tourists filter into the square.

A motorcycle dodged around a group of students taking pictures of an old horse-watering trough. The rider killed the engine, coasting to a stop at the far end of the cart.

Dismounting, Boon pulled her helmet off and tossed it into Ju's lap. "Strawberry or plain?"

"Strawberry." A slow smile spread across the man's face. "Please."

"Only because you're the best drummer in town." Boon reached into her messenger bag and took out a waxed food container. Leaning in, she rested her forehead against Ju's and stared into his eyes. "Missed you last night."

Ju wrapped his arms under the sides of her leather jacket and kissed her.

After a moment Boon leaned back. "What did Otter hit you with this time?"

"I have to clean the bathroom before meeting up for practice tonight."

Groaning, she shook her head. "You should tell him watching his bike while he uses the toilet here counts toward housecleaning."

Ju shrugged and put his hands on her hips, drawing her in for another kiss.

Boon put her hand on the side of her headset and stepped away. "On it, Patty." Mouthing an apology, the courier took her helmet out of Ju's lap and walked back to her bike. She blew him a kiss and started up her machine.

He held up a hand as she took off, smiling as she darted around another cluster of startled tourists.

▽ ↗ ◢

On the Straight, Boon checked her mirror and crossed over to turn onto East Market Street. She drove under the Midtown Byway and followed Timber Street until it merged onto High Street. She parked under an old maple tree outside of 110 High Street and dismounted. Her bike's exhaust flung leaves into the air as she left it idling. *"Clouds kiss the sky and the heavens shiver,"* she sang as she jogged up the stairs. *"Your lips burn cold."* She rang the bell next to the slate blue entranceway. *"Like stars falling in the river."*

A portly woman in a prim suit opened the door and Boon held out her thumb recorder.

"Good morning, I'm here to pick up for 81 Cygnet."

"Yes, yes, I have it right here." The woman flapped a red packet at the courier and jabbed her thumb on the device. "It's not working."

Boon cracked the recorder against the side of her helmet and held it out again. The device beeped as the woman placed her thumb on it.

"Thanks." The courier slipped the packet into her bag and spun on her heel, bounding down the steps to the sidewalk. "Patty, I've got the package." Humming, she kicked her bike into gear and waited for a produce truck to go by before pulling into traffic.

"This should put a little more into your tour savings, 22-77. The client has just upgraded it to white hot. Fifteen minutes and counting."

"Hell, yeah." Smiling, Boon kicked into a higher gear. She took to the centerline, passing the truck on the right.

Out of her line of sight, a sports car cut in from the left. The truck driver leaned on her horn and shouted at the car. In response, the driver put his hand out the window and flipped three fingers up.

Caught between the car and an oncoming bus, Boon twisted her throttle fully open, accelerating. Her motorcycle leapt forward to dart in front of the vehicles as the bus went by. "Fucking unbelievable." She watched her mirror as the sports car sped up, tailgating her. She switched her turn signal on and downshifted, taking a left onto Manson Street.

□ ♍ ♏ ♋ ■

Avery parked his motorcycle outside the Dove Cot Bakery and consulted a street map. Flipping open his visor, he traced a route with his gloved forefinger. He glanced up as a trio of laughing tourists crossed the street on their way into the Custom House Hotel.

"62-91, give me your status."

"I'm at Market Square, Patty."

"62-91, emergency transfer at the corner of High Street Extension and the Straight. Pick up the package from 22-77 and get it to 81 Cygnet. Package is white hot and 22-77 is down. I'm sorry, Avery, you're the closest."

"On my way." Avery shoved the map into his jacket and zipped it closed.

He took Manson to East Market and changed lanes. One block further, the traffic started to crawl as it entered the rotary. The cars stopped moving and Avery rode onto the double yellow lines in the center of the road. No oncoming traffic appeared as he traveled along the pavement down the Straight.

On the other side of a stopped bus, the front end of a mail delivery truck was hung up on the granite steps of a brownstone. In the center of the road, a sports car lay upside down in the shattered remains of its windshield. The courier stared as a cluster of bystanders tried to shift the mail truck.

As the truck rocked back and forth, Avery dropped his kickstand and dismounted, racing over to the mangled motorcycle underneath. One of the witnesses shook his head as the courier got down on his knees next to the exposed wreck of the bike. There was no sign of the rider. Avery got up and ran around to the stairs on the far side of the truck.

Throwing packages and sacks aside, he dug until the back of Boon's riding jacket became visible.

He heaved the debris off her. "She's here! She's here!" he choked and backed away, bringing the back of his hand to his mouth.

A baritone voice shouted through Avery's headset. "62-91, get the package out of her bag! Do it now!"

The courier started to back away. "I'm not ..."

"Open her bag. Take out the packet."

"I can't."

"You are. Right now. Do it."

Avery rolled Boon's body to the side and opened her bag. His hand closed around the packet as someone grabbed his shoulder.

"We'll take over now, son. Go on with your job." The S&P officer patted him on the back.

The dispatcher's baritone voice sounded over the radio. "62-91, get back to your bike. Now!"

Avery stumbled back to his bike. He swung his bag around and shoved the blood-smeared packet into it.

"Delivery to 81 Cygnet. Repeat it!" The voice commanded.

"81 Cygnet." He walked his bike out between two ambulances and stared at the stretchers being carried to the scene of the accident.

"Take the next left. Status."

Avery passed two cars and spotted another emergency vehicle in the oncoming lane. "I'm on High Street Extension, in the thirties."

"Take your next left and go up the Southern Prom. Status."

"On the Prom now."

"Take the turn onto Mariner's. Status."

"Turning onto Mariner's."

"Take the next left onto Willow."

"On Willow."

Traffic began to slow and the courier edged his bike toward the center of the road.

"Go ahead and cut around those cars. The package is white hot."

Avery pulled in the clutch and snapped his gear lever up a notch, accelerating down the centerline to pass. He skimmed the road, inches away from the side of a delivery truck.

"Get over to take the next right. Status."

The courier downshifted and counter-steered, swinging between two cars to take the turn. "Right on Trawl Street." He glanced at the parked cruisers outside of the S&P station ahead.

"Left on Cygnet. Status."

"On Cygnet."

"Repeat."

"*On Cygnet.*"

The man's voice crackled through static. "Give me the addresses on the buildings on the left."

"23, 35, 47, 59, 65, 73 ... 77, 81."

"Park near the flowers. Keep your helmet on."

Avery stopped, releasing the clutch before shifting into neutral. His motorcycle lurched and stalled out.

"Leave it, the package is white hot."

Avery staggered across the street, running blindly through traffic. Breaking

46

into a sprint, he leapt up the front stairs of the building, surprising two office workers.

His new dispatcher continued to give him instructions over the radio. "Take the stairwell on your right."

Avery crashed into the red fire door and ran up the stairs. A woman carrying a mop bucket squeezed out of his way as he took the stairs two at a time.

"Exit this floor and take a right."

He bumped into an intern entering the stairwell. She shouted as her papers sailed through the air. The courier ran down the carpeted hallway.

"Next door on the left."

Avery clipped his hip on the doorknob and bumped his knees into the reception desk. His bag hung open at his hip and he shook the red packet at the man seated in front of him.

The voice in his headset prompted. "Record his thumbprint."

He fumbled the device out as the office worker kept typing.

"Your new, aren't you? Just made it." Without looking up, the receptionist placed his thumb on the recorder and took hold of the corner of the packet.

Avery let go of it and walked out into the hall. He ran down the stairs and bolted out of the building.

"62-91, sit down."

"*I'm not your fucking dog.*"

A woman on the sidewalk looked at him in surprise and crossed the street.

"Avery, please sit down. Now."

The courier sank onto the steps next to the marigolds.

"Take off your helmet and take a few deep breaths."

Complying, he took his helmet off and set it on the ground. There was a bright red smear on the back of his left glove. He vomited into the flower bed.

▽ ↗ ◢

When he arrived at Maddy's, the bar was already crowded with couriers talking in hushed tones. Without saying a word, Kitty took Avery's gear and washed it in one of the bathrooms before bringing it back to the table. The pint of beer in front of Avery kept being replaced no matter how many times he emptied it.

A chair scraped the floor. Two shots of whiskey appeared in front of him, and another two shots were set to their left.

Dis sat down in the chair and pushed the shots closer to Avery. "Drink."

"This going to become a habit with you?" Avery stared into the dispatcher's visible eye.

"You needed help getting the package there on time and Patty needed to go be with Boon." The other man indicated the shots again. "Drink."

The courier glared at him and his voice rose petulantly. "I don't work for your company, so stop telling me what to do."

Dis's expression hardened as he sat back in his chair. "Drink it."

Avery gave Dis a miserable look and threw back the shot.

Dis drank one of the other shots and kept watching him.

"How did you know I was going to puke?"

"I didn't." The older man glanced over at the door as a new group of couriers entered.

"Then why did you have me take off my helmet?" Avery downed his second shot and pushed the empty glass across the table.

"You were in shock and full of adrenaline." The dispatcher sat back and pushed Avery the last shot. "I needed to keep you from trying to ride."

They sat in silence and watched a pair of drunken couriers stagger past on their way to the restroom. One started crying and the other helped him by holding open the bathroom door.

Avery trailed his fingertips along the side of the shot glass. "Aren't you going congratulate me on the double?"

Dis cocked his head and watched the younger man. "No."

"Everyone else is."

"Then you don't need to hear it again."

"Today was the first time I've ever been afraid of ..." He threw back the shot. "When I signed the waiver, Patty told me couriers have a two-year life expectancy, like we have cancer." Avery rested his forehead on his hands. "Boon died for a piece of paper ..." Then he sat up, glaring at Dis. "Why are you here?"

Dis lifted his beer. "For Boon."

Roy came over to their table, carrying more shots. He raised an eyebrow and Dis shook his head. Roy vanished back into the crowd, taking the unserved alcohol with him.

Dis took a sip of his beer and looked down at the glass. "There are two kinds of riders ..."

"Those who have been down and those going down." Avery rolled his eyes. "I know."

Dis shot him a warning look. "There are two kinds of riders, those who want to die and those who want to live. The difference is knowing this could be the last moment of your life, or wishing it was."

Otter tousled Avery's hair as he yanked back a chair. "Congratulations on your first double."

Zade took a seat next to Otter and greeted Dis in a low voice. "Hey." Her eyes were red and swollen.

Otter put his arm around her and raised his glass. "To Boon."

Dis lifted his pint and watched tears drip down Zade's face. "To Boon."

Zade drained her beer and glanced at Dis.

Another courier picked up the toast and soon the fallen rider's name echoed throughout the bar. "To Boon."

Otter got up. "Patty's going to give Boon's leather to Ju. I should go be with him."

"I'll be over in a minute." Zade slumped forward, resting her head on her folded arms. Otter squeezed her shoulder as he left their table.

"Who's Ju?" Avery asked.

"Boon's boyfriend and the drummer in her band. He's Otter's roommate."
Zade stared into her empty glass. "Otter was off today, so he got the phone call
and had to go break the news to Ju."

Dis pushed his beer over and she nodded as she lifted it.

Avery reached out and touched her hand. "Are you going to the funeral
tomorrow?"

Zade sat up, flinching away from the contact, her eyes wide.

Dis watched her reaction. "OC is running deliveries for YC."

Avery stared at Zade. "What? Oh, right."

"I'm going to go see how Ju's doing." Zade stood up and nodded to Dis.

He held her gaze and gave her a sad smile. "Tell Otter I'm not expecting
either of you to be on tomorrow."

Zade shrugged and her mouth turned up for a moment. "I'll tell him, but
he'll think I'm making it up."

She found Otter leaning against a wall with his shoulder resting on an
antique photograph of the bar.

He nodded at the table of cart workers and couriers. "I'm going to get him
home."

Zade glanced over to where Ju was sobbing with his head in his hands. "We
could all do with a change of scene. You want me to stop by the liquor store on
the way over?"

"Yeah, that would be a help. Thanks." Otter started over to Ju's side. "I think
we might want to get you home." He gave the others huddled around his
roommate a sad smile. "You're all welcome to come over."

Zade waited as Otter helped Ju up and they started for the door.

A young woman walked up to her. "Beer run?" She asked, touching Zade's
elbow.

The courier nodded and set her empty glass down on the table. "Yeah, Liz,
you want to come with me?"

"Yeah." The cart seller watched Otter half-carry Ju out of the bar.

Zade looked thoughtfully at the woman's sneakers and lightweight jacket. "You all right with being on a bike?"

Liz dipped her head and shrugged. "Yeah."

"I have to get my keys from the bar, I'll meet you out front?"

"Okay." Liz nodded and then eased her way through the crowd.

When she got out of the bar, Zade found Liz waiting by the parked motorcycles. She handed her helmet to the woman and put on a pair of goggles. Zade flipped down the passenger pegs and started up the bike, and Liz got up behind her. She waited until her passenger's arms were wrapped firmly around her before easing out into traffic.

▽ ↗ ◢

Inside the beverage center, the clerk behind the counter glanced up as Liz and Zade walked in. He looked back at his newspaper as they walked over to the cold cases, arm in arm.

There was a small bucket of single roses at the counter, each wrapped in cellophane. Zade eyed it as she set her armload of alcohol down. While the clerk rang up their purchases, she removed all of the flowers from the bucket and added them to the pile.

When they returned to the motorcycle, Zade crammed cans of beer into the storage box and settled a stuffed messenger bag on her passenger. She rubbed at Liz's fingers as the woman got on the bike behind her. "One more stop, okay?"

"Yeah." Liz squeezed Zade's sides.

"Here, put your hands in my pockets." Zade unzipped her side pockets and put her passenger's hands inside.

They rode down the block, then turned onto High Street Extension. Zade flipped on her right signal and glided over to the curb, parking beside 68 High Street Extension. A hundred candles glowed from the front stairs of the brownstone. The flickering light cascaded over flower bouquets, band posters, photographs of Boon, and notes and letters, spilling down the stairs and out onto the sidewalk. Pieces of windshield glass glittered along the base of the curb.

The two women dismounted and stood looking at the offerings stacked at the site. Someone had written song lyrics in green chalk on the brick building. Others had covered the remaining bricks with messages and prayers, filling the wall around the first floor windows with colored scrawls.

Zade wiped away tears and opened the bag cradled in Liz's arms. With a sad smile, she took out the flowers and handed half of them to Liz. They silently set about tucking the roses into the few empty spaces left on the stairs.

Zade went back to her motorcycle and opened the storage box, taking out two cans of beer. She nestled the alcohol and the bar of chocolate under the chalk-covered wall, took off her gloves and picked up a piece of pink chalk from a window sill. Kneeling, she brushed fallen leaves away and drew a simple design on the sidewalk. Liz used a blue piece to write on the edge of the window sill.

They took one more look at the shrine and got back on the bike. Zade tucked Liz's hands back into her jacket pockets and they drove toward the harbor. Turning west onto the Southern Promenade, they continued onto Mariner's Way to Grant Street and stopped outside of 1262.

Zade took her bag and helmet back from Liz and held the apartment door open. Liz stood on her toes and kissed Zade on the cheek. She joined her friends in the living room while Zade went into the kitchen.

Seeing her, Otter hauled Zade into a drunken embrace. "Thanks for going to the store."

Zade rested her head on his shoulder and hugged him. "It'll be okay." She knocked the side of her head against his and stepped away to empty the contents of her bag onto the counter.

"Eventually." Otter propped himself against the refrigerator and gave her a sad smile.

His friend scrunched her nose at him. "Dis said we can take tomorrow off."

"You're making that up."

Zade snorted and handed him a beer. "I told him you would say that."

"Good of him to keep an eye on Avery. Today must have been hard on the kid." Otter cracked open his beverage and nodded.

Opening a handle of whiskey, Zade gave Otter a look. "He always watches out for us, you know that."

Otter watched her take two glasses out of his cabinets. "He didn't hit on you, did he?"

Zade stared at him. "Dis? He would never …"

Her friend shook his head and gave a soft laugh. "I meant Avery."

"Oh." Zade poured three inches of amber liquid into two glasses and gave one to him.

"Mala asked about you again. The girl who works at the Blue Lotus."

"The blonde or the one with her hair down to her ass?"

"Blonde." Otter tapped his glass against hers. "Boon, may she rest in peace."

"To Boon." Zade drank, then wiped her eyes with the back of her hand. "You got me started again."

Otter poked her and leaned back against the fridge. "Remember when you switched on that guy who thought he was going down on you at Ella's?"

Zade grinned. "Pervert had her trousers off before I was even out of the booth!"

"Boon said, 'The table service here is fucking fantastic!' Do you remember the look on that guy's face? Oh, Mother." Otter bent over laughing.

"Shush. Someone will hear us." Zade held onto the edge of the counter, taking gulps of air.

"Screw it. Could be any of us going dirt-side tomorrow." Otter slid down the front of the fridge to sit on the floor and pillowed his chin on top of his crossed arms.

Zade joined him on the floor and poured more whiskey into his glass. "Then

I'm just happy my last drink is with you." She lifted the bottle to her lips.

"Me too." Otter drained his glass and reached for the bottle.

▽↗◢

Zade gave Liz a ride back to her apartment. Liz took Zade's hand and led her up the stairs. When they were inside, Zade buried her face into the smaller woman's neck. Her lips and tongue traced their way across Liz's collarbone. Whispering, Liz brought Zade's face up and crushed her lips against hers.

Zade used her hips to pin Liz to the wall and slipped off the other woman's coat and shirt. She swung her up, cradling her head. Liz leaned in for a lingering kiss as Zade carried her to the living room couch.

"My bedroom's the next door on your left." Liz nipped at Zade's earlobe.

"Anyone else home?" Zade set her on the couch.

Liz laughed and linked her hands behind Zade's head. "No."

"Then this will do fine."

"They might come home!"

"Then we better hurry." Zade knelt down and untied Liz's sneakers.

Liz's trousers came off and she hooked her ankles over Zade's shoulders. She moaned as Zade ran her tongue up her thigh. Liz's hands twined in her lover's blue hair as Zade's mouth traveled higher.

"Get up here with me."

Zade grinned up at her and climbed onto the couch as Liz worked her hands into the back of Zade's trousers. They rolled over and Liz gasped as Zade smoothed a hand along the cart seller's thigh.

"Is this okay?" Zade stroked the slick skin under her fingers and kissed along the other woman's jaw.

"Oh, yes."

THE COLD WINTER RAIN was changing to sleet as Zade went into the Cold Pail Bakery. She picked up a to-go cup from the stack and depressed the toggle on the self-serve coffee dispenser. Joining the queue at the counter, she watched the translucent splotches of half-frozen rain hit the glass above the window seats. She slid a few bills across the counter and nodded at the young man behind the register. Smiling, he put her money in the till and turned to help the next customer.

She wedged a lid down on her coffee and walked over to the exit. Hunching her shoulders, she stepped out onto the sidewalk and wrinkled her nose as bits of cold, wet slush landed on her face. Putting her head down, she made her way up Pioneer toward Bravery Crossing Station.

A teenage Underground employee sprinkled salt on the entranceway stairs. Zade watched a decrepit man in a filthy trench coat snag the open bag of salt from behind the bored-looking girl. The man hid his prize under his coat and descended into the station, blending in with the influx of late morning travelers.

Dropping her change into the turnstile, Zade headed over to the inbound platform. She cracked open the lid on her coffee, watching the salt thief walk to the far right of the platform. When the man reached the end of the chipped tile wall, he hopped down into the gravel and disappeared into the train tunnel.

The sound of brakes squealed in the distance and Zade squinted at the opposite end of the platform. Light flared along the curved walls as the next train rounded a corner on its way into the station. "That's cutting it a little bit too close, mister." She sipped her coffee and boarded the train.

▽↗◢

Coming out of Mercy Station, Zade was pelted with needles of ice as she ran across the street to St. Anna's. The loose belt of her messenger bag rang against the gate as she entered the churchyard. The other couriers sheltering under the archway made room as she jogged over.

"Couldn't just snow, could it?" A man with stripes of purple hair griped.

"At least no one's out on delivery in it," Mo answered. He brushed the clinging slush off of Zade's rain gear as she stepped in under the stonework.

"Is it better or worse if it's nice weather when you have to go to your shitbag friend's funeral?" Kitty extended a flask to Zade.

"I'm glad the sun was out for Boon's last month." Zade swallowed a mouthful of whiskey and passed the flask down the line. "I wish it was nice out today for Ox."

"Ox probably ordered this mess, hoping we'd fall on our asses." Mo accepted the alcohol. "He always thought it was funny when one of us dumped."

Zade tilted her head and looked out at the dull dark clouds above the cathedral. "Only when we got back up afterward."

Nodding, Mo passed the alcohol. "I heard you gave your two weeks."

The purple-haired courier shrugged.

Kitty shoved him with her elbow. "What the fuck, Fen. You weren't going to tell us?"

"I've got two kids. The money's not worth leaving them like this." He upended the flask. "It was one thing when we could pretend a few weeks laid up was the worst that could happen. Now we're all waiting to see who's the next poor fuck to take the ride out to Rest&Be."

"Grow some balls." Kitty rolled her eyes. "I'm not ending up in a fucking rotbox."

"We all go down, Kitty." Fen capped the flask and slipped it into the inner pocket of his yellow and blue riding jacket. "You better get used to the idea."

Turning away, Zade went into the warm vestibule of the cathedral. The stained-glass windows cast muted pools of light over the pews and the air reverberated with the thrum of low-pitched conversation.

The pews closest to the casket were filled with the grieving family. An elderly man in the front wept uncontrollably while a haggard-looking woman tried to comfort him. Strangers twisted tissues in their hands and looked away as Zade made her way down the aisle.

"Zade." Dis beckoned to her from a pew on the left.

"Thanks." She sat down next to him.

Further down the bench, Otter, his eyes raw and red, leaned forward and gave her a half-wave.

Dis pointed at the rack on the back of the pew. "There's a prayer sheet if you want it. Mother Ida should be starting in a minute."

"Unfortunately, I've got it memorized."

Dis put his hand on hers. He squeezed her fingers briefly before letting go.

A bell signaled the beginning of the funeral Mass and the assembled mourners rose to face the sanctuary at the side of the altar. A young boy entered, swinging a brass censer. Another appeared behind him, stiffly supporting a chalice on a purple cushion. A girl followed, holding aloft a slim silver and gold sword. An elderly priestess in a white and scarlet robe appeared, leaning on the arm of a white-robed novice. The novice smiled gently as the cathedral's matriarch patted her arm and then released it.

The censer-bearer circled the casket three times while the chalice-bearer and sword-bearer assumed their posts on either end of it.

"Please be seated." Mother Ida raised her arms. "We are here today to honor the passing of Henry Oxwall. While we grieve his loss, we must remember that being a motorcycle courier was the path Ox chose. It now brings him into the eternal embrace of our Holy Mother. May we all come to it by the way of our joy. Amen."

"Amen." The mourners' collective voices resonated through the cathedral.

"Join me now as we recite our first prayer. Our Holy Mother who delivers us from villainy, hallowed be thy heaven and hallowed be thy earth. Thy blessings come as thou accept our follies and forgive us our failures. Give us this day thy sacred milk of compassion so we may show others mercy in thy name. Guide us to understanding and save us from deception. Lead us always to thy divine embrace. For thy love is eternal, the passion and the promise, for now and forever. Amen."

"Amen." Zade dragged her sleeve over her face.

Dis offered her his handkerchief. "Amen."

▽↗◢

Sitting by herself in the back bar of The Crossing, Zade ordered a drink. The venue was full of couriers and cart workers, all in different states of intoxication. Every few minutes a new toast was proposed in Ox's name. Zade took the crumpled handkerchief out of her bag and flattened it out on the bar.

Pushing his way through the crowd, Clink slid onto a barstool next to Zade. "Hey, why aren't you sitting with us?"

Shrugging, Zade folded the square again and put it into her pocket. "Needed a few minutes to myself." She lifted her beer toward his cast-covered right arm. "When's that thing coming off?"

"Doc said two more weeks." Clink jabbed her with the fingers of his left hand. "Come on, everyone's waiting for you."

"All right, I'm coming."

Couriers from both companies were hovering over the table. They looked up nervously as Clink and Zade approached.

"Are you planning a bank heist?" Zade asked.

Clink used his hip to move aside a bigger man and take a place next to her.

Kitty squinted at her from across the table. "You remember to take your earpiece out, dispatcher's pet?"

"Yes, Kitty. What's up?" Zade crossed her arms, returning the other woman's haughty look.

"Avery here has an idea for cheering us the fuck up. Don't you, snotball?" Kitty clapped her hand on Avery's shoulder.

Avery eyed Zade hesitantly, then gestured at a map rolled out on the table. "A race through the city on the Winter Solstice. Just like the Summer Solstice race, only a different route."

Zade moved in to get a closer look at the map. She glanced from the map to Kitty. "Mother Ida is doing a blessing of the bikes on the Solstice."

"After that, we race. At night, so no ragsuckers whine to S&P." Kitty leaned against the railing overlooking the dance floor.

"We'll use the major landmarks in town as checkpoints." Avery traced his finger across the map and looked at Zade. He swallowed rapidly.

Zade shook her head and stepped back. "YC and OC won't go for a winter race. Especially with the current body count. Four people quit this week. No way would they allow us to risk bikes and bodies. And there's no fucking way they can justify a permit at this time of year."

Kitty smirked at Zade. "Right. So we don't fucking tell them. The route is in town, so the roads will be clear. Easy as kicking a dog down a hill."

Zade crossed her arms and turned to Otter. "What's the prize?"

Avery continued to stare at Zade. "We all throw in and get a suite at the Pierce."

Otter shrugged. "We could do that without racing."

Kitty leaned over the table to plant her hand on the map. "Listen, kiddiefuckers, this is about the goddamn challenge. First one around the city who makes it to all the checkpoints wins the hotel suite and bragging rights. Adrenaline addicts only."

"You know, Patty will just fire *our* asses," Clink interrupted. "Dis will skin you alive if he finds out."

"Are you too fucking scared of him to risk it, Zade?" Kitty demanded.

Zade leaned in, bringing her face close to Kitty's. "I'm in. But everyone needs to keep quiet. If Dis finds out …"

"He won't. It will be a courier-only event," Avery added.

Zade glanced back at him. "Who'll be in charge at the checkpoints then?"

"Cart sellers," Kitty offered. "I've asked and they said they wouldn't miss it." Withdrawing her hand from the map, she put her fists on her hips. "You won the summer route, but I'm going to win this winter race, touchhole."

Zade grinned. "Not with your times, slowpoke."

"Yeah, well, when your cash is paying for me to scream my fucking head off in the big bed at the Pierce, we'll see."

"I'd pay for that bed right now, if you want." The other couriers hooted as Kitty looked away.

Otter grinned and raised his beer in a salute. "You made the lady shy!"

"You in, Zade?" Avery asked.

"I already said I was." Zade shot him an impatient look. "Where's the starting line?"

"Point of Graves and ending at the Victory Monument. Eight stops in between, tagging each landmark."

"Show me on the map."

Avery shook his head and rolled up the map. "You'll get a copy once you're officially in."

"How much is the entrance fee?" asked another courier.

"Hundred each for the Victory Suite at the Pierce."

Zade chewed on the side of her thumb as she watched Avery stow the map in his bag. "People better keep their mouths shut."

Dropping her hand to her hip, Kitty rolled her eyes. "No one wants to get the cranky fuckhead on our cases, Zade, relax."

Zade sighed. "I need another beer."

Clink waved a waitress over.

Ȥ♓⑩ɸȣ

On the thirtieth floor of the Pierce Tower, Nash tapped on the double doors of a conference room. All of the twelve people at the long table watched the doors open. "Pardon my intrusion. I have an important message for Chairwoman Pierce." He stepped in and walked to where Mercy Pierce sat at the head of the table. Handing her a piece of paper, he stepped back as she read it.

She gestured to the presenter. "Do continue, Mr. Washbo."

"Thank you, Chairwoman. Now, if I can have the next image, I will go over the Continental investment speculations for next quarter." Washbo cleared his throat and nodded to his assistant, who changed out the transparency of the bar graph for a candlestick chart.

Pierce lifted her hand, gesturing to her assistant. Nash approached and leaned forward. "Immediately arrange a private consultation with the City Manager. It has priority over the rest of my schedule." She handed him back the piece of paper. "You will also inform S&P that failure is unacceptable in this matter."

▽ ↗ ◢

Mother Ida carried an evergreen branch in one hand and a sword in the other. Her attendants followed behind with an urn filled with water from the holy well.

Dipping the branch into the urn, the priestess traversed the row of parked motorcycles, shaking drops of water over the riders and their machines. The couriers and dispatchers from the two delivery companies waited as the ritual blessing was performed. Friends and family of the assembled waited on the sidewalk as an S&P officer redirected traffic around the proceedings.

"May God in her infinite wisdom grant you a long and healthy life. Ride safely, for you are also her precious children." Mother Ida raised the sacred sword and made ritual passes in the air. "May you be free from harm and envy. Amen."

"Amen." A cheer rang out from the crowd as the cathedral bells began to ring.

"Right, see you later." Otter nodded to Zade.

She wiped the water off her bike's fairing. "Where you off to?"

"The Blue Lotus. Jeniel and Mala are doing another blessing for those of us not so church-minded."

She snorted. "Heretic."

"Hey, I'll take all the blessings I can get!" He threw his hands up as he started back to his bike.

"Later."

Zade waited in line until the S&P officer waved her out into the road, then took the turn into the wet street.

❧ ⌘ ⑨ ❶ ❧

A woman in coveralls under a long dress coat watched the line of motorcyclists merging into the holiday traffic. She glanced over at Dis and Frankie. "I think I can get the 500 Denton that Ray dumped up and running."

"It's the Solstice, Iris. Go spend it with your family." Dis shook his head at her.

"Why? Miserable louts. Whining about their office jobs and wanting to

62

know when I'm going to retire and sell OC. I'd rather spend tonight in the garage. At least the riders only complain when something is broken." Her eyes twinkled as she watched the couriers depart. "We could order in from Lou's, my treat."

"I'd love to, but I have other plans." Dis shook his head.

"Oh?" The older woman scrutinized him. "You have a date?"

"She's waiting for me over there." He pointed to the churchyard.

Iris spun around. "With Mother Ida?"

The corner of the man's mouth lifted. "Yes, Mother Ida."

Iris turned around and smacked him on the arm. "You'll know where to find me and Lou's red-hot spicy chicken." She looked over at the young woman standing next to her. "You too, Frankie. You can come have chicken and I'll show you how to change the bars on the new 350 Smarrow. Those monkey hangers it came with have to go."

"Maybe tomorrow? I have to go get ready for a family thing I have to go to later."

Dis turned to leave and raised his hand to the two women. "Happy Solstice to you both."

"Happy Solstice." Iris scowled at his back. "I wish he'd get over that man and move on."

"Have a great Solstice." Frankie kissed Iris on the cheek, then ran across the street to Mercy Station.

&ᴈ⑨❶ᴖ

As the last of the parishioners left, Dis waited inside the cathedral, looking at a statue of a shepherd cradling a vague animal shape. He ran his fingers over the worn marble, examining the indistinct form in the figure's arms.

"It looks more like he's holding a bunch of seaweed than a hound of God, doesn't it?" Mother Ida waved the tip of her cane at the statue.

"Could be a seal." Dis smiled down at the priestess.

She pursed her lips and narrowed her eyes. "Come have a cup of tea with me, child."

"If it isn't an inconvenience." He fell into step with her. "I know you have the big show to do later. Happy Solstice to you, by the way."

"Happy Solstice to you." The elderly woman's wrinkles dimpled as she smiled up at him. "I've done it every year for over fifty years. I think I've got it down by now."

They walked together slowly, their canes tapping on the stone floor. A novice rushed ahead to open the door to the office. Ida shot Dis an amused look as the girl opened the door for them.

The priestess frowned suddenly. "Your mother was always doing that too, until your father stole her."

"I believe you gave your blessing to his theft." Dis waited while the novice helped the priestess out of her formal vestments.

"I thought it would bring your father closer to the Holy Mother. Fetch us some tea, would you, Lily?" Ida put her hand on the edge of her desk and smiled benignly as the girl bowed out of the office. When the door shut, she turned back to Dis and glared. "Now, are you going to tell me why you are here, boy?"

"I'm here to celebrate the Solstice with my godmother." He lowered himself into the chair opposite the priestess's desk.

"When you want something, you call me that to remind me of my obligations to you," Ida addressed him sternly. "My only obligation as your godmother is to bring you into the Church's care."

Dis rubbed his eyes under his glasses. "I missed you, not your god."

"Don't you try and enchant me with that glib tongue of yours. Your father couldn't do it and you certainly can't."

"You liked him enough to marry them at the high altar."

"That was for your mother's sake and, I had hoped, for your own." There was a knock on the door and the novice entered with the tea. "Ah, thank you,

Lily." The priestess resumed glaring at her guest. "I'm not sure what you get up to with your witchery and I don't want to know, but I doubt your spirits want you anywhere near this sacred house of the Holy Mother and her Saint."

Lily served them tea in dainty porcelain teacups before fleeing the room.

"I'm here because of the unexplainable increase in courier deaths." Dis sipped his tea.

The priestess sniffed. "What would I know about that?"

"You didn't offer that particular blessing on this specific day because of tradition." Dis laid his saucer on the desk and looked pointedly at her.

"I offered it as a service to the community, God's divine care to the *orthodox* believers." Ida blew on the surface of her tea. Her eyes narrowed as Dis grinned wolfishly.

"You offered it because you know someone's tampering with the luck, Mother."

"Superstition!" Ida set her cup down and frowned until he stopped smiling.

"You don't normally use the sword for blessings. Church protocol is to use it for severing malicious attention or, in other words, clearing bad luck."

"Your generation is in love with death. You, in particular, are chasing it right out of this world and into the next." She sighed and looked up at him sharply. "That's what luck is, you know, love of life. Love life, and the Holy Mother directs you to happiness. Love death, and it draws you to your grave. There are so many dying now, too many looking to death. All of them so young."

"Tell me about the others."

She stared at him for a moment. "There has been, as you say, an increase. Primarily among the homeless. We've had sixteen charity funeral Masses in the last three months. Poor dears, dying down there in the tunnels or falling into the streets. They race on the rooftops for some harebrained reason. The Church covers the costs. The Department of Safety & Protection says they're all accidents, but …"

"There are too many."

"Far too many! We've had more funerals than I can remember, between your couriers and the city's orphans. I keep asking for more funds for the outreach programs, as there aren't enough beds in the shelters. Your generation is too busy escaping in entertainments to be charitable to those in need." The priestess puffed out her cheeks. "And you, what power do you call upon during those heretical rites of yours out by the sea?"

Dis lifted his cup. "I call only my ancestors, stretching back to the first three: Amrwyn, Mammor, and Ournok."

"The same false gods that your father worshipped. There is only one true way and that is the Church's. *When will you accept that salvation is through the Church, not through magic?*" The priestess smacked her hand on the desk, rattling her cup.

"You were performing magic half an hour ago."

"God's blessing is not magic! Your father had the excuse of being the last of the Ornish clans. With your mother's blood, you don't have his excuse. She brought you here to be baptized and I blessed you in the name of our Holy Mother thirty years ago. The teachings of the clans are incompatible with those of the Church. You need to turn to the true teachings of the Holy Mother and her Church."

Looking past the priestess, Dis stared out the window at the garden behind the cathedral. His gaze moved over the bare flowerbeds and rested on the arbor obscuring the holy well. "My father carried me to the sea and dedicated me to the Eldest, Father Earth, Mother Ocean, and Parent Sky. We've certainly never harmed anyone …"

"Don't be a horse's ass." The priestess's voice was stern. "I think you misunderstand me intentionally sometimes, boy. I'm afraid *for* you, not *of* you. Of the powers you barter with. He died because of his beliefs, *your* beliefs. They killed him in his own home."

Twisting in his chair, Dis turned his face away. "As you performed the funeral rites there, you know very well my father died in the hospital."

"He poisoned himself! Then you stole his body!"

He kept his gaze down. "I did what he asked of me. I gave him to the sea."

"You threw away his chance to be at rest. You ignored the traditions of the Church. You choose death over life, proving once again that you are in love with death."

"I am not." He kept his gaze on the polished wooden floor. "This is an old argument between the Church and the clans. You know we do not worship death."

"The clans are gone." She frowned. "Your morbid adherence to their ways is what drove Bone away."

Dis gave her a pained look. "That's not …"

She pursed her lips. "Will you give up your unhealthy fascination with the past? Let go of the clans, child. They are dead and gone and their ways should go too. Do you understand me? I want you to live in the present. Your father never could, and it killed him."

Dis dropped his head. "I already come to Saturday services."

"Clean your ears out, boy. I'm telling you to reconcile with Bone. No one will ever love you as much as that man."

Avoiding her gaze, Dis set his cup down on her desk. "I will see his band when they play in a couple of months."

"Good." Ida watched her godson as he rose from his chair. "Have faith. The Holy Mother loves you as She loves all of Her children. Even the stubborn, willful ones."

She watched him walk to the door. "I had a terrible vision." Her eyes were distant and unfocused. "Two months ago, on Victory Night. It was terrible. Blood flooded Victory Square. A voice spoke to me. It was a young woman's voice." Trembling, the elderly woman looked at Dis. "She said, '*Death comes for the blessed and the cursed alike.*'"

He stopped with his hand on the doorknob and looked back at her. "A nightmare."

"I thought so, but the next morning I received a phone call from the monastery in Sweet Meadow. There's a holy sister there, a secluded mystic of our order. She woke up that very night, screaming. She dreamt of the city drowning in blood."

Dis smiled reassuringly and shrugged. "People have nightmares all the time."

"Holy Mother and her Saint, I shouldn't have to justify holy visions to *you*, of all people."

"I'm sorry you were upset by it. Thank you for sharing it with me, and for the tea." Dis inclined his head to her, opened the door, and exited her office.

"IF YOU'RE DONE, can I borrow the tape?" Otter looked at Zade and put out his hand.

She chucked the roll at him. "I think it's stupid to use our numbers."

Frowning, Zade hauled herself up onto a granite memorial stone inscribed with the outline of a shepherd flanked by two hounds. "We should be covering them too."

"You worried about Dis getting a call, or S&P?" Otter ripped a strip of tape and slapped it over his bike's license plate.

"Fuck S&P. What are they going to do, give me a ticket?" She surveyed the Point of Graves and turned to look out over the harbor. The lights of the fishing boats moved slowly toward the docks near the Warehouse District.

"So that means you're worried about our sweet-tempered dispatcher. What's he going to do? If he fires you, Patty will hire you in a second."

Zade glanced up at the city's skyline. "I don't want to work for Patty."

With his head down, Otter grinned and kept working on his task. "What, don't want to get one of the fancy-colored jackets?"

She started chewing on the side of her thumb and looked back at her friend.

"I hate having him mad at me."

"When has he ever been mad at you?" Otter tore off another piece of tape and patched a crack on the cover of his motorcycle's air filter.

"When I punched that cabbie last summer." Zade hopped off the headstone and kicked at a piece of gravel on the graveyard path. "You've heard him yell at Mat."

"Mat deserves it. He's a fucking asshole for riding trashed. Dis is okay. He's got our best interests at heart. Worst he can do is give you that disapproving look, then tell you how disappointed he is, and how you've disgraced your company …"

She rolled her eyes at him. "You done?"

"No, but I'll save it for when you've had a drink and revived your sense of humor." He threw the tape at her.

"You put some over your helmet camera?"

"No."

"Well, you better." Zade tossed the roll back. "Hurry up, looks like they're lining up."

"How many can you make out?" Otter slapped a piece of tape on the camera aperture in his helmet.

"Looks like twenty. Thought there would be more."

"It's a holiday. Who in their right mind wants to race when they could be eating and getting properly intoxicated with their adoring families?"

She grinned at him. "Us."

"You'll note that I said, 'In their right mind.'" He hung his arm around her neck. "Let's go show the babies how to waste company gas."

They got on their bikes and rode along the cemetery path among the fallen slate headstones until they reached the parking area outside the wrought-iron gates. Most of the couriers wore their regular leathers and armored boots, with a few extra pieces of padding. Kitty wore a sleek one-piece black racing suit with her company number stitched on the back in hot pink. Instead of his livery jacket, Avery wore a black leather jacket emblazoned with hand-painted scarlet symbols.

"Nobody told me there was a fashion shoot!" Otter hollered.

"Lick me." Kitty glared at Otter. "Everyone know the route? Each rider needs to make contact with each of the eight landmarks. First one to touch all of them and the Seat of Victory wins. Any questions, touchholes?" She surveyed the group. "Five minutes and then Ton drops the flag. Good luck, shitbags."

A cacophony of rumbling, spluttering engine noise filled the small park and echoed over the water as the riders started their bikes. A man walked out in front of the assembled riders and held a fluorescent green flag over his head.

"Don't fucking run me over!" Ton consulted his watch, then circled the flag overhead. "Go!" He snapped the flag down.

Zade waited until the first motorcycles blazed by the cart seller. She watched Avery outmaneuver the lead rider, smiled, and kicked her bike into gear. She took up the rear as the racing pack claimed the Southern Promenade from the Point of Graves to First Landing, spreading out over the empty two-lane road. The riders circled the monument in a line. Each stuck a hand out to swipe the bronze plaque near the entrance of the Underground station. Cart sellers with clipboards screamed profanities at the riders while scribbling down their numbers.

The pack divided, spilling around the cars on the rotary at Glory Avenue and Cart Street, shouting and laying into their motorcycles' horns, startling the drivers. Many of the cars frantically pulled over as the bikes entered the circle at highway speeds. The couriers jostled for position on Dolphin Lane, cutting down Carlisle to go under the Midtown Byway. The motorcycles roared up Milk Street, heading up Gallows Hill.

Zade continued to hang back, letting the others loop through the grounds at the top of the hill. She was the last in the line to graze the marker stone with her gloved fingertips.

As the pack disappeared back down the hill, Zade veered off by the park's outdoor toilet hut. The race judges' mouths hung open as her bike plunged down the footpath. The beam from her headlight bounced madly over the trail leading down the backside of Gallows Hill.

With her boot heels skimming the path, Zade ducked to avoid tree branches. A man jumped out of her way as she slammed through his makeshift campsite on the side of the trail. Clearing the trees, she drove up onto the sidewalk on Maple Street. She cranked her throttle open and blasted across the street, heading the wrong way into one-way traffic. Horns blared as she zipped by.

She merged onto the Midtown Byway on the northbound ramp and hopped lanes. Holiday lights from the upper floors of nearby buildings cast bright colors over her motorcycle as she traveled along the raised roadway. She took the exit ramp without slowing, spiraling down to the westbound side of the Riverway. An icy wind billowed up from the river, buffeting her and pushing her to the far edge of the lane. Flattening her upper body against the gas tank, Zade cracked open the throttle. She glided into a hard right turn at the top of the turnoff and went up on her pegs on the cobblestones along the Shipwreck Memorial.

The race judges were drinking and chatting as she approached. She tapped her horn and the cart workers stared at her in dismay as she parked her bike and ran up the steps to lay a glove on the side of the statue.

One of the women shouted. "You couldn't be here already!"

Zade jumped back on her bike. "Mark it!" She gunned her engine and merged back onto the Riverway.

She drove through a service vehicle exit and passed through an alley, kicking heaps of trash bags and surprising the restaurant workers taking breaks by the dumpsters. Turning onto the top of Mercy, she crossed the centerline and ran two red lights. She parked at the curb outside of St. Anna's and dodged by the parishioners heading into the church for the holiday Mass. A group of cart workers cheered as she tagged the side of the cathedral.

A bus barreled out in front of Mercy Station and Zade cranked on the throttle to avoid being struck. The bus driver swore at the courier as she snaked around the vehicle to get onto Granite Lane. Cutting through a nameless alley, Zade merged onto Charity Street.

She swung around the back of the Station, gunning her motorcycle up the steep hill to the Captain's Monument. Avery was getting on his motorcycle as she rode her bike up the grassy patch. He shouted in surprise as Zade reached out with her boot and kicked the base of the obelisk.

As the rest of the competitors climbed the hill, Zade plunged by them, going the opposite way. Otter yelled and she flipped three of her gloved fingers up. She drove her bike west and navigated a maze of neighborhood districts, dodging between alleys and one-way streets. On Pearl, she parked her bike and climbed the chain-link fence, dropping down onto the miniature battleship of the War Monument.

"Happy Solstice from 90-32." She waved at the departing judges who were in the process of getting into a taxi.

The race judges looked on in shock as Zade scaled the fence and vaulted over the top. One of the judges started applauding while his companion shook his head and wrote down her number.

On Pioneer, an S&P cruiser with the lights on appeared behind Zade. She started to pull over and the cruiser sailed by, turning its siren on as it passed. She whooped with glee and followed in the vehicle's wake right into Post Office Square. The cruiser turned as they entered the square and another S&P vehicle appeared in the oncoming lane.

Zade spotted a group of people congregated at the fountain. She went up the crosswalk, laying into the horn, scattering holiday shoppers from the ice sculpture they had been admiring.

"Shit." Zade craned her head, scanning for the race judges. She eased her way around the fountain.

"I would have thought you'd be at the front." Liz ran up to her.

Zade grinned at Liz and the large man with her. "Going the other way."

"Well, go on and tag it. We'll vouch for you." The man laughed as Zade hung over the barrier and smacked the fountain.

Zade crossed the square, tapping out a rhythm on her horn. She cut off two cars and nearly dumped her bike on Tulip Lane when a food cart skipped out in front of her. At the end of the lane, she went up onto the sidewalk and cut over a holiday display. A shower of mud rained down and she had to keep her boot heels dug in to avoid dumping.

Market Square was a dense clot of last-minute shoppers and holiday celebrants. A brass band played and shrieking children ran about. The pedestrians drifted back and forth across the street in waves. Zade revved her engine. Her back tire squealed as she clamped the front brake and fishtailed, burning a black mark onto the pavement. People cowered away from her as the smoke and stink of burning rubber filled the air.

Zade leapt into the brief corridor through the crowd and the square vanished behind her. As she merged onto the Straight, she shifted into fifth gear and lay over her tank, behind the fairing. A sliver of the crescent moon appeared between the skyscrapers and she decreased her speed as it slipped into a tangle of clouds. Tires squealed as cars braked to avoid hitting her as she ran a light, turned onto the northern extension of Watt Street, and cut over onto Pierce Street.

Veering up onto the pedestrian walkway, Zade's trajectory brought her out onto the wide marble expanse of Victory Square. She shouted as the monument came into view. In her left mirror, a single headlight appeared, swinging in from the Straight.

Using both brakes, Zade dropped her anchor leg down as the back of the bike swung in a wide arc. Snapping her faceplate up, she launched upward, dropping her bike against the steps. Metal scraped on stone as another motorcycle bounced into the marble steps of the monument.

As she was reaching for the stone seat, a camera flash went off. Zade tripped, the corner of the seat catching her on the cheek. "Shit!" She flung herself forward, landing sideways in the Seat of Victory.

"We have a winner! 90-32!" A woman leaned over the stone back and looked down at Zade. "Are you okay?"

Zade wiped the blood from the cut on her face as Avery stood on the step below her, glaring. "She went the wrong way, Vicky."

"Rules said we had to get to all eight stops, but not in what order. Courier's prerogative to get the job done as fast as she can, however she can." Zade sprawled in the seat. "I have witnesses at all locations, including the Post Office fountain." She removed her helmet as the other riders parked below. "Avery, quit looking at me like I stole your puppy."

"Look at *you!*" Otter pointed from the back of his bike.

"Time to drink!" Zade climbed off the monument.

A girl with a first aid kit charmed Zade into letting her put a surgical strip on her cut before the entire pack rode around the corner to the hotel. The couriers parked in rows on the opposite side of Pierce Street. Outside the hotel, the doorwoman winced at the din until they killed their engines.

▽ ↗ ◢

"I can't believe you went the wrong way." Avery unlocked the suite's door.

"Get over it," Zade laughed. As the door opened, she came to a full stop.

"Move your skanky ass, I want a beer!" Kitty tried to push by, but Zade blocked her with an outstretched arm. "What the fuck?" She followed Zade's gaze. "Oh, shitballs."

Looking into the suite, Avery slumped against the door frame.

"I hope you don't mind. We started without you." Patty gave them a smug smile, raising her glass of sparkling wine. "Zade, close your mouth, dear, you look like a fish." Turning, Patty swatted at Dis. "Stop hovering, I think she's afraid of you."

"I hear congratulations are in order." Dis offered his hand. Zade managed to shut her mouth as she shook it.

"You knew?" Her eyes flickered to Patty and then back to Dis.

"That all of you planned to risk your lives racing illegally, causing Holy Mother knows how much damage, while wearing your company numbers in our temperamental winter weather?" Patty walked over to the buffet table by the balcony windows. "Or that you're all a bunch of adrenaline addicts who talk about everything with your headsets on?"

"Uh …"

"Yes. Though my feelings are a bit dented that you didn't think to ask us to attend this fabulous party. Why are you standing there, we should be toasting!" Patty raised her glass again.

"You knew and didn't say anything?" Zade looked at Dis.

He gave her one of his rare full smiles. "Things have been bleak lately and we thought you could use something to look forward to. Consider it a Solstice present."

"Where's the bed? I want to see how big it is." Kitty looped one arm around Avery and the other around Clink's shoulder.

"Fuck that. I want to see how big the bar is." Clink shrugged her off and started across the room.

▽↗◢

Couriers and cart folk stacked the suite's living room furniture against the wall as over a hundred people streamed into the rooms of the hotel's premier suite. A brief squabble between two couriers over the music was settled by the dispatchers and soon the main section of the suite was transformed into a dance floor. Dis retreated to a corner and watched as Zade took up a position in front of the largest speaker as a bass line started to thump through it. Within a few minutes, she was encircled by admirers.

"She doesn't even know they're there." Wearing a white dress, Jeniel walked closer to Dis and nodded toward Zade.

"She tends to focus on one thing at a time." He turned to reply.

"I'm Jeniel. I own the Blue Lotus." She tucked a piece of her long hair behind her ear. "My employee Mala is out there, hoping to catch her eye. She has quite a crush on your courier."

"Dis." He shook the hand she offered.

"You gave a lecture at the Shining Star on the ritual use of sacred pathways in the city." Jeniel's eyes sparkled. "My favorite one, though, was on how the legends of the Ornish shaped the design of the city."

"That was quite some time ago." He watched her fingers trace through her hair again. "You may be the only person who attended both."

"Mala and I have been talking about having a lecture series at the shop." She gave him a warm smile, placing her hand on his arm. "Would you be interested?"

Shaking his head, Dis looked down at his empty glass. "I wouldn't have anything new to present."

"We've only been open for a few months, but we have a solid customer base. We want to branch out a bit, and lectures by local experts would be ideal. It would be fine for you to offer the same lectures again."

Dis shook his head. "I wouldn't call myself an expert."

"Mr. Quail does, on the Ornish in particular." She indicated his glass. "What are you drinking?"

"Whiskey. Thanks." Dis watched Jeniel walk over to the impromptu bar. He dug out a coin, flipped it, and caught it in the same hand. Opening his palm, he smiled and pocketed the coin.

A woman with long black and purple hair began a sultry, hip-heavy dance, tracing a path around Zade. She spiraled into the courier's embrace and managed to lure a third woman in. Soon the dancer led the spiral wider, gathering people into the line and drawing them out one by one.

Jeniel reappeared and waved her empty hands. "It seems they've misplaced the whiskey."

Grimacing, Dis glanced over at the bar, which was overrun with couriers. "They should have kept it under lock and key."

"I have a bottle of Newton ten year at my place if you would care to come back and have a drink with me." She tilted her head.

Dis arched his eyebrows. "The celebration has just started."

"I've been looking forward to meeting you for some time." She held out her hands to him. "Now that I have, I know how I want the night to end."

In the taxi, Jeniel straddled Dis's lap. Curling her fingers behind his head, she laid her thumbs against the underside of his jaw and lightly brushed her lips against his. She ran her thumbs along the sides of his face and tightened her grip. Tilting his face to the side, she traced a line with the tip of her tongue to his neck. Dis pressed her closer, sliding his hands up her back. As her teeth grazed his skin, he hefted the silken length of her hair.

Jeniel's eyes blazed as she pulled back, staring down at him. Leaning in suddenly, she crushed her mouth against his. Her eyelids fluttered closed as she sank into the passionate kiss. When they arrived at the Blue Lotus, she tugged him inside by the lapels of his coat, laughing as she opened the apartment door behind the counter.

In the bedroom, she unzipped his trousers as he slid her dress up over her hips. The white dress sparkled as it puddled on the rug by the foot of the bed. Sitting astride his hips, she reached down for his glasses. He caught her fingers.

"Let me see you." Jeniel tried to get her hands free.

"While the lights are on, they stay on." He released her hands and hooked his thumbs through the strings of her thong. He looked at her questioningly.

She nodded and he tore the strands. Jeniel fell forward to grip the metal bar of the headboard. Her hands groped blindly for a moment, then she arched backward, gasping. She collapsed onto him and kissed her way down his chest as he laughed. His laughter cut off abruptly as she dug her nails into his side.

There was a challenge in her voice. "Too much?"

"No."

He sat up and began undoing the straps on his left leg. The brace hit the floor and then the two of them peeled his trousers off completely. Keeping her eyes on him, Jeniel opened the drawer of her nightstand and took out a condom. She leaned over him with a predatory smile and set it on the pillow next to his head. Grazing the side of her neck with his teeth, he coiled her hair loosely in his hands. Sweat trickled down her back as they moved. His hands caressed her stomach and breasts as her hips traced a figure eight. She rose and fell until he wrapped his arms around her and flipped them both sideways.

Jeniel's fingernails cut into the backs of his shoulders as he licked the hollow along the rise of her left hip. Blood welled up in the crescent impressions under her nails and she gave a sharp cry. She seized a handful of his hair, twisting it. "Kiss me."

Glancing up, Dis laid his tongue on Jeniel's skin, eliciting another cry from her.

"Now." She twisted her hand in his hair until he winced.

With a mischievous grin, he reached over to turn off the light on the nightstand and complied.

$$\triangledown \nearrow \blacktriangle$$

In the Victory Suite at the Pierce Hotel, Zade bolted upright in the king-sized bed, shaking and dripping sweat.

"You okay?" Kitty swatted at her from under the covers.

"Had a nightmare. Go back to sleep." Naked, Zade climbed out from under the scarlet sheets and stumbled into the bathroom.

"Hey, what's happening?" Raising his head from a pile of blankets and pillows on the floor, Clink watched her walk across the room.

"Zade's had a bad dream. Go back to sleep, fucker." Kitty rolled over.

Clink's voice drifted out from his nest. "Tell her, flip the pillow. It always helps me."

Zade closed the bathroom door and turned on the light. She walked over to the sink and looked in the gold-framed mirror. She stared at the dark smudges under her eyes and turned on the faucet. She splashed cold water over her face and wrists, then rested the top of her head against the mirror and stared down the drain. "Shit." Walking out, she turned off the light and went over to the balcony doors. Laying her fingers on the glass, Zade stared out over Victory Square, then glanced up at the looming shadow of the Pierce Tower.

"Come back to bed." Kitty's voice was muffled by a pillow.

"Go back to sleep." Zade left the window and searched the floor for her clothes.

Moments later she was dressed and descending in the elevator. The night clerk scrutinized her as she crossed the lobby. The doorman inclined his head and held the door open as she exited the building and walked over to the row of motorcycles parked across the street.

Riding in the pre-dawn blackness, she shivered. The city's early morning traffic vanished as she took the ramp onto the Riverway. The lights of the bridge hovered above the black expanse of the river as the eastern sky lightened. The courier stopped at one of the gas stations beyond the bridge and watched the stars fade above Rest and Be Thankful Cemetery while she filled the tank.

She crossed the Hinterlands, passing the few other vehicles on the road. The silhouettes of bare trees framed the highway as the outline of the Ouring Ridge shifted from black to gray. At the tollbooth, Zade threw change into the basket and kept riding as the rising sun poured warmth over the back of her jacket. She cracked her faceplate and wiped the tears away as she turned onto the first exit. Parking her bike on the shoulder, she tore her helmet off and closed her eyes.

"Fuck. Why won't you let me leave?"

$$\nabla \nearrow \blacktriangle$$

The next morning, when Zade left her apartment, a crow chattered from a

80

nearby tree and a smaller bird replied with a territorial warning. The black bird's raucous response was interrupted by the motorcycle's engine noise. The startled crow flew out of the tree and perched on the roof of the apartment building, cocking its head.

Zade rode to the Pit wearing goggles but no helmet, letting the air wash over her. When she got there, she swapped her goggles for her earpiece and helmet. "Dispatch, 90-32 at the Pit." She cinched her waist strap and stared up at the cloud-heavy sky.

"Pickup at 19 Grove, Suite 2082. Going to 110 Turtle Drive, out in Hinterlands. Doctor Greyer's office."

"On it."

▽ ↗ ◢

The law office's intern stared in awe at the courier as she took the packet from him. He followed her out of the building and down to her parked motorcycle. His eyes darted over the machine and its rider.

"Did you need something else?" Zade started her engine and glared at him.

The young man shook his head, still staring as she drove away.

The morning outbound traffic in the tunnel was sparse compared to the backed-up oncoming lanes. The courier groaned. "Dispatch, this run is going to cost me the whole morning."

"Same pay regardless, unless a bonus comes in."

"I'm going to be stuck on the wrong side of the tunnel for it."

▽ ↗ ◢

Outside the doctor's office, several birds were fighting for space on a feeder. The metal cylinder rotated madly as feathered bodies whirled around it. As Zade rang the bell, one of the birds crashed into the main window. The courier jumped at the noise, and the stunned creature fell into the bushes.

"Poor thing. We had a hawk come right through last week." The receptionist reached for the packet. "Had to replace the glass."

Zade shook her head as she held out the recorder. "Could you please give me a print?"

"Of course, dear." The woman thumbed the recorder. "Have a good day."

The bushes rippled as a gray cat emerged, carrying the twitching bird in its mouth.

Zade walked back to her bike. "Dispatch, I have a hunch it's going to be a while before I get back into town."

"Take your time, 90-32."

□ ♍ ♏ ♋ ■

The first accident she drove by was a minor fender bender. She watched the drivers exchange information amicably in the breakdown lane. The second was at the entrance of the tunnel. A man sat on the guardrail, holding his head in his hands. There was blood splattered at his feet. Zade's eyes lingered on the slick pavement.

She watched him in her left side mirror. "Dispatch, is S&P on it?"

"S&P trauma unit ought to be there any second now."

She watched the ambulance inch through the heavy midday traffic as cars tried to pull over. Soon she was riding the double line back through the tunnel. "90-32 city-side. Anything, dispatch?"

"Pickup 15 State Street, main desk. Going to 165 Pierce Street, Suite 22."

"On it."

At the pickup location, her thumb recorder failed to operate. She knocked it against her thigh and held it out again. "Sorry, could you try one more time?"

The woman in a gray skirt and suit jacket poked the device again and gave the courier an annoyed look. "Did it work this time?"

"Yes, thank you. Battery must be dying." Zade shoved the packet into her bag.

"Have a nice day." The woman reached for the phone.

"You too." The courier sidestepped a delivery person with a dolly full of boxes to avoid a collision.

At the curb, her motorcycle backfired and stalled out when she tried to start it. "Dis, can you ask Iris if she's got time to check my bike later?"

"I'll ask. Hold."

At the corner of State and Green, a black luxury sedan braked abruptly and Zade cracked her throttle open to sprint around it. She cut between cars, kicked her bike up into the highway gear, and zipped down the centerline until she cut across the oncoming lane. She thumbed on her right turn signal at the corner of Watt and Pierce Street as a landscaping truck's gate fell open and a riding mower tumbled out, slamming into the middle of the street.

Zade pushed down on her rear brake and clamped her hand brake lever in, throwing her right hip sideways. The back end of her motorcycle slid forward. With her left boot on the ground, she came to a complete stop in the center of the intersection, two feet away from the mower.

Before she could catch her breath, a taxi plowed into the front of Zade's motorcycle, throwing her backward onto the hood of a parked car.

"90-32, status! Zade!"

"Dispatch …"

The headset squealed with feedback. Zade slid off the hood.

An older man in tweed helped her up, peering at her through his bifocal glasses. "Good God! Are you alright?"

Dis's voice crackled in her ear. "S&P headed to your location. Stay where you are. Pickup is coming."

Zade pulled off her cracked helmet and winced at the wreckage of her motorcycle. "Might as well cancel that appointment with Iris." She stumbled out of the grasp of the concerned bystander.

"Stay put, 90-32. Wait for 11-46 to pick up."

She kept walking. "I'm right at the location, dispatch." The sirens became audible as she pushed open the glass doors of 165 Pierce Street and limped to the bank of elevators.

"Sit your ass down. Now, 90-32."

Zade pushed the elevator button. "Shut up, dispatch."

The elevator bell sounded and she got on.

"Is that blood?" A man in a beige suit gave her a stricken look and took a step back.

Zade looked at the blood dripping off her gloved hand. "Sorry." She sagged against the wall, keeping her eyes on the ascending floor numbers.

The receptionist stood up as Zade limped out of the elevator toward her desk, holding out the recorder and packet. "Oh my, what happened?" Grabbing a tissue, the woman offered it to the courier.

Crossing the carpet, Zade smacked the malfunctioning recorder against the reception desk. "Sorry to rush you, but I've got an ambulance waiting."

Static electricity snapped between the two women as the courier handed the packet over. The receptionist flinched. "Have a good day," the woman's voice quavered and she dropped the envelope on her desk, recoiling from the blood on her fingers.

In the elevator down, Zade clung to the wall, watching the floor numbers winking on and off. She lost her balance coming through the lobby doors and started to fall.

An S&P medic caught her. "Easy, I'm just going to have you lie down on the stretcher."

Zade slapped at his hands. "Don't cut my leathers."

"Your dispatcher will have my hide if you hit the pavement. He's been on our asses to find you. I don't want to make him any angrier."

"He's not that bad …"

Dis roared through her headset. "90-32, sit down and shut up!"

▽↗◢

A nurse in scrubs approached Dis as he stepped out of the elevator. "Your courier's ready to leave, but Doctor Mwsyr wishes to speak with you." The man guided Dis to a curtained bay. "I'll tell the Doctor you're here."

"Thank you."

A doctor with a clipboard and an entourage of nurses rounded the corner. The group stopped and the doctor glanced over the top of her glasses at Dis. She murmured to the nurses and they retreated to the emergency room's nursing station. As the doctor approached, the older woman's gaze flickered over the darkened left lens of the dispatcher's glasses. "The courier works for you?"

"Yes." He inclined his head to her.

"The laceration on her scalp required ten stitches, but there's no indication of a concussion. Hairline fractures are possible. However, they often will not show up on X-rays. I'm recommending a follow-up in a week. She's bruised and scraped and is to be on bed rest. The nurse will give you a prescription for the pain. She's to go home directly, no celebratory trips to the bars. I want you to make sure she stays in." The doctor's expression intensified as she looked at Dis more closely. "I find I am relieved to patch up one of your people so easily. Foolish of me, as I expect you will only send her out to do it again tomorrow."

Under the doctor's scrutiny, Dis shrugged. "It is the job she has chosen."

"I hope it pays well." She looked pointedly at his leg brace and cane.

His expression hardened. "We know the risks."

Mwsyr frowned as she looked over the clipboard in her hand. "The hospital report to the city manager shows an increase in fatalities, a dramatic rise from one fatality per year to seven. The rate of minor injury remains at one incident per every twenty hours worked." She glanced up sharply.

"They were experienced riders. All of them had over two years." A nurse appeared and gave Dis a prescription slip. "Thank you."

"She's not to be on a motorcycle for a few days." Mwsyr hugged her clipboard. "If it was my decision, cousin, she'd never get on one again."

"Feel free to try and convince her."

The doctor inclined her head. "If I am unable to convince you, I will not try to influence your employees."

The corner of his mouth twitched. "I appreciate your, and your staff's, care of my people, cousin."

She turned away. "I wish it was not required so often."

He watched her walk to the end of the corridor, where she passed an orderly pushing Zade in a wheelchair. The doctor bent and spoke to her for a moment and then continued around the corner.

Zade made an apologetic face at Dis as the orderly pushed her closer to the bay. "Sorry, they had me sign a million things." She got up and collected her gear from the bed and returned to the wheelchair.

"I don't mind waiting to get good news." Dis started walking alongside her as they moved toward the elevator.

"Maddy's?" Zade looked up hopefully as the doors opened.

Dis shook his head and shared a look with the orderly. "I promised your doctor I'd get you home without stopping at the bar."

"Oh, come on."

"I have a prescription for you that doesn't play well with others." He showed her the slip.

"Not the same at all." Zade pulled on her leather jacket. "I already have that one at home."

When they reached the ground floor, the orderly waved to one of the cabs. The driver stepped out to open the door.

"54 Pioneer." Dis got in next to Zade.

The woman nodded at him in the rearview mirror. "Gotcha."

Resting her head against the top of his shoulder, Zade looked up at Dis. "How's the bike? Salvageable?"

"Iris said, 'Broom, dustpan, and a tiny box.'" Dis gave a small shake of his head. "Sorry."

"Fuck." She closed her eyes and relaxed against him.

He watched her for a moment, then turned to look out the window.

Zade gasped suddenly, then cringed forward with her chest on her knees.

Dis glanced up at the driver. "Bring us back to the hospital entrance, please."

"No! I'm fine." Zade panted in pain. "Take me home."

"It could be …" He set his hand on her back as the driver looked at them in the mirror.

"I'm fine. I just want to go home."

He smoothed his hand down the back of her leather. "I'm not sure …"

"Please, Dis."

"What will it be, folks?" The driver waited for a response.

Dis kept his hand on Zade's back. "54 Pioneer."

Zade rested her head on the back of the front passenger seat until the taxi pulled up outside of her brownstone. Dis paid the driver and helped Zade out of the car.

He took her house keys from her hand as she slumped onto the top step. "We could go back."

"They can't do anything for me except give more of the same prescription." Zade rocked back and forth as he unlocked the door to the building.

He helped her inside and began the slow process of getting her up to the third floor. As he unlocked her apartment door, Zade crouched with her arms wrapped around her stomach.

Glancing through the doorway, Dis frowned at a solitary metal folding chair in an otherwise empty living room. He looked at the bare rods above the bay windows and then down at an empty glass next to the chair leg. "I hate to tell you this, but it looks like you've been robbed."

"I don't own a lot of stuff." Zade stumbled through her apartment and into the bathroom.

Without looking up, she gripped the bathroom sink, opened the medicine cabinet, and grabbed a bottle, shaking out two pills and swallowing them. She ran the water and splashed it over her face.

Dis watched from the doorway as she perched on the edge of the tub, took a heating pad out from under the sink, plugged it in, threw a towel into the tub, and attempted to tug off her boots without untying them.

Dis came in and sat on the toilet lid, lifted her feet up into his lap, and untied her bootlaces. He removed her boots and placed them neatly next to the toilet. Zade pushed off her riding trousers and lowered herself the rest of the way into the dry bathtub.

"You look like you're planning on staying in there for a while."

"Yes."

He nodded toward the rest of the apartment. "Tell me you own a bed."

"I don't want to ruin it." She placed the heating pad on her stomach and dragged the towel over her lower body. "It's the only nice thing I own."

He looked down at the blue-stained bath mat. "You take three days off to sleep in the tub every month."

"Two days in the tub. Third is for laundry."

"They make rubber sheets."

She glared at him and adjusted the setting on the heating pad's controller. "Why are you still here?"

"I'm trying to ascertain if this fulfills my promise to your doctor or if I have to call another ambulance."

"Don't. They can't do anything, and I couldn't stand being treated like a freak right now." She closed her eyes.

He looked back at her boots and rumpled leathers on the floor. "You weren't expecting it today."

"I'll be fine." She dragged the towel up higher.

"There might be something they didn't find causing it to start early."

"It happens. Stress ..."

After a moment of silence, Dis looked at her. "Can I get you anything?"

Zade opened her eyes slowly. "There's a pitcher of water in the fridge. Thanks."

He got up and went through the empty living room into a large kitchen devoid of any cooking supplies or appliances. The refrigerator contained a jug of water and a battered takeaway container. He glanced back at the unadorned walls of the apartment and at the single drinking glass in the living room.

He returned to the bathroom and set the jug and glass next to the tub. "Jeniel at the Blue Lotus might be able to suggest an herbal remedy."

"What is it with you guys? Otter's always trying to get me in there too."

Dis went over to the towel rack. "I'm staying for a while to make sure you don't need anything else."

Zade closed her eyes again. "Fine."

"Raise your head for me." He placed a towel under her neck. His hand hesitated for a moment before moving her hair out of her eyes.

A faint smile curled the corners of Zade's mouth and her breathing deepened. Dis rested the back of his hand against her forehead and watched the pulse in her neck settle.

Walking back into the bedroom, Dis laid his hand on the queen-sized bed's clean white comforter. He quietly returned to the bathroom and sat on the closed toilet. Zade was curled into a fetal position. A ribbon of blood ran along the bottom of the white porcelain tub and into the drain.

Zade opened one eye. "Frankie says you keep a cabinet of weird things in the dispatch booth."

"Frankie talks too much."

"Is it for magic?"

"Yes."

"What do you use it for?"

Kiarna Boyd

"To keep the couriers safe." Dis gave her a crooked smile. "It doesn't always work as well as I'd like."

Trying to focus her eyes, she shifted the towel under her head. "How does it work?"

"This may not be the best time to try and explain."

"I'm not going anywhere."

"No, but you're half-asleep." He glanced up, meeting her eyes. "It can wait until we go out for a drink. Next week's your fourth anniversary running for OC, isn't it? We should celebrate."

"Yeah." She reached out of the tub to poke his knee. "Are you avoiding the question?"

He filled the water glass. "It helps to think of it as indirect action or influence."

"Like manipulating people into doing what you want them to do?"

He held out the glass. "When I was young, my father said magic was for hunting what a person desires and making sure it happens. A full net of fish, a warm fire in the hearth, and a strong family to share them with. The oldest magic ensured the basic things we need to survive. Food, shelter, health, and safety."

She took a sip and moved to set the glass on the floor. "What about love?"

He took the glass from her and set it down. "That too."

"Ever use it for love?"

"If you mean to make a person fall in love with me, no. I have used it on behalf of someone I loved. To improve their chance at fame."

Her words slurred again as her eyes unfocused. "It worked."

He dropped his gaze to her clothes by the side of the tub. "You shouldn't listen to gossip."

"It's true, though."

"He was, is, talented enough not to need my help." He lined up her boots and grabbed her discarded leathers.

"What's it like?" She had closed her eyes again and her voice faded off at the end of her sentence.

"Magic?" Dis looked at her as he folded her leather trousers.

Zade's eyes stayed closed. "No. Being in love."

The man's lips curled up on one side of his mouth. "You'll have to get me drunk if you want to hear that story."

"Deal."

A BLACK SEDAN WITH TINTED WINDOWS took a right onto Grant and a left onto Jenkins, slowed to a crawl while it followed the old railway tracks, and disappeared behind a row of derelict shipping containers stacked against the back of the Quayside Fish Market.

Stopping outside an unmarked warehouse, a meticulously dressed older man stepped out, retrieved a white bucket from the trunk, and walked over to unlock a door into the rust-mottled building. Entering, he relocked the door and descended a metal ladder six feet down into a concrete room. Moving beyond networks of dusty pipes and a cold furnace, he opened a second door. A miasma of urine and sweat rolled out, filling the cellar.

Within a cage of mesh fencing, a young man shielded his eyes from the sudden brightness. He retreated to a cot in the far corner, his white underwear hanging loosely from his emaciated body.

The corners of the older man's eyes crinkled as he set the bucket down by the door. "I am sorry to disturb you at this hour." He dragged a wooden chair from the wall, placing it close to the fencing. "Please accept this as an apology for the inconvenience." He extended his hand and passed a plastic bottle filled with juice through a small hole in the mesh.

His captive cringed against the wall and wept.

&~౭౩⑨➍౩~

Dis let Zade's deadbolt lock behind him. Outside, he glanced back up at her windows before walking down the street. At the Cold Pail Bakery, he purchased two pounds of cheese, a fresh loaf of sourdough bread, and a pint of heavy cream. He waited at the crosswalk until the light changed and made his way to Gilbert's Market. Inside, he purchased three pounds of salmon, two lemons, six leeks, and a pound of fingerling potatoes. He asked the counter staff to triple-wrap the fish and to put it in its own plastic bag. Casting a speculative look at the sky, he walked over to Bravery Crossing Underground Station.

▽↗◢

Dis was greeted at the door by a happy trill from Stinky. He ran his hand down the cat's back, entered the kitchen, and set about prepping the food. Once the chowder was simmering on the stove, he went upstairs and took a shower. As the hot water sluiced over his back, he stared at the shower tiles. He shut the water off and reached for a towel. He held the ratty terrycloth for a moment, watching the last of the water drain out of the tub.

Stinky butted her head against his legs when he came downstairs. She followed him as he went through cabinets, took out a silver tray and a large silver tureen, and rinsed them in the sink. He tore the loaf into chunks and arranged the bread on a separate plate. The cat yowled until Dis dropped a piece of salmon into her bowl.

▽↗◢

Pouring the chowder into the tureen, he placed it and the plate of bread onto the tray and carried it up to the third-story attic. He set the food on a steamer trunk and struck a match. The hurricane lamp's wick smoked, then changed to a steady flame. The light wavered over an altar adorned with an eclectic assortment of framed photographs, ritual tools, and seashells. Many of the faces in the black and white portraits shared a resigned expression.

Along with the cluster of family portraits, the altar contained a basket of hand-dyed yarn, three tarnished metal boxes, a cabinet giving off the rich scent of imported spices, and a motorcycle's speedometer. A jumble of marine-animal vertebrae lay adhered together by the spent wax of numerous white candles. On the top of the spice cabinet were a pair of cracked motorcycle goggles, the dusty lenses crusted over with dried blood.

Dis unlatched and opened the window, filling the attic with the cold tang of brine from the tidal river below. "I invite you, my family, to be with me now. I ask for your aid and your wisdom. I ask you to be with me now." He unraveled several arm-lengths of red and white yarn and set a short tree branch on the altar.

The wind stirred the strands of fiber. The white ball of yarn bounced off the basket and onto the attic floor. A ball of unused black yarn followed, rolling to his feet. Laying aside the other strands, Dis picked up the black ball and unwound a length of it.

Tying three knots in the end of each string, he coiled the three lengths around his hand and elbow, winding them into a small skein. He began a complicated series of loops and knots, tying the strands through each other. Behind him, the steam from the chowder swirled and billowed out the window.

□ ♍ ♏ ♋ ■

On the roof of the Pierce Tower, a maintenance worker grumbled under his breath as he angled his flashlight to inspect the non-functional elevator motor in the dark machine room. He swung the light over the steel ropes resting in the elevator's pulley system and scratched at his jaw through his thick beard. With a quiet clicking sound, the lights of the control panel and the fluorescent overheads suddenly switched back on. Raising his eyebrows, the man glanced over at the motor as it began rotating the cable sheave. He watched it operate for a few minutes, then turned off his flashlight, opened the machine room door, and stepped out into a cold wind, frowning.

□ ♍ ♏ ♋ ■

In the main gallery of the Imperial College at 144 Dunaway Street, a lithe woman danced with a sword in the center of her practice space. Other performers in monstrous animal costumes danced around her, swiping at her with shaggy paws. Seated in the shadows, the accompanying musicians quieted their instruments one by one until there was only a single frenetic drumbeat. When the drum abruptly stopped, the sword dancer vanished under the mound of her attackers.

□ ♍ ♏ ♋ ■

Dis hooked one of the anchor strands with a finger and pulled, contracting the strands of yarn. He used a forefinger and thumb to transfer the remaining loops to his right hand. Spreading his fingers wide, he opened the tangled mess into the next sequence. The new pattern condensed, the strands leaving three tiny knots visible along the web. Dis stretched his fingers apart and contemplated the knots as he transferred the yarn onto the tips of the branch on the altar. "Not one, but three others to contend with."

▽ ↗ ◢

Frankie watched Dis hang up his coat. "Nothing in the queue. Weather reports are on the desk. Clear and cold. 11-12 and 30-84 are in the Pit. I let the others go. Is that okay?" She pulled her wool coat on over her fluffy pink sweater, her eyes following the senior dispatcher's movements.

"Sounds fine." Dis handed her the book she had left next to the keyboard. "See you at six."

"How's 90-32? 30-84 was asking …"

Dis looked up at Frankie. "She's fine. I expect her to be in on Monday."

Frankie flipped the ends of her braids out from under her collar and settled the strap of her messenger bag across her chest. "Okay, see you later."

As soon as the booth door closed behind the night dispatcher, Dis was up and out of his chair. Bowing, he opened the wooden cabinet, removed a white pillar candle and a box of matches, and brought them over to the control displays. He put on his headset, checked the terminal display and live helmet feeds, then read through the weather report Frankie had left for him.

"30-84, pickup at 60 Philmont, main desk. Going to 15 High." Dis lit a candle and set it between the monitors.

Otter's voice crackled over the radio channel. "On it, dispatch. How's 90-32?"

"Bruised. I noticed you were out yesterday."

"Felt sick."

A woman's voice cut over on the speaker. "Dispatch, 11-16 at the Pit."

"Nothing for you yet, 11-16." Dis flipped on the courier's helmet feed and lines scrolled on the queue terminal. "31-24, pick up at 76 Terrace. Going to the Pierce."

"On it."

The dispatcher took out a deck of cards and began to shuffle. "Breakdown in the Tunnel, southbound through the Artery. S&P blocking off all lanes. 31-10, pickup 6 Victory Court, Apartment 3, looks like pickup's a residence. Going to 19 Grove, Suite 2082." Dis split the deck into thirds. "11-62, status."

"Just coming down the elevator. Hit me, dispatch."

"111 High, main desk. Going to 72 Market, it's the doorway next to the store entrance. You are to persist until the occupant answers the door."

"It's not a fucking eviction, is it?"

"Not our jurisdiction." Dis reassembled the deck. He closed his eyes and then fanned out the back of the cards and selected one.

"Dispatch, 31-40 at the Pit."

"31-40, I've got a red hot coming in."

"Yes!"

"Pickup at 1023 Doyle, going red hot to the Pierce Hotel. The name on it is Elgar." Dis set the rest of the deck down and watched the camera feeds. Tapping the single card on the desk, he turned his head to study the queue and punched a phone number. "Good morning, Merril, I've got an urgent package coming in for one of your guests, a Ms. Elgar." He glanced at the feed again. "The courier should be there in about five minutes."

"Morning, Dis, 11-22 at the Pit."

"Morning, 11-22. Nothing at the moment."

"I'm getting a coffee."

Dis studied the card again and then put it back in the deck, on top of the others. "31-40, status."

"Almost there, getting on Pierce now."

"Dispatch, 11-62 here. Delivery is not answering the door."

"Keep knocking."

"The lady from the shop next door is yelling at me. If this keeps up, I'm quitting."

"Tell her somebody died."

"They did? Shit."

"Take it easy, Kay, happens all the time. Hold." Dis typed another phone number. "Yes, good morning, I'm calling about a delivery sent from your office this morning, ID number 6-6-300-A. The courier is reporting difficulty. It appears no one is at the address to receive the package. Certainly. I'll tell him. 11-62, keep knocking."

▽↗◢

When Frankie appeared for her next shift, Dis was straightening his black tie in the mirror. He nodded to her as she stared at him from the doorway.

"Queue is empty. 31-32 is waiting for the next one. 11-68 is taking a break. Weather is going to get bad tonight, whatever the report says. Possibly snow." Dis removed his headset, setting it on the desk. "Cancel any runs if it gets too slippery. They can wait for the morning."

She swept him with an appraising look from head to toe. "You look good in a suit."

"You've seen me in one before." Dis took his black trench coat out of the closet.

"You didn't look this good." Frankie's gaze swept from his boots to his face again. "Did you do something different with your hair? And …" She sniffed the air. "You smell yummy. I take it you're going to be out late on a school night?"

He shook his head. "I'll see you on Monday."

Buttoning his coat, Dis headed for the Underground station, taking his time navigating the puddles. By the time he got out of Market Station, patches of ice were forming on the sidewalk.

Crossing Belmont Street, Dis went into Halley's. The elderly hostess squinted at him when taking his coat, then led him to Jeniel's table. He bent over to kiss her, ran his hand over her unbound hair, and then sat down. "I hope you haven't been waiting long."

"Only a few minutes." She handed the wine list across the table, her gaze lingering. "I went out to the Hinterlands to do a reading for a client. I had three new home cleansing visits this week." The diamonds in Jeniel's necklace glittered as she sipped her cocktail. She ran her finger around the rim of the glass. "Otter mentioned Zade had an accident yesterday ..."

A young waiter appeared at the side of the table and waited until Dis looked up before speaking. "Good evening, sir. Would you care to start with a cocktail?"

Glancing at Jeniel's drink, Dis nodded. "Yes, please, Newton whiskey. Neat, please."

"Very good, sir." The waiter handed him a red leather-bound menu.

"I'm not surprised you've been so busy with clients." Dis leafed through the pages. "The last few days have been unusual."

"Why do you think so?" Jeniel touched the back of his hand.

"The luck's gone sour." He narrowed his eyes at the menu. "Their new menu seems to be mostly seafood."

"I'm thinking about the salmon." Her eyes widened as he grimaced. "Is it bad here?"

"No." He shook his head. "I'm sure it's very good, I've just always disliked seafood. I can recommend the steak tips, however." He gave her a half-smile as the waiter set his drink on the table. "Thank you."

Jeniel gave him a teasing smile. "A Mthdys not liking seafood. What must your ancestors think?"

He paused. "It did cause a fair amount of conflict with my family. They expected certain traditions to be carried on."

"I know what that's like, too." Lowering her gaze to her cocktail, she swirled the amber liquid. "As only children, parents place a great deal of expectation on us. Everything that must be done, we alone must accomplish." With a sudden intake of breath, Jeniel looked up and gave him a dazzling smile. "I'll have the steak tip salad, then."

□ ♍ ♏ ♋ ■

Zade woke up shouting and flailing. Her foot caught on the shower curtain and the suspension bar fell into the tub on top of her. The bathroom light bulb blew out with a pop, leaving her in total darkness.

"Shit." She sat up and groaned. She shoved off the fallen curtain and threw the heating pad to the floor. Groping her way into the kitchen, she heard a pop as another bulb died. "Fine. Be that way." She went back into the bathroom and hauled the shower curtain out into the living room. "There better be hot water, damn it."

She stripped off her shirt and underwear and turned on the water. Using the light coming in from the living room through the open door, she located the soap and washed the dried blood from her body. She wrapped herself in a maroon towel and slid her feet forward one at a time on her way into the bedroom. Crawling under the pristine covers, she wedged the towel between her legs and went back to sleep.

▽↗◢

The light through the bedroom window was pale gray when she woke up. Tugging the comforter all the way to the footboard, she inspected the white sheets and brushed reddish towel lint onto the bedroom floor. On the way to the kitchen, she nudged the shower curtain with her foot. She looked over at her keys on the chair in the living room. She walked over and picked them up, then stood in front of her tall bay windows, looking at the spires of St. Anna's peeking over the top of the brownstones.

▽↗◢

Snowflakes shimmered outside the windows of the Sunshine Clean Laundromat as Zade dumped the contents of her laundry bag into one of the industrial machines. Heaving herself onto one of the dryers, she watched a car crawl by on the slick street outside. By the time she finished her laundry, a cold rain was erasing all traces of the snowfall.

▽ ↗ ◢

She changed the bathroom light bulb and stood on the folding chair to change the one in the kitchen. After she stacked the clean towels in the rack, Zade scrubbed out the tub and the rest of the bathroom. At the kitchen sink, she stared at the water glass before rinsing it, shrugged on her leather jacket, and left.

▽ ↗ ◢

Outside of the Cold Pail Bakery, Zade stood next to a black touring motorcycle, longingly examining the covered, heated grips. She walked around the machine a few times before heading inside the shop. In line at the register, she watched the motorcycle's owner push water off its saddle and start up the machine.

Zade sat on the window bench and warmed her feet on a heating vent under a coffee table covered with magazines and newspapers. After she finished her coffee and the paper, she got up and headed for the payphone in the back of the shop.

"It's Zade. Yeah, I'm fine. Thanks for getting me home." She started to raise her thumb toward her mouth and then stopped abruptly. "I don't think anyone's ever taken my boots off for me or folded my stuff before. I should hire you to do all my cleaning." Grinning, she pinned the phone between her head and shoulder and draped her arm over the top of the payphone. "Do you still want to hang out tonight? Yeah? Where do you want me to meet you?" She turned to get a better view of a woman bending over to select a magazine from the nearby coffee table. "What time? Okay, see you then." Zade hung up the phone and went to sit on one of the couches. She flipped through a magazine and occasionally glanced over at the other woman.

▽↗◣

An hour later Zade walked out of Market Station. She spotted Dis standing by the entrance. His wide-brimmed hat was pulled low over his face.

As Zade walked up to him, Dis pushed his hat back and held out a hot pink shopping bag. "Congratulations on making it four years, 90-32."

"Shut up. You got me a present?" She looked at the giant glittering font in horror. "Should I be afraid?" She reached out for the bag slowly.

"Yes."

She gave him a doubtful look and rummaged through the tissue paper. "They really do make rubber sheets."

He smiled. "Friends don't let friends sleep in tubs. You look better."

Shoving the gift into her messenger bag, she shrugged. "I'm okay. I haven't eaten yet. You?"

He glanced down at her through his glasses. "I thought we might try BB's. I didn't know what you had in mind for this evening."

"They've got my favorite burger." She shot him a mischievous look. "How do you feel about bad movies?"

He narrowed his eyes. "How bad?"

"Really, really bad."

"Now *I'm* afraid."

▽↗◣

Zade held the door open for him as they entered the crowded restaurant. She waved at an older waitress. "Booth for two please, Evelyn."

The waitress winked at Zade and they followed her to a high-backed wooden booth. The window mirrored the waitress's movements as she set the menus down and took out her ordering pad.

Zade tossed her gear into the booth and slid in. "Pint of Black Dog, cheeseburger, no onions, fries."

"Sure, cupcake." Evelyn smiled, her pen skittering over the pad. "Do you need a minute with the menu, hon?"

Dis set his gear down and put his hat on top of his bag. "No, I'll have the same. Thank you."

"You are most welcome. Be right back with your beers, kids."

"Iris will have a twin Denton for you on Monday." Dis stretched out on his side of the booth, extending his legs. "And a replacement helmet."

Zade started chewing on the side of her thumb, then wedged her hand under her thigh. "I figured she'd have something."

Dis dropped his head and cleaned the right lens of his glasses on his t-shirt. "It won't be exactly like your last one."

"It's company property, not mine. I'm not like Otter, buying them presents."

"I got from your apartment that you're not into ownership."

"I like sleeping there and keeping my clothes there. Renting's like using OC's bikes. Easy."

The corners of his mouth curled up. "You've never ridden on your own motorcycle. It changes things when it's yours."

"So long as the one on Monday is as good as the last one, I'll be happy. Besides, that's less for someone to clean up when I get scraped off the road into a box."

A woman escorting a toddler back from the bathrooms smiled at Dis as the child's hands fumbled along the edge of their table. She quietly whispered in the boy's ear and directed him toward another booth.

"I hope that box is a long way off." Dis watched the child tottering down the line of booths.

Evelyn set two glasses down. "Be right back with your food, kids."

Zade grinned over the top of her beer at Dis. "I bet you have a ton of stuff."

"Most of it came with the house." He nodded his thanks to the waitress. "The cat is mine. Or I'm hers, depending on how you look at it."

"I've thought about a cat, but I'd worry about what would happen if I didn't make it home to feed it."

"You can leave food out for them or have a neighbor stop in. They are usually fine with a night or two on their own."

"Who will take care of yours if you don't go home? Your family?"

Dis shook his head. "They're all gone."

She winced. "Sorry."

"The cat is enough to take care of."

"To cats?" She raised her pint glass.

"To cats." Dis touched his glass to hers. "It does make it easier if you have roommates."

"Then there are always arguments about who ate what out of the fridge and who used what in the shower. At least if I run out of toilet paper, I only have myself to blame."

"Otter was a good roommate." Dis angled his head, centering his gaze on her. "Though, that was a long time ago."

"You lived with him?" Snorting, Zade slouched back against the booth. "He's like an old man. Everything needs to be clean and in its place. Plus now his apartment is full of all his lucky magic doodads." She sat forward, looking at him pointedly. "Hey, you promised you were going to tell me about magic."

Dis sighed as he set his beer down. "It's not as exciting as you or Frankie think it is."

"Otter believes in it. He's always going into the magic shop to buy stuff." She narrowed her eyes. "Is it in those things, or is he getting ripped off?"

"He's buying talismans to attract luck and amulets to ward off ill luck. Any given item may be a product of a magical process, or it may be only necessary that he believes it will help him."

She scrunched up her face, leaning back into her side of the booth. "Magic is about luck?"

"One is more structured than the other. Or you could say one is more intentional work than the other."

"That doesn't make any sense. People don't make luck."

Dis laughed. "Tell me what you think magic and luck are, then."

Zade poked at her fork, causing the utensil to wobble on the napkin. "Luck is everything falling into place, or out, if it's bad. Magic is doing the impossible, like flying."

Dis watched her play with her silverware. "So it's luck when Otter tries to make everything fall into place the way he would like."

"No, that doesn't sound right. People can't make luck."

The waitress reappeared and set their food down. "Here you go. Two cheeseburgers, no onions, and fries. Can I get you anything else?"

Draining her glass, Zade nodded. "Another round, thanks." She grabbed the ketchup from the end of the table and upended it over her fries. When the contents failed to pour, she looked at the bottle in annoyance.

Dis held his hand out and recapped the bottle before smacking it against his palm three times and handing it back to her. "The goal of the magic I create is to cause events to fall into place in accordance with my desired outcome. Or to change what I desire."

As the ketchup plopped out onto her plate, Zade grinned. "You can make luck? Otter should come see you."

"You could say the magic I use intentionally influences individual and collective luck." He picked up his burger. "Otter has his talismans and many people already influence it through prayer and ritual."

"Why do some get the good kind and others the bad kind?" Zade gulped her beer. "Is it limited? Only so much to go around?"

"Mother Ida was telling me the other day that she thinks it is a measure of how much someone loves their life." Dis pulled a napkin from the dispenser and offered it to her before pulling another for himself.

They ate in silence for a few minutes. A group of teenagers invaded the booth behind Zade, shaking the seat partition. She leaned away until it stopped moving. She wedged her back against the window and glanced over at Dis. "You sound like you don't agree with Mother Ida?"

He waited until he had finished his mouthful before replying. "Too many good and loving people have suffered grave misfortune for me to ever believe it was their fault."

"We all go down." She absently pushed a fry around her plate. "Seems like it's happening more now, though. Isn't it?"

"Your doctor had statistics on the increase." Dis lifted his pint. "Mother Ida thinks I'm superstitious, Jeniel thinks I'm being pessimistic."

She gave him a confused look. "Jeniel? From the Blue Lotus? Oh, right, Otter mentioned you've been keeping company with her."

"I had hoped to keep it private." He dropped his gaze back to the table. "We share common interests."

"I'm sure you have a great time talking shop." Zade smiled knowingly as she crunched on her last fry.

Dis reached for another napkin. "It's been all right so far, but ..."

"You think she's eyeing you as her next improvement project?"

"Maybe. Or I'm being paranoid."

Evelyn set the next round on the table. "You all set? Can I bring you anything else?"

Zade handed over her empty glass. "The check, when you can. We've got to catch a movie." She looked back at Dis. "Is that why you kept blowing me off? You thought I was trying to make a project out of you?"

He finished his first beer. "I appear to be a charitable cause to some."

"So why did you change your mind?"

"Your attitude when I brought you back to your apartment after the hospital."

"I don't really remember much." She pointed at his pile of fries. "Are you done eating?"

"Yes." He smiled as she attacked the remaining food on his plate.

"So you figured you would be safe from me? Because I'm a freak?"

"Because you resent people trying to fix you, too."

"How does it work, then?"

"How does what work?"

Zade stretched out her arms, taking up her side of the booth. "Magic. How does it work?"

"It's complicated."

"You don't think I'll understand it?"

"No, I think it might bore you."

"If it's killing my friends, it won't." She looked up as the waitress brought the check over.

"Take your time, sweetie." Evelyn winked and picked up an empty glass.

"Many of the people I know view it as a transaction. They use sacrifices, offerings of effort, offerings of treasured objects, like coins in a vending machine." Dis picked up the check and examined it. "I was taught it's not about the specific exchange. It's about building and maintaining a balanced relationship with the world. If you care for others, they will care for you. We can't avoid certain things entirely, like sickness and death."

"That sounds like what Mother Ida told you about luck being about love."

"It's similar, when not used to blame victims for causing their own tragedies."

She tugged the check from his fingers. "Okay, why would people use magic to hurt other people?"

"It's a tool like any other. Same as a knife that can cut bread or stab people. Though I think magic would be a poor murder weapon."

"Why do you say that?" Zade dug out her wallet.

"Magic doesn't always work the way you'd expect it to. If I wanted to kill someone, it would be more efficient to do it with a brick than a curse. Magic doesn't move in straight lines, it follows the threads of interactions and works subtly, indirectly. A love spell can make the target of your intentions more inclined to be interested in you or help you run into them at the most advantageous time. But it can't create a lasting relationship out of nothing. And a curse is more trouble than it's worth."

"What about magic changing one thing into another? Or doing the impossible?"

"You're thinking of stage magic, illusions, like sleight of hand." He leaned back, pulling something out of his hip pocket. "If the action appears impossible, and it isn't pure misdirection, it would qualify as a miracle, a verifiable, tangible alteration of consensual reality. Most magic is more a matter of personal revelation." Dis showed her a silver coin in his palm, then closed his fist around it. When he opened his palm again, the coin was missing.

Zade grinned as Dis reached over and appeared to pull the coin out of the napkin dispenser. "Can you do that for real? Change one thing into something else?"

"Without using illusion, the process is called transubstantiation and you can talk to Mother Ida about it. She does it at every Mass."

"So if you are only doing small things, not miracles, how do you know if it worked? How do you know it wasn't just coincidence?"

"You don't, not completely. On some level, it's always a matter of faith. Did that guy break his arm because of the revenge spell you laid on him? Did that girl fall in love with you because you prayed to the Saint, or because you remind her of her first girlfriend?"

Zade laughed and put on her coat. "It sounds like horseshit. Can you do the thing with the coin again?"

▽↗◢

On the subway ride over to the Plague Monument Station, Dis pointed out the graffiti tags obscuring an advertisement. "I think that one's an occult symbol used to tap the influence of the city directly. I've collected about 200 distinct ones throughout the Underground. They're often linked to offering sites for the dead." He looked quizzically at her. "You're laughing at me."

"It means the surveillance cameras have been vandalized in here." She started laughing again at the look on his face.

He took out his journal and flipped it open to a set of pages covered in symbols. "Do you know what this means?"

"That one means there's a safe place to store gear nearby and there would be another tag to follow. This one means you can trade sex for food at the restaurant it's on. That one means there's clean drinking water …"

"This one?"

"Someone died there. We're coming into the station now."

They walked up to street level in silence and turned onto Stricken Lane. "Yes!" Zade pointed at a picture of a giant robot threatening a skyscraper on the side of Outlander Movie Theater.

"You're serious about this." Dis eyed the poster.

She clapped her hands. "It needs to be so bad it's funny."

Dis put his hand on his hat and shook his head, visibly cringing. "That one looks bad."

"Oh, we have a winner!" She laughed and pointed at another poster.

"I'd rather sit through the robot one." He glanced at the exotic costumes and pining expressions of the actors in the poster.

She walked backward toward the ticket booth. "You too chicken, dispatch?"

He shook his head, following her under the marquee.

▽ ↗ ◢

Outside of the theater, Zade sighed deeply and hefted her bag over her shoulder. "Now I really want a cat."

"The cat was the best part of that awful movie. You should get one." Dis paused on the sidewalk. "If you didn't make it to your next anniversary, I'd take care of your cat."

"Really?"

He nodded and started walking back toward the Station. "Really. You'll need to buy more furniture for it to lounge on. Cats need nice things to ruin."

Chewing on her thumb, Zade walked alongside him. "I'll think about it. Where did you get yours?"

"My furniture came with the house."

She cuffed him in the arm. "I meant your cat."

"I got her at the city shelter. She lost her rear legs in an accident."

Zade stopped walking. "Do you carry her everywhere?"

"She has her own cart and gets around fine on her own." Dis kept walking toward the Underground. "I built her a litter box with two ramps so she can get in and out."

"Huh."

Dis glanced into the station entrance. "I need to go feed her soon."

Zade looked up at the bank clock rotating on the corner of the intersection. "I should get going too. Thanks for coming out."

"I'm sorry I haven't come out before. Had I known what you had in mind…"

Zade started jogging away from him. "You would never have come out."

He cupped his hands around his mouth. "Zade, you can call me if you ever need anything."

"Shut up!"

With a slight smile, Dis watched her jog away, round a corner, and disappear.

THE OIL PAN SLOSHED PERILOUSLY as Zade nudged it across the concrete floor of the depot. She began wandering among the twenty or so motorcycles in different states of disassembly. She pushed the rear brake on a spray-painted red and black 350 but stopped abruptly with a guilty look as the stained door in the dingy back wall opened.

"I've got one for you over here, 90-32." Iris waved the courier over to the side of a twin. "Had to bribe the scroungers to give it back to me in one piece."

"Street wreckers?" Zade tugged on the bike's clutch lever with two fingers.

The mechanic muttered something obscene as she flicked the kill switch back to the on position. "S&P tow crew got a little overly enthusiastic. As if they couldn't see my brand right there." Iris pointed at the Uptown Delivery sticker on the fender.

The two women grinned at each other over the machine's saddle as Iris started up the bike and revved the engine.

"Newish tires, and I adjusted the timing. Should keep you running packages, no problem. There's your new brain bucket. See if it fits okay."

"Thanks." Zade picked the black helmet off the bike's hardcase and tugged it on as Iris stepped back, letting the throttle fall back to idle.

The mechanic nodded, stepped forward, and rapped on Zade's helmet. "Any more accidents and he's going to make all of you wear bright orange safety vests. We've been having words over it. Just keep the rubber side down."

Zade nodded and paddle-walked the motorcycle backward in a curve. She held up her hand to Iris and downshifted into first, letting the engine pull the bike gradually out of the bay.

▽↗◣

"Dispatch, 90-32 at the Pit." Zade yawned and scratched her face as she looked around at the other couriers.

Static crackled over the radio. "You haven't gone to the Blue Lotus yet."

Zade shoved her gloves into her helmet and looked over at the store. "What? Oh, you wanted me to see your girl, sorry."

"She's a knowledgeable herbalist and I told her I'd recommended you consult with her."

"Drumming up business for your girlfriend?" Zade mouthed the next words as Dis spoke them.

"She's not my girlfriend."

Grinning, Zade started walking through the Pit toward the Blue Lotus. "Sure she is. Your only, your sun, your moon …"

"Shut up, 90-32. I can't believe you got me to watch that movie."

"You up for seeing another this Friday with me? At seven? I'll tell you what the rest of the tags you've collected mean."

"Only if you use your present tomorrow."

"I'll try them out. Do you know if you're supposed to wash them first?"

Dis paused. "I have no idea. I will be there at seven."

"Call the sex shop for me and ask about how to care for my new sexy rubber sheets, will you?" She laughed as she stopped outside the shop entrance.

"90-32, pickup at 32 High Street. Going to the Hinterlands, 55 Daisy Circle."

Groaning, the courier turned around and trotted back to her motorcycle. "You are making that up, there is no such place as Daisy Circle."

"It's a new development. Shake it to make it, 90-32."

"Only if you swear you will embrace the power and the passion ..."

"Shut up."

▽ ↗ ◢

It was noon when Zade parked her bike next to Otter's and looked down at the granite benches on the level below. "Hey, where's 30-84?"

A courier scraping a parking ticket off his bike's hardcase paused and glanced up at her. "He went to get lunch with 62-91."

"Thanks." Zade hung her helmet off her handlebar and walked over to the Blue Lotus, removing her headset before going in.

"May I help you?" Mala glanced at the door as it opened. "Oh, Zade. How are you?" The shopkeeper's eyes flashed.

"Hi, is Jeniel around? Dis told me to ask her about a tea or something." Zade glanced around at the shelves.

"I think she's in the back." Mala went over to the door and pushed the button on the intercom. "Jeniel? Are you available? Zade's here and she'd like to see you."

"I'll be right out."

"It will just take her a minute. How have you been? I haven't seen you since the Solstice." Mala smiled broadly.

"Busy. You?" Zade went over to one of the bookcases and peered at the titles.

"I've been doing more here since Jeniel's been picking up more client work. I heard about your accident. Are you okay?"

Zade glanced up as the door in the back opened and Jeniel stepped out. "Yeah, I'm fine."

The herbalist rounded the counter and approached Zade. "I'm Jeniel. It's a pleasure to finally meet you." The woman extended her hand. "What can I help you with?"

Zade shook her hand carefully. "Dis suggested I ask you for a tea."

"Let's go over to the herbs." Jeniel guided Zade to the racks of jars as Mala returned to her work. "Any particular issue you'd like to address?"

Zade shrugged. "Painful menstruation with a lot of blood. It puts me down for a couple of days every month."

"I'd suggest two teas, then. The first blend is a daily supplement, the second is for when you are menstruating. Do you know if you are anemic? Do you get enough iron in your diet?" Jeniel looked at her.

Staring at her boots, Zade scrubbed at the back of her head. "I eat mostly bar food."

The brunette smiled and then turned to look at the rows of jars. "Much of your discomfort may be from a nutrient deficiency. How bad is it?"

She stared at the herbalist's long legs. "I take prescription pain medication and sleep through it."

"How long do you bleed?"

"Two days, normally. Maybe some on the third day, but it doesn't hurt by then."

"Classic menorrhagia. It will take me a minute to make those teas up for you." Jeniel gathered up several of the glass jars, took them to a separate counter, and began sifting the herbs.

Zade followed her, inhaling the spicy fragrances. "Dis mentioned he took you to the symphony last week."

"It was lovely. It was very thoughtful of him to get tickets." Jeniel smiled at Zade through the veil of her long hair. "Do you hear about me as much as I hear about you?"

Zade leaned on the glass counter. "I hope he has better things to talk about than me. I would have thought you would be talking about ..." She waved her hand. "All this stuff."

"We do, a bit. I have to badger him to talk at times. It took me weeks to get him to talk to me about his family." Jeniel shook her head as she recapped one of the square jars.

Zade's smile faltered as she stood up. "Oh?"

"His father wrote *Under Blue Hill* and *Star River City*. You remember those?" Jeniel opened the smallest jar and scooped out a measure of yellow flowers.

Zade turned away, looking out the shop's window. "No."

"Well, they're classics, take my word for it. They're all about the myths of the Ornish clans."

Zade stared out at the Pit through the shop's window. "Huh."

"He wouldn't tell me his birthday either." Jeniel laughed. "Can you believe I had to read it off of his ID while he was sleeping?"

The courier's hand went up to check her ear as she stared at the shopkeeper.

Jeniel sifted a pungent-smelling mix of leaves out of another glass jar. "You should steep a teaspoon of this one for ten minutes every day in the morning. This other one is just for when you're bleeding. Steep a teaspoon for five minutes. You can add honey to either of them, but don't cook the honey." She folded the tops of the two bags and wrote on them with a marker. "Has he told you about his accident?" She brushed her hair back over her shoulder and walked to the register.

"No."

The herbalist shot her a knowing smile. "He's the reason the bartenders at Maddy's make all of the couriers give over their keys." The woman's long manicured nails tapped the register keys.

Zade sagged against the counter. "He was drunk?"

"After a knockdown fight in the middle of the bar with his ex, Bone." The herbalist retrieved a shopping bag from under the register. "Did you know him?"

Avoiding the other woman's eyes, Zade shook her head and took out her wallet.

"They had to be separated by half the bar, the fight was so bad. Dis crashed his motorcycle and Bone left town on tour while he was in the hospital. I suppose it's understandable he's the way he is, considering." Jeniel held the bag out, smiling. "We'll call it five. Friends' discount."

Handing over the cash, Zade kept her head down. "Thank you." She put the packet into her messenger bag and walked quickly toward the door.

"Come back and tell me if the tea helps at all. Oh, and Zade, do try to eat something besides bar food."

"Okay." Zade waited until she got back to her bike before she put her headset on. "Dispatch, 90-32 at the Pit."

Dis's voice was full of humor. "Gloria says you don't have to wash the sheets."

"What? You called? I was kidding."

"You went to the Blue Lotus. Did you meet Jeniel? What did you think?"

Zade winced, looking up at the sky. "She's very beautiful."

Laughter rang over the radio. "That sounds bad."

"I think you might be right about the project thing. I could be wrong, though, it's not like I'm any kind of expert. My only relationship lasted two days. Don't listen to me." She fumbled her helmet off the bike.

Dis laughed again. "I have to listen to you. It's my job."

▽↗◢

On Thursday night, Dis rode the train from Claremont Station to Victory and walked to the Blue Lotus. "You look lovely." He bent to kiss Jeniel in the doorway.

"I was just locking up." The woman's white wool sweater hung off one of

116

her shoulders and her hair was in a long single braid, stretching in a dark line down her back. "How was work?"

"Nothing exceptional."

Jeniel locked the door and turned around. She looked him over from head to toe. "Any luck pinpointing the sources of the negative influences?" She started toward the back of the shop, stopping as he paused to examine the contents in one of the display cases. He shook his head. "No? If it makes you feel any better, I can't discover as much as you have. My divination is all noise and nonsense recently." She began to tally the register. "It's frustrating. It feels like intentional interference."

"Despair, calamity, obstruction, and being haunted by the past. Ending with romantic love and a hard-won victory through great sacrifice." He glanced over. "I'm considering consulting with Quail."

Jeniel looked up at him in surprise. "I thought you said …"

"I'm allowed to change my mind." His smile softened his reply.

She put the day's earnings into a register bag. "I have dinner simmering on the stove. I hope you like lamb stew."

He walked over to her and leaned down to kiss her exposed shoulder. "I can't stay over tonight."

"Is someone expecting you tomorrow morning?" She watched him closely.

Moving the side of her braid out of the way, he kissed the side of her neck. "Just work. Then Zade's meeting me for a movie tomorrow night."

"If you can't stay long, perhaps dinner can wait?" Jeniel unlocked the door to her apartment and took his hand in hers.

"As you like. You've got me for a few hours." Wrapping his arms around her waist, he kissed the side of her neck again.

She drew him into the apartment and locked the door behind them. "The stew will keep, unless you're starving?"

"I'm fine." Dis eyed the sword on the top of the table by the door. "I see you have a new acquisition."

"It's an heirloom I've borrowed for a ritual." She set the cash bag into a drawer in the table. "When did you eat last? Do you need to use the bathroom?"

"It's going to be one of those nights." He cupped her face as she turned back to him. "I ate a late lunch. I should be all set for a while."

"Any new injuries I should know about?" She brought him into the bedroom and went over to the stereo.

Dis sat down on the bed, watching her lower the needle on a record. "No. The safe word is orange."

As strange, lilting music began to play, she slipped off his jacket and unbuttoned his shirt. "Lie down on your back." She kissed him and slid his shirt off.

"As you wish." Dis kissed her on the cheek, lying down on the black satin sheets. "I always feel like I'm going to slip off these." The sides of his mouth turned up as he inched himself further up the bedding.

"Not tonight you're not."

"Do you want me to take my brace off?" He propped himself up on his elbows, watching her.

"It can stay for now." She pushed him back roughly. "Lie down."

Jeniel went over to the wardrobe and retrieved a canvas bag. She walked back to the bed and lightly tossed bundles of white hemp rope onto his bare stomach. Lifting his left hand, she kissed her way up his arm, positioning it near the metal headboard.

"If I say the safe word, you will untie me." He watched her shake out the first bundle and run the length through her hands.

Using the looped end of it to cuff his wrist to the headboard, she slipped a finger in between the rope and his skin, testing the fit. She threaded the restraint through the metal and brought it over to his other hand. She drew the slack tight, pulling his arm against the headboard, and tied the length off. She straddled his chest and kissed him on the mouth. "I had my rope-maker create this set especially for you." She reached back and lifted another of the bundles from his stomach.

"You have a rope-maker." Dis grinned as she picked up another twist of the white rope. "I've only used cotton clothesline."

"The burn rate on cotton is atrocious. You could be injured quite badly." She snapped the next bundle loose. "I only use the best hemp rope in the world." She began to kiss her way down his body, running her tongue along his stomach. Dis bit his lip, raising his hips against her.

At his thighs, she selected a larger bundle, fed the rope under his left leg, and tied it to the rail along the side of the mattress. She cuffed his right thigh high above the knee and used her hands to spread his legs wider, tying the end of the rope to the other bedrail. Sliding her hands up the insides of his legs, she removed the last two bundles from his stomach and began cuffing his shins above his boots.

She brought up the end of a wide leather strap from under the bed.

"What else do you have under there?" Dis watched her tighten the strap across the tops of his legs, binding him further to the bed frame.

"All kinds of things." She climbed back onto his hips and deployed more leather restraints. Her playful smile disappeared as she finished testing a wide strap across his throat. "Can you get free? Any chafing?"

Dis tugged on the restraints and bucked his hips under her. "No."

"Good." She reached down for his glasses.

Dis shied away. "I'll call it if you try to take them off with the lights on. That's the rule." His body tensed under her.

Jeniel sighed and sat back on his hips with her hands on her thighs. "You have to trust me for this to work."

"I'm willing to trust you with a great deal, but I need you to respect my boundaries."

She lifted the glasses off of his face. "I was hoping you'd trust me by now…"

"Orange." Dis kept both of his eyes closed. "Untie me. Now."

"How long are you going to keep your eyes closed? You can't hide what you are from me."

Under her weight, Dis clenched his jaw. "Let me up, Jeniel. This is over."

"Then open your eyes." She ran the tips of her fingers over his face. "Believe me. I'm trying to help you, child of Mammor."

"Jeniel, I'm asking you not to do this." Keeping his eyes closed, Dis raised his head.

"Before your accident, both of your eyes were normal. Hazel is listed on your license, along with your birthday and full name. How do you pronounce it properly?"

"I don't want to play this game. Let me up."

"You must be lonely with your family gone, no one to talk to, no one to share anything with. I don't want to hurt you. I'm here to help you. Open your eyes. Let me see your true self." Her voice fell into a cajoling lilt.

He unclenched his hands. "There is nothing magical about my eye. It's blind."

Her playful tone dropped away, replaced by one of command. "Open it." She put her fingers on either side of his face and squeezed. "You're not going anywhere until you do."

"Untie me, now." Dis opened his eyes.

With an indrawn breath, she sat back. "What did the doctors say when it changed?"

Dis closed his eyes again and his hands went limp in the ropes. "You're not going to untie me."

She smiled triumphantly. "Not right now."

"I'm not going to tell you anything else. You might as well let me go."

"That's okay, baby, I already know what I need. We're going to find out a few new things, together." She kissed his closed lips. "My powers told me it transformed after your accident when your body tried to heal by shifting you into your animal form. You don't have enough skill on your own, so I'm going to help you finish. I'm going to help you change completely, the way the ancient clans did."

"It's only a myth." There was an edge of desperation in his voice as he opened his eyes to look at her. "I'm human, I can't change. Don't do this."

"I can help you. You just have to trust me. Can't you trust me a little?" She licked her lips as she traced the line of his collarbone with her fingers. "You know I can make your pain feel wonderful."

"Don't fucking do this!" He thrashed under her. The bed shook beneath them. "Let me go! Now! Jeniel!" He screamed her name and arched his spine against the straps.

"Hush, baby. It will be okay." She got off of him and walked over to the wardrobe, taking off her sweater and skirt. The naked woman's eyes shone with a feverish light and her tone was one of absolute authority. "I will help you, and I will see it, the magic of your people. I will make it mine. Through you, I will acquire the means to save us all." She removed a lacquered black box from under the bed and set it on the nightstand.

Dis stared at her as she opened the box. Seeing the contents, he closed his eyes. "It won't work. I've never changed. I will never change …"

"Your eye changed." She looked down at him. Her smile was predatory.

"It's fucking blind. I can't see anything out of it."

"Blind human eyes don't look like that, so dark, so beautiful. Only animals have eyes like it. I can't wait to see what you look like when you transform completely." She smoothed back his hair and touched the scar next to his black left eye. "You don't have to keep lying to me. I know what both your names mean. You are the son of the sea, born to the seal clan." She ran her fingers over his exposed chest, caressing his body down to his groin.

The speakers above the bed went silent. There was a faint crackling as the needle rode the groove across the surface of the album and then the next song started. The bedroom was suddenly filled with the sound of a drum roll, followed by the droning voice of a male singer.

Dis enunciated each word carefully, both of his eyes opened wide. "Don't.

Do. This."

Jeniel switched on the overhead lamp. "Is there anything I can say that will get you to trust me? I swear by my powers, I mean you no harm."

"If you mean it, let me go."

"If you try to work with me, it may go faster. Embrace the pain and use it." She set a gag over his mouth. "Don't fight me, baby. I know what I'm doing, and you'll thank me when we're done. We'll both have what we need." Shoving the strap under his head, she fastened the buckle into place. Her smile became possessive as she stroked the leather lying over his cheek. "This is the solution for both of our problems."

As Jeniel's attention returned to the lacquered box, Dis turned his head away, closing his eyes. The woman snapped on a pair of sterile surgical gloves. The antiseptic smell of rubbing alcohol filled the air as she opened a packet and swabbed his chest with it. She raised a scalpel and its blade glittered in the light. Jeniel licked her lips again as she set the knife against her victim's collarbone.

࿐ࡄ⑨𝟎ࡅ

A black sedan with tinted windows eased into a garage bay next to the Old Port Storage building. The metal shutter rolled down behind the car, each slat of the garage door making a clacking noise as it locked into place. The driver exited the vehicle, smoothing his suit jacket as he walked to the rear of the car. Lifting out a plastic bucket, he gently shut the trunk and started toward the back of the garage.

He unlocked a scarred and pitted metal door and stepped into a side corridor. Setting his bucket down, he selected another key from a heavy-laden key ring and activated the service elevator with it. As the industrial doors slid shut behind him and he pressed the button for the tenth floor, he started to hum a shanty.

The elevator opened into a small vestibule containing another fire door. Turning the key and opening it, the man walked into a long white corridor, set the bucket down outside of a door bearing a small sign numbered 1054, glanced over his shoulder, and unlocked it.

He hit the switch and the fluorescent lighting flickered on, revealing hundreds of unmarked white buckets stacked around the walls.

He walked over to the far left wall and set the bucket in his hand on top of one of several long metal tables. He removed his suit jacket, hung it up on a hook on the wall below a poster of a snow-dusted Basilica of St. Anna, and tugged on a stained lab coat.

After buttoning the coat completely closed, he turned and took a belt of tools off another hook and buckled it on. Pulling on a pair of sterile gloves, he settled a clear face shield over his gray hair and turned on another switch. Ventilation fans kicked in, cycling cold air throughout the space.

Still humming, he spun open the bucket he had carried in and lifted out a completely flayed human skin, still lumpy with bits of fat and meat, crusted with a crystalline layer of salt. Clear liquid dripped off the flesh as he examined it, carefully running his gloved fingers over the surface. He began to sing. *"When they tell me I'm wrong, when they tell me you've gone ..."*

After laying the skin out with its inner surface facing upward, he stripped off his gloves and dropped them on the floor. Procuring a fresh pair out of his tool belt, he slipped them on and reached for a second bucket. Ladling salt out of it, the man covered the skin in a thick layer of white and massaged it in. *"I will sing my pirate love song ... "*

He replaced his gloves a second time, selected one of the many buckets stacked against the wall, and carried it over to a table underneath a round translucent plastic barrel bolted sideways to the wall. A motorized six-inch wire brush wheel protruded from the back of the makeshift trough.

"Yo ho-ho, yo ho-ho yo ho. For the brawny maidens bright and the gentlemen of the night ..." A sharply acidic smell permeated the room as he opened another bucket. Using a set of tongs, he removed a human skin and draped the saturated hide on the clean table. With a pair of scissors, he began to

meticulously cut away the chunks of fat, throwing the snippets of flesh into the bottom of the trough. "*I will sing my pirate love song! Yo ho-ho, yo ho-ho yo ho...*"

Setting the gore-crusted blades down, he tapped a pedal under the table with his foot. "*I will sing my pirate love song! Yo ho-ho, yo ho-ho yo ho ...*" The wire brush inside the barrel whined as it spun. He lifted the skin up and pressed it against the wheel. "*Sail on, sail on, sail on ...*"

$$\triangledown \nearrow \blacktriangle$$

Zade waited for two hours outside of the theater, scanning the faces of people stepping out of the Plague Monument Underground station. She chewed on the edge of her thumb, checked the bank clock on the street corner, and went inside to the payphone. She dropped a coin in the slot and watched the door as the phone rang.

She replaced the receiver in its cradle, tapped the back of it, and then spun on her heel and walked out to the parking lot. When she reached her bike, she dug her headset out of her bag and put it on before her helmet and gloves. "Dispatch, this is 90-32."

Frankie's voice crackled over the radio. "Hi, Zade. I didn't think you were working nights?"

"I'm not, I'm looking for Dis. When did he leave?"

"He didn't come in today." Frankie's voice wavered. "Iris had to work his shift."

"Is he okay?"

"He didn't call in. Iris is worried, she says he's never done this before."

"Did she check his house?"

"No, she called S&P, but they said it has to be over seventy-two hours before they'll consider him a missing person."

"Can you call his girlfriend over at the Blue Lotus, Jeniel?"

"Iris had Otter ask her. She told him she saw Dis last night and then he left."

"Did she … did Iris … check his house?"

"No."

"Will you give me his address?"

"Zade, I really can't."

"I promised him I'd check on his cat if anything happened. Please, Frankie?"

"Well, I shouldn't …"

"His cat's only got two legs."

"Wow. Okay, but if he gets mad at me …"

"Tell him I made you."

"Okay, it's 44 Manning Street. Out on the Point."

"Thanks, I'll buy you a pint."

"Tell me if you find anything."

Zade got onto the Straight. She rode down State to Duncan until she merged onto Market and then took the exit for the Riverway Bridge. Below the bridge, darkness obscured the river as she crossed over to the Point.

Cars bouncing through a giant pothole on the outbound lane sent up sheets of filthy water. Droplets streaked off her faceplate and fairing as she dodged through the traffic. When she turned onto Fremont, a man on the corner waved and called out to her and she watched in her mirror as he did the same to the next vehicle. On the next corner, a group of young women beckoned to her. On the next, a trio of young men lifted up their shirts and blew her kisses.

She passed a parked car being broken into. People yelled from the windows of nearby buildings. In her mirror, she watched a drunk stagger into the road to pound on the hood of a taxi waiting outside of an apartment building. She watched as S&P cruiser lights appeared in her rearview mirror.

Parking her bike, she ran up to the door of 44 Manning and rang the bell. It buzzed inside the dark brownstone, but no one answered. She held down the button with her ear pressed to the door. She heard something squeaking followed by a cat's yowl.

"Kitty, is your dad in there?" Zade leaned back and looked up at the three-story house. "Shit." She went around the side of the backyard and jumped up, catching the top of the wooden fence. Landing on the grass, she walked to the back door and knocked. "Hello?" Walking backward while looking at the windows, she scanned the tiny basement window and the bars across the larger ones on the ground floor.

Zade knocked again and the cat cried in response. "I hear you." She dragged over one of the patio chairs and pulled herself up using the granite lip above the kitchen window. Scaling the outside of the building, she moved from handhold to handhold, finally dragging herself up to sit on the wide ledge of an open second-floor window. The wooden window frame protested as she pushed it completely up and swung inside. She untangled the lace curtains from around her legs. "Hello?"

Zade ran her hand over the neatly made bed, pausing as she touched the crocheted throw blanket folded at the foot. She checked the bathroom off the hallway and the other rooms on the second floor. Flipping the lights on and off, she quickly went through the master bedroom and scanned the large tub in the adjacent private bath.

"Dis?" The cat yowled from downstairs. "I'm coming kitty, sorry."

Stinky mewled as Zade came downstairs. She extended her fingers to let the cat sniff her. The cat yowled again and then started toward the kitchen. Zade followed, turning on the kitchen light, then went to check the living room and the dining room. The cat wailed impatiently and Zade returned.

"Sorry, do you need food?" She opened the fridge and took out a covered can. "Is this still good or should I open a new one? Sorry, I don't know how to do this."

The cat banged her head against the woman's legs, purring loudly. Zade searched the drawers until she found a spoon. She took a plate from the dish rack and scraped the food out.

"Where's your dad, kitty?" She crouched down and watched as the hungry cat chomped and purred.

The cat finished her food and banged her head against Zade's hands. Abruptly, the cat went over to her pillow under the kitchen table and started to wash.

Zade squatted on the floor, watching Stinky. "I think that means you're all set for a while?"

The cat blinked at her and curled up to sleep. Zade watched her for a moment, then grabbed a pen and paper out of her messenger bag and scrawled a note, leaving it on the counter before turning out the kitchen lights. With the front door locked behind her, she got back on her motorcycle and headed back toward the other side of the river.

A bus lumbered in front of her on Market as a limo veered into the lane from the right. She warily watched two sleek new sports bikes speed past her, one dipping too low as the pair took the corner.

She parked next to Otter's bike at Maddy's and eased her way into the thick Friday night crowd.

"Otter!" Zade pushed through to the table of couriers.

Otter moved so she could sit down. "Hi. Didn't expect to see you until Monday?"

"Did you hear Dis is missing?" She looked around the table at the others.

Cradling her pint glass to her chest, Kitty leaned away from the table. "Good riddance to that shitbird."

Zade frowned at her and looked back at Otter. "He was supposed to meet me at seven at the Outlander. I waited until nine."

"Iris had me ask Jeniel, but she hasn't seen him." Otter handed over his beer. "We could go check his house, maybe?"

"I was just there, no sign."

"He'll show up. Maybe he's got an emergency." Otter nodded at the waiter. "I'll have another and can we have some more shots? Thanks."

The waiter looked at Zade. "What will it be?"

"Pint of Black Dog and whiskey." Zade stared at her keys before dropping them into the waiter's outstretched hand. "His cat wasn't fed. He didn't show up to work, his girl hasn't seen him, and he didn't show up at the theater."

"Hey, did you know Avery has a sister? Met her the other night. She looks just like you, only maybe more …" Otter waved his hands in the air. "Girly."

"I'm serious, Otter. When was the last time Dis was ever late to anything, let alone stood us up?"

"I don't know, maybe way back when he was running deliveries. He was different, less serious. Used to smile and come out with us a lot more."

"Dis used to hang out?" The courier to Otter's right looked surprised.

Otter looked down at his beer. "Yeah. He used to come out all the time. Well, more often when Bone dragged him out."

"He said you used to be his roommate." Zade hung her jacket on the back of her chair. "Did you live with Bone too?"

"Yeah. You'd like him." He pushed his glasses up the bridge of his nose. "He told you about Bone?"

"Jeniel mentioned him."

"That's fucked up. What's she doing telling you about his ex?"

"No idea. She just said his name. Some other stuff about the accident."

Otter looked shocked. "She knew about his accident? What did she say?"

"Ah, thanks." Zade took a beer and shot from the waiter as he set drinks down. "They got in a fight and he dumped his bike riding drunk."

"She doesn't know fucking shit, then." Otter frowned. "Dis never risked trashing his bike. He loved that machine."

"Did he get fucked over by his cocksucking boyfriend?" Kitty asked.

"It's none of your fucking business, trash mouth." Otter threw back his shot. "Besides, who cares? People have drama all the time. I don't want people talking about my business. I. Mind. My. Own. Business. You should too."

Zade lifted her beer and then set it down again. "This isn't like him."

"I'm sure he'll come in on Monday. Iris will be pissed, and Jeniel too, probably, but …"

"Maybe." Zade looked down at the table. "I think there's something weird about Jeniel. She seems too … I don't know, obsessed with him."

Otter raised his beer. "Midnight Excursion tickets are going on sale tomorrow. You should come with us."

"Where are they playing?"

"The Crossing." Kitty smiled. "In two weeks. I can't wait to see them. Drake Bonnrey's a tall order of fuckme."

"Dinner at the Palace before." Otter tapped Zade's arm. "I want you to meet Vicky."

"Who?"

"Avery's sister I was telling you about. Eight o'clock. Enough time to order, eat, fight over the bill, and then stagger across the street. You're not going to believe how much she looks like you."

Zade stood up. "I'm going to take a piss. Keep my seat?"

"Yeah." He waved her on. "If you see Mon, tell him we could do with another round."

Mat stood up from a nearby table and followed Zade through the crowd as she made her way toward the restrooms. Stepping into her path, he put his face close to hers. "Hi, Zade."

"I'm not in the mood." Zade tried to get past him.

Mat put his arm out across the entrance to the bathrooms, blocking her. "I heard you were looking for Dis. I thought you'd like to know where he was."

"You don't know shit."

"Why don't you try asking me nicely?" He reached out to touch her.

As she pushed him out of her way, he grabbed her arm. Zade swung her other fist up, punching him in the jaw. Staggering, he yelled and then rushed at her. Zade's eyes narrowed. She drove the heel of her palm into his nose.

He reeled back with his hands over his face, blood streaming through his fingers. *"What the fuck is wrong with you?"*

The entire bar fell silent and Otter pushed his way through the crowd. "Let's all calm down." He clamped a restraining hand on Zade's shoulder. "Come on, let it go." He gently tugged.

Mat grabbed a beer bottle and flung it at Zade's head. She dodged and lunged at him. Her fists rose and fell with the entire force of her upper body. He grabbed the neck of the broken bottle off the floor and slashed at her, cutting into her arm. Otter's attempts to haul Zade off failed until Kitty and Avery wrapped their arms around hers. As she was dragged away, Zade landed a solid kick to Mat's ribs.

"Get her out of here! S&P is on the way!" The bartender lifted a phone from its cradle as Otter and the others hauled Zade out of the bar and onto the sidewalk.

"You're bleeding." Avery held out a wad of napkins.

"How bad did he cut you?" Otter tried to look at her arm but Zade pulled away, trying to rush back into the bar. Blocking her, he pushed her backward. "You need to go to the hospital. That needs stitches."

"I have to get my jacket and bag."

"Avery, go get her gear, please."

Avery hesitated before heading back into the bar.

"You need to calm down. Now. Put some pressure on it." Otter shoved Zade further down the sidewalk.

She growled, looking back at the bar. "I need to put my boot down his throat."

"What do you think you'll accomplish if I let you curb-stomp him?"

"Public service."

"Let it go."

"I feel like beating the shit out of him. Okay?"

As they walked, blood began to drip from the front of Zade's black T-shirt, leaving a trail on the sidewalk.

"I think you've pretty much accomplished your goal, then. He looked like a

130

fucking truck hit him." Otter made her stop and lifted up her shirt. Zade hissed as he peeled back the bloody fabric. "Shit, when did he cut your stomach? You're losing a lot of blood."

Avery walked out of the bar and held out her bag. "I couldn't get your keys. Mon said you'll have to come back tomorrow for your bike."

"Shit!" Zade grabbed her bag and opened it with one hand. She dug out a roll of gray tape, tore off a piece, and clamped it on the cut on her arm. She tore off another piece, hissing as she pinched the sides of her stomach wound together. "Will you?"

Otter shook his head and dropped her shirt. "I'm not taping your guts together. You need to go to the ER."

"You put it on yourself all the time."

"That is your abdominal cavity, not a goddamn wart." Otter glared at her.

Avery watched Zade. "Mon said the ambulance should be here in a minute."

"I am not waiting for S&P to arrest me for taking out the trash." Zade shook the strip of tape at Otter. "Do you want me to bleed to death?"

"This is crazy, you know that?" Her friend waited until she had the wound pinched together and then gingerly applied the tape. "Boon was right." He shook his head as she held out another piece for him to apply. "You're a fucking mental patient. You belong in the Stat."

In the distance, the sound of sirens grew louder. Zade put her jacket on.

"Do you want a ride to the hospital?" Avery followed behind as she strode down the sidewalk. "I can drop you off."

"No. Thanks for getting my gear."

He halted, watching Zade heft her bag over her head and start jogging down Pioneer Street.

She ducked into Market Station and rode the escalator down. At the turnstiles, she glanced over her shoulder before going through to the inbound platform. When the train arrived, the conductor announced over the speakers that it was going out of service at Victory Station. She got on and made her way to the end of the car, keeping her gaze on the rubberized floor.

□ ♍ ♏ ♋ ■

At Victory, she trailed behind the rest of the passengers on her way to the escalator, where she stopped to stare at a dead mouse sandwiched in the cycling treads of the automated stairs. She pried the animal's body free and carried it outside, laying it under a bush by the station entrance. Squatting over to a puddle to wash her hands, she stared up at the sky as pieces of mouse fur floated away from her fingertips. The speeding clouds flowed apart, revealing a patch of stars between the skyscrapers.

"I know you know where Dis is." Looking up at the stars, she slipped her arm out of her jacket and peeled back the tape. Blood dripped from her cut as she pressed on the skin around it. "Tell me where he is." She stared at the sky, letting the blood run down her fingers to mix with the grimy water.

An empty beer can careened onto the white marble walkway, rattling as it tumbled across the square. Looking in the direction it had come from, Zade smoothed the tape back over her wound and stood up. There was a commotion on the far side of the square. The red and blue flashes of an S&P cruiser shone through the bare tree branches along the Straight. She started toward them. She watched two officers under a tree shout at a teenager clinging to the trunk, high up in the branches.

"Get your ass down here, now." A burly officer pointed at the sidewalk as he stared up at the offender.

The boy hurled down another empty beer can. It bounced off the top of the cruiser and into the street. He held up three fingers defiantly at the officer and climbed higher.

"Call in for jumper netting and a ladder." Adjusting his uniform cap, the officer glanced over at his partner. "Looks like we've got ourselves another rescue mission. At least it's close enough for them to walk over here."

Zade looked across the street, where a woman inside a phone booth was yelling and hammering the receiver repeatedly on the cradle. The lights of the cruiser flickered over the glass enclosure, making it appear as if the woman was moving in slow motion. Her cries of outrage stopped as she bolted out of the phone booth.

Crossing the street, Zade entered the glass booth and stared at the dangling handset. Sagging against the side of the enclosure, she put the beeping receiver back into its cradle. "Where is he?" Her eyes focused on a defaced sticker above the phone.

The center of a band logo was peeled off the glass and the reflection of the cruiser lights filled in the gaps, creating the image of a flashing arrow. Zade stared at it and back at the S&P cruiser across the street. She touched the glass, leaving a bloody fingerprint. Pushing open the door, she shoved herself out of the booth and ran down the sidewalk.

Ahead of her, a taxi screeched to a halt and the driver got out of his car, shouting. He pounded on the roof as his passenger scurried out the opposite door and into the street.

"Thief!" The taxi driver screamed and pointed. "Thief!"

Zade changed direction, pursuing the fleeing man. He veered onto Appleton Lane, grazing his shoulder and hip on the corner of the brick building. She slowed as they entered the top of the outdoor mall. Catching her breath, she watched the man run through a group of people talking outside the Blue Lotus.

A young woman in a quilted coat cried out as the thief knocked her down, scattering her armful of books. One of her companions bent down to help her up as the others collected her belongings. Jeniel appeared in the shop's doorway. She spoke soothingly to the woman and then beckoned her students to come back inside.

Keeping out of sight, Zade watched as the concerned expression on Jeniel's face dropped away, replaced by one of annoyance. She made a strange, exaggerated gesture before shutting the shop door.

Kiarna Boyd

Zade crossed the mall, listening to the door click shut. She sat on a bench opposite the shop, watching the silhouettes through the drapes in the display window. She glanced up at the narrow strip of sky over the mall and peeled back the tape on her arm. Squeezing the cut, she watched the blood splatter onto the weeds growing through the cracks below the bench.

JENIEL BADE THE LAST of her students goodnight and shut the shop's door. She folded the chairs and stacked them behind the counter, then sat down in the one chair left. She was making a few changes to an attendance list when the bells on the shop door jangled madly.

"Did you forget something?" Jeniel looked up from her notes. She stared at Zade. "What are you doing here?"

Zade's eyes blazed. "Where is Dis?"

"I don't know, I haven't …"

Zade angled her head away, scanning the shop. "He's here."

"You're wrong, Zade. Dis isn't …"

"Get out of my way or you'll regret it, Jeniel." Zade approached the counter, heading for the door to the apartment beyond.

"No!" Jeniel jumped up, grabbed the ritual sword from the counter, and pointed the blade at Zade. "No further. I command you in the name of the Sea and the Sky, by …" Jeniel cut a star shape in the air with the sword. "I'll have S&P arrest you for trespassing!"

135

With a stony expression, Zade grabbed the blade and dragged Jeniel to her, blood dripping down the hilt from her arm. She pushed Jeniel against the counter and threw the sword away. It clattered to the floor.

Finding the apartment locked, Zade kicked the flimsy door open and walked through to the candlelit bedroom. Beneath a cloud of incense, Dis lay on the bed, unmoving. Zade's expression softened for a moment and then was replaced by a look of cold fury. Sections of his chest glistened where the top layer of skin had been removed.

"Dis?" She carefully laid her hand on his neck.

Taking the utility knife from her bag, she cut the ropes and straps binding the unconscious man to the bed. With quick fingers, she unbuckled his gag, tore the curtain from the rod above the window, and wrapped it loosely around her friend. As she lifted him, Zade's knees began to buckle. She set her jaw, straining. Blood leaked from the tape on her stomach as she struggled to lift him. She straightened under his weight, cradled him against her chest, and exited the bedroom.

As Zade emerged from the apartment, Jeniel gave a sharp cry. "No! I haven't finished it!"

Wordlessly, Zade carried Dis through the store and out into the empty mall.

▽↗◢

"I assure you, doctor, we will not bother your patient any longer than we have to." A woman with short, silver hair entered the hospital room. She held the door open for her partner and gestured for him to take the chair by the bedside.

Her companion stopped a few feet from the chair. "I'm Detective Bray and this is Detective Fuller. Dr. Mell mentioned that she already cleared our visit with you? Mister Mw ..."

"Mthdys." Dis loosened hair from behind his left ear and let it hang over his blind eye as the S&P detectives stood watching him.

"We've been assigned to your case and have reviewed the statements you and your friend Zade gave about the kidnapping and assault." Bray eased himself into the chair and set a pair of business cards on the bedside table. "We wanted to personally assure you we are taking the matter of your safety very seriously. If you have any questions about the investigation, you can call us at any time, day or night."

"Thank you." Dis glanced at the cards and crossed his hands over the top of the bedding. His thumb hooked onto the medical bracelet around his other wrist, straining the plastic band.

"Detective Fuller and I have spoken with the hospital's therapist, Dr. Gray, who feels you are able to discuss the attack with us. Please let us know if you would like to take a break or to stop at any time."

"I'm okay." Dis continued to toy with his hospital bracelet.

"We're assigning you an officer escort for the next few days. There will be an officer outside your room, and when you are released …"

Dis sat up. "I'm fine, she won't …"

"It's necessary." Fuller watched Dis as he struggled with the pillow behind his back. She walked over to the other side of the bed and picked up another pillow from the floor.

"Thanks." Letting out a hiss of breath, Dis stuffed the pillow next to the others. "I don't need any protection from her."

"Victims of assault, sexual assault in particular, often feel safer with an officer posted for at least twenty-four hours." Bray shot a look at his partner before continuing. "It's normal procedure."

"I don't need a bodyguard."

"The docs have glued you back together and they seem happy to let you out soon." Fuller shrugged, then leaned against the wall. "I'm sure you won't accept any rides from strangers this week. But it's still necessary."

"Why?"

"We got to the crime scene what, thirty minutes after you arrived here at the hospital? So let's say with that walk your athletic friend made over here to Harbor Hospital, that's maybe sixty minutes before a cruiser showed up. Maybe an hour and a half, tops. The apartment behind the shop was empty by the time we got there."

"She threw out the evidence." Dis watched the detective pace.

"No, not 'attacker throws the evidence in a garbage bag' clean. We're talking 'no fingerprints on the premises, not one stray piece of hair, no dishes in the sink, no soap scum in the tub, no change in the couch' clean. Professionally sanitized. The mattress was gone, the rug was cut and removed, and all the potential evidence of your assault in the apartment turned to vapor." Fuller ticked off the points on her fingers. "Whole place reeked of bleach. We got fingerprints out of the bookshop to run, but nothing corroborating your statement."

"You think I did this to myself."

"Not at all." Bray glanced at his partner.

"What I'm saying is that there's someone who cleans up after this … Jeniel. We can't find any record of her. The landlord rented it through a management company, and they rented it to a curtain manufacturer for a showroom. All the ads for the store were purchased by the employee, one Mala Frankel. Who is now on our persons of interest list, by the way." Fuller glanced at Bray. "It gets worse. The sexual assault kit they ran on you during your intake is missing. All the photos, all the samples, everything that was under lock and key and logged per procedure got up and walked out within two hours of being taken. So yes, it's necessary." Fuller snapped one of the window blinds down and peered out at the morning sky. "We have reason to believe your case overlaps with an ongoing murder investigation and that there is more than one person working with your alleged assailant. We need to make sure that you stay available to us. Understand?" She turned back to face Dis.

Dis looked at his hands resting on the blanket. "Fine."

"Your friend Zade said she was going to get you some clothes and feed your cat. With your doctors' assessment, you'll probably get out tomorrow or the next day, so I wouldn't worry too much. You work as a dispatcher for one of the motorcycle messenger companies in town, right? Well, consider this a vacation for a few days. Or if you can't, the officer will go with you to your workplace. Anything happens, you call straight off." Fuller pointed her chin at the cards on the table.

Dis stared at the ceiling. "Is that it, detectives?"

"I'm sure you're tired after everything you've been through. We have your home and work numbers. Thank you for your time." Bray stood up and looked pointedly at his partner.

"Don't worry, we'll keep you safe." Fuller patted the side of the bed and headed for the door.

Dis frowned. "Thanks."

Bray closed the door and nodded to the S&P officer seated in the hallway. He turned to his partner as they walked down the hospital corridor. "I'm not clear on the reasoning behind going into so much detail with the victim at this time."

"He would have ditched anyone we put on him unless we impressed the needfulness of the thing, explicitly. Would've been troublesome to keep track of." Fuller shrugged and shoved her hands into her pockets.

"You may have traumatized him further."

"Oh come on, I didn't say anything that would scare that one after what he's been through. Made a point not to mention the slice-and-dice we hauled out of the harbor on the way over here."

"Dot!" Bray stopped and put a hand on his partner's shoulder. "He could be involved."

"Horseshit. He couldn't carve up a chicken, let alone another human being. Besides, with his injuries he's not exactly going to be hauling weighted body bags quayside, now, is he?" Fuller continued toward the elevators, still digging through her pockets. "You have any gum? I left mine in the car."

▽↗◢

"90-32, pickup at 28 Duncan Ave, Suite 6. Going to 207 Victory Square."

"On it. How you feeling today, dispatch?" Zade kicked down a gear and swung right, skirting the extended ramp hanging off the truck in front of her. Her eyes lingered on the motorcycle's left side mirror as she drove by the side panel featuring the company's mascot.

"Like a celebrity."

"Okay otherwise?" Zade turned her head to watch a group of pigeons settle under a bench close to the sidewalk. She toggled her turn signal and dipped the bike into the on-ramp for Fisher Tunnel.

"Yes. Keep your eyes roadside, 90-32."

"You sure you don't need anything?" Inside the tunnel, the motorcycle's headlight bounced off the reflectors.

"Yes." The dispatcher sounded annoyed.

"You've any plans for dinner?" A knot of fur by the bottom of the road divider caused Zade's eyes to dart back to her mirror.

"No, just going to head home with my shadow."

"You could come out with me and Otter tonight instead. He wants to introduce me to Avery's sister." A dog in the back seat of a car barked as Zade passed the vehicle. The animal's muzzle flashed open and shut, its saliva flecking across the glass.

"Otter will protect you from 62-91's attentions. You don't need me."

Daylight cut across the lanes as the courier came up the Duncan Avenue exit. A trash can rolled off the curb and Zade zigzagged to avoid hitting a rat that ran out from behind it.

"Otter says she looks like me."

"Who?"

"Avery's sister."

"I'm staying in tonight, thanks."

"I'll swing by later to see how you're doing." The kickstand snapped out and Zade swung off the back of the motorcycle.

The dispatcher's sigh was audible over the radio. "I'm fine."

"Iris wants me to bring the bike by anyway. I want to make sure you're okay."

"Don't get all maternal on me, Zade."

"I'm not that kind of mother." A smile curled the courier's lips as her dispatcher's laughter rippled through her earpiece.

$$\triangledown \nearrow \blacktriangle$$

At six, Zade hit the engine's kill switch and glided into the depot, throwing out a hand to the mechanic as she dropped her heels to the concrete floor.

Iris waved the courier toward the back of the bay and came over with an oil pan. "Running fine?"

"Seems fine. How is he?" Zade pointed her chin up at the booth above.

"Dis? He stormed out about an hour ago."

"An hour ago? I thought he was in the can when I got you on the radio to check out. I was only running a drop through the Straight. He could have told me …" Zade rested her helmet against her leg.

"He took off so fast, that S&P girl had to run to keep up." Iris looked up from the cable she was inspecting. "I had to call Frankie in early."

"Everything okay?"

"I shouldn't tell you his business. Plopped everything on me until Frankie got in, all because he got a hand-delivered letter."

Zade leaned back, setting her helmet on the top of a nearby chest of tools. "Fuck. He didn't happen to mention what it was, did he?"

"No, he's private about his affairs. None of my fucking business."

"He makes me worry." Zade chewed on the side of her thumb. "I've got to go meet Otter soon. Do you think he'll be okay?"

"I think he'll be fine, Zade. He's got that S&P officer in tow." The mechanic tested the brake lever. "You're good friends with him now, aren't you? Looking after him like you do." Iris' voice dropped to a whisper.

Zade stopped chewing and stared at the other woman for a moment. "What happened?"

Iris stood up with a hand on her lower back and dipped her shoulders forward. "Don't usually get visitors during the day here. Only OC with flats and leaks and whatnot. Sometimes food deliveries, you know. Those kids Lou hires can't find the booth even though it's right in front of them. I tell them to go up, they knock a few times, he tells them to wait, opens it, gives them cash, and gets his food."

Zade kept her gaze locked with Iris's as the mechanic rubbed her neck.

"This one I've never seen before. He came in and marched right up there like he knew where to go. Knocked like he owned the place. Dis, he opened the door and then the guy in the suit made him sign a ticket before he handed over the letter. Soon as he had it signed, the suit turned around and marched down the stairs. Out to a limo. That thing must suck gas like a pig." Iris pointed over to the stairs. "Dis stood right there and opened it, so I wasn't spying on him or anything. He stared at it and then threw it over the railing. He slammed the door so hard I thought it would come right off the hinges." Iris shook her head. "Then he came down those stairs as fast as, well, as he can with that leg, shouting at me that he was leaving. Scared the hell out of the S&P girl, tell you what. No one's safe when he's like that."

"Thanks." Zade headed over to the stairs, the sound of her boots hitting the metal steps ringing through the garage.

At the top, she peered over both sides of the railing. She raced back down and climbed into a disused corner of the shop. She emerged from behind a row of tarp-covered heaps with a rumpled envelope.

"Well?" Iris stood watching her. "Is it anything important?"

"I'm not sure." Zade held up a laminated piece of plastic. "It's a VIP backstage pass for the show at the Crossing tonight." She shook the package but there was nothing else.

"Oh, well, lemme see that then." The older woman took a pair of reading glasses out of her coveralls and shoved them up the bridge of her nose. She put her hand out, impatiently flapping her fingers.

With a bemused expression, Zade handed over the pass and envelope.

"This would send him off like that." Iris shook her head and looked at Zade over her glasses. "He'll be in that foul mood for months now, but he'll be fine, eventually." Iris handed the pass back to Zade and dipped her shoulders. "Well, if he doesn't throw himself in the river."

"Over a VIP pass?" Zade held it up by its red cord.

"Not going and then regretting is what would do it. He acts like he doesn't care, but I know. He's been waiting all this time for him to come back." Iris went over to the cabinets and took out two containers of oil. "Every time the other one plays in the city, this one gets all worked up over it. He tries to not let it show, but I know. Shame he's in no shape to go tonight. He should punch that one square in the face again."

"Who are you talking about?" Zade pried apart the sides of the package and checked inside it again.

Iris stopped and threw her an odd look. "Thought you said you were friends with him now?"

"Who are you talking about and why are you looking at me like that?"

"Because …" Iris cleared her throat. "That man left him alone at such a dark time, I don't know how fate would reward him with success. But then, what do I know?" She waved her hand above her head. "He best never step foot in here again." She cleared her throat again and looked at Zade out of the corner of her eye. "Shame though, Dis being too low to go over and give him a proper piece of his mind." The mechanic sniffed and dragged the clean end of her rag under her nose. "Those two were always causing me problems. Racing other couriers

or dumping bikes trying for bonus pay. But when they fell in love, it was …"
She gazed through the open garage bay doors at the street outside, sniffed again
and wadded the rag tightly in her fist. "Well, at least we know why he left mad
as hell." Iris shoved the rag into her pocket.

▽↗◢

Car horns added to the background din as the evening commute out of Uptown
inched forward. Zade took the Southern Promenade, heading west. Behind her,
the skyscrapers of the Financial District stood out silver against incoming storm
clouds. Only the Pierce Tower still reflected the setting sun, its opalescent
windows rippling gold.

The harbor curved to the south and Zade cracked open her helmet, letting in
the scents of seaweed and salt. The empty park stretched down from the
roadway to a line of flotsam stranded on the gray sand of the shoreline. Beacons
out on the shipping route twinkled as the tugboats' horns echoed off the
embankment. Farther out, the incoming tide crested white against the dimming
horizon.

After her headlight reflected off a dark glistening streak on the pavement,
Zade flipped her turn signal on and coasted over to the breakdown lane. She
sighed as the motorcycle's light illuminated a twisted mound of fur and flesh.
Killing the engine, she dismounted and got a plastic bag out of her bike's
hardcase. She slipped her gloved hand into the plastic and bent down next to
the corpse. "How many times did you make this run before today?" As she lifted
the body up, the animal's snout sagged open.

Fresh blood oozed out, candy-red in her headlight. She carried the body on
top of the bag and a loop of intestine dropped over the side. She grimaced,
angling her wrist up to guide it away.

The thin plastic squelched between her fingers as she carried the animal into
the park. Sharp pieces of bone pressed into her gloves where the animal's outer

layers had been sheared off. She brought it down the slope, stooping by the first tree. The sea wind dispersed the stink of musk and meat.

"I hope someone does the same for me." She lowered the dead animal between the roots of the tree. While she was turning the bag inside out, a gust of air inflated it, trying to snatch it away. She wedged it under her boot heel, then wiped her gloves clean on the grass. Leaves fluttered over the animal's corpse, continuing in the direction of the road. Zade stood up and followed.

▽↗◢

Otter smacked Zade on the arm and handed her a flask. "Fuck, it's cold tonight. Thirsty?"

"Thanks. I wanted to ask you about the bands." She upended the container and looked back at the restaurant.

"Avery and Vicky said they'd grab a table. I want to know what you think of her." Otter held open the door. "For me, though. You have to find your own cutie to take home tonight." He accepted the flask back from her.

Zade smirked and stuck a finger in Otter's ribs. "Not my fault if beautiful girls like me better."

"Do me a favor, and let me have the first try, okay?" Otter lowered his voice as they entered the dining room. He took off his glasses and put them in his jacket pocket.

"You've had enough time with her."

"You haven't even seen her yet!"

"I'm just giving you a hard time." Zade laughed. "It's good to see you excited about a girl."

Otter's frown faded as he spotted Avery standing up from a table. A slender woman in a blue cocktail dress sat next to him. She looked up with a smile.

"Zade, meet Vicky, Avery's older and lovelier sister. Vicky, this is Zade." Otter settled his riding jacket onto the back of the chair closest to Vicky.

"I'm very happy to meet you, Zade. Avery has told me so much about you." Vicky rested her hand on her brother's arm, smiling as Avery scowled at Otter.

"We've ordered drinks." Avery looked down as he sat next to Zade and handed over the beer list.

"The resemblance is uncanny, isn't it?" Vicky reached across the table and touched Zade's hand. "We must be related."

Zade glanced up from the beer list and stared at the other woman's hand.

"Stranger things have happened." Otter grinned and pried the list from his friend's grip.

"After my birthday party, we'll have to look into it. I'll have some free time to start a new project then." Vicky sat back, taking her hand off of Zade's.

"You're having a birthday party?" Otter tapped the list. "Is it soon?"

Vicky kept her eyes on Zade. "Yes."

Avery glanced quickly at his sister. "It's in two weeks, on the twenty-first."

"When is yours, Zade? We must be close in years as well." Vicky returned her hand to Avery's arm.

The waiter placed a cocktail and a beer in front of the siblings and looked expectantly at the other two guests.

"I don't celebrate it." Zade turned to the waiter. "I'll have a Black Dog, please."

"A pint of Settlement." Otter nodded to the man and turned back to face Vicky. "Are you always very busy? Avery mentioned you were coming here from work?"

"She manages the Pierce Hotel." Avery offered his beer to Zade and she shook her head, declining. When he then held it out to Otter, Vicky gave her brother an odd look. He shrugged in response. "Couriers share their drinks if someone hasn't been served yet."

"Very chummy of you." Vicky pointed at Zade. "Are you anti-birthdays, Zade?"

"No." Zade kept her gaze on the table.

Vicky gave her a wide smile. "Then why not celebrate?"

"You might as well tell her. She'll find out eventually." Avery winced as his sister squeezed his arm.

Zade threw a pleading look at Otter.

"Oh, right, you were asking me about the bands. What was it you wanted to know?" Otter handed Avery back his beer.

"Were any of them OC?" Zade's eyes darted sideways from Avery to Otter.

Vicky looked questioningly at her brother.

"Almost all the couriers are in bands." Avery eyed the significantly lower volume of beer in his glass.

"Not me!" Otter laughed. The waiter set the two pints down, and Otter handed his to Avery. "You're after which cutie, the drummer?" Otter poked Zade in the shoulder.

Zade batted his finger away and shook her head.

"Lana Newton. She's the drummer for Midnight Excursions." Avery lowered Otter's pint. He shrugged when the others turned to look at him. "I like girl drummers."

"Oh, I bet you like girls who play with sticks." Otter winked.

Vicky leaned forward. "Drake Bonnrey plays lead guitar and sings." Setting aside the swizzle stick from her cocktail, she smiled at Otter. "I like men who are good with their mouths *and* their hands."

Otter snorted as he caught sight of the expression on Avery's face. Vicky squeezed her brother's arm lightly.

"Sel Mudon is the other guitarist, and what's her name, or is it the guy on bass?" Otter closed his eyes. He cocked his head and tapped the side of his nose. "So he told you about Bone's band?"

"Which one is he?" Zade set her glass down.

"Who is this 'he'?" Vicky reached across the table to poke Otter.

"My guess is it's their dispatcher. I told you about him." Avery watched Zade's expression change. "See, I'm right."

"Don't be rude, Avery." Vicky's tone was sharp. "You'll have to forgive my brother, Zade. His ego isn't used to women who don't pay attention to him."

"Whose is, really?" Otter beamed across the table at Vicky.

"Our dispatcher has had a rough few weeks." Zade picked at the hem of the tablecloth.

"Oh? I'm sorry to hear it." Vicky extended the menu out to her. "We should order dinner now, or we'll miss the whole show, not just the opening act."

▽↗◢

A pulse of music enveloped them when Otter flung open the inner doors. Vicky laced her arm through her brother's and Otter dropped his arm around Zade's neck.

Otter put his head against his friend's ear as the two of them threaded their way down to the lower level. "What do you think?"

"Of what? Vicky?"

"Yeah." Otter waggled his thumb.

Zade grinned and gave him a thumbs up.

"Not sure if she's up for slumming." He sighed dramatically.

She laughed. "Could be your lucky night."

"What?"

Zade shoved Otter in the direction of the bar.

Excited shouts erupted around them and the crowd at the bar thinned as the stage crew finished setting up the next band's equipment. Otter pressed against the tide of fans and waved money at the bartender. A moment later, he handed Zade a shot glass.

"I told Vicky I needed to talk to you." Otter tossed back his whiskey and winced.

The house lights dimmed and the music cut out. The audience cheered as the headliners took to the stage.

Otter held up two fingers to the bartender and then turned to face Zade. "The handsome fucker with the red hair is Bone."

As his fans screamed and applauded, Bone waved and picked up a black electric guitar. Under the blue-white spotlight, the front man's hair blazed. Bone screened his eyes, surveying the edges of the crowd.

"I'll get this one." Zade dug a bill out of her pocket.

Otter leaned against the bar and watched the stage. "He used to work for OC when I started."

"You were friends?" Zade traded her empty shot for a new one, hooking her boot heel on the bar's footrest.

"Still am. I've had drinks with him when he's played in town over the years." Otter nodded as the crowd cheered again.

Zade rested her back on the edge of the bar and watched Bone as he swung his guitar behind his back.

"Good evening." With his guitar pick resting between his fingers, the musician cupped his hand around the mike and adjusted the stand's height. The audience roared a greeting and his throaty laughter cascaded over the speakers. "If I didn't know better, I'd think you were happy to see us."

Voices called out amid whistles and howls as the band members checked their equipment.

"We're delighted to be here with you this evening." He cradled the mike close to his mouth, amplifying the sound of his breathing.

A male voice shouted something from the edge of the stage and the singer laughed.

"Do you fine people know anything about how the booze you are drinking tonight comes into existence? No?" Bone let go of the mike and brushed his auburn hair out of his eyes. "We took a tour of the distillery in Grava and the owners showed us how the flowers and fruit are fermented and distilled. Imagine big bubbling vats simmering this thick, sweet mash, and warehouse walls with high-water marks from years of floods." Shielding his eyes from the spotlights, Bone surveyed the dance floor and then looked over his shoulder at the rest of the band. "The first bit of condensed vapor out of the pipes is called the head, the second is the heart, and the third and last is the tail. Heads, hearts, and tails. The heart is the prized essence we drink, once it's flavored and aged. They use the other parts for cleaning the equipment. People think the best part, or the most important, is at the beginning or the end, but it turns out it's in the middle. Not the romantic falling in love part, or the tragic falling out, but the routine mundane daily business no one ever writes songs about. Being with our beloved, that's where you find the essential meaning of our everyday lives. Our lonely, lovely lives. Love is nothing more or less than the distilled heart of our fucked up lives." He brought his guitar to the front of his hips and the crowd cried out as he began to play.

▽↗◢

After the third encore, Bone raked his fingers through his drenched hair and grabbed the mike. "If you want more, you'll have to wait until we come back on the next tour." He laughed as the other guitarist threw water at him. "Sel says to tell you to buy our new album, it's back there at the merch table on your way out." He shook the water off. "Friends, I hope you all find what your heart desires, or the closest approximation they are serving at the bar. Good night, and thanks for coming out to see us, you sweet-hearted fuck-ups."

Otter made his way to Zade's side. "Vicky wants us to go back to her place for drinks, all of us. You up for it?"

Zade used the front of her shirt to wipe the sweat off her face. "I've got something I've got to do first. Can I catch up with you?"

Otter handed over Zade's jacket and bag. "How long you going to be, do you think?"

"Maybe a half-hour, tops?"

"We'll have another round and if you're not back by then, I'll leave the address on your bars. Deal? You won't bag out on me?" He gripped her arm.

"I won't bag out; I'll probably be back in a few minutes." She grinned. "Why are you so nervous to be alone with her, anyway?"

"It's her little brother that's making me nervous. I need you to distract him for me." He slapped her shoulder.

Zade hauled her bag over her head, adjusting the weight of it on her lower back. She watched Otter work his way up to the bar as she dug the backstage pass out of her pocket and dropped its cord over her head.

She joined a queue of other pass-holders at the far end of the stage. Most of the VIPs were dressed in high fashion and giggling over slender fluted glasses of wine. The socialites' passes were checked and they were waved behind the red velvet rope sectioning off the exclusive lounge. When it was Zade's turn, the security guard inspected her pass thoroughly, then indicated she should step out of line. After a short exchange with his radio, he addressed her.

"Third door on the left." The guard pointed down the backstage corridor. "Knock first."

"Thanks." Zade made her way down the dark hallway, hefting her jacket across her arm.

She knocked on the door to the third dressing room. There were sounds of movement and then the door was jerked open. She stepped back as Bone, in a fresh T-shirt and tight-fitting trousers, loomed over her.

"Do you require my thumbprint for a package?" His eyes widened as he caught sight of the laminated pass around her neck.

"No, I was hoping I could talk to you for a minute, Mr. Bonnrey." Zade looked up at him apologetically, then dropped her gaze. Bone's bare toes curled into the stained carpet.

"Iris thought ..." She glanced back up as he continued to stare. "It's about Dis."

"I suspect I am far too sober to hear what you have come to say, friend." Bone shoved the door open and waved her toward the black leather couch taking up most of the room. "If you could be patient a moment more, I will fetch anesthetic."

Zade took off her messenger bag and sat down on the couch. She eyed the battered acoustic guitar at the other end of the couch, then looked over to the dressing room table, where her host was filling two tumblers with a rose-colored liquor. She started chewing on the side of her thumb, then shoved her hand under her right thigh.

Bone glanced at Zade's reflection in the mirror and then turned around, extending one of the drinks to her. "What kind of machine does Iris have you out on, is it a 350 Denton or a 500 Smarrow? She always loved rehabbing the twins."

"I'm on a 500 Smarrow, yeah. Dumped the 350 a few weeks ago." Zade leaned forward to accept the tumbler, wrapping her hands around the heavy glass. She sniffed the contents and sipped slowly, earning an amused smile from her host.

After twisting his wet hair into a knot, Bone sat down in a chair across from her. "It's called Constalia. I buy it by the case, so there's no need to go too easy on it." He swallowed half of the contents of his tumbler, then dangled it loosely from his calloused fingertips. "You wanted to talk to me about Dis?"

Zade drank more of the fragrant alcohol and sunk into the cushions of the couch. "Iris said if your invitation had come at any other time, he would have come to see you."

"She overthinks things. If he wanted to see me, he wouldn't have given you his pass." He reached back to grab the squat bottle off the table.

"He didn't give it to me." Frowning, Zade looked at him as he turned and poured more into her glass. "He threw it away."

"Of course he did. Idiot." Bone's voice was bitter as he refilled his own glass. "That's me, not you. Then you are here to tell me what, exactly? Never to chase after your man again?" Even as he continued to smile at her, his eyes were sharp with pain.

Zade's mouth gaped open and then she gave a spluttering laugh. "Dis isn't enough of a woman to be my man, Mr. Bonnrey." She grinned at him over the top of her glass and then emptied it.

"Call me Bone." He splashed more liquor into it and then sat back with a contemplative expression. "So then, what have you come to say?"

Rolling the glass between her palms, Zade looked down at the rug and then back up into his eyes. "I think Iris is right. If it had arrived last month, he would have come to see you. We've been putting couriers dirt-side for months. We had three more quit OC this week, and everybody's scared." She took a large swallow and hunched over with her hands between her knees. "A week ago, the woman he was dating tried to skin him alive. He's got an S&P tail babysitting him in case she comes back to try and kidnap him again. Shit's bad all around for him right now."

Bone squeezed his tumbler as the muscles knotted along his jaw. "They haven't caught her?"

"No." Zade locked eyes with him. "He came to work yesterday and today. He says he is fine, but ..."

The muscles in Bone's jaw clenched as he stood up and looked away. He set the bottle down on the dressing table and leaned forward until his forehead was resting against the mirror. He stood motionless for several minutes as the distant noise of the club's music filtered into the dressing room.

Standing up from the couch, Zade finished her drink and set the glass on the far end of the dressing table. She picked up her bag and turned to leave.

Pushing off from the mirror, Bone rotated to face her. "You came here to ask me to go to him."

Zade flinched, then nodded.

After a moment, Bone extended his hand to her.

"Thank you for coming to see me tonight." His hands were warm as they pressed around hers. "What is your name, sugar?" He gave her a dazzling smile.

"Zade." She smiled nervously. "Please don't tell him I came to see you, or he'll be mad at me."

"It will be our secret, Zade." Bone walked her to the door. "Thank you."

She grinned as he opened the door for her. "It was a great show tonight. I'm going to have to get your albums now."

"Avoid the first one. It's maudlin trash." Bone leaned against the doorframe and watched her as she walked down the hallway.

▽↗◢

Otter looked relieved when she joined them in front of the club.

"Did you get your autographs?" Vicky reached out to take Zade's arm as they crossed the street.

"Ah … yeah." Zade threw a glance back at Otter.

He gave her a wide smile. "Told them you'd fallen in love with the band."

"I'll play their new album for you when we get back to my place." Vicky glanced back at her brother.

"We should go get beer." Avery tugged on Otter's arm as they approached the parked motorcycles.

"Zade can run me home." Vicky squeezed Zade's arm. "That way, we can have a few minutes to ourselves."

Otter sighed. "Sure, why not."

Avery handed his sister a helmet hanging on the side of his motorcycle and looked at Zade.

"Don't worry, I'll go slow."

"You've been drinking all night. I'm not sure if it …"

"So have you! Besides, I'm the more experienced rider."

"She's got you there, Avery." Otter clapped him on the shoulder.

Avery opened his mouth, but his sister cut him off with a dismissive gesture.

"Go." Vicky locked eyes with him, then put her helmet on.

Otter sighed, watching Zade help Vicky settle herself into pillion position, then started his bike up. Zade waited for her passenger to pin the edges of her coat under her legs.

"Where to?"

"Across from St. Anna's, down from the U." Vicky's gloved hands locked around Zade's waist.

"You're not dressed for riding; would you like my jacket to go over your coat?"

"It's close. You can go as fast as you want to. I'm used to being on the back."

At Pearl Street, Zade slowed to let a person in layers of old coats drag a broken shopping trolley across the road. The taxi driver behind them beat out an impatient staccato on his horn. In response, Zade dropped her boot heels and came to a full stop, waiting until the bedraggled pedestrian hauled the trolley completely onto the sidewalk.

Vicky kept her high heels notched against the passenger pegs and squeezed Zade's waist. Zade revved the throttle, casting a glance back at her passenger. Vicky responded with an exaggerated nod of her helmet. The motorcycle leapt forward and cut around a couple crossing against the light, leaving the taxi honking impotently behind them.

When they reached State Street, Zade dropped her hand off the clutch and moved Vicky's hands off the healing cut on her stomach to rest higher around her ribs. Taking a left, Zade cracked the throttle. Neon signs along the shopping district blurred as the motorcycle accelerated into the center lane. Zade laid the bike into the curve, counter-steering the right bar up to shoot around the corner of Mercy Street.

Vicky kept a tight grip as Zade righted the motorcycle and glided into a parking spot across from St. Anna's. She only released her grip when Zade paddle-walked the bike back to the right of the parking space.

Zade waited as her passenger dismounted, then clicked the kickstand down and pried off her helmet. "You know how to keep your seat." She grinned as her passenger removed her helmet.

155

Vicky smoothed her hair and produced a set of keys. "I've ridden behind Avery on steep mountain roads, on the Continent."

"I've heard the roads over there are spectacular." Zade followed Vicky up the steps of a brownstone.

"You've never been? Perhaps we should all go this summer."

"I'd like that." Zade waited as Vicky unlocked the front door.

"Please come in. You can put your bag down under the coat rack." The woman kicked off her heels.

Zade waited under a brick arch until Vicky guided her into the living room.

"There was a fire when I was young. When my parents remodeled, they decided to leave the beams and bricks exposed. The result is quite beautiful, but it can get very cold in the winter." The hem of Vicky's dress swayed along the tops of her stockings as she crossed the living room. She knelt down at the side of the room's fireplace, ran her hand along the white facade, and turned the gas jets on.

"You've lived here your whole life?" Zade watched as she adjusted the height of the flames.

"I was sent away to school on the Continent when I was a child. I came back to take care of Avery after our parents died. I've tried my best to make it feel like a home for him."

"I'm sorry." Zade scratched at the side of her head and looked around the elegant living room.

"I should be the one apologizing to you. I'm sorry I was hounding you about your birthday over dinner." Vicky gave her a concerned look. "Otter told me afterwards you don't like talking about your childhood."

"It's okay. It's just not a story anyone wants to hear." Zade took a seat on the edge of the couch closest to the fireplace.

Vicky watched her for a moment. "After my parents died, I found out my father had been having an affair with Avery's mother. We're only half-siblings, you see. Avery's mother killed my parents and then herself when our father wouldn't end the marriage after years of promising he would. She discovered he was keeping company with other women and lost hope." She warmed her hands near the flames.

Zade watched her for a few minutes. "I've never known who my parents were. I barely remember my mother. It seemed like she was always crying, and then one day she was dead."

"It might not be a coincidence that we look alike, Zade." Vicky held out a hand to her. "Our father might have had other families ..."

"That sounds like the plot of a movie. Anyway, you're much more beautiful than I am."

"We do look alike, admit it. They have tests in movies, don't they? Blood tests? We could have it confirmed." Vicky twined her fingers into Zade's. "It would mean so much to Avery to have more family, especially if it was a person he admires as much as you."

"What if it came back negative?" Zade locked her thumb around the back of Vicky's.

"We could have the tests done without telling him, so as not to get his hopes up."

"I'm not big on hope either." Zade gave her a wry look. "Seems like everything always breaks and everyone always dies, no matter what you do."

"I'll call Dr. Crysal and set something up for tomorrow." Vicky fiercely squeezed Zade's hand. "We can make a pact right now, to be sisters no matter what the results are."

"Sisters?"

"Haven't you ever wanted a sister or a brother? Or wondered who your family is? Your flesh and blood?"

"When I was young. When I was older, I had friends, so I didn't think about it as much."

"Friends like your dispatcher?" Vicky relaxed her hand and slid her fingers free from Zade's.

"Other kids. We were always running on the rooftops or racing in the Underground. Then Iris gave me this job and I made friends with Boon and Otter."

"How did you meet Iris?"

"I learned to ride by bombing around on stolen bikes before I'd sell them to the chop shops. She caught me stealing one of her bikes."

Vicky laughed as she turned back to the fireplace. "How long have you been a courier?"

"Four years."

"That's a long run for a courier. Avery told me there's a short life expectancy. Only two years, and then what, you're all supposed to retire?"

"Most people quit after a few months and some make it a year or two. It's hard to adjust to almost getting killed every day. Only a few of us are lifers. Otter's got almost ten years and he's never been in a bad spill." Zade paused. "Does it bother you that your brother's running deliveries?"

"Nothing bad will happen to him." Vicky rose and went over to a pair of ornate wood panels on the wall. She rotated one and operated a tap in the recessed bar sink to fill up a pitcher. When it was full, she turned off the tap and wedged the stems of two matching goblets into her other hand.

"How can you be so sure?"

"Oh, I'm a bit psychic. It runs in our family. I've read Avery's cards and he won't die until after I do, and I plan to live a long, long time." Vicky paused in the middle of the room, listening to the rumble of motorcycle engines approaching. "That will be the boys with the beer now."

DIS WAS SCRAPING THE REMAINS of his dinner into the compost bin when the doorbell rang. Setting the plate on the kitchen counter, he wiped his hands on a dish towel and walked out of the kitchen. Stinky looked up from her pillow under the table as he walked by. "Officer Dobbs, you are more than welcome to let yourself in if you have to use the washroom again …" He opened the front door.

Leaning into the light, Dobbs coughed into his fist. The young S&P officer's eyes were bright. "Mr. Drake Bonnrey would like to know if you are receiving guests this evening, sir." He glanced over to where Bone stood on the sidewalk. The young officer's smile faded when he caught sight of Dis's expression.

The two men locked eyes over the top of the officer's head. Bone took his hands out of his pockets and gave Dis a wide, radiant smile. Dis inhaled sharply and sagged against the doorframe.

The officer looked back and forth between the two men and coughed again. "What should I tell him, Mr. Mthdys?"

"You can tell Mr. Bonnrey he can come in." Dis walked back into the kitchen, leaving the door open. He went to the sink, turned on the taps, and started washing his dishes.

Bone hung his leather jacket on the coat rack and retrieved a bottle of Constalia from his bag before stowing it under the hallway table. Holding the bottle of liquor, he leaned in the kitchen doorway and began removing the foil seal. "Shall we have a drink in the living room with your venerable ancestors and their relics? Perhaps the ghost of your Da will join us?"

After dropping a handful of forks in the cutlery drainer, Dis started scrubbing a pot. "He's not here."

"No? I hope he comes around for Sunday dinner?" Walking through the kitchen to stand next to Dis, Bone opened the cabinet under the sink.

Stepping out of the way, Dis scowled as Bone tossed the foil into the trashcan. Bone then opened the cabinet to the right of the window, taking out three juice glasses, glancing up, and watching Dis. Unscrewing the cap on the Constalia, Bone poured two fingers of the rose-colored alcohol into each glass. "I'm canceling the rest of the tour."

Dis set a pot into the drying rack. "You appear to be in fine health."

Bone placed the first glass onto the windowsill and then pushed the second to the side of the sink. "Family emergency." Lifting the third to his mouth, he gave Dis a wicked smile.

Bone's eyebrows shot up as Stinky emerged from under the table. She stretched out her front legs and walked over to him, her cart squeaking. "Let me guess. At night this lovely beast transforms into her war form and the two of you fight crime." He crouched down and extended his hand to the purring cat. "What's this lovely girl's name?"

Dis started washing a plate. "Stinky."

Bone glanced up in surprise. "Truly?"

"Truly."

"Your dad's an unimaginative, paranoid shut-in, darling, but you mustn't hold that against him. Is it okay to pick her up?"

Dis lifted the glass of liquor from the side of the sink and drained it. "Yes."

"I know you can string more than three words together at a time. Bring the bottle, we'll get drunk in that grim memorial your family calls a living room and you can tell me what life is like up in the dispatcher's booth." Bone gathered Stinky under his arm and headed out of the kitchen.

Turning the taps off, Dis stared out over the sink, watching the first few drops of rain hit the window. Glancing at the libation Bone had left on the sill, his mouth twisted into a sad smile. He dug a coin out of his pocket and tossed it into the air, catching it on the back of his right hand. With a solemn expression, he shoved the coin back into his pocket, then carried his glass and the bottle out of the kitchen.

Reclining in the dark, Bone occupied the couch with his legs stretched out, keeping the soles of his boots off the velvet seat cushion. He watched from under half-closed eyes as Dis carefully made his way into the room. He waited until Dis turned on the lamp before holding his glass out for a refill.

A small bit of liquid dripped off the neck of the bottle and onto the rug. Bone smiled and shook his head. "You used to be a bit more mindful of your Ma's imported rug."

"It's mine now." Dis set the bottle on the coffee table. He sat down in the wing-backed chair, pressing his back into the corner and stretching his left leg out.

"Would you be more comfortable …" Bone stopped as Dis glanced away. He watched Dis for a moment. "Your Ma made me promise, right here, in fact, that I would look after you. It looks like I've defaulted on my promise quite badly."

"She shouldn't have asked it of you." Dis stared at the heirloom rug. "I don't need to be looked after like a child."

"Elspeth knew she was dying. She knew what your Da would do when she went, and she didn't want you to be alone." Bone's tone was harsh. "She was afraid you would do something stupid. And you, her only son, did exactly that."

Dis hooked his left thumb on the top of his leg brace. "It was an accident."

"What? That you survived?" Bone laughed bitterly. "I don't know what corrupted instinct makes you believe half the nonsense in your brain, but suicide is not an appropriate action in this day and age. You need to stop trying to martyr yourself." He lifted the cat off of his lap and set her on the couch cushion. "I know why the heroic Officer Dobbs is assigned to you, and while there is a chance you are still in danger, I'm not leaving you with only a bunch of mother-mugging S&P lackeys to watch over you."

Abruptly, Dis leaned forward, glaring. "I don't want your ..."

"Too bad. I'm not interested in what you don't want." Bone swung his boots onto the floor and sat up, locking eyes with Dis. "As far as I can tell, you have no idea what you *do* want."

Dis dropped his gaze to the rug. The two men sat in silence. The cat made small wheezing noises. The clock on the mantel ticked.

When Bone spoke again, his voice trembled with emotion. "After your Da went, you told me, in no uncertain terms, to leave you the fuck alone. I thought that was what you wanted." He sighed. "The night you crashed your bike, Iris called to tell me. I sat in the fucking hospital all night, waiting until you got out of surgery, convincing myself that if I gave you up, you would find someone who would make you want to live. Idiot that I am."

"I never knew you were at the hospital. Not that it matters." Dis looked at Bone over the top of his glass. "You found someone else. It was in the papers."

Shaking his head, Bone gave him a sad smile. "I'm sorry to disappoint both you and the press, but no, I have only ever been in love with one man. I stayed away because you told me to leave and never told me to come back. Recording and touring are all I've been doing for the last five years. Well, and learning how to spend more money annually than any courier makes in their besotted, stunted lifetime. I thought if you wanted to contact me, you would have done so by now."

Dis stared at him.

Bone lifted the bottle of Constalia and refilled their glasses. "Besides a mutinous uprising at OC and having a lunatic attempt to skin you alive, what have you been getting up to?" He set the bottle on the coffee table and started to sit back.

Dis grabbed Bone's hand. He stroked his thumb over the rough callouses on his fingertips and laced his fingers through Bone's. The two men sat without speaking.

When the clock on the mantel began to chime, Bone squeezed Dis's hand. "It's late. I should go and let you get some rest. I can lecture you another time."

Without looking up, Dis shook his head. "Finish the bottle with me."

"You're already drunk, love." Bone stood up and started pulling his hand away. "I should go."

"I'm not drunk." Without letting go, Dis stared up into Bone's eyes. "Like the stars above and tides of the silvery sea, the moon always comes back to me."

"You certainly are drunk, if you're reciting poetry." Bone stared down at his trapped hand and set his drink down on the coffee table. "It's late and this should wait until daylight and sobriety."

"I want you in the water with me." Dis lifted Bone's hand to his mouth and kissed along the edges of his fingers.

"I'd forgotten exactly how quickly your mood changes." With a hiss of indrawn breath, Bone closed his eyes. "What is it that you want, plainly?"

"I want your hands, I want your mouth, and all the rest of you." Dis trailed the edge of his teeth on the inside of Bone's wrist.

"Sweet Heavenly Mother. You're serious about this." Bone opened his eyes and leaned in to thread his fingers through Dis's hair. "I'm not fucking you tonight. Do you understand me?" His voice was low and level. "If you regretted it tomorrow …"

"Stay. Finish the Constalia with me in the tub."

"As long as you understand I am not allowing you to set this up so you can play the martyr in the morning. If I stay, you will run and hide, and then we will have to start all over when I find you again."

Dis released Bone's hand and dropped his gaze back down to the rug. "I'm not going to, Drake." When he spoke again, his voice was filled with anger. "If you don't want me anymore, just say so."

Leaning down, Bone set his hands on either side of Dis's face. "You know I want you, Dulyn. Every scar, every bolt, and every other gorgeous, sullen inch of you. I do very much want to fuck you, in the tub, in your bed, and on this couch." Bone raised Dis's face and lifted off his glasses. "You're a slippery creature, my beautiful love." He held him in place as he tried to shy away. "If I give you the chance, you'll leave me crying on the shore, all alone. I've been crying after you for so long now, you'll have to forgive me if I can't risk …"

Dis leaned in and stole a kiss. He slid his hands through Bone's hair until it hung loosely around both their faces. Extending his hand slowly along Bone's thigh, Dis drew him closer, pushing his fingertips underneath Bone's t-shirt to rest against his bare skin.

The kiss began to transform into a passionate embrace and Bone pulled back. "If we keep this up, you will ruin my self-restraint. Are you certain you've healed enough for this sort of …"

Dis answered by digging his thumbs into Bone's hips. Bone groaned, sliding his mouth along Dis's jaw, letting his teeth lightly scrape the skin. Trailing the tip of his tongue over the other man's neck, Bone kissed his way to the collarbone.

Kissing him on the jaw in return, Dis pressed him onto the couch. "Stay and I will promise to come to your hotel tomorrow." He buried his face in the side of Bone's neck.

With a rough bark of laughter, Bone wrapped his long arms around Dis's back. "Of all the possible outcomes I was prepared for tonight, this was not one of them."

□ ♍ ♏ ♌ ■

At the foot of the garden, the river sparkled beneath the winter sky. The back door clanged shut and Dis stepped out into the morning sunlight. He carried a bucket down the stone path to a steel drum resting on cinder blocks. Removing the cover of the drum, he inspected the interior of the fire-blackened container.

A red and black songbird scolded him from a nearby tree as he picked up a shovel and used it to push aside a layer of charred shells. He sifted through the crumbling white remains and scooped them into the bucket.

A gust of wind buffeted the garden shed as he opened its narrow door. Inside, he set the bucket on a worktable and began transferring its contents into a granite mortar. Wings fluttered in the brambles outside. He glanced up, his gaze coming to rest on the boat dock out on the river.

▽ ↗ ◢

Slate-colored clouds marred the blue sky when he came out of the shed, shutting its door with the toe of his boot. Carrying the empty bucket in his left hand and the jar of freshly prepared whitewash in his right, he followed the stone path back to the house. The river flashed silver as the clouds broke, only to dull again when Dis set the bucket down and opened the back door.

He crossed the kitchen, pausing to look into the living room, where Bone sat on the edge of the couch, tuning an acoustic guitar. He strummed two strings together, then adjusted one of the pegs along the guitar's neck. His fingers ran over the strings once more and then moved on to the next pair. Stinky sat on the couch next to him, her eyes following his movements intently.

"I'm going into the city for a few hours. Will you be here when I get back?" Dis flexed his wrist, swirling the contents of the jar.

Bone took a guitar pick out of his mouth. "No. I have a band meeting at five. Will you be done setting your traps by eight? Sorcery permitting, I was thinking we could have dinner at the Melborn."

"I could be doing something non-magical in town."

"Certainly. However, you were down at the dock at dawn whispering sweet nothings to the sun."

The side of Dis's mouth curled up. "I will meet you at the Pierce later."

Bone nodded and returned his attention back to the guitar. He set the pick between his teeth and played a chord. Dis smiled and continued down the hallway.

He hoisted his messenger bag onto the narrow table there. Opening it, he rearranged a collection of paintbrushes, a white painted brick, and a journal to make room for the jar. He carefully placed it between several bundles of yarn and a sack of bread. He put his old leather jacket on, closed the bag, and slipped it over his head, shrugging it into place against his back.

In the living room, Bone muttered to the cat and repeated the chord. As Bone's singing filled the house, Dis opened the front door and stepped out, locking it behind him. He paused on the last stair, scanned the street, and then slowly stepped onto the sidewalk.

At Point Station, he got on the inbound train. At Claremont, an older man in front of him stumbled on his way off the train. Dis caught his elbow and guided him onto the platform.

"Are you arresting me?" The man blinked with crusted eyelashes. "I told you I didn't steal any fish, officer." Saliva ran from the corner of his lips and his clothes stank of urine.

Dis averted his face from the full force of the man's exhalation. "No one's arresting you. I didn't want you to fall. That's all." He let go of the man's arm.

"I fell into the ocean once. Off the Long Pier. Went for a swim." The man's eyes focused on Dis. "You ever seen them, boy? All shining under the moonlight or sunning themselves on the rocks? The tugs scare them off, but they're out there. They stole all the fish." The old man turned and staggered away.

Dis watched the man wander down the train platform, took out his journal, flipped to a fresh page, and wrote down the man's words. He then made his way to the exit. He didn't notice a whirlwind chasing cigarette butts and wrappers through the turnstiles behind him.

☐ ♍ ♏ ♋ ■

Near the corner of Langham and Spencer, he ducked into an alley. Gulls occupied the dumpsters and a few jousted over several ripped garbage bags. Their squawking quarrel subsided as they caught sight of Dis. The older white-winged gulls shuffled to the side while the younger brown ones flew up to safety. All fixed their eyes on the man's movements. He twisted his bag around his hips and opened it. The squawking echoed through the alley again when they saw the bread.

"Trade me, cousins." He tore off a chunk of bread and tossed it. Three older gulls swooped down. They snapped at each other and flapped their wings, trying to bat the others away from the prize.

A second wave of birds glided in, landing on the first. As he threw more bread, the rest of the flock sailed into the air, piling in to join the fight. Dis emptied the bread bag and the birds' heads darted around, seeking out the last crumbs.

When they were finished, the birds returned to the tops of the dumpsters, making low strange cries and shuffling along the metal edges. Under their scrutiny, Dis knelt down and selected four white feathers that had been shed during their squabble. He ran them through his fist and tucked them into the outside pocket of his bag.

A salty blast of air followed him as he walked the remainder of the way to the delivery depot. The clouds tumbled and shredded apart as he set his bag down against the shuttered garage entrance. He eased the jar out from the nest of yarn and angled it into a sunbeam until its metal lid glittered.

Dis cut off the tip of a gull feather and stroked it through the limewater. He began retracing the outlines of shapes along the border of the garage door. By the time he refreshed the ghostly patterns on the ground, the winter sun was high enough to make him sweat inside his jacket. He continued until the serpentine white lines flowed all the way from the right side of the entrance to an equal height on the left. He recapped the jar and started walking back toward Claremont Station.

☐ ♏ ♍ ♋ ■

A pair of children with matted hair crept along the edges of the subway exit ramp at Unity Station, mimicking his uneven gait with exaggerated limps. They fell in, dogging his steps, and Dis tightened his grip on his cane.

"Give us some change, mister." They ran closer.

"Give us all of your change, mister." One of the boys kicked at the bottom of his cane as the other aimed for his knee brace.

Dis took a diagonal step forward to the right and changed his grip on the cane, bringing it up against his shoulder. He threw a handful of candy behind him and continued to move away, keeping the cane ready as the children fought over the sweets.

In the middle of the block on Mason Street, he entered a paved lot set behind a high chain-link fence. At the far end, yellow and blue motorcycles stood parked in rows outside the garage bays. On his way into the one open bay, Dis ran his hand along the surface of a column covered in faded white spirals.

"Mr. Lew?" Dis looked around the white-walled expanse of the garage and then walked back out to the column. He set his gear down and began to refresh the spirals. Upon completing the last flourish, he rolled his neck and circled his arm.

"I found my favorite hammer." A weathered man walked toward him. "In the storage room, on top of the toilet paper. Went missing three years ago."

"Good afternoon, Mr. Lew." Dis turned to greet him.

Lew absently wiped his hands down the front of his coveralls and nodded. "Used to lose them every day. Thought the kids Patty hired were always walking off with them." Lew looked at Dis over the top of his glasses and slipped his hands into the pockets of his coveralls.

"Sorry to hear it."

"Not sure now. Been finding them this last month." Lew's eyes narrowed as he nodded at the column. "All started coming back not five minutes after you put the first coat on that there post. I found a drill bit in the fridge. In one of the egg holders in the door. I'm getting old, but I know it wasn't there in the morning when I had coffee. No one else went into the kitchen."

"My mother once found one of my father's favorite books in the freezer."

"Patty used to drop her keys every morning unlocking the office door. Like clockwork for years. Couldn't let her in the place without a mess following behind. Spill coffee all over a bike and claim someone pushed her. Always used to think she was making it up."

"Patty's not a morning person, I'd imagine."

Lew let out a snort of laughter. "No, that she isn't."

"I should do the other pillar before it gets dark." Dis nodded his head at the far end of the awning.

"As you like." Lew followed behind as Dis carried his jar and feather over to the second column.

Lew stood and watched Dis work, occasionally turning his head to compare the finished column to the one in progress. When Dis set the feather down and started to close the jar, Lew said something under his breath.

"I'm sorry, I didn't catch that." Dis looked up.

"No mind. You'll come back again?"

"For a few more months. Eventually I shouldn't need to."

"Why's that? It'll either be enough or it won't, by then?"

"Yes, exactly." He nodded.

Lew walked back with Dis to the open garage bay door. "Anything you recommend for keeping them sweet?" The mechanic jerked his chin at the rows of motorcycles.

"Mother Ida's offering a blessing for the Equinox. She'll likely be willing to give you extra water to bring back for the ones your couriers don't bring to her." Dis packed up his gear.

"I appreciate ..." Lew's eyes welled up. "Been nice having a break from all the funerals."

"I agree." Dis held out his hand. "Though we all have to take that ride eventually."

"May it be a long time from now for both of us." Lew clasped Dis's hand in his.

❧ ೮ ⑨ ❶ ☙

Zade looked at the slip of paper in her hand and squinted back up at the brass plate on the brownstone. Ringing the doorbell, she shoved the note into the side pocket of her jacket with her other hand. While she waited, she looked out over the trimmed hedges, watching an elderly woman be pulled across the street by her tiny wheezing dog.

"Good afternoon." A young nurse opened the door. "Do you need me to sign for something?"

"My friend Vicky set up an appointment for a test." Zade turned back around, taking off her goggles.

"Oh, yes. Please come in." She waved Zade into the marble entranceway and led her past a reception desk and through a sitting room with an ornate fireplace.

"I have everything set up for you." The nurse opened a pair of glass doors, revealing the consultation room within, and gestured to a padded chair.

Zade slipped off her jacket and eased into the seat. She watched the nurse carry a tray covered with sterile cloth over to the side of the chair. The nurse

170

snapped on a pair of sterile gloves and began to unfold the cloth on the instrument tray. "Doctor Crysal asked me to explain that you will need to go to the city hospital's secure facility to obtain a genetic test admissible in court, if that is what you want." She gave Zade a reassuring smile. "This is a favor to the family to see if there is any reason to go through all that. Are you comfortable? Shall we start?"

"Sure." Zade held out her right arm.

"Oh, no, we don't use blood tests." Picking up a steel cheek retractor, the nurse turned back to her. "I'm going to need to scrape the inside of your mouth for a sample."

Zade grimaced and opened her mouth as the nurse brought the device close to her face.

"You'll just feel a bit of a pinch."

□ ♍ ♏ ♋ ■

On the train to Victory Station, a group of teenagers started singing. Dis put his canteen away and watched them clap and chant the words of a playground game. His fingers twitched as the complexity of their movements increased.

One by one the players dropped out until only two girls were left, swaying in the middle of the train car. Their hands flew back and forth as the others cheered them on until the train lurched into the station, ending the game. The laughing group tumbled out the doors past Dis and one of the girls smiled shyly in apology.

Reaching the Pit, Dis glanced at the newspaper-plastered windows of the closed Blue Lotus and descended the steps into the seating area. A couple using a set of granite benches looked up at him and then returned to comparing their purchases.

Dis walked around the circular pool at the bottom of the Pit before setting his messenger bag down on a bench and pulling out his tools. He dipped a wide brush into the jar and approached the rim of the pool. After casting a glance upward, he knelt to spread a thick layer of paint around the base. He shifted his weight as the wet bristles fanned out, coating the granite in white. The soft sounds of the paintbrush and the bubbling water were interrupted by the rasp of metal on stone each time he forced his leg back to begin a new section.

When he had finished, Dis stood up, went over to his bag, swapped the paintbrush for a feather, and stretched his shoulders and neck. As he looked up, his eyes met with those of a woman inside the bakery storefront on the other side of the brick walkway. Noting his attention, she frowned and retreated behind a display case of pastries.

Dis resumed his work. Moving in the opposite direction, he dipped the feather in the jar of limewater and traced the lip of the pool. He bent over, his attention fixed on the emerging calligraphy. When the last stroke was done, he set the jar down and lowered himself onto a bench. He rubbed the strained muscles along his neck.

A shadow fell across his back. Dis looked over his shoulder to see a scowling teenage boy standing on the other side of the bench. He rotated to face the boy and raised an eyebrow.

"My Gran wants you to have this." The aloof teenager held out a crinkled bag.

"Thank you." Dis accepted the bag without opening it.

The youth walked away abruptly, leaving Dis alone with the unexpected gift. He packed up all of his gear, including the waxed food bag, and hissed as he put weight on his leg. He drew the telescoping cane out of his bag, snapped it open, and leaned onto its expanded length.

The baker watched him from the doorway of the pastry shop as he walked out of the Pit. He waved to her and she disappeared back inside.

□ ♍ ♏ ♋ ■

The sidewalks began to fill with pedestrians as the sky faded. Dis was forced into the street by a trio of drunkards taking up the entire expanse of the walkway along the edge of Victory Station. A lattice of stars shone above the monument as he reached the center of the square. He unwound white ribbon from his bag and examined the marble seat, peering into the recess behind it.

Dis scratched at a rust-colored stain running along the back of the seat. Taking out the feathers, he bound them together, the unused one at their center. Swabbing them into the last of the limewater, Dis muttered as he painted over the old bloodstain. When he was done, he wrapped the base of the seat in a cat's cradle of white ribbon. He threaded the satin ends together, securing the feathers into the heart of the layered knots.

▽ ↗ ◢

As he made his way along the carpet on the sidewalk in front of the main entrance of the Pierce Hotel, a couple walking in front of him were directed by the doorman into the building's revolving glass door. The hotel employee noticed the cane Dis was heavily leaning on, and immediately opened a wide door to the side.

"Thank you." Dis gave the man a pained smile as the cold night air rushed into the lobby around them.

He approached the reception desk and waited.

"May I help you, sir?" A smiling woman in the hotel's black and gray pin-stripe uniform set her phone into the cradle.

"I'd like to leave a message for Mr. Bonnrey in the Unity Suite, please." Dis rested his weight against the reception desk.

"Do you have a message already prepared, sir, or shall I write one for you?"

"If you could, thank you. Just a message that his friend is waiting for him in the bar."

"Very good, sir. I will put it in the Unity Suite box now. May I help you with anything else?" The woman's eyes sparkled as she wrote the message out. She paused, giving Dis a flirtatious smile.

"No, thank you." Dis turned away and started across the lobby toward the hotel lounge.

"Have a good evening, sir."

▽↗◢

He was nursing a pint of Black Dog at the bar when Bone arrived. Many of the ongoing conversations ended when he entered the crowded lounge, and startled whispers followed him as he approached. Dis moved aside, offering the seat next to him, and pushed his glass toward Bone. "How was your meeting?"

Bone picked up the beer and drank a quarter of it. "Once Sel said she was quite happy to have a reason to take a break for a couple of months, everyone else followed. She made me promise I'd remind you of her offer to kick my ass on your behalf." He glanced around the hotel's bar lounge. "Where is your watchdog?"

"Haven't had one all day. Wasn't around when I left home and none appeared later."

"Rather odd, considering the floor show they put on for you at the hospital."

"It made my day easier. Except for getting hassled by some street kids."

"Did you engage with the dirt babies over a magical territory dispute?" Bone turned as a young woman approached him, ringed by several of her friends. "Yes, ladies?"

"We were wondering if we could take a picture with you, Mister Bonnrey." The fan smiled shyly.

"We're going to have to get out of here before you cause a riot."

"You must keep my friend out of the picture, ladies. His aura will ruin the negative." Bone finished Dis's beer and set the glass on the bar.

After posing, Bone shooed his fans away and watched Dis step down from the barstool. Bone's mouth twitched as Dis hefted his messenger bag and began taking careful steps.

"You fought the rats off by hand?"

"No, I'm just stiff from my errands."

"The Melborn can wait. I'm putting you in the tub to soak, love." Bone hooked his hand under the strap of Dis's bag. "Give it up, granddad." He gave Dis a stern look and took the bag off his shoulder.

"I'm younger than you are."

"Proving your single vice is distinctly more debilitating than all of mine combined." He waved Dis into the elevator.

▽ ↗ ◢

A harlequin pattern of onyx and white marble decorated the Unity Suite. Bone put Dis's bag down on an enameled table and held out his hand for his jacket.

"The tub is in through there." Bone gestured to the right of a white leather couch. "I'll order dinner. Any requests, besides no seafood?"

"No, thanks." Dis handed over his jacket and set his cane against the side of the table.

▽ ↗ ◢

After plugging the drain and opening the taps in the master bath, Dis sat on the wide edge of the tub to loosen his bootlaces. He unfastened the straps on his brace and undressed, folding his clothes and placing them in a pile on the edge of the bathroom vanity. Steam billowed up from the black tub as he eased into it. The rising water lapped over the tops of his thighs.

By the time Bone came in and switched the vent fan on, the water was the height of the fresh scars on Dis's chest.

Bone retrieved a towel and washcloth and came over to the side of the tub.

He lifted Dis's head and slid the rolled towel under his lover's neck. Handing Dis the washcloth, he sat on the edge of the vanity and kicked off his boots and socks.

Taking his glasses off, Dis set them on the side of the tub and draped the washcloth across his eyes. When the water reached Dis's neck, Bone leaned over and shut off the taps.

"You're not getting in."

"Not completely." Bone folded up the cuffs of his jeans. "I will need to sign for our dinner when it arrives. Move yourself." Bone sat on the edge of the tub behind Dis and began to massage his neck and shoulders.

"I have dessert in my bag." Dis grunted as Bone squeezed his shoulders. "Old lady who runs the bakery in the Pit gave me a couple of those sweet potato cake things you like."

"Gave you?" Bone dug his knuckles into the sides of Dis's spine. "Was washing her floor one of your errands?"

"I whitewashed the bubbler pool." Dis dropped his head to his chest as Bone kneaded the muscles under his shoulder blades.

"Nice of her to give a starving artist yesterday's stale leftovers. I'm amazed S&P didn't arrest you for vandalism. Hand me the bottle … No, the other one. Dunk your head."

Lying on the bottom of the tub, Dis blew all of the air out of his lungs and watched the silver bubbles ripple up to the surface. After a moment, Bone poked him with a toe and Dis sat up quickly, sending cascades of water into the air and soaking Bone.

"I could sell you to the aquarium to entertain the tourists." Bone grabbed a handful of Dis's hair and gave it a playful shake. He lathered his hands together and began washing his lover's head, massaging his scalp with his fingertips.

"I only do tricks for you." Dis grinned.

Bone bent down to kiss him. "Brat."

"Bully." Dis slipped out of Bone's grip, submerging again. Suds floated from his black hair as he resumed his position on the bottom of the tub. Dis watched through the water as Bone stripped his wet shirt off and threw it onto the floor. When he was prodded with a toe, Dis twisted out of the water, emerging between Bone's thighs. He wrapped his arms around the top of Bone's jeans.

Dis transferred his grip to the sides of the tub, pulling himself further out of the water. He nipped at Bone's lips while Bone laughed. Kissing him, Dis cradled the back of the other man's head. Bone gave a whoop of surprise as his lover pulled them both into the tub. A sheet of water flew up and smacked the marble floor, washing Bone's t-shirt to the base of the toilet.

They sloshed in the water, laughing, as Bone pinned Dis down and bit his neck.

Dis's hands flexed open and he shuddered. "How long did they say dinner would take?"

"Fifteen minutes." Bone kissed his way up to his lover's mouth and released his grip. Dis's freed hands locked around Bone's waist.

As they kissed, Bone ran his hand over the side of Dis's ribs. Spiraling his knuckles along the other man's hipbone, he opened his palm against his body. Dis made a low groan in the back of his throat and tugged at the top of Bone's jeans. They traded lingering kisses and teasing bites as Dis unzipped him.

"Open your eyes." Bone growled. "See me. Be here with me. I am yours and you are …"

With his right eye focusing, Dis matched his movements to Bone's. "Mine."

"Yours."

Dis groaned and his eyes half-closed. "Yours." As Bone's hands moved over his skin, Dis's breath came in shallow gasps and he bit down on his own lip, muffling a low cry.

"Mine." The word turned into a sharp cry as Bone's back arched.

After a moment, Dis adjusted his arm and moved Bone's head to rest in the crook of his shoulder. "We've most likely flooded the hotel."

"Considering what they charge, they can afford it."

□ ♍ ♏ ♋ ■

In the Generosity Suite of the Pierce Hotel, Jeniel threw a vase of roses at the wall. The vase ruptured on impact, sending glass, water, and white flowers tumbling over the stereo cabinet, causing the record to skip.

Naked and covered in small cuts, Jeniel turned away from the stereo, covering her face with her hands. Her long brown hair fell in tangles over her shoulders. She stumbled forward and fell to her knees in front of a full-length white mink coat hanging from a coat rack in the middle of the floor. Plates filled with untouched slices of white-frosted lemon cake and dark chocolate cake alternated with fluted glasses of white wine and tumblers of whiskey to form concentric circles around the rack's wooden pedestal. The offerings radiated out from under the hem of the coat to form a five-pointed star.

"*Stop saying that!*" Jeniel raised her hands and brought them down, scoring her thighs with her jagged fingernails. "I tried! I did!" Fresh blood trickled down her legs as she sobbed. She made a strange keening sound in her throat and smeared the blood onto the floor over older, reddish stains. She worked her way around the star, crawling on the floor and mumbling. "*I did!* Why didn't you stop her?" With desperate eyes, she looked up, staring at the fur. As she lifted her filthy hands in supplication, the reek of her unwashed body mixed with the aroma of the food and alcohol.

"You said he was mine, you said he would change. You told me I would be …" Tears trailed in streaks down her face as she pleaded. "No, I didn't mean it like that. I'm sorry … *Don't!*" With a sudden cry, Jeniel rolled over on her side and thrashed her arms and legs, sending the carefully arranged glasses and plates tumbling. Splashes of liquor and wine mingled with sticky frosting. The resulting mess clung to her feet and legs amid chipped porcelain and broken glass.

The turntable's needle entered the last groove in the record and the device's arm rose, resetting into its holder. Jeniel abruptly froze and lay panting in the silence. Staring up, a look of awe dawned on her face. Her breathing evened out as she smiled adoringly at the fur.

Sitting up, sweat coursed down her breasts and over the crusted scabs on her ribs and stomach. She bowed her head. "Of course I understand. You had to be sure I can perform the ritual properly. I understand now, you were only testing me. You've been so disappointed before, so hungry. She doesn't know how to feed you properly." She looked up in rapture, her eyes blazing. "Of course, I promise, I'll keep feeding you. I would never let you starve. Never." Linking her hands together, she rose to her knees. "Thank you for this. I promise." She went over to the cabinet and reset the needle on the record. With a blissful expression, she walked through the master bedroom into the bathroom.

The sound of a female voice and an acoustic guitar played over the noise of Jeniel's shower and continued through the drone of the hair dryer. During the last song on the album, Jeniel reentered the sitting room in designer jeans and a long-sleeved white blouse. She wore her combed hair in a bun and full makeup concealed the bruises under her eyes. Her nails were filed smooth and lacquered with clear polish.

In three-inch black heels, she picked her way carefully through the wreckage leading to the coat rack. A haughty, confident smile played over her lips as she lifted the mink off its padded hanger, slipped it on, and ran her hands over the plush white fur. Raising her chin, she took a pair of oversized designer sunglasses out of an inner pocket.

She locked the door behind her, slid on the sunglasses, and went down the hallway, smiling as the hem of the coat brushed against her calves. Laughing quietly in the elevator, she bit her rouged lower lip as the doors opened into the hotel lobby. She walked over to the reception desk and beckoned to one of the young men behind it.

She lowered her glasses and looked over the rims at him.

The receptionist smiled at her.

179

"How may I be of assistance?" His eyes lingered on her glossy lips.

She leaned forward and pitched her voice so only he could hear her. "I'm afraid one of my drunken artist friends made a bit of a mess in my suite. I'm going out for a while. Can you see to it that it's cleaned up before I get back? You can add the extra cleaning charge to the room bill."

"Of course, miss."

"Thank you." Pushing her glasses back up, she smiled at him, spun on her heel, and headed for the lobby doors.

Outside, she waved away the doorman's offer of a cab and strode down Pierce Street toward Pier Alley. A man in a winter overcoat in the doorway opposite the hotel folded his newspaper under his arm, watching Jeniel pass the line of taxis. He stepped out onto the sidewalk, shoving his gloved hands into his coat pockets. As he walked by a parked sedan, the black car's headlights turned on and the vehicle pulled away from the curb. It drove slowly down the street behind him.

As she walked, Jeniel whispered to herself and then laughed loudly. She reached Pier Alley and took neat, small steps, navigating the cobblestones. Unnoticed, the man entered the alleyway, trailing several feet behind her. Its headlights switching off, the sedan slipped into a loading zone and sat idling.

The bell of the East End Church began to toll. Jeniel stopped outside the brick archway of a wine emporium, frowning at the shuttered door. A blast of cold air whipped through Pier Alley and she folded the edges of her fur collar closed. The icy sea air churned, tumbling down the corridor and driving the few other pedestrians on the cobblestone walkway to seek shelter.

Jeniel headed toward the bronze statue of the fisherman at the entrance of the pier. As her heels struck the wooden boards, the man dropped his paper and sprinted up silently behind her. He swung his arm forward and clamped a damp rag over her mouth. Ignoring her hands clawing at him, he held her and waited. It only took a few seconds before Jeniel went limp. He picked her up and carried her to the waiting car.

ZADE BRAKED HARD, the back end of her bike skidding out as she stopped.

"90-32, your cam jumped. Status."

"Sorry, dispatch. On it to drop off the package." Zade shook her head and took the turn onto Manson.

"Status."

"I'm fine." The courier kept looking at her side mirror as she veered through dense traffic.

On High Street, a car swerved into her lane. She sounded her horn and gave the passenger-side door of the car a hearty kick as she sped by. Sweat beaded along her forehead and she cracked her helmet open.

Riding the elevator up to the drop-off point, Zade clenched her shaking hand into a fist and kept her eyes on the door. After she got the legal aide's thumbprint, she headed for the stairwell. Swinging down, Zade cleared several flights.

At the Pit, Zade tore her helmet and earpiece off, slamming them on the bars before running for the restroom. She avoided looking into the mirror as cold water from the faucet coursed over her wrists. She splashed her face, rested her chilled hand against the nape of her neck, and stared at her reflection. "You're okay."

She jumped when the door to the restroom suddenly swung in. Kitty entered and kicked open a stall door.

Zade returned to her motorcycle. She hefted her helmet and then set it back down. "Where's Otter?" She asked the assembled couriers.

"Not in today." Mat glared at her over his cup of coffee.

"Thanks." Zade picked her helmet up and put her earpiece and gloves back on. "90-32 at the Pit."

"Nothing in, 90-32."

"Shit." Zade rubbed her gloved hands down the sides of her thighs. "Nothing? Not even a milk run?"

"You'll be the first to know as soon as something hits the queue, 90-32."

The courier made a face and started up her motorcycle. "I'm changing over to Market."

"Sit tight, 90-32. The Pit's better for this time of day."

"I can't sit here." Zade's voice rose as she let out the clutch.

"Status."

"Nothing. I'm fine." She glanced at her right mirror, and then the left, and back again.

"90-32, pickup at 62 Manson Ave, Office 5, third floor. Going to 207 Victory Square."

"On it, dispatch."

At the pickup location, Zade banged her recorder on the desk. "Sorry, it does this sometimes." She whacked it again and held it out to the dour-faced young woman.

"I have to kick the copier once a week."

"Thanks." Zade bolted into the elevator. "On it to 207 Victory Square."

As the bike accelerated on the Straight, she slapped her faceplate closed and shifted to highway gear. The tachometer's needle hit the red as she leaned out over the tank. Tears started streaming down her face, unchecked. She closed her eyes for a moment, blindly riding the centerline.

A security guard held the door open as Zade thundered up the granite stairs.

"Excellent time." The receptionist nodded as he took the package from her.

"Thanks." Her voice was a mumble as she headed back through the lobby.

She parked next to the curb on Trellis and sat on her motorcycle, staring at the avenue. Abruptly, she flicked the kill switch into the run position and roared out of the parking space. At the intersection of Trellis and Parker, she snapped in the clutch and hit both brakes hard, swinging her boot to anchor the bike. "Dispatch, tell me you saw that."

"I didn't see anything in your feed, 90-32."

"You didn't see it? Were you *watching* my feed, Dis?" Zade walked her bike to the side of the road.

"Playback shows an empty crosswalk."

"No, it was right fucking there."

"Are you seeing things?"

Zade stared at the crosswalk. "I thought I saw Boon."

"Take the rest of the day off, 90-32. I'll call you later."

"I don't want …"

"I'll call you when I get done today. Go home."

"I'm fine."

"I'm not giving you any packages, Zade. Go home."

"I'm …"

"About to get fired, 90-32."

Zade got on the Riverway and rode over the bridge to the highway. Rain clouds and trees with closed buds framed the road as she exchanged the urban smells of exhaust and oil for the countryside's early preview of spring. At the tollbooth she threw change into the basket without fully stopping. She kept riding as a light warm rain began to draw mist from the asphalt. Taking the first exit, she parked her bike by the side of the road and clawed off her helmet.

"Fuck." She sat on her bike and watched the mist creep through the forest.

□♍♏♋■

When she made it back to her apartment, Zade headed into her bedroom and flung open the closet door. She dragged out an old set of boots, a hooded gray sweatshirt, and a worn pair of cargo pants. After she changed into the clothes and boots, she squatted, dropping her hips all the way to the floor. She bounced there while keeping her heels down as she adjusted the boot's laces.

Leaving her motorcycle gear on the floor by the apartment entrance, she checked her pockets, snapping all the buttons closed. She tucked her house key under the strap of her motorcycle's saddle and walked down the street.

A block away from the Central Parking Garage, she slipped her hood up and hunched her shoulders. When the building came into view, she stamped each of her boots and surreptitiously eyed the few other pedestrians in the vicinity. After a moment, she broke into an easy jog and hip-checked the ground-floor stairwell door open.

Zade's hands flew up the yellow rails as she clambered into the gap in the center of the stairwell. The toes of her boots barely made contact with the railing as she hauled herself to the next level. She climbed the ten levels of the parking garage and swung up and over the uppermost railing, landing in a crouch.

She jogged across the roof lot, leapt onto the trunk of a parked sedan, and began running over the row of cars. Her loud footfalls rocked the cars as she broke into a sprint. Her boots touched the surface of the half-wall as she pushed off and vaulted over the side of the garage.

Her momentum carried her across the gap between the buildings. She landed just beyond the other building's edge, then tumbled through a puddle on the tarred roof. Distributing the impact from shoulder to opposite hip, she came up lightly and continued running. Reaching the edge, she dropped off the side of the building, grabbed a water spout, and swung her legs, pushing out over the next expanse and landing on a fire escape. Hand over hand, she climbed down the metal bars. Halfway down, the ladder stopped. Zade looked up at the pigeons flying overhead and let go.

෨෴ⒸⒼⒾⓞ෴෴

Dis switched from watching the scrolling text on one screen to the grid of cam feeds on the other. One of the pillar candles on top of the monitor sizzled as the wick burned low. He used a spent wooden match to lift the flame from it to a replacement, then set the carbon-coated glass on the floor. Dis hit the speaker button when the phone rang. "Uptown Deliveries, hold please."

The fingers of his right hand typed on the number pad of the keyboard as he spoke into his headset. "70-22, keep cooling your heels in Market." He hit the speaker button again. "Thank you for holding. May I have your account number?" Dis turned the chair to watch the monitor displays.

"I am Oliver Nash, personal assistant to Chairwoman Pierce of Pierce Shipping Exports. Our company does not currently have an account with Uptown Deliveries. However, we would like to create one immediately."

"I will have a courier bring over the paperwork for you now, Mr. Nash."

"Chairwoman Pierce would like to meet with you directly, Mr. Mthdys. I am speaking with Mr. Mthdys, yes?"

The chair creaked as Dis turned to look at the phone's speaker. "Yes."

The office door rattled open and Frankie walked in with more pillar candles. She mouthed an apology and carried them over to the table against the far wall.

"Due to a cancellation, the Chairwoman happens to have an available appointment slot in an hour. Please bring the required paperwork with you to our offices at 207 Victory Square."

Frankie poured a drop of oil from a cut glass bottle into one of the candles and placed it into an empty slot on a shelf on the wall.

"If you insist." Dis leaned back, watching Frankie.

The sharp tang of rosemary and pine filled the office as Frankie lit the candle. She opened the nearby cabinet and set the bottle within.

"Excellent. I look forward to meeting you this evening. Goodbye." Nash severed the connection.

Dis listened to the line click for a few seconds before hitting the release. He opened the file cabinet next to the desk and took out a slim folder.

"New account?" Frankie brought two candles over to the desk, swapping them with older ones.

"Possibly." Dis stood up. "11-20 and 31-06 are the only ones in transit. 70-22 is in Market in case there's a last-minute order out of City Hall." He nodded at the rack of candles. "Thanks for picking these up. You've modified the recipe."

"Yeah, I hope you don't mind. The owner of the Shining Star suggested adding vetiver."

"Quail's good with herb lore. You should take one of his classes if you can." Dis grabbed his coat and cane.

"I'm having a hard enough time remembering all the things you've been teaching me."

"Have a good night. I'll see you in the morning." He smiled at her and opened the booth door.

"Bye." Frankie turned her attention to the monitors.

At the bottom of the stairs, Dis stopped to flip a coin. After tossing it a second and third time, he put the coin in his pocket and started walking to the subway. At Claremont Station, there was a line of grumbling commuters.

An Underground employee waved people away from the locked turnstiles. "Sorry, the inbound line's shut down. There's a shuttle bus coming in ten minutes."

"I heard it was a jumper." The man next to Dis frowned.

"Jumpers go in the morning or the last run. The one in the paper last week was a murder-suicide." A woman hugged a small dog to her bosom.

"It's just a downed cable, ladies and gentlemen. Nothing serious. Scheduled service will resume as soon as the crews have it secured. Until then, there's a shuttle. Here it is now." The station employee waved as the vehicle pulled up to the curb.

"That's what they say when one of the bums living down there gets crushed to death on the tracks." The woman with the dog squeezed him tightly and looked at Dis as they sat down. "Terrible way to die, like getting hit by a car. That's why I don't let Cazzie off the leash when we go outside." She stroked the elderly terrier. "All that steel rips right through you. Terrible way to die."

"There are worse." His thumb hooked the strap on the outside of his brace.

"True. I was having lunch with my lawyer last summer. We were arguing over the trust I wanted to set up for Cazzie, at one of those cute outdoor cafes, when a boy hit the ground next to us. It was terrible. Blood everywhere, people screaming. I thought it was the end of the world. A tooth landed in my salad! I was lucky it wasn't his whole head. S&P said he was racing around on the rooftops. Can you believe that? Terrible."

When he got on the train at the next station, Dis quoted the woman in his journal. More passengers crammed in at each stop and he gave up his seat to a weary woman in a leg cast. She smiled in relief, trying to keep her crutches out from under the feet of the other passengers.

$$\triangledown \nearrow \blacktriangle$$

At Victory Station, Dis loaded his jacket pockets with candy from a vending machine and went to a payphone, cradling the receiver against his shoulder. "Hi, Zade. My friend Bone and I are having dinner at the Melborn if you would like to join us at eight. Good. See you then." He hung up and took the square side exit out. Office workers were flooding into the station on the descending side of the ramp as he emerged onto the street. He lobbed a candy bar into the underbrush where the children had tried to knock him over a few days before.

A soda can made a tinny noise as it bumped along the steps of the Victory Monument. Dis looked up at the base of the marble seat and prodded the can with the toe of his boot before going up the monument's steps. He ran his fingertips through the empty groove behind the seat. Dusting his hands on his trousers, he walked back down and sat down on the steps, pinning the soda can under his heel.

He tossed a coin. He let it hit the marble step and tumble to stillness before he picked it up. Holding it between his thumb and forefinger, Dis raised the coin in front of him, obscuring the front of the Pierce Tower from his view. He shifted it from his right eye to his left and set it back in his pocket. He deposited a candy bar on the step and slowly made his way over to the building.

$\triangledown \nearrow \blacktriangle$

"Mr. Mthdys, I'm Mr. Nash." The chairwoman's assistant held out his hand to Dis as he entered the lobby.

"Mr. Nash." Dis clasped his hand as Nash directed him toward an elevator.

"The Chairwoman is very pleased that you were able to accommodate her schedule. I'll be happy to fill out the paperwork while she goes over the account details with you." Nash deftly selected one key among the many on his keyring, inserted it into the elevator's control panel, and pressed the button for the top floor.

Dis pulled the folder of paperwork out of his bag and handed it to Nash.

"I half-expect you to ask for my thumbprint." Nash smiled as the elevator hummed upwards.

"You have an existing account with the other courier company in town."

"The Chairwoman wishes us to move the account to your company."

The arrival chime sounded and Nash gestured for Dis to proceed into the atrium on the top floor. Afternoon sunlight poured through the wall of windows overlooking the square and onto the tall glass cases of artifacts filling the space.

"This way, please." Nash led Dis past a case of nautical log books opened to display their venerable notations. He guided Dis toward a corridor situated alongside the atrium's internal wall. "The Pierce Museum is one of the best in the world for preserving the ethnographic and zoological heritage of the Ornish Archipelago. We have three curators engaged in research and preservation and each is the leading expert in their respective fields. Besides the Chairwoman's office, the rest of this floor contains our expansive research laboratory. The majority of the collection is housed in temperature-controlled vaults in the basement levels."

"Strange, I've never heard of it."

"It's the family's private collection. Open by invitation only, I'm afraid." Nash knocked on a double door.

"Enter."

"Chairwoman, Mr. Mthdys is here as you requested."

"Do come in, Mr. Mthdys. I am Mercy Pierce." The chairwoman cast an appraising look over her guest. "Shall I have Nash bring us tea, or do you prefer coffee?" Pierce came around her large mahogany desk and extended her hand.

"Tea will be fine." Dis averted his eyes, looking instead at a brass astrolabe mounted to the wall below a shelf of antique ledgers.

Retracting her hand with a frown, Pierce indicated the upholstered leather chair facing her desk. When Dis was seated, she sat on the corner of her desk.

"Thank you, Nash." Pierce kept her gaze focused on Dis as her assistant wheeled a tea service over. He poured dark tea into ornate blue and white porcelain cups and handed them to Dis and his employer.

Dis sat back, cradling his cup. Nash withdrew from the office, shutting the double doors.

The chairwoman considered her guest. "I was given a sample of your work on the Ornish legends. I found the analysis of archetypal motifs quite intriguing, though I disagree with your assessment of the underlying polytheistic religion."

"This is not about changing accounts, then."

"Oh, Nash will transfer everything to your company, Mr. Mthdys. His research indicates your company has noticeably improved performance over your rival's."

"Usually when someone wishes to speak to me about the clans' history it is in reference to my father's work." Dis set his cup and saucer on the arm of the chair.

"I read your father's books to my daughter when she was young." Pierce indicated one of the framed pictures on her desk and watched her guest closely. "Brilliant retelling of the myths, certainly, but written for children. I'm interested in specialized expertise of a more adult nature."

"Nash mentioned your private museum employs several experts."

"Indeed, I have Dr. Argu, Dr. Miller, and Dr. Fasu."

"I am unclear as to what I could add to such a distinguished list."

Pierce straightened, placed her untouched tea on the desk, and walked to the window to gaze down on the square. "My family's collection is greater than the few items you saw on the way to my office, Mr. Mthdys." She turned and watched his face carefully. "The Pierce family has been accumulating artifacts since Captain Pierce's original contact with the Ornish clans 300 years ago. Very rare and precious relics, including animal skins of immense size and unparalleled beauty. They have been preserved with the utmost care, I assure you."

"I have no expertise in, or use for, taxidermy, antique or modern." Dis rested his head on his curled fist.

"Your father would have had great interest in these particular skins. His work referenced the use of them for certain magical undertakings. Seal skins such as these were believed to allow those possessing them to change into seals themselves."

"As my father is dead, he is beyond interest in ancient beliefs … or wanting anything at all, for that matter."

"Another point on which we disagree, Mr. Mthdys." Pierce lightly touched the window, returning her attention to the square. "My brother, Honesty, was murdered in front of the Victory Monument twenty-one years ago, and I am very aware of what *he* wants."

"Unless it requires delivery to an address in the city, I am unclear as to how I may be of service to you."

Pierce's expression grew fierce as she stepped away from the window. "It seems the advice I was given to be direct with you was correct. Very well. I know the method by which your couriers are being killed and I wish to have your assistance in discovering why and by whom."

"They died in accidents. S&P has verified none of the parties involved were acting maliciously."

She gave him a haughty look and then smiled condescendingly. "True, but just as the cutting of a brake line can be fatal to a driver, so is siphoning off their luck."

"You have asked me here to discuss superstitions."

"I have asked you here to discuss methods of harvesting life force. Do you know how it is done?" Pierce resumed her position on the corner of the desk.

"I have never had any reason to study the topic."

"Yet you have been working diligently these last few months to counteract those very methods, haven't you? Come now, it is not the time to be coy about your use of magic. As I said earlier, I am familiar with your research."

"Then you are familiar with my techniques."

"No sorcerer worth their salt publishes their core practices, Mr. Mthdys. Only enough to impress their peers with the effort involved, or titillate acolytes with the risks."

"Nor would she gossip them away over tea with a stranger."

Pierce gave him a small, sharp smile. "Your point is well taken. I will offer this in trade, then. I will explain to you the mechanics of how it is being done in exchange for your information regarding the mechanics of thwarting it."

"It may not be happening at all. Therefore I may not be responsible for thwarting it."

"While the quality of writing in our newspapers may not be of the caliber of those from the Continent, the obituaries are concisely correct. Following weeks of an unprecedented spike in courier fatalities, not one motorcyclist from either company has died in the last two months. Not even the usual drunken after-hour collisions."

His gaze wandered over to a vase of lilies. The large white blossoms filled the space with a funerary scent. "Our employees are more cautious in the winter."

"There has been, however, an increase in deaths among the homeless, as well as employees of a certain diversified multinational family-owned corporation."

Dis stared at Pierce.

"My family built this city. It belongs to us. Now someone wishes to destroy it by destroying my company. Literally, killing it. They are after my family, Mr. Mthdys." She struck out as if to ward off a blow. "You of all people know the pain of losing a loved one."

"I also know, Chairwoman Pierce, the pain of losing an entire people."

Pierce inhaled slowly. "Will you agree to the information exchange?"

Dis sampled his cooled tea and looked at the family pictures on Pierce's desk. He froze, then looked down at his porcelain cup. The muscles of his jaw twitched.

Pierce's eyes flickered over her guest. "The technique is called the Black Cake. At the time the spell is activated, the person in possession of it dies, usually from natural or accidental causes."

Dis leaned forward, inspecting one of the photographs. "Terribly inconvenient if the sorcerer is still in possession of it when it is activated."

The woman raised her chin and looked down her nose at him. "The technique for triggering it and redirecting the life force is highly complex, so much so that it would never be subject to such an accidental miscalculation."

"If it worked, and wasn't merely coincidence, what you are describing would be murder."

"It is a random lottery, I assure you."

Dis stood up, setting his cup on the table between the chairs. "Non-voluntary death, caused intentionally, is a legal definition of murder."

"Share with me how you have prevented the Black Cake from killing your employees."

"I have given you my attention in return for your hospitality. That is the only exchange we will have this evening, Chairwoman." Dis walked toward the door. "We all die, Pierce. Even if not all of us are unlucky enough to end up well-preserved in museum collections."

"My enemy is your enemy, Mr. Mthdys. They will break through your barriers eventually and you will return, begging for my help. You may not have family left, but you have much to lose."

Dis reached for the doorknob. "Not if your enemies are successful in finishing their campaign against you."

"Is that a threat? Are you already allied against me?"

"My only ally is a cat, and I'm told it is our destiny to fight crime." Dis walked out the door, bumping into Nash, who was hovering in the corridor.

Pierce scowled. "See to it that Mr. Mthdys finds his way out."

Nash glanced at Dis nervously and gestured toward the atrium.

As they walked down the corridor, Dis paused. "The Chairwoman was saying she read my father's books to her daughter when she was young."

"Oh yes, Miss Generosity is a fan. Your father's work is a family favorite." Nash waved Dis toward the elevator.

Dis bent forward to examine an ivory comb in the closest display. "If she lives in town, I could drop off a signed edition. As a favor to the Chairwoman."

"She's studying in Newton, on the Continent, but I would be delighted to pass it on." Nash anxiously ushered the other man into the elevator.

"I will address the dedication to Miss Generosity Pierce."

"She prefers Gen." The assistant relaxed visibly as they entered the elevator.

After a few minutes of silence, Dis looked at Nash's reflection in the mirrored surface of the elevator car. "I will bring it by next week."

"Thank you, Mr. Mthdys."

Dis left the building while Nash returned to the upper floor. Dis cleared his throat and spat a glob of mucous onto the glass exterior of the lobby. Watching from the inside, the security guard took a step back. Dis rolled his left hand away from his body as he went down the stairs and walked away.

ZADE NERVOUSLY LOOKED UP at the sign outside the Melborn, then at the laurel topiaries on either side of the establishment's polished oak entrance. The warm glow of candlelight emanated as the door opened, and a rich scent of roasted meat and butter rushed out. She stepped aside, letting a departing couple pass. She glanced at their formal attire, then frowned at her own riding gear and boots.

She hefted her helmet in one hand, pulled open the door, and walked into the landmark restaurant. The host looked up from the podium and gave her a genuinely welcoming smile. "Good evening, miss. Do you have a reservation with us tonight?"

She winced apologetically and shifted her helmet from one hand to the other. "Um, I think it's under Bonnrey?"

"Ah. Right this way, please. Mr. Bonnrey has already arrived." The host picked up a menu, inclined his head, and led her through a candlelit dining room adorned with oil paintings. Reaching a stone archway, the man indicated the linen-covered table within.

"At last, some company." Bone rose and greeted Zade with a crushing hug.

"Is it okay that I'm here?" The courier glanced around the snug.

"You are always welcome at my table, Zee." Bone waved her into the chair the host was patiently holding out for her. Pushing her gently toward the table, he addressed Zade with another smile. "Would you care for a cocktail?"

She looked at Bone. He indicated the wine in front of him. "Share the joys of civilization with me, Zee."

A waiter appeared, with Dis in tow. "Sorry I'm late." He looked between the two of them. "You've already given her a nickname? A double Newton sixteen year, neat, please."

Zade watched Bone pour the wine and avoided looking at Dis.

Dis drummed his fingers on the table, stopping when his lover touched the back of his hand. "Sorry."

Bone lifted an eyebrow. "I count not one, but two apologies in mere minutes, and have taken note of your impatience for anesthetic. What's happened, love?"

"Mercy Pierce tried to bribe me with a seal skin." Dis glowered at the arrangement of lilies on their table.

Zade looked at him. "Is that code?"

"Unfortunately, no."

Bone put his hand back on Dis's. "You didn't accept it?"

Dis looked up as a waiter returned with his whiskey. "Thanks." He drained the tumbler and set it roughly on the table. "You know I wouldn't accept anything from a fucking Pierce. They're all treacherous maniacs."

As Dis's expression hardened, Bone's tone turned playful. "Then you'll be needing us to help dispose of the body after dessert, love?"

Shaking his head, Dis looked at Zade across the table. "I want to know how you are."

"I'm fine. I haven't been sleeping well."

Bone gave her a questioning look.

"Nightmares." She shrugged.

"You might have been hallucinating from sleep deprivation earlier." Dis put his arm over the back of his chair.

"Maybe." Zade shrugged. "I don't know. I thought I saw people I knew and then they weren't there."

"You said you saw Boon."

Draining her glass, Zade set it back down and stared at a tiny wine stain on the white tablecloth. "It might have been a person who looked like her."

"Boon is one of the couriers who died recently?" Bone set his menu on top of Dis's.

"She worked for Lew's … her band was just about to go on tour." Zade looked over at the speckled, red-throated flowers. "She was my best friend."

Bone poured more wine into her glass. "Does your nightmare change?"

"Parts are always the same."

Dis leaned forward, his eyes focused intently on her.

Zade swallowed. "There's something chasing me and I can't see it. I'll see someone I know, like Boon, walk into the U Station and I try to catch up. But they aren't on the platform, only a bagger on the far end."

"Bagger?" Bone raised an eyebrow.

"Homeless guy with his gear."

"Then what happens?"

"He starts getting nearer. He's on the end of the platform by the wall and then suddenly he's right next to me. I realize he isn't a bagger at all. He's wearing a yellow and blue leather and is carrying a messenger bag."

"They will keep strafing us unless we give them something to do." Bone indicated the waiter returning to the table. "Do you know what you want to order?"

"Would you care to hear the specials for this evening?" The waiter smiled at Zade and her friends.

"Skip anything with seafood in it." Bone tipped his hand in Dis's direction.

"Then I would suggest the locally-raised seared rack of lamb, which is finished in a sweet plum reduction. It is served on an eggplant ragout and accompanied by a thrice-baked potato."

"Thrice? Once should have sufficed, friend. I will attempt to appreciate your chef's enthusiasm and try it." Bone handed over his menu. "We'll start with your cheese selection."

"I will have the same. Another whiskey as well, please." Dis held out his empty tumbler.

"Might as well make it thrice." Zade handed her menu over to the waiter.

Her response won a grin from Bone. "Do you recognize him, the courier in your dream?"

"No, he has this weird hood thing on, so I can't see his face. When I first see him, he's up to his knees in trash. That's why I thought he was a bagger. When he gets closer, I realize it's moving." Zade made a face and reached for her wine glass.

"The garbage is moving?" Bone raised his eyebrow.

"I think it's garbage until he's right next to me. I can see the maggots."

"That sounds like garbage."

"It's not, though. It's dead animals … all roadkill. All these gory parts writhing around his feet and legs. At first, I think they are eating him, but they're not."

"What are they doing, then?"

"They're petting him. Reaching out with broken paws and wings, trying to climb up him and falling back down, crawling over each other to get to him."

"That's pitiful, in a gross sort of way."

"The bones are showing through the backs of his hands. He's all safety-pinned and stitched together. Patchwork." She toyed with her glass. "I can hear the train coming and I keep praying to the Holy Mother it will arrive before he's able to touch me."

Dis rolled his right hand toward himself. "You sound like you know what will happen if he touches you."

Zade locked eyes with him. "I'll end up in the roadkill pile with the squirrels, rats, and pigeons."

"Adoring him."

"Maybe, but I'll still be roadkill." She sat back as the waiter returned with the appetizer and Dis's whiskey.

"Sounds like a classic subconscious representation of motorcycle courier anxieties to me, Zee. Ending up squashed or stuck waiting with a pestiferous fellow courier who is subjecting you to unwanted advances." Bone used his fork to spear a grape on the cheese plate and offered it to her.

Zade snorted, accepting the fruit.

"Did he say anything to you? Was there anything else odd?" Dis warded off Bone's offer of impaled cheese and fruit.

"Mm. There was a sharp smell. I could see the maggots in the pile when he was right next to me, but it smelled like Rest&Be when they cut the grass."

Dis looked thoughtful. "Visions of Amrwyn often contain the scents of growing things and cemeteries."

"Visions of who?" Zade scrunched her face. "This non-moldy one is great." She directed Bone's attention to a chunk of orange and white cheese.

"That's the Delmont."

Dis's mouth curled as he watched her and Bone. "The Earth-Father. One of the first three ancestors of all living things."

"This guy was not living, Dis. He was skin and bones and ..."

"Powers often appear layered in dreams. Mysteries dressed in symbols we can recognize."

"It's probably like Bone said, an anxiety dream."

Bone lowered his wine glass and looked between the two friends. "You mentioned seeing things when you were awake. Did you see him?"

"Who?"

"Your king of roadkill." Bone mashed a chunk of blue and white cheese onto a piece of bread.

Zade speared a grape and traded him for the mini sandwich. "No, just regular people."

"People who are dead." Dis lifted his whiskey.

"I didn't recognize all of them, so ..."

"Amrwyn is also the God of the Dead. If he has taken an interest in you, that might account for seeing apparitions. It could be he's given you his blessing, chosen you as his own."

"Mother." Bone stabbed at the back of Dis's hand with the tines of his fork. "She could have a complication from hitting her head in the accident you told me about. Don't foist your personal psychological poetry onto other people."

"In this city, it's a valid option." Dis removed his hand from the table. "This is their city, and they speak through dreams."

"To you, maybe. Try and remember what you think is right is not the same for others. Mercy Pierce surely thinks she was being magnanimous by offering you her gruesome token."

Dis frowned and stared into his drink, then tilted the honey-colored liquor down his throat.

Zade turned to Dis. "Why was she trying to bribe you?"

"She claimed an enemy was killing her employees to harvest their luck and wants my help."

"Is that even possible?"

"Depends on your point of view." He averted his eyes from Bone.

"I see I am in disfavor, Zee. He gets very disagreeable, as he dislikes it if one disparages the wisdom he seeks to dispense."

Zade grinned. "Perhaps you have a way of distracting him from his distress at your disposal?"

"In his current state of distemper, it will only make him more distraught if I sought to change the topic of discussion." He grinned back at her. "Back in the day, he would spend days being dysfunctional like this."

Dis groaned. "Enough. I'm not even drunk yet."

Bone held the palm of his hand across the table and Zade slapped it.

"Did you know, Zee, in other cities couriers use bicycles as well as motorcycles?" Bone tumbled the last nugget of cheese across the plate. "Have the last bit of Delmont."

She wedged the cheese into her mouth. "Bicycles?"

"Hundreds of bicycles, even thousands in some big cities."

"Maybe they can't handle the rain."

"I've seen bicycle couriers hauling ass through a downpour in Newton, the original city this one is named after. You should come travel with me, Zee. I'll take you on tour. Bikes, bands, and brethren in a whole new land. Cities that are ancient. Some are even thousands of years old, not just a paltry 200 like this one. The Imperial Temple in Grava is 3,000 years old."

"Grava, that's where you said your favorite liquor comes from?"

"Yes." Bone glanced at Dis with a speculative look. Dis kept his attention on his own glass, seemingly oblivious to their exchange.

"I've never been out of the city except on delivery to the Hinterlands. My friend Vicky has invited me to go with her and her brother Avery to the Continent this summer." Zade picked at the tablecloth where it draped over her leg. "She's having her birthday party next Saturday, and she said to invite you, Dis."

"Next Saturday is the Equinox." Dis shook his head. "I'm already booked after Mother Ida's spring blessing of the bikes."

"Oh." Zade teased a thread loose with her thumbnail. She looked up as two waiters approached their table.

Bone sat back, holding his wineglass, as their dinner was served. "It appears the slaughtered innocents we ordered have arrived."

▽ ↗ ◢

Pockets of blue peppered the cloud cover over the spires of St. Anna's, allowing only a few sunbeams to stray into the yew trees in the front garden. A passing produce truck backfired, sending a wave of pigeons up into the air. Mother Ida blessed the last motorcycle in the line parked along the curb as Iris spotted Bone leaning against the cathedral's wrought iron fence. She marched through the spectators crowding the sidewalk. The white silk flowers on her hat bobbed as she poked her finger into him.

"You should be ashamed of yourself."

"Oh, I am, for many reasons, dear. Yet I'm not exactly clear what exact mortal sin you are chastising me for." Bone retreated further down the ironwork to evade the woman's anger.

Iris drew herself up and grabbed his earlobe. "Five years. Not one visit, not one phone call, not one card, and then you send an errand boy in a limo." She tightened her grip and Bone hissed in pain.

"Ah, ow, I understand. You are upset I didn't come myself. Ow, let go, harridan." He pulled himself from her grip. "I thought it best not to bother him at work. And you might not have let me in."

"I wouldn't have, but you would have figured out some way, and then you would have seen him yourself rather than me having to …"

"Having to do what, Iris?" Dis materialized out of the dispersing crowd.

Iris blinked as motorcycle engines began to start. "Yell at him right now." She turned back to Bone and shook her finger under his nose. "You be good to him, do you hear me?" She purposefully strode away, not meeting Dis's eyes.

He looked at Bone. "I have to find Otter. I'll be back in a few minutes."

"Take your time, love. I'm apparently the on-duty whipping boy."

The sides of Dis's mouth curled up as he went back along the fence to the churchyard. Entering under the canopy of ivy, Dis headed to the rack of devotional candles. Otter glanced up as Dis dropped a coin into the offering box and lit a candle.

"I remember watching my mom do this when I was too short to do it myself."

Otter adjusted one of the candles in the offering rack. "She used to hold one out for me to pray over, then she would set it up on the very top row for me. I was too heavy for her to lift. Before she died, I was doing the same for her."

"My mother did the altar arrangements here. I remember when I was a kid, she always smelled of flowers and incense when I came home from school. I could tell the last Mass she had attended that day, depending on if she smelled more of cedar or juniper." Dis turned to look at the baskets of spring blossoms on the high altar.

Otter extended his hand to him. "I feel a bit weird bringing this to you here."

"Safest place in town." Dis opened his palm. The courier placed his carved gray stone into it. Dis raised his glasses and examined the worn item.

"I've never told anyone about it." Otter peered at the object. "Have you seen one before?"

Dis lowered his glasses and rolled it between his fingers. The finger-length stone was carved into the shape of a boat, with a pear-shaped nub in the center. "Yes."

Otter smiled guiltily. "It was one of those school trips out to the outer islands when I was in middle school. Whale watching and crap like that. I was bored and wandered away like they tell you not to do. I guess the teachers figured it's an island, not like there's any place to get lost, right?"

"You managed to."

"Yeah. Don't understand how, really. Not that big of a place, but I couldn't find my way back. Then it got dark, and then it started raining. Big storm came in. I was a total crybaby back then." Otter's expression shifted into a full grin. "I remember being hungry and tired and crying for my mom."

"You could have died from exposure or been washed away."

Otter grimaced. "That's what my mom said when I got home. I told her I found an old boat to sleep under."

"You were lucky to find one."

"There was no boat." The courier glanced up at the top row of candles. "I

203

lied because I thought no one would believe me."

"Go on."

Otter hesitated, then nodded. "I looked for hours, but I couldn't find anyone or even the stupid boat dock. I was cold and wet and scared. I huddled up against a big granite boulder, trying to get out of the wind. I cried for my mom. I must have fallen asleep at some point. When I woke up, the side of my body against the boulder was warm. It was pitch black by then, but the boulder felt like it was breathing. Expanding and contracting next to me, and warm. I touched it and it was furry, like a big dog."

Dis rolled his right hand toward himself.

"I thought I was dreaming. I was warm on all sides and the wind wasn't howling anymore. Just the sound of big things moving around me, over the rocks nearby. I wasn't afraid, either, just tired from the warmth. When I woke up in the morning, I was alone between three boulders, but I had that in my hands." He indicated the tool Dis held. "I woke up knowing how to use it, but nothing else, not even what it's called."

Dis smiled. "It's called a tyn. It's a tool to divine your luck for the day."

Otter looked relieved. "I've used it every morning. Never missed one." His eyes flickered over Dis's cupped hand.

"Nor should you." Dis handed back the stone.

Otter paused with his hand half-extended. "I thought you wanted to borrow it?"

Dis set the stone into Otter's palm. "When you call out of work, I'll know what I need to know. Or I will ask you to spin it for me."

"It seems like it should be in a museum." Otter ran his thumb over the convex side of the stone.

"It was given to you so you might know when to take your boat out or to stay at home."

"You've used something like this before?"

"I've never seen one given directly by the children of Mammor. It's a priceless gift."

"I wasn't dreaming, then?" Otter held the other man's gaze. "They were really there?"

Dis gazed up at the buttresses above their heads. "Dreams are often more real than our waking lives." He glanced up at the sunlight sloping through the stained glass. "We should get going."

"You going to make it tonight? By seven?" Otter slipped the carving into his jacket's inner pocket. "Bone's coming too?"

"Yes. We'll be there by seven."

"Okay, cool. I have to run." Otter slapped Dis on the shoulder. "Hey, thanks for the florist recommendation, by the way. Vicky was blown away by the birthday arrangement I sent her. Wish me luck tonight." Backing away, Otter flashed him an enormous grin.

Dis stared up at the stained-glass windows as the last tendrils of incense drifted through jewel-colored sunbeams.

▽ ↗ ◢

"I know you're trying to be romantic, but I'm pretty sure having it delivered would have been fine." Zade made a face at Otter through swaying pink cherry blossoms.

The two couriers stood in the middle of a subway car with a sapling cherry tree jostling between them. Each held the ends of two straps wrapped around its potted base. Tiny pink petals floated to the floor as the train rocked, adding to the amusement of the other Saturday night passengers.

Otter shrugged and readjusted the ends of his straps. "They didn't have a night delivery option and I want to give it to her at the party."

"You're trying to impress her friends."

"I'm trying to impress *her*. I appreciate you helping me get it there. Sorry about making you late."

"I'm happy to help you out." Zade puffed as one of the petals settled on her face. "Nice to see you excited about a girl."

"Are *you* interested in anyone?" Otter cocked his head.

Zade shrugged and widened her stance in the aisle. "Not really. Can't we set this thing down?"

"Not on this nasty train. Whatever is on the floor might get up through the holes in the bottom of the pot and poison it."

She shifted her grip. "I wish Boon was here."

"Floating's playing at Maddy's next Tuesday." Otter sighed. "It will be their first time out without her. Ju's still having a hard time with her being … gone."

"I'll go with you …" Zade trailed off and looked over Otter's shoulder.

"He'd be into that. Might help him."

Zade's expression froze.

"What?" Otter craned his neck around. "Something up?" He looked back at Zade.

Sweat was standing out on her forehead and she was breathing heavily.

"You okay?"

"I'll be fine." She closed her eyes and swallowed. "We're almost there."

"You need to sit down?" Otter tapped his friend's boot with his.

The train began to slow as it entered Mercy Station. The other passengers stood up around them.

"I just need a drink after we deliver this to your girl."

"Not my girl yet, but this might help my chances." Otter angled the top of the tree out of the train as Zade waddled behind him.

"Here, swap the sides so you can face forward." She directed.

"You all set?" Otter turned his back, switching the straps, and started across the station.

"Yeah." Zade's eyes went round as they shuffled through the evening crowds swarming the platform.

As they started up the escalator, she bit her lip and stared back at the platform.

"Everything okay back there?" Otter peered at her over his shoulder. "You're yanking on the straps."

"Everything's fine. Sorry."

A bagger with her hair matted into a single clump thrust an upturned hand under Zade's nose. "You have eleven cents?"

"No, sorry." Zade made an apologetic face. "Next time I come, though."

"Liar. Liar." She ceased abruptly and started walking backward down the rising escalator, still glaring at Zade. "Liar!"

"Fuck off already!" Turning to look at Zade, Otter shook his head. "Mother. Is it a full moon or what?"

They exited the station and carried the tree two blocks to Vicky and Avery's brownstone.

"Okay, let's set it down here. Can you go get Vicky?" Otter indicated the front door. Muted laughter and music were audible in the house. Zade knocked. "They won't hear that. Use the bell."

Zade rang the bell and waited.

"Is it even locked?"

Zade opened the door and stepped into the suddenly quiet brownstone. "No. I'll go get her. Be right back." She walked down the hallway and into the darkened living room. "Hello?"

"Surprise!" The lights flipped on, revealing a room crammed full of people. "Happy birthday!" Confetti sparkled in the air as Zade stood in a daze, staring at her friends.

"Happy birthday!" Vicky laughed and squeezed Zade's arm.

Avery went out and helped Otter bring in the tree as the assembled guests swarmed to greet Zade.

"You shouldn't have." Zade ducked her head as Patty planted a kiss on her cheek.

"We should have done this for you before. Consider it a late payment with interest." The dispatcher hugged her.

"Come open presents!" Kitty and Clink dragged Zade into the living room.

"Can I have a drink first?"

Bone rescued her from the other couriers. "Of course you can, Zee." He delivered her to the side of the bar. "What will it be, birthday girl?"

"Whiskey, please."

Dis went into the dining room across the hall, where Avery and Otter were setting the cherry tree. "Your sister is a very thoughtful woman."

"Which one?" Otter grinned.

Avery frowned. "She thought Zade deserved to have a surprise party." He dropped his straps abruptly.

"Your sister hopes Zade is related to you." Dis touched one of the tree's tiny green leaves.

"I hope she isn't." Avery stiffened. "She deserves a better family than this."

Dis glanced over at him. "She deserves to be a part of a family, no matter what problems it has."

Avery's frown deepened as he turned away. "She doesn't need one that's cursed." Avery fled the room with his head down.

Surprised, Otter glanced from the dining room door back to Dis. "He did just say '*cursed*,' didn't he?"

"He did." Dis bent, picked up the end of the strap, and began to wind it up.

"Figures, I finally meet a girl I think I could settle down with, who seems to like me ..." Otter sighed, grabbing the end of his strap.

"What Avery said doesn't make it true. It only means he thinks it is." Dis handed Otter the finished bundle. "Curses are fairly rare and tend to weaken with time."

"Thanks." Otter slapped Dis on the shoulder. "I need a drink, you?"

Dis nodded. "Just one. I have to go after I give our birthday girl her present."

"I should check in with Vicky and see if she needs me to do anything before I start drinking. Is this what being in a relationship feels like?"

"Could be." Dis clapped him on the shoulder.

Neither man noticed the draft of air lifting the fallen petals from the carpet. The miniature whirlwind dogged their steps and then dissolved, leaving a spiral of petals on the floor of the hallway. The blossoms were scattered a moment later when the front door opened.

Finding Bone on the couch by the fireplace, surrounded by a group of Vicky's friends, Dis laid a hand on his lover's arm. "Where's Zade?" he asked.

"She went upstairs with Vicky. Something about a birthday present." Bone smiled up at him. "Everything okay, love?"

Glancing up the stairs, Dis shook his head. "I was thinking we could give her the card and then go."

"Oh no you don't." Patty tugged Dis down onto the couch. "I know you. If we don't chain you down, you'll be sneaking out the door. Here, Bone, you give him your drink and have one of these girls get you a fresh one."

Bone put his arm around his lover's shoulders and handed him his whiskey. "Might as well make the best of it."

A door slammed on the second floor. Dis looked over to the living room entrance as someone ran through the hall. He started to rise from the couch. "Zade?"

She stopped, grabbed at the doorframe, and stared at him with wild eyes. "Don't …" She turned away from him and flew out of the house.

Dis crossed the living room, heading toward the open front door. Pink petals which had drifted over the hallway floor floated down the front steps as he scanned the street. He walked back up the steps, shaking his head. "She's gone."

Vicky leaned against Otter in the doorway. "I don't understand what happened. She was so happy and then she just …"

"Let's go back inside." Otter ran his hands over the woman's bare arms. "She'll be back."

The guests in the living room were talking in low voices. Dis shook his head at Bone as he followed Vicky and Otter up the stairs and into the upstairs parlor.

In the sitting room, Dis waited until Vicky indicated a chair on the other side of a coffee table. "You were giving her a birthday present." He glanced at a series of cards laid out on the table, then quickly averted his eyes.

"I did a reading for her first. It was all very positive." Vicky nodded at the table. "Then I told her the laboratory results, which I got back from my doctor today. She seemed so happy until I teased her about our names …" She paused and looked at the spread of cards. "Then she just ran out."

"It wasn't the test result she reacted badly to?" Dis went back to the doorway as Avery walked back into the house and came up the stairs.

"No, she seemed very happy." Vicky looked up as her brother appeared in the doorway next to Dis. "Ever since Avery told me about her, I've been hoping for this. Zade is our half-sister. We all have different mothers but share the same father." Her smile faded as Avery stomped back down the stairs.

"She was happy after you did the reading and after you told her she is your sister." Dis walked over to the coffee table and gestured at the cards. "This is the spread you did for her?"

Vicky looked up at Otter first, then over at Dis. "Since we're sharing secrets, I don't see any harm if you want to look at it."

"You said this was a positive reading?" Dis settled into the chair on the other side of the table and examined the cards. "Your style of interpretation must be very different from mine." He reached out a finger to touch the image of a flower-wreathed skeleton riding a black horse.

Vicky pointed at the individual cards. "A lonely past, a challenging present, and a future love with a dark-haired woman. Helpers surround."

"Very different styles." Dis looked up. "Then you teased her about her name."

Vicky bent to gather up the cards. "Only that it was too bad Avery already has the name that best describes her." Vicky's eyes welled up with tears. "I hope she knows I wouldn't make her change her name for a silly …"

Dis closed his eyes. "Family tradition."

◻♍♏♋■

Zade ran along the side of St. Anna's cathedral. She wiped away her tears and jumped up, catching the lip of the brick wall enclosing the novices' garden. Vaulting over the top, she dropped down onto the gravel walkway and resumed running. The light of the spring moon slipped through a tangle of clouds, casting her silhouette onto a hedge of cypress.

Coming to the end of the path, Zade shied away from the darkness under the arbor enclosing the holy well. She stumbled back along the path and landed on the freshly turned ground underneath the rose bushes. Crawling out of the flowerbed, she left a trail of crushed daffodils and tulips.

Blinded by tears, she pushed her way through a row of juniper bushes and found herself in the center of the meditation garden. In front of her, the marble icon of St. Anna knelt in supplication at the feet of the shrouded form of the Holy Mother. A third figure lay draped across the god's lap. Zade ran a muddy hand across her eyes, trying to clear her vision. Taking a step closer, her eyes went wide at the oddly dark human shape pressed into the curve of the sculpture's arm. Rivulets of blood seeped down the white marble, and the flayed corpse's exposed muscle and tendon gleamed wetly. Zade gasped and staggered back into a pair of waiting arms.

"My lucky day, yes?" A man clamped a rag over her face.

Book 2:

The Heart Distillers

ZADE WOKE UP ALONE and in darkness, dressed only in her underwear, a thin blanket covering her prone body. She ran her hands along the bare metal frame of a cot, over the bolts securing it to the floor, and along a slotted metal grate. Getting up, she traced the confines of her prison with probing, blind hands. The small cell was tiled on three sides. The fourth was rigged with a metal mesh fence, closing her in. A faint vibration emanated from the tiles behind the cot. She listened as the rumbling grew louder.

She attempted to leverage the fencing with the weight of her body but to no effect. She repeated her exploration and discovered a small round hole in the mesh, near one of the support poles. Straining, she wedged her arm through the hole up to her bicep and reached into the darkness. With a growl, Zade withdrew her hand and groped her way back to the cot.

The sound of a door unlocking woke her. She sat up as the overhead lights flickered on.

A man entered the room. "Good morning." He dragged a wooden chair from the wall and placed it close to the mesh edge of the cell. His weathered face wreathed into lines as he smiled at her through the fencing.

"Is it?" Blinking in the bright light, Zade examined her captor.

"Oh, yes. Sunny and sweet. I'm afraid the only breakfast I can offer you today is water." The gray-haired man passed a plastic bottle through the hole in the mesh.

"Thanks." Zade cracked the top off and drank half the contents of the bottle.

"You are most welcome." His eyes grew bright as he watched her movements.

She picked at the blanket. "How long are you going to be keeping me locked up?"

He watched her fidget. "Oh, I'm waiting for instructions from my employer on the matter. I was in the process of delivering our last guest when I, rather you, bumped into me. Quite an unexpected fortuity, yes?"

"I would have to disagree." Zade recapped the water bottle as the tiles began vibrating, rumbling against her back.

"Understandably so."

She nodded at the door. "Do I have to ask to use the bathroom?"

"Oh, the drain should suffice." The man pointed to the slotted grate.

Zade made a face at the grate and then looked back at him. "Really?"

"I am afraid so. As I will only be offering you water, it should not be a difficulty much longer." Smiling, he returned the chair to its former position next to the door. "Until tomorrow morning."

She watched him push open the door and leave. The lights snapped off, leaving her alone and blind. The wall cycled through three sets of vibrations before she stretched her hand out to feel along the cage floor again.

The phone continued to ring downstairs. Dis untangled himself from his bedding and sat on the edge of the mattress for a moment before tugging on a pair of boxers. Shuffling down the stairs to the kitchen, he blinked at the sunlight streaming in through the kitchen window. He looked at the phone and picked up the receiver.

"Hello." He rubbed the heel of his palm into his eye, opened the refrigerator, and took out a can of cat food and a carton of milk. "Okay, please tell her I'll be right over." Dis thumbed the switch hook, then hooked a finger into the rotary face and dialed. "I'd like a taxi, please. 44 Manning Street, out on the Point. Thank you."

Stinky looked up from her spot on the bed as Dis came in and swiftly got dressed. She gave a soft meow as he rigged her back into her cart. She was purring loudly by the time he set her on the downstairs floor. He scraped cat food onto a fresh plate, leaving the forgotten milk carton on the counter. Dis stepped out of the house and locked the front door.

A taxi eased up to the curb. Dis got into the back. "St. Anna's, please."

A pink rosary dangled from the taxi's rearview mirror and a tiny statue of the Holy Mother was glued to the dashboard. "No Mass this morning, man. Somebody got murdered there." The driver glanced at his passenger in the rearview mirror.

"You can drop me off at the rectory." Dis raked his fingers through his dark hair as the car bounced through a pothole. He took out his journal and began flipping the pages back and forth, comparing notations.

The cabbie's attention shifted from the occupant of the backseat to the other vehicles on the road. He clicked on the radio. A song crackled through the speakers in the rear of the cab. Dis glanced up for a moment before shifting his attention back to his journal.

"You heard about the murder, right?" The driver's eyes darted from the road back to his mirror. "Been all over the radio."

"Not all the details." Dis kept scribbling and didn't look up.

"Missing girl S&P was looking for got dumped, all creepy-like. 'Macabre,' they called it. You think we got a serial killer loose? I think we do. I bet S&P's been covering it up. There's talk of the City Manager imposing a curfew."

Dis tabbed to the front of his journal and ran a finger down a page. "A serial killer would require more than one victim."

The taxi stopped at a red light and the driver leaned back over the seat. "Don't you listen to the radio, man? This is the fifth body been found in six months. That's some serial killer shit if you ask me."

"People get murdered, doesn't mean it's a serial killer."

"I figured it out. All of them have been dumped on the full moon. Some serious weird shit going on, man." The driver nodded as the traffic began to move again. In front of the taxi, the 53 bus belched a cloud of exhaust and changed lanes.

"Full moon will be in another week, on the thirtieth."

"Damn, you sure?" The driver thumped his hands on the wheel. "Man, this city just loves coming up with new ways of killing folks."

Dis quoted the driver in his journal and then put it away. Crossing over the bridge, the radio chattered static. The driver turned it off, muttering as the Mam River twisted into view below. As the vehicle merged onto the top of Mercy, its passenger watched an elderly couple unfurl an awning outside Magda's Tea Shop. In the shop window, the couple's black cat paused in its ablutions, leaving his pink tongue sticking out as the cab went by.

The driver parked outside of the rectory. "Ten fifty."

"Thanks." Dis handed over the money and got out. He looked over the property surrounding the church, which was cordoned off with hazard tape. S&P officers patrolled near the churchyard.

"I'm told Mother Ida wishes to see me." He glanced over the shoulder of the sister who answered the rectory door.

"Thank you for coming so quickly." The woman averted her eyes from his.

"She's had a terrible shock, but will not let me administer a sedative. She insists she needs to see you." The sister showed him through the front parlor crammed with religious icons and hand tatted lace up to a private set of stairs leading to the second floor.

"Weather permitting, Mother Ida meditates in the garden at dawn every morning. She discovered the poor soul and managed to return here and call S&P." The sister shook her head. "They asked her dreadful questions, those detectives. I can't imagine why on earth they would say such things to her."

"Send him up, Mareil. I will tell him of their blasphemous falsehoods myself." Mother Ida stood at the top of the stair in a white dressing gown, her long hair in twin braids. "Come up, boy. I need to see you before they put me under. Come up."

Dis climbed the stairs to join Mother Ida in her bedroom. The old cleric was standing by the window, watching the S&P forensic team photograph and examine the church garden.

"Blasphemers. Every one of them." She dropped the lace curtain back into place and glared at her visitor. "I would threaten to excommunicate them for stupidity if I thought they knew what the word meant." Mother Ida waved him toward a chair by her bedside as she climbed back under the covers.

"The Holy Mother's Church doesn't excommunicate members."

"Ignorant louts like those wouldn't know that. They're ignorant of everything about the Holy Church." Mother Ida slapped her hand on the top of her comforter. "Do you know what they asked me? Right down there in the room I counsel my parishioners in?" She shook her finger at the floor.

"No."

"If we keep records of known rapists or pedophiles among the clergy. Among the clergy! As if the Holy Mother Church, as if I, would allow such an abomination to occur. If one hair on one child's head was out of place, I would know it or the other sisters would know it. We would never cover for an insult against God such as harming a child! If I ever found such a person amongst my flock, I would march them right down to S&P and pray for their soul while I

219

made damn sure they were being fingerprinted." The elderly woman slapped her hands on the bedding again.

"I'm …"

"I thought Lily was in the garden waiting for me this morning. She does that sometimes to make sure I don't fall asleep, not that I could out there in the cold." Mother Ida pursed her lips and looked toward the window overlooking the garden. "The novitiate can be hard for the young ones. So many dreams to say good-bye to when they decide on the Calling. It can be very lonely." She glanced at her guest. "So I wasn't surprised to hear a girl crying in the garden, as I've heard it many times before. But what I found in the arms of the Holy Mother … that was a crime committed against God herself." Ida shuddered.

Dis rolled his left hand away from his body. "There was someone else in the garden?"

"No, only the poor murdered girl and the sacred figures of St. Anna and the Holy Mother. It was the well I heard."

"The well."

"Go and listen to it yourself if you don't believe me." Mother Ida snapped. Her expression softened. "Remember when it ran dry? Or were you too young?"

Dis took the elderly woman's outstretched hand. "I remember."

"You must have been what, four or five? Your mother spoke to your father about it and he sent her back with you. Your mother held your hand and you sang to the well. Do you remember?"

"I remember being afraid of the statues and seeing the fireflies come out."

"St. Anna had a holy vision there and the waters flowed up from beneath her feet."

"The clans said it was a sweet water spring created by the tears of Mammor long before the saint came to these shores."

The cleric's gaze sharpened. "Mammor, as the Holy Mother was known to the clans before St. Anna came to them."

"The Ocean-Mother is a bit more playful than the Holy Mother. Mammor likes to play tricks, and once she played one too many on the Earth-Father. He went below ground, shunning her company and causing the first winter. The well is where she wept for the loss of his company."

"Your father said it went dry because of the wickedness of this city."

"Construction nearby could have shifted the water vein."

"Ha! You sound like Bone." Mother Ida squeezed his hand. "I saw him with you last week at Mass." She gave him a knowing smile. "I'm pleased you listened to my advice and reconciled with him."

Shrugging, Dis gave her a half-smile.

She squeezed his hand again. "I don't want the well to go dry. Go sing to it, for me, child."

He looked at her in surprise. "You're asking me to perform magic in the church garden."

"If that is what it takes."

"S&P might not want me in their crime scene."

"I will send Mareil with a note telling them to let you through on Church business."

"You're asking, telling me, to go sing a prayer to the Eldest behind your Cathedral …"

"I will bless it in the name of the Holy Mother when I can bring myself …" She squeezed his hand and turned away as tears welled up in the corners of her eyes.

He squeezed her hand and stood up. "I'll get the sister to come up for the note and to bring the sleeping draught."

Mother Ida called out to him. "I'm pleased to see you are not hiding behind your glasses anymore."

At the top of the stairs, Dis started to raise his hand to his face and then set it on the banister.

Watching the pigeons roosting on the Cathedral, he waited on the rectory steps for the sister to return. Individual birds launched out over the churchyard and then settled back into the communal ranks. A contingent of the flock wheeled above the spires before tumbling down to graze.

"Mr. Mthdys." Detective Fuller walked up with Sister Mareil. "Where is your escort?" Her gaze lingered over his left eye.

"I haven't had one in two weeks." He nodded to her as the clergywoman went back inside the rectory. "Thank you, Sister."

Fuller chewed her gum and then spat it into a napkin. "I thought I told you to call me if you didn't see an officer." The S&P detective folded the napkin and put it in the pocket of her raincoat.

Dis hesitated as his fingers touched his scar instead of the familiar eyeglasses.

Fuller narrowed her eyes at him. "You didn't tell me you were an employee of the Church."

"I wasn't, until this morning."

"Mother Ida …" Fuller unwrapped another piece of gum. "…wants us, me, to escort you immediately to the holy well, which, by the way, happens to be in the middle of the scene of a crime. Would you care to explain why I should drop what I'm doing and piss off the evidence collection team by bringing in a civilian?"

"A sacred place has been desecrated and it would set its guardian's mind at ease to have me address any damage."

"Since when does the Holy Mother Church hire occultists?" She watched Dis frown. "Oh, I know all about you, Mr. Mthdys. I had a lengthy chat with S&P's expert regarding your family."

"Then you know Mother Ida is my godmother."

Fuller snapped her gum and turned toward the churchyard. "You will stay behind me and you will not touch anything."

Dis stayed behind the detective as she walked by the S&P officer guarding the cordoned-off perimeter. Fuller veered off the gravel, tramping through the dark green vegetation and flowers. She followed a route marked out by a neon orange cord, then waited until one of the forensic specialists looked up.

"Are we clear to go to the well yet, Graver?" Fuller scanned the row of plastic bags laid out on the trampled ground.

"Mind the tag lines." The man returned his attention to his task.

"Stay with me and don't step beyond any of the orange lines. Don't touch anything." The detective held up the cordon for Dis to pass under.

On their way to the well, the pair walked by a number-tagged flower bed. Another number was clipped to the break in the junipers behind it. More tags rested on the gravel path and several more were attached to shrubs. The S&P specialists working by the statues did not look up as they passed.

The detective waved Dis under the arbor with a flourish. "Would you have any witnesses who can vouch for your whereabouts last night at nine?"

"I was at Victory Pierce's, across the street, for her birthday party." Dis looked at Fuller. "I was there until three."

The woman inhaled and then coughed rapidly. She took out a napkin and spat her gum into it. "Did you hear or see anything unusual between eight and ten? Did any of the other guests mention anything to you?"

"One of our friends left early." Dis turned toward the moss-covered granite stones. "She was upset and didn't come back. It was around nine when she left. I need to touch the rocks."

"Hold it." Fuller turned to the officers by the statues. "Graver? Is the well clear?"

The group by the statues stopped their examinations and conferred. Graver held up a thumb. "All clear."

"Go ahead." She shoved her hands into her trouser pockets and nodded in the direction of the well.

Dis lowered his bag to the ground and knelt in front of the low stone wall protecting the spring. Brushing away the fiddleheads growing from the cracks, he rested his hands on the stone curb and looked down into the well. A frog darted from its hiding place and plopped into the spring below. Dis turned his head and listened to the sound of the water threading its way through the earth. His baritone voice resonated against the stones and water as he began to sing.

Fuller's mouth opened momentarily. She rocked back on her heels, looking over her shoulder at the other S&P officers. The evidence team froze, listening to Dis's voice echoing off the stones. The wind kicked up, tossing the remains of crushed flowers out of the garden beds.

□ ♍ ♏ ♋ ■

In the Hinterlands, a family stood around an open grave in Rest and Be Thankful Cemetery. The officiant offered words of comfort from a silk-bound book. The mourners grabbed onto their hats and prayer sheets as a sudden breeze swirled through their midst. A funeral wreath tumbled over, showering the coffin with white flowers.

□ ♍ ♏ ♋ ■

In a disused storage room in the East Municipal Garage, a group of teenagers squatted around one of their own. The boy gasped for breath as blood pooled around him. Another teenager with a bag of first aid supplies tore open his shirt and winced at a piece of white bone showing through the boy's skin.

He turned and shook his head at the girl standing guard. She looked down at a candy wrapper that rustled into the room. When she kicked the door shut, the bright yellow and white foil skittered until it came to rest against the injured boy's leg. He smiled feebly as the girl flicked open a knife and walked toward him.

□ ♍ ♏ ♋ ■

In the darkness of her cage, Zade lay under the cot. She used the lip of the water bottle to pry up a piece of metal. After freeing one end of the slat, she slid sideways on the cement floor and began to work on the other. She muttered as she worked, turning the bottle's mouth to keep it from breaking. A strange sound traveled up through the floor grate. She turned her head, listening to the distant oscillation of the wind singing through sewer pipes.

☐ ♍ ♏ ♋ ■

Dis sat with his back against the well. He looked up through the arbor at the pigeons in flight. When he started to stand, Fuller extended her hand to help.

"What language was that?" She stood next to him and watched the evidence team gather up their equipment.

"No language. Not all prayer requires words."

"Islo Quail told me you are an expert in Ornish occult practices."

"I suspect he has told that to most of the city by now."

"Is it true?"

"Chairwoman Pierce has the leading expert on her staff."

"Pierce says you threatened her." Fuller watched his face.

"I only declined being on her payroll."

"We identified one of the recent murder victims as Mala Frankel. You mentioned her in your statement after your alleged assault."

"She worked at the Blue Lotus, for Jeniel." Dis brushed the hair out of his face. His expression was stony.

"There's some speculation regarding the manner in which she was killed. Quail thinks it had ritual significance."

Dis cocked his head and looked at her. "We're a ritualized species, we do things that create meaning for us."

"I assigned you an escort detail for a reason." The detective rocked back on her heels and looked up at the spires of the cathedral as clouds covered the sun.

"You think I'm involved." He watched the pattern of shadows move across the woman's upturned face.

"You have a motive." Fuller tilted her head and locked eyes with him. "Since the Autumn Equinox, we've had four victims of varying age and sex. No overlapping patterns except one, which, by the way, has historical significance. We've been trying to keep the case out of the news to prevent copycat incidents or full-blown panic."

"All clear, Fuller!" The last of the S&P team moved away from the pair at the well.

The detective gave Dis a considering look. "I take it you've completed your work for the Church for today?"

Dis nodded and came out from under the arbor.

She fell into step with him, moving toward the statues. "There's a handful of old families left in this city, and old money likes old, familiar things. Gets comfortable, knowing everyone, knowing the right people, going to the right events, right schools, even the right churches." Fuller glanced up at the Cathedral's stained glass rose window. "I don't have to tell you how the Pierces got their money or how much they hate spending it, but they will spend it if they want to destroy someone. I will say, for Mother Ida's sake, that I'm relieved to know Victory Pierce doesn't share her aunt's opinion of you."

The white marble figures were checkered with numbered evidence tags. Dark brown stains ran from the crook of the Holy Mother's left arm and down the carved creases of the statue's veiled gown. The stain spread out across her bosom and the crocuses blooming at the seated figure's feet were crusted with dried blood.

Fuller began to walk around the figures. "The city manager's office likes to say we have a homeless problem because the winters are mild. I've been to Newton in the winter and it's much harsher, comparatively. We've got ocean currents and whatnot. Though that doesn't explain the higher rate of alcoholism or mental illness here, which is funny, considering Newton's supposedly got the market cornered with the Statler Institute." The woman threw another glance at her companion. "Best musicians in the world are from here, by the way. You would think, being so scenic, we would attract more painters here. We have galleries that import work for the money to browse, but not much of a visual art community of our own. Seems all our artists crack up and get shipped off to the Stat."

Dis glanced at her. "The clans believed it was unbalancing to live in a sacred place. It's like using alcohol instead of water in everything, though it doesn't affect everyone the same way all the time."

As they approached the rear of the marble pedestal, Fuller stepped off the gravel path and into the yew bushes. She held back the evergreen branches, allowing Dis to stand with her in the mulched area behind the statues. "The Pierce family commissioned this from a local sculptor who ended up in the Statler before it was finished. Had to import another one to complete it." She patted her coat pockets. "I left my glasses in the car. Will you read the inscription?" She dug around in her pocket and tore the foil off a new pack of gum.

Dis raised an eyebrow at the detective. "Dedicated to the memory of …" He looked at her and she nodded for him to continue. "… to the memory of Captain Sincerity Pierce, founder of the first settlement on this spot and hero of the Great Insurrection, who made the supreme sacrifice for Victory."

Fuller wadded up the ripped foil. "Ever since its founding, this city's been great at producing three things. Two of which the Pierce family excels in." She shoved through the bushes to the other side of the statue. As shouts came over the wall, she cocked her head. "That is the sweet sound of Officer Low yelling. I can trust you to walk back out the way we came in? I'm going to have to go rescue members of the press before she handcuffs them for standing on the grass."

"Thank you for allowing me to attend to the well, Detective Fuller." Dis stepped out onto the path. "I appreciate you taking the time to escort me."

She shrugged her shoulders and began walking toward the front of the Cathedral. "By the way, I heard Victory's little brother Bravery is a motorcycle courier now. You'll have to let me know if he joins any of the bands you people always seem to be in. A Pierce musician would be a novelty I'd like to see."

▽↗◢

"I'm getting old, love." Bone dropped onto the bench next to Dis, grinned, and wiped his sweaty face on the side of his lover's arm. "I like those kids. They have the good sense to abuse their audience."

"They were okay, yeah." Otter upended his beer and took a seat across the table from the couple. "Miss the hell out of Boon's voice, but they were doing a fine job." Otter lifted the bottom of his t-shirt and toweled off his face. "If you're old, I must be geriatric. I need a nap."

Dis began to reply but stopped and turned toward a scuffle breaking out by the bathrooms.

Kitty ran up to their table and grabbed Otter. "Batshit Mat's warming up to beat the fucking piss out of Avery." She flinched as she spotted Dis.

"Let's go see if we can't talk him down." Dis stood up.

Kitty looked at him in surprise and then took a step back as the other men followed him.

"Excuse me." Dis put a hand on a bystander's shoulder. He pressed to the front of the gathering crowd.

"Where the fuck is she? What did you fucking do to her?" Mat screamed, grabbing Avery by the throat.

"Put him down, Mat. He didn't do anything to her." Dis glanced at Avery gasping for breath.

"Horseshit. He asked all kinds of questions about her." Mat slammed Avery into the wall. "He's been fucking stalking her and now she's missing."

Avery gasped again and tried to push Mat's hand off his throat.

"He's Zade's fucking brother." Otter stepped around and put his hand on Mat's shoulder. "Let go. Now."

"Then why was he asking who was the best rider? Why was he asking who won all our races even before he was with YC?" Mat shook Otter's hand off and knocked Avery's head against the wall. "I remember this rich boy came in asking last fall. What the fuck did you do to her?"

Dis sighed. "Enough, Mat. Let him go. If you want to find Zade ..."

Meeting Dis's mismatched eyes, he snarled. "Don't you start in on me, you fucking freak."

"*What the fuck did you just say?*" Bone stepped around Dis, grabbed a fistful of Mat's hair, and yanked.

Mat dropped Avery and grabbed Bone's hand. Bone stepped forward and smashed him into a picture hanging on the wall, cracking the glass. Mat yelled as Bone put him in an armlock.

"Let him go, Bone." Dis closed his eyes and pinched the bridge of his nose. He looked over at Avery. "Are you okay?"

"Yeah." Avery coughed. "I'm fine."

Dis turned back to where his lover held Mat against the wall. "Bone." He took a step forward.

Bone whispered something into Mat's ear, then released him.

Mat glared at him and then turned to look at Dis. "She wouldn't have missed tonight. She wouldn't have missed Boon's band." He rubbed his shoulder and gave Dis a withering look. "I cut her and she still went out to find you. What's so fucking special about you?" Mat tried to shove Dis but he shifted sideways. Mat sneered and walked away.

Dis watched him go and then cocked his head at Avery. "Explain."

"Come on, you know Mat's fucking nuts." Otter looked back and forth between the two men.

"Vicky saw Zade deliver a package to the hotel and thought she might be related to us. That's why I signed up with OC and asked about her." Avery straightened his jacket and t-shirt. "We're both worried about her." He met Dis's eyes for a moment and then looked at the floor.

Bone straightened the broken picture. "It hasn't even been three days. She's most likely thinking things through about finding out she's a Pierce and getting seriously inebriated, hopefully with a bevy of beautiful women. You're all overreacting." He clapped his hand on Otter's shoulder. "Let's buy the band a round on her behalf."

"That's the best plan you've had all evening." Otter threw his arm around Bone's neck.

Bone winked at Dis. "I'm saving the best for last."

Dis stopped Avery. "She will come back to us, soon." He met his eyes. "Or

I will tear this city apart to find her."

Avery nodded and Dis let him go.

Kitty was leaning against a table, watching. "You believe that shitbag?" She looked at Avery as he walked away. "Mat wasn't making that up about the questions that snotball's been asking."

"Keep an eye on him for me, Kitty." Dis looked at her and went to join the others.

She made a dismissive noise and flipped three fingers at his back.

▽↗◢

Bone sat on the central counter of a converted warehouse, chewing on a piece of raw pasta while Dis flipped sizzling ingredients in an iron skillet. Bone stretched, watching. "You ought to open a restaurant and call it 'No Fish.'"

"Did you buy plates yet?" Dis lowered the flame under the saucepan. "Or forks?"

"At the same time, I bought the pots you are currently employing to create dinner." Bone hopped off the counter and went over to the newly-installed cabinetry to collect the place settings. He surreptitiously washed his plates before setting them on the counter next to the stove.

Dis arranged the portions and gave them to Bone to carry over to the coffee table. Setting the pots in the sink to soak, he stood at the edge of the kitchen, dragging a dishcloth between his hands as his host sat down. "Start without me."

Bone put his arm over the back of the couch and looked at him. "Worrying is a down payment on something that may never happen, love. Come eat."

"The divination …"

Bone groaned and stared up at the metal rafters. "Your imaginary friends need to go on tour."

"Vicky's cards …"

Bone dropped his head and looked at Dis over the back of the couch. "You said that woman could not do a proper reading to save her life."

230

"Her interpretation was flawed, but the spread in question may have been…"

"Enough. Come eat."

Dis turned away, folded the dishtowel, and laid the compressed square on the counter. Bone jabbed his fork into a piece of meat. "There's no reason to worry yourself sick."

"She's in danger. We can't find her and she's on the verge of death."

Bone set his fork down and got up. He walked over to face Dis. "Stop it." He put his hands on his lover's face. "None of that is true. She could be in Newton or Grava, or even in …"

Dis broke free and retreated toward the sink, leaning heavily on his right leg. "I need to …"

"You need to stop convincing yourself of these ridiculous things." Bone raised his voice. "Hire a private detective."

"Vicky already has." Dis kept his gaze on the wooden planks of the kitchen floor.

"Then go make friends with the dirt babies and give them her socks to pick up her scent. Hand out missing person flyers outside of hotels. Do whatever sane action you can think of, but stop trying to propitiate fantasies. Stop playing at being a mystic or you'll end up like Quail, flouncing around and moaning while ripping off the rich and the gullible."

"She saved my life."

"Don't fabricate a disaster just so you can ride to her rescue, love."

"I told you what Fuller said. It's not my fantasy, there is a serial killer."

"Did it occur to you that they might think their cause is righteous? Keeping the sun running through the heavens on greased rails of sacrifice? Or that it's just to fuck with people who buy into all of this idiocy? An egomaniac writing themselves into history." Bone dragged his hands through his hair. "You really think your imaginary friends can help you find Zade? They can't even help you deal with your own life. You know what brought me back to you? Your real live human friends, the people right here who love you and want to see you happy. Not some bowl of chowder you left out for your beloved dead."

"I know Zade went to see you." Dis clenched his fists against his thighs. "That's one more thing I owe her for."

"How do you know she even needs your help? A seagull bring you a secret message? Or are you having visions now? Are your extinct deities finally responding to your daily devotions? Does it soothe your ego to think of yourself as the last of your kind still practicing the fading traditions?"

Dis spoke evenly, but his tone was sharp. "Not all of us worship at the altar of our own talents."

"*For that, one needs a talent.*" Bone spit the words out.

Dis gave a short bark of laughter and shook his head. "The only one I seem to have is repeating my mistakes." He shook his head again, collected his gear off the side of an unopened furniture crate, and walked out.

"You're excellent at running away. You may even be the world champion of fleeing." Bone gripped the edge of the counter. "Your noble ancestors must be proud of your evasion skills."

"My beloved dead give me more credit than you ever have." Dis paused next to a brand-new touring motorcycle parked by the loading dock doors. "Don't bother showing up again at my door, Drake." The door clicked shut behind him.

"*What about dinner?*" Bone flopped on the couch and picked up his plate. He ate several bites, then tossed it back down. "Idiot. Serves you right for dating a magician."

▽ ↗ ◢

The shop doorbell jingled as Dis entered the Shining Star. He frowned as he came abreast of a statue of the Holy Mother.

"Are you here for the astrology class?" A middle-aged woman beamed at him. "You're early. The class won't begin for another half an hour."

"I'm looking for Quail." Dis scanned the shop's rows of books and occult paraphernalia.

Her smile faltered. "Oh. Do you have an appointment?"

"No." He stepped around her and headed for the back of the shop.

"You mustn't bother Mr. Quail before he teaches." The woman followed at his heels, wringing her hands.

Dis ignored her and opened the office door, revealing a cluttered room lined with bookshelves.

"You mustn't ..." The woman nervously tugged on his jacket.

"Ah. It is quite all right, Swan." Quail snapped shut the book he was reading. "My friend here is just stopping by for a brief chat."

"But the class ..." The woman looked from her employer back to Dis.

"We will only be a moment." Rising from his chair, the balding man came around the side of the room and eased the door shut. He pursed his lips and walked back to his chair with his hands clasped behind his tweed suit jacket.

"You are working for S&P and Mercy Pierce." Dis glared.

"You have not been casting your horoscope regularly." Quail opened his desk drawer and lifted out a wooden box. He began tamping an herbal mixture into a pipe. "If you were keeping your hand in, you would have been standing there last week."

"I'm standing here now."

"I went to great lengths to teach you how to identify the pivotal moments when events can be influenced with minor effort rather than requiring heroics." Quail's match flared and filled the room with the smell of sulfur. He set the match against the bowl of his pipe, sending up a plume of fragrant smoke.

"I'm not here to discuss astrology with you." Dis leaned forward to loom over the desk, glowering. "You told them about me."

"There are advantages to maintaining formal working relationships within the community." Quail sat down and leaned back, looking up at his former student.

"I'm not interested in their money."

"To gain information, one must be willing to barter something of equal value."

"I will not …"

Quail sighed. "Your ascendant makes you so unreasonable at times."

"I'm not here to …"

"Through my contacts, I know the times of death, method of death, and identities of the recent murder victims. Including the one deposited at St. Anna's last Saturday night. I also know the perpetrator was interrupted by a witness."

"What did the witness say?"

"Nothing. It appears they were most likely abducted." Quail waved a hand at Dis. "Do sit down. It must inconvenience you to hover like that."

Dis put his hands on the desk. "My friend went missing that night."

"What method did you use to locate her, dowsing or pebble mapping?"

"I haven't been able to locate her."

Quail's eyebrows went up. "You thought to demand my assistance by waving my client list under my nose? Or did you think I would be moved to guilt for listing your qualifications to potential employers?"

"S&P is one thing, but Pierce? Why would I work for …"

"The wealthiest family in this city?"

"For the descendants of a genocidal lunatic!"

Quail sighed. "I've had members of the Pierce family as clients for my entire career. I have known Generosity Pierce ever since she was a child. I even had her as a student, not too many years ago. I advised her mother to send her away to the Continent last year, as her chart indicated she would suffer a breakdown. Though given her treatment of you, I can understand if you lack compassion regarding her demise."

Dis sagged into the chair in front of the desk. "Her demise?"

"Dental records have confirmed that she is the most recent murder victim. Starved for days and then killed by a blow to the base of the skull. It appears I interpreted her horoscope incorrectly." The older man examined his guest's drawn features. He retrieved a silver flask from his lower desk drawer and passed it across to Dis. "My contacts informed me that Mercy Pierce used her influence to suppress the S&P report. She is telling the press her daughter was killed in a traffic accident in Newton. Apparently, the family is well-enough connected there to get it corroborated."

Dis mechanically opened the flask. "I would not have wished that death on Jeniel." He tipped it back and then put it back on the desk.

Quail returned the flask to the drawer, keeping his eyes on Dis. "Yet, by your reasoning, the daughter of Mercy Pierce deserved it?"

"I need to find Zade." Dis looked down at his clasped hands and then back at the other man. "I will give you whatever you ask."

Quail laughed. "I see. In your mind, I am the forest witch who will ask you to barter your remaining eye or your true love's beating heart. All because I add a touch of theatre to suit the expectations of my clientele."

"Will you help me or not?" Dis stood up and began to pace.

Quail knocked ash into his palm. "The class will be over at ten. Come back then, unless you wish to sit in? I'm covering planetary transits through the seventh house."

Dis shook his head. "What should I bring for payment?"

"I'm going to take a holiday. All of this extra work is quite doing me in." Quail stirred the contents of his pipe. "I would like you to fill in for me while I'm gone. You will have the use of this office and the shop to see clients. No, you don't have to roll around on the floor in body paint with a drum. A suit will suffice."

"Anything else?"

"You will give at least one lecture a month. You will cast a weekly horoscope and pay attention to it."

"How long will you be gone?" Dis narrowed his eyes.

Quail let the smoke roll out of his mouth lazily. "Oh, not very long. Just a short jaunt up to Awyton."

"I will be back at ten."

"I look forward to it. Do you know your missing friend's birth data?"

"No. She doesn't either."

"Interesting. Make sure to eat something before you return."

Swan was visibly relieved as Dis left Quail's office. She gave him a timid half-wave as he latched the door.

▽ ↗ ◢

Dis walked down High Street to Maddy's and took a seat at the bar. "Cygnet and a menu, please, Roy."

The bartender set a menu down in front of him. "Otter's in the back with YC."

"If I join them, it will be an all-liquid dinner."

▽ ↗ ◢

He was finishing his meal when a hand dropped on his shoulder. "Roy said to leave you alone with your burger." Otter looked down at his friend's empty plate. "Looks like I'm free to hassle you."

"What are you drinking?"

"Settlement." Otter took the barstool next to Dis. "Thought you were cooking for Bone tonight as a housewarming present?"

Dis gestured at the bartender. "A Settlement and another Cygnet."

Otter watched Dis's face. "Well, at least it wasn't a big fight, or else you would be ordering whiskey."

"I have an appointment later I need to stay sober for."

"Mother. He wasn't riding his new toy hammered, was he?"

"No."

Roy brought their pints over.

"Thanks. You guys were doing so well. I thought maybe this time …" Otter tapped his glass against Dis's. "Well, here's to our girl coming home soon."

"To Zade." Dis lifted his beer and stared at his reflection in the curved glass.

236

THE STINK OF SWEAT AND STALE URINE permeated the dank space. When the vibrations in the walls and floor of the storage room settled into silence, Zade tried thrusting her arm through the hole in the mesh again. She clung to the front of the cage and ran her fingers over the supports and fencing. In her teeth, she held the piece of spring steel she had pried from the cot. The ends caught on the mesh as she clambered from one side of the cage to the other.

She hauled herself back onto the cot and listened to the sound of the subway train hurtling by somewhere on the other side of the wall. She stopped suddenly, clenching her hands over her lower stomach. Laughing, she slid to the floor in the darkness. When the tears started, she put the back of her hand against her mouth and sat up, reaching for her latest water bottle. She pressed it against her face and started giggling, then howling.

Leaning over the side of the cot, she hid the strip of metal and then pulled the blanket over her head and fell asleep. She woke a few minutes later, stumbling off the cot and knocking over the stack of water bottles. Hyperventilating, she crawled underneath the cot and curled up against the wall.

Eventually she fell asleep with her back against the tiles.

▽↗◢

When the lights flipped on, Zade was sitting on the cot, the blanket straightened out and the bottles stacked neatly beside it. Her captor dragged a wooden chair from the wall and placed it close to the fencing.

"I am sorry to disturb you at this hour." The corners of the man's eyes crinkled as he smiled apologetically. "I thought you might like to know my employer has sent instructions. They've seen fit to set me the challenge of skinning you alive. The skin must be unbruised. This requirement limits the use of restraints, which would in turn limit the length of the cuts. My employer requires the skin to be in one piece with as few incisions as possible. Blunt trauma is not permitted, which is a pity for both of us." The chair creaked as he leaned forward, his eyes bright.

"In a few hours, I will bring you fresh juice." He smiled warmly, watching her dig her fingernails into the exposed skin of her leg. "Ah, you are not feeling talkative today. I won't take it personally. This can be a challenging time, yes." The man's eyes swept over his prisoner. "You will feel better after the juice." He left the room, turning off the lights.

She slipped off the cot and leaned over until she was lying on her side on the floor. A backdraft of sewer air rushed over her foot. Zade bent her knees and rolled onto her back. She took the piece of metal out from under the cot and hugged it to her chest.

□♍♏♋■

Dis waited near the register while Swan packed up an astrology book for one of the students. The customer gave Dis a shy smile.

"Please lock up when you're done with this gentleman." Quail came to collect Dis. "We will be using the main salon and cannot be interrupted."

Quail indicated a seat at the round table in the center of the salon. Dis remained standing as the other man shut the room's doors and lit a brazier.

"You're not using your pipe." Dis watched as the briquettes started to spark.

Quail fanned the brazier until the coals grew cherry red and then took a jar down from a nearby shelf. "Have you contemplated what might be the source of your block?"

"I'm too emotionally entangled because Zade is the one who rescued me from Jeniel. That's why I can't find her."

Quail looked thoughtful. "Yet you sense she is in danger."

"I feel a sense of immediate panic when I think of her."

"Things are easy for you in the lowest kingdom. Growth and decay you understand intuitively, but you fear losing yourself in the changeable chaos of the middle kingdom." Quail sifted a mixture of resins and herbs over the glowing coals. "Why are you hiding the answer from your conscious mind?"

"If I knew, I wouldn't be ..." Dis coughed as blue smoke churned through the air.

Quail lowered the lights. "Tell me about your friend who doesn't know her birthday. Zade?"

"She works for my company. Courier 90-32."

"Your answer avoids the necessary intimacy. Breathe. Who is she to you?"

"You're not sitting." Dis looked at Quail in alarm.

"To uphold your promise to tend to my clients, you need to regain your proficiency with this technique. You will find your friend and I will guide you. Breathe. Who is she to you?"

After a moment, Dis inhaled deeply. "Zade is my friend."

"An improvement. Why her, what makes her special?"

Dis stared at his mentor through the dimness of the room. "She went out of her way to become friends with me."

"Why?"

"I don't know."

"You don't want to know. Who is she to you?"

Dis put his hands on the table as the intoxicating smoke enveloped him. "She is the one who saved my life."

"Better! She is the one who saved me from …"

"She is the one who saved me from being skinned alive."

"She saved your skin. She is the woman who saved your skin. Work through the words. Use them to dance your mind down. Begin."

"Skin saver, she who saves sin, skin." Dis breathed deeply. "She who saved me from the sins of the skin. From the sins of her kin."

"Who are her kin?" Quail threw another handful of herbs into the brazier and lowered a perforated screen over the smoking coals.

"Zade saved me from Jeniel. Vicky is her sister. Avery is her brother." Dis began to sweat in the increasingly warm room. He sank into one of the two chairs at the table.

Quail walked quietly to stand behind his chair. "The one who saved your skin is also a Pierce?"

"Lab test says they share the same father, same blood. Blood, blood best, brother best, contest."

"When you became friends, you did not know she was a Pierce."

"Pierce skin, cut skin, girl skin, slide skin, slide sin. She who saved me is a sin. She who cut me is dead." Dis laughed.

"Say it again. Breathe." The older magician rested his hand on the back of the other's head. "Find the bond between you and the one who is missing."

"Sister skin, sister kin, sister sin, the sins of the sister. She who saved my skin. She who let me in."

"She let you in, this sister in sin?" Quail lowered his mouth next to his ear.

"She bleeds a rose in the tub. Blood and pain down the drain. She carried the Black Cake and got up again." Tears began to roll down his face. "Now she belongs to Amrwyn."

"The ritual of the Black Cake belongs to the Pierce family, not to the Earth-Father. Where did you hear of it?"

Dis's right fist crashed on the table. "She sent it out and back again."

"Breathe, go deeper. The skin saver sent the cake?"

Dis pinched the bridge of his nose. "No, the mother did, that is how she controls it. She knows it, knows where and when it goes. She sends herself the birthday cake, black cake. Birth cake, white cake, Black Cake, death cake." He stared up at his mentor, the pupil of his hazel eye fully dilated. There was only the faintest distinction between the oversized dark brown iris and black pupil of his blind eye.

"The skin saver is where?"

"In the underneath. With him. In the dark. He will take her skin, my sin."

"She is your lover."

"No, she is my ..." Dis's head lolled forward. "She is bleeding in the dark, waiting for death."

"Can you see her?" Quail put a piece of paper on the table. He pressed a pen into the man's right hand and started to move it. "Show me where she is."

"It's too dark. I'm blind. I gave the forest witch my eyes." Dis's voice was hollow. "She's dying in the dark. She's bleeding in the dark." His hand sketched on the paper in swooping movements while his other hand covered his face.

"Where is she going? To the lower kingdom?" The older man gently moved Dis's left hand back to the table.

"Mammor is teaching her. Showing her the way to the middle kingdom."

Quail glanced at the repeating symbols forming on the paper. "Tell her she must be brave."

Dis shook his head. "I don't want her to be one of them."

"Where is she?"

Dis shook his head again. Tears fell onto the paper as he continued sketching. "I don't know."

"Start again. Saved skin ..."

"Saved skin, girl skin, seal skin, turn skin, shift kin, seal kin, bleed skin. Blood sin." Dis began to sob. "Pierced the ocean's skin, they skin the ocean's kin. They stole it from her daughter, they stole it from her son, they stole the luck from everyone."

"Ah." Quail slid his hand over Dis's shoulder and placed it over the man's heart. "This is what blocks you from finding her. I will shape it for you." The older man inhaled deeply and then extended his fingers over Dis's chest. "When the luck thief caught you, you changed to stone to break her knives. Her first knife broke here, and another of her knives, here." Qual's fingers traced the line of keloid scar tissue through Dis's shirt. "The luck thief's sister stole you away and brought you to the sea. The Sky-Parent taught her what song to sing to change you back, but she who saved you stopped singing when she saw your outer form change in the moonlight. She stopped too soon and left your heart still made of stone. Your stone heart is hardened to the sister of the luck thief."

"Stone-hearted." Dis's sketching hand raced over the paper, layering the image of a heart among the other designs.

"Even so, you know where the unfinished song is." Quail released him and walked over to the wooden shelf near the brazier. He closed an outer lid over the smoking bed of coals and selected a slim book. The book unfolded into a map of the city and Quail set it on the table by Dis's left hand. "Show me where the woman with your heart-song is right now. Where is your heart-song?"

With his right hand still scribbling on the paper, Dis moved his left hand slowly. His fingers scrabbled over the map's surface, dragging the heel of his palm behind. "Here."

Quail moved the map and circled the spot with a red pen. "Lend her your strength to stay alive a little longer. Ask the Eldest to save her."

Dis's head lolled back. He stared at the smoke writhing along the ceiling in blue tendrils. "Oldest of the old, hear me. I am the voice of the gull, the wail of the injured child, the cry of the lost people, the moan of the dead. I am a ghost crying over the waters. Please do not take her from me."

The older magician furrowed his brow and glanced at his former student. "You will not offer anything for her return?"

Dis rolled his head to the side. "I have nothing left to offer. I have no skin, no heart, no bones." He laughed as his right hand raced on the table. "Today I threw my bones away. Should I offer them my pain again?"

Quail reached out to quiet the moving pen. "Your ancestors have laid their notice upon you. Their pain lives in you and haunts you." He moved to stand behind Dis. Both men closed their eyes. Quail laid his hands on Dis's head. "I will name the winding road you walk. I will tell you the places you must go and the songs you must sing." The older magician sighed, lowering his forehead onto the back of his hands. After a moment he straightened, still touching Dis. "Through you, your ancestors seek the return of what was stolen. Only when it is returned will you be able to forgive the theft. When you are able to forgive, they will forgive and move toward rebirth. When they take rebirth, then you too will be reborn whole."

"I won't forgive them. *I can't.*" Dis stretched his hands out on the table. His fingertips dug into the sheet of paper, crinkling the swirling symbols as he dragged it toward his chest.

Quail sighed. "You cannot swim with a stone for a heart. It will drag you down to the ocean floor for the crabs to pick you clean. You must let yourself change. The Eldest will work through you, whether you wish it or not. You must change."

With his eyes closed, Dis slammed his hand on the table. "Why should the murderers have everything when we have nothing? When we are dead, when we are broken, when we are …"

"Would you bring more suffering into this world? Use your words, use the smoke. Shape the world as you would have it be. Breathe. Say it as you would have it be. Speak the truth of it, son of my heart, and it will be as you say. Speak it. Saved skin …"

"Saved skin, turned skin, stone skin, seal skin, ocean's kin. He said they were shining under the moonlight, heart light. Swimming in the darkness, chasing silver fish, heart's wish." Tears streamed from his eyes, unheeded. "Stars fell into the river and swam out to sea. What is lost, return to me."

243

As the lights in the cage fluttered on, Zade's captor halted at the threshold of the room, dropped the white plastic bucket in his hand and shrieked. The bucket bounced onto its side and rolled across the floor, coming to rest against the mesh fencing. The duffle bag in his other hand slipped out of his grip. He rushed to the fencing and pressed himself against the mesh. *"What have you done?"*

He stared at the words *"FUCK YOUR JUICE"* painted in long streaks of scarlet blood on the wall above the cot. Shaking the fencing, he yelled at the woman lying on her side on the floor. Enraged, he marched back to his bag and lifted out a pair of bolt cutters. "Stupid, filthy thing, you've ruined it!"

As he cut the fence apart, he stared at the blood dripping down the grate and into the sewer. Once he had made a hole large enough, the man dropped the cutters and climbed through. He reached down and grabbed Zade by her right shoulder and flipped her limp body over.

Using the momentum generated by his action, she brought her left arm up off the floor and plunged the spring steel slat into his chest. She hooked her right hand behind his head, clinging to him as he stumbled backward, screaming. Biting into his face, Zade shoved her fingers into the chest wound, tearing it wider. He thrashed, slamming his fists into her as they fell to the floor.

He choked and gasped as she scrambled off of him. As she pushed away, her hand fell on the handle of the bolt cutters. Zade grinned, stood up and swung the tool from her waist, hitting him on the side of the head and knocking him into the fence. He bounced off and landed on the floor.

Keeping a grip on the tool, she backed away from his unmoving form and stumbled over to the duffel bag. She sorted through the contents, lifting out a pair of handcuffs, a set of keys and a bottle of juice. Securing him to the cot with the handcuffs, she watched his chest rise and fall. She tossed the bottle at him, walked out and switched off the lights.

Warm moist air tumbled through an open door at the end of a narrow hallway. She leaned against the wall and slammed the bolts shut on the inner door, locking her former captor inside. She turned around as the windows of a subway train hurtled by at the other end of the hallway.

The light of the maintenance passage spilled out over the empty tunnel as she stared into the darkness the train left in its wake. The bolt cutters thudded to the floor of the hallway. Taking several deep breaths, Zade jumped down onto the gravel floor of the tunnel and began to run barefoot over the uneven surface.

She kept her fingertips in contact with the bricks on the right side of the unlit tunnel. After a while her pace lessened to a jog and she hung her head, stumbling through the dark. When the air began to buffet her back, her head snapped up and she started to sprint. The rumble of a train in the distance grew louder.

The darkness gave way to the approaching train and the tunnel curved under her fingertips. Just as the lights flared behind her, Zade found the metal lip of a ventilation duct. She squeezed into it, wedging herself in. Inside the duct, the bricks under her shifted. The wheels of the subway train screeched on the curving tracks, drowning out her scream as she fell.

≈∽෴⑨❶∾≈

Bone wandered down the middle of High Street Extension with a nearly empty bottle in his hand. Car headlights swept over him and the oncoming driver honked furiously. "Fuck off!" He turned and threw the bottle at the car's windshield. The driver swerved and crashed into a parked car. Bone stared at his now empty hand. "Idiot, you're going to get yourself arrested." He laughed and ran down the Straight.

He ducked into the entrance of Market Station and jumped the turnstile, running down to the inbound platform. He jammed his shoulder through the closing train doors and collapsed into a seat, smiling broadly at the few other late-night passengers. Taking another liquor bottle out of his bag, he cracked the foil off the top and raised it in a silent salute.

The train swayed as it swung onto a new set of tracks and Bone stowed the alcohol back in his bag. He started humming and then singing loudly. He stopped, yawned, and pillowed his hands behind his head as the subway car rocked. He fell asleep, snoring softly as the other passengers left.

ຈ໐ౚ❾❶ ๛

A plastic cup scratching against Zade's cheek woke her. Water pressed her against a barred sewer outlet. Buoyed up by trash, Zade floated, half-submerged, caught in the currents rushing out to the sea from the storm drains. She laced her fingers through the grating over the end of the sewer and tried to shake it.

She cried out, beat her hands against the barrier, and with a resigned look, stared out at the winking lights of the fishing boats. She then rotated in the water to face the cement interior of the culvert.

She attempted to make her way back up the sewer line but was knocked off her feet by the force of the run-off. She spluttered as she bumped back into the mound of trash against the sewer grille. Brushing a bag away from her face, she lifted her hand to look at the little blue and green flecks. She whispered to the luminescent marine life coating her skin and wept.

ຈ໐ౚ❾❶ ๛

Bone woke at the last stop on the line. The unmoving train sat with the doors open. Yawning, he staggered out onto the platform and lifted the liquor out of his bag.

An irritated voice admonished him from the station speakers. "No drinking in the Underground." A station employee glowered at him from her post in the ticket booth.

"I would be delighted to share." Bone offered.

"I'll call S&P if you don't leave immediately." She snapped the intercom off.

Bone sauntered by the vending machines and exited through the turnstile. He leapt up the stairs leading out of Landing Station. A salty wind blew in with the tide. He wandered from the station entrance over to the monument, hopped up onto the marble encasement and began walking heel to toe with his arms outstretched out over the water, the liquor bottle in his hand.

Reclining on the edge of the encasement with his legs stretched out, he looked up at the sky and started singing. *"Like the stars above, and tides of the silvery sea, the moon, my love, always comes back to me."* Laughing, he stood up, his voice becoming a howl. "You can't say it, can you? You've never said it even once to me in fifteen years! Do you hear me, you disagreeable, disloyal, distrusting, disobedient ..." Bone wobbled and dropped the bottle. "Fuck."

☐ ♍ ♏ ♋ ■

Lacing her fingers through the grille, Zade floated on her back in the trash, watching the faint reflections of light play across the arch of the culvert six feet above her. The water under her shifted, the waves mixing the warm runoff from the sewers with the colder salt water. With each pulse of the incoming tide, the light in the culvert grew brighter as patches of iridescent blue began to cover the interior.

"Disavow, disapprove, disbelieve, discount, discover ..." The words became a chant as the level of water in the culvert continued to rise.

☐ ♍ ♏ ♋ ■

Bone sat, looking at the upright and unscathed bottle in the brambles below. He lowered himself down into the underbrush and careened forward. "Disgusting, disobliging, disgraceful, disinterested ..." His fingers wrapped around the neck of the bottle. "Disowned!" He put the Constalia to his mouth and upended it.

Lowering the bottle, he cocked his head and looked up at the sky. He spun around, searching the undergrowth with a confused expression. "Idiot, chasing after echoes." Sloppily recapping the bottle, he slid it into his bag, then climbed through the brambles toward the Underground station.

The wind dropped away. He looked over his shoulder to see a white shimmer

247

breaking the horizon. Rising, the full moon spun a luminous silver bridge across the water. The wind returned, carrying the clear sound of a woman's voice calling his name.

Bone lost his footing and slid down the gradient on his backside. Getting up, he brushed the dirt off the seat of his jeans and stumbled through the brush toward the water. Climbing over granite boulders, he gazed out at the ascending light. "Who are you? Where are you?" He raised his voice to carry over the sound of the waves.

"Bone? Here! Bone! I'm here!"

Bone sprinted to the edge of the culvert and dropped onto his stomach, looking over the edge into her face. "What are you doing in there, Zee?" He grabbed hold of the grille and tried to lift it. "I thought you were a sea witch come to drown me."

"It's welded shut. The tide's coming in." She thrashed against the grille. "The crabs are going to eat me."

Bone put his fingers over hers. "I'll be right back, Zee. Don't you let any of those fucking crabs touch you."

▽↗◢

He ran uphill over the rocks and into the Underground station. He snatched up the payphone's handset, put it to his ear, and then smacked it back into its cradle.

"The phone's out. My friend's trapped in the sewer pipe. Call emergency services to come get her out." He panted and sagged against the ticket booth.

The intercom clicked on. "You came in alone, and drunk."

"There's a person trapped in …" Bone stopped as the woman lifted her newspaper and blocked him out. She continued to ignore him as he pounded his fists on the glass.

Bone backed away with his hands up and went over to the row of vending machines. He wrenched the fire extinguisher off the wall and went back to the ticket booth. "Will you *please* call S&P?"

"Go sleep it off." The intercom snapped off.

Bone picked up the fire extinguisher and hefted it like a bat, smashing it into the glass of the booth. "*Now* will you call S&P?" He began using his impromptu weapon on the vending machines.

A sedan pulled up outside the station and an annoyed-looking man got out just as Bone ran by and pitched the extinguisher onto its hood. Two S&P cruisers flew into the lot with their lights and sirens on.

One of the uniformed officers walked over as the other officers pursued Bone. "Are you responding to the disorderly, Detective Todd?"

"No." Hauling the metal cylinder off his car, the detective shook his head. "Just checking out a tip from the Chief's crystal ball, Mr. Quail." He winced at the dent in his car's hood. "I hate working night shift on the full moon."

▽ ↗ ◢

Zade was sitting in her hospital bed, watching the saline and glucose drip through her IV, when Bone returned, carrying two cups of soft serve ice cream.

"I was inspired to give the officer outside a portion." He handed over one of the cups to her. "Don't worry, it was the vanilla. How are your hands? Do you need any help?"

"They're just scraped. The nurse said I have to keep them wrapped so they stay clean." Zade spooned some of the chocolate ice cream into her mouth.

Bone settled into the chair by the window with his breakfast. His reassuring smile faded. "Can I ask you something, Zee? You can, of course, tell me to fuck off. I'll understand completely."

She pushed her spoon into the melting ice cream and looked over at him expectantly. "Go for it."

"Why did you run out of Vicky's?"

"I dunno. I guess I thought Dis would hate me for being a Pierce." She shrugged and glanced away. "I got scared thinking about how he would treat me when he found out."

Bone narrowed his eyes. "You think that would matter to him more than your friendship?"

"You heard him at dinner that night we went out. He hates them."

"He's one of the last descendants of the Ornish clans. Hatred is possibly too tame a word to describe how any of them feel about that family. But that's not how he thinks of you."

"I don't know that much about them." She poked her spoon around her cup. "I didn't go to school, so I only know about Captain Pierce."

"As it turns out, they don't teach you everything in school anyway." Bone jabbed his spoon upright into the remains of his ice cream and set it on the bedside table. "It was only after I met Dis's family that I heard the clans' version of what happened." He glanced at her bandaged hands. "I'm not certain this is the best time for us to talk about this."

"So I'm right, he'll hate me."

"I was referring to you learning the Pierce family's history." Bone sighed. "The Ornish clans mostly kept to themselves on the little islands after Pierce's ship came down the coast and took this one. Captain Pierce was batshit crazy and thought the native people were using magic to turn into animals. Wolves, deer, seals, herons, that sort of thing. Under the auspices of the fur trade, the Pierce family started trapping all the animals in the area to prove it. That all changed when the Captain decided that seal skin was the best for magic." He grimaced. "The clans were already hostile to the fur trappers, but the seal slaughter enraged them. The clans came in their fishing boats in the middle of the night and set fire to the settlement. Supposedly, the clan elders took the Captain into the middle of the burning town and, well, only brought Pierce's skin out with them. Though Dis's father said that's Pierce propaganda. After that, the Pierce family sent for reinforcements, hunted the clans down, and killed everyone they could lay their hands on."

Zade looked horrified. "How did Dis's family survive?"

"His great-something grandmother and other clan elders were at St. Anna's in Newton trying to gain support for banning the fur trade. The Church stepped in to stop the war, taking the remaining Ornish under its protection." Bone glanced over at the door to the hospital room. "His father's family's intense grief, mixed with guilt, is very much alive for him, Zee. They grieve intensely for what is gone. Dis's father committed suicide a few days after his wife died. Dis says otherwise, but I believe he was trying to do the same when he crashed his bike five years ago." His head dropped. After a moment, he looked up at her with a kind smile. "I saw how he reacted when you went missing. You're like family to him, Zee. He could never hate you."

"He always sounds like he's on top of everything, you know?" Zade blinked back tears. "Keeping tabs on OC, keeping everyone moving, all the packages on time, always having all the detours and timetables. Getting the best route so you can get a chance at a triple. I feel like I've always had his voice in my ear, keeping me safe."

"Weird sullen little lump in the corner with a funny name, he was always getting bullied in school." Bone smiled. "Wouldn't fight back and didn't have any friends. I always thought he didn't know how to throw a punch. Idiot that I am." He held out the box of tissues.

She took the entire box. "You met him in school?"

"Oh, I was his number one tormentor. All the shit I got at home, I dumped on him." Bone picked up his melted ice cream. "Then, I made the mistake of following him to the swimming pool one day with a plan to ambush him."

Zade twisted her tissue. "What happened?"

"I watched him swim. Love can be an affliction, Zee. Completely mysterious, it strikes you down until you can't eat, sleep, or play a guitar. All because you saw your true love's unguarded joy and wasted away for want of being a part of it. To be the source of it."

▽ ↗ ◢

The mid-morning sun disappeared behind rainclouds. Dis knocked quietly on Zade's hospital room door and entered. Zade held her finger to her lips, nodding over to where Bone slept in the chair by the window. Dis set a coffee tray down on the table by the door and sat down in a chair on the other side of her bed. Rain tapped against the window. He looked down at her bandaged hands.

Bone yawned and blinked. He sat up rapidly when he saw Dis. The three sat in silence, listening to the rain grow louder. Bone got up, went over to the tray, and busied himself with a cup of coffee.

"I'm going to head home for a shower and a change of clothes. Shall I bring you anything when I come back later, Zee?" Bone kept his back to the room while he put on his coat.

"A cheese pizza would be great, thanks." She watched Dis. He kept his eyes on her hands.

"I'll plan to be back by two."

As the door shut, Dis looked up at Zade.

"Did they find him? Is he dead?" She plucked at the blanket fitfully until Dis cradled her bandaged hand between his.

"He's in ICU, under guard and shackled to the bed. I went and checked. He's not going anywhere."

"Can't be a very good guard if they let you get that close." She gave him a half-hearted smile.

"S&P is feeling kindly toward me at the moment." He paused, looking down at her bandaged fingers. "He killed Jeniel. It was her body you …" He clenched his jaw. "I'd rather the others didn't know about it yet."

Zade squeezed his hand.

He glanced up, scanned her face, and frowned. "You haven't slept. If you ask, they'll give you a sedative."

She shook her head. "I told Dr. Gray I want to stay awake to eat. Only my feet hurt."

"I will stay and watch over you if that will help you sleep."

She started to say something, then stopped when the door opened. Dis released her hand.

"Zade!" Vicky set down a shopping bag and rushed over. She bent over and stroked Zade's hair. "I was so worried. I came as soon as Dis called me. Avery wanted to come with me to see you, but I thought it for the best …" She dropped her hand and rushed through her words, looking at the floor. "Our cousin Generosity died in a car accident overseas last week and we've been with our aunt. Avery was very close to Gen, and when the news came of what you had been through, it was too much for him."

She sat on the side of the bed. "When he's a bit calmer I will bring him to visit, and when our aunt is less upset, we will introduce you to her." She gave a weak smile. "I'm so glad you're okay."

"I'm sorry to hear about your cousin." Dis watched Vicky.

"Thank you." She shifted on the bed and indicated the bag to Zade. "I brought a few of my things for you to wear. Can I get you anything?"

"No, thank you." She shook her head. "I'm sorry about your cousin."

"I wish you'd had the chance to meet Gen. I think you would have liked her." Vicky stood up and a guilty look flashed across her face. "I'm sorry I can't stay longer. I have to get back to my brother. He's not doing well. I just needed to see you were okay with my own eyes. You're so lucky." She bent down and kissed Zade's forehead.

"90-32 has impeccable luck, don't you think?" Dis propped his head up on his fist. "Wins at everything from motorcycle races to surviving serial killers."

"If she called heads or tails, it would be as she wished it." Vicky stroked Zade's hair again.

"The best luck." Dis kept his eyes on Vicky.

"The finest." Vicky smiled at him. "Call me if you need anything." She squeezed Zade's hand and waved to Dis.

Zade waited until the door closed. "It's all about the heart, isn't it?"

Her friend angled his head to look at her. "Depends on what you are referring to in particular. Often, it is very much a problem with the brain."

"If you wanted to make the coin go a certain way, heads or tails, you'd need to influence its heart." Zade leaned back into the pillows. She stared out the window at the clouds moving over the city, then closed her eyes. "I wish the patient in the next room would stop crying."

"What patient? Zade?" Dis fell silent and watched her sleep.

☐ ♍ ♏ ♋ ■

Quail waited for the ink to dry before folding the letter neatly into thirds and placing it into an envelope. He wrote a name on it in elaborate cursive script and set it on the pile with the rest. Standing up from his desk, he adjusted his vest and patted the watch in his pocket. After a moment, he removed it and unhooked the chain, letting it pool next to his pipe on the desk.

He brushed his fingertips over the surface of the desk on his way toward the door of his office. Upon reaching it, he paused and squared his shoulders. He exited, shutting the door behind him. He stared down at the crystal doorknob and tapped it three times.

When he reached the door of the shop, he turned back. "Thank you." Bowing his head, Quail stepped out of the Shining Star and into the spring night.

He locked the door, tapping the latch three times before withdrawing the key. As he walked toward Unity Station, white plum blossoms rained down from the trees along the sidewalk. The petals clung to his clothing and swirled around his feet.

The dumpster stench rolling out of Plum Alley prompted him to hold his breath as he approached the narrow break between the buildings. Quail gave a muffled cry as hands wrapped around his neck and mouth and violently hauled him into the alleyway. His assailant rammed him into the dumpster and forced his head up, exposing his throat. Quail kicked and struggled, clawing at the arm holding his head. His legs were kicked out from under him and he fell forward onto his knees. He stared up in shock as a curved blade bit deeply into his neck.

His assailant rifled through his pockets, dropped him, and walked away. Quail collapsed sideways, clasping his throat. As he gasped for breath, a white petal slipped off his shoulder and landed in the blood pooling around his head.

AS THE LIGHT CHANGED TO RED at State and Duncan, a courier fell in behind Zade. Grinning, she dropped her hand off her throttle and flashed it behind her. The other courier responded by revving the bike's engine and releasing the clutch to bring the yellow motorcycle alongside hers. Avery flipped his helmet visor up and nodded.

He revved his throttle again and Zade nodded, indicating the street. Avery flashed his left hand over his tank. Zade revved her engine in response. The instant the light turned green the two motorcycles raced through the intersection.

Zade slipped ahead, banking a hard left onto Green. She led Avery across Market Street, through a series of alleyways to East Market, and across a parking lot to the Straight. She swung around the gray concrete base of the Central Municipal Parking Garage and drove in, skirting the arm of the automatic barrier. Glancing into her mirror, she watched Avery follow her, then gunned it through the ground floor.

She hopped her bike onto the pedestrian walkway, with an inch-wide gap between her machine and the wall, and exited through the north side entrance.

Avery exited the garage a full block behind her and accelerated, dodging the door of a taxi as it opened. A car length behind her, he kicked into a higher gear to pass. Dropping her speed, she let him by and took a sudden left onto Carlisle Lane. She got up on her pegs, coming out onto the Straight a full two blocks ahead of him.

She had her helmet off and was standing next to her bike at the Pit when Avery pulled up next to her. She gave him a wide smile. "Someday, you might even beat me."

Taking his helmet off, Avery frowned. "If I knew the same shortcuts …"

Snorting, Zade started to walk away, shaking her head.

"I can beat you on any standard route right now." The young man's challenge rang out and the other couriers glanced over. "I'll beat you on the Solstice."

Zade turned to look back at him. "You think so?" She shared a grin with the other couriers.

Avery dismounted and set his helmet on his seat. "I bet you a week's pay I can do it."

"Deal." Zade held her hand out and he shook it.

▽↗◢

The waxy green leaves of summer replaced the spring blossoms. Zade sat on her stoop and watched the northern sky darken until the street lights began to hum. She walked down to her bike, started the engine, and rode off.

▽↗◢

Outside his loft, Bone casually sat on his motorcycle, waiting for her to park. "I'm not certain this is a good idea, Zee."

Zade flipped up her faceplate. "Otter's tailing him and piping the info back to Frankie for me."

"I am not questioning your ability. I'm questioning your sanity. If he wanted us there, me there, he would have asked." He looked at the ground. "He'll be fine on his own."

"Iris said after he got back from Quail's funeral, he was in the worst mood she can remember him ever being in. Worse than when you sent him the backstage pass. Now he's going to see Pierce alone." She watched as he dragged his fingers through his hair. "Are you willing to risk him going by himself?"

Bone took a pair of clear riding glasses out of his pocket and started up his machine. The huge black and white touring bike roared to life. He dragged his boots on the pavement, easing out of his parking space. He flexed his jaw muscles and nodded to her.

"Frankie, I've got the backup. Where's the package?" Zade was forced to shout over the rumble of her companion's engine.

"30-84's just gone through the tunnel. Coming up in the Hinterlands. I called over to the Red Star dispatcher and got confirmation. The taxi is headed to 1111 Long Shore Way."

"Crafty, Frankie. Dis would be impressed." Zade grinned as she and Bone headed north.

"Pissed, more likely."

"How many you got on tap for us in case we need to make a scene?"

"OC has fifteen, YC is lending ten. Want me to stage them at Shipwreck?"

"How'd you get to be so good at this?"

The sound of the night dispatcher's laughter came through Zade's headset.

Bone rode behind her down Market with his feet up on his highway pegs. When Zade flashed her hand at him, Bone grinned and lifted his hand up. She smacked her faceplate down and opened the throttle, racing down the remaining length of Market. Bone's bike thundered alongside hers as they merged toward the Riverway Bridge.

Dis sat in the back of the taxi, examining the handle of his cane. He traced the fossil ivory down to the silver band and wrapped his hands around the blackthorn stick. He rested his forehead on the handle, then sat up.

The car swung off the main road. The suburban landscape fell away behind trees as the properties increased in size. Dis watched the treetops rustle in the sea breeze as the road curved around the edge of the cliff and into a private drive.

They passed a gatehouse and Dis turned to look out the rear window at the last glimmer of the sky above the sea. He gripped his cane as the taxi approached the main house.

"You want me to wait?" The driver leaned over the back of the seat.

"No, I'm not sure how long I'll be." Dis pressed a couple of bills into her hand. "I'll call for another."

"I can wait until morning." She smiled at him as he got out of the back seat. Dis straightened his suit jacket and started toward the main entrance.

As the tip of his cane struck the lantern-lined walkway, the front door opened. Nash inclined his head. "Good evening, Mr. Mthdys. Please allow me to express my sincere sympathy for your loss. Mr. Quail was always very kind to me."

Dis did not reply.

"This way, please." Nash led him through the mansion's ground floor, passing through the treasure rooms displaying the family's collection of rare antiquities. Statuary and gold and silver ritual objects from around the world lined the corridor in temperature-controlled exhibit cases. Dis scanned the shelves in the library on the way to the rearmost section of the house. Nash quietly slid open a set of white paneled doors and gestured for Dis to enter.

"Thank you, Nash." Chairwoman Pierce rose from her chair. A vase of lilies complemented the floral pattern of the ornate brass screen covering the cold fireplace next to her. She indicated a chair opposite her own. "Please join me, Mr. Mthdys."

"Shall I bring any refreshments?" Nash paused on the threshold.

Pierce glanced at her guest and shook her head. "I will ring if we require anything." She watched Dis settle into his chair and then took her own. "I appreciate you coming here this evening. Islo was a dear friend to both of us. I understand he has left his clients in your care? I am hoping you will include my family."

"Your message stated you had information regarding his death you wished to tell me in person." Dis spun the blackthorn cane in his hand.

"It's about Islo's last phone message. He had discovered something regarding the man the papers are calling the Cutter." Pierce rose from her seat and began pacing. The older woman twisted at the rings on her fingers. "My family is still in danger, Mr. Mthdys. You must help us." She paused and glanced at him. "Vicky tells me you know her and her brother Avery socially. Surely, you must have some concern for their well-being?"

"I've gone through the records of both courier companies and correlated the spike of last year's accidents with pickups and deliveries. The majority may be random incidents, but there is enough of an overlap with pickup locations at known associates of your company to confirm my suspicions. I know you sent the Black Cake out with my couriers, Pierce."

She turned away from him. "My family was, and is, being attacked. I am using the skills at my disposal to protect them. If anyone died from my actions they were selected randomly and without malice. It was a chance event."

"Neither you nor your family are eligible for this particular lottery." Dis settled back, looking at her. "It's still murder."

"No court would find me guilty." Pierce looked over her shoulder at him.

Dis ran his fingers over his cane and arched his eyebrow at her. "I'm not a court."

"I am telling you the person responsible for killing Islo was behind kidnapping your courier."

His expression was contemptuous. "Last time you said this same person sent out the Black Cake."

The woman clung to the side of her chair. "You think I killed him."

He watched her for a moment and then shook his head. "No. I don't believe you would. I believe you valued him as a means to ensure your family's future, even though he failed to protect your daughter from being murdered."

She inhaled sharply and turned to face him. "Then why will you not help me?"

"You intentionally caused the death of my couriers." He rose from his seat. "Your daughter betrayed my trust and assaulted me."

"My daughter is … Generosity was very sick." Pierce sagged against the side of her chair. "But I can't believe you would kill Islo to stop him from helping us."

Dis shrugged, leaning on his cane. "I haven't, to my knowledge, killed anyone. Directly or indirectly. I may be guilty of assigning a delivery leading to a legitimate accident, but it is a risk I have taken myself."

"Your hatred is strong enough to allow you to watch us die without lifting a finger to help," Pierce stated bitterly. "After all this time, you hate us so much that you would permit our enemies to take away our future?"

"Has the possibility occurred to you that I do not want your family to *have* a future?" His expression hardened. "I live without my people daily. I live in a city built on their graves. Imagine schoolchildren taking trips through this house and seeing your possessions behind ropes and glass. Your holy places renamed to honor your killer, the person who slaughtered your family. Perhaps my heart will feel compassion for you on that day."

"You also curse us." Pierce's look was icy. Her hands trembled. "There is no one who will stand with us now. Everyone is against us. Quail was wrong. You will not help us. You stand against us. You also wish to see us dead."

"I haven't called up your death, Mercy Pierce, nor your family's."

"Why should I believe you? Your word is dust, just as your precious clans are dust." Her eyes burned with wild rage. "All of our family's enemies will be dust. If I must, I will sacrifice every life in this city to protect them."

Dis looked at her in disgust. "You know I have bound your attempts to harvest the lives of my people. I can and I *will* prevent you from using the Black

Cake to kill anyone else. I will break your magic into grains of salt and scatter it to the winds. This hallowed city is under my protection, Pierce."

Pierce's face twisted into a mask of rage. With a howl, she lunged, reaching behind the fire screen.

She leveled the point of an antique sword at his chest. Dis froze. "If you kill me with that, a court will indeed find you guilty of murder."

"I will not leave an enemy alive on the battlefield to attack again." She thrust the sword at him. "*You will not take everything from me.*"

He knocked her thrust away with his cane and retreated. "Nash?" Dis rapped on the door. "The Chairwoman may need a cup of tea, or something stronger."

The assistant slid the doors apart just as Pierce lunged toward Dis. Missing Dis, she impaled the door.

"Where's your car, Nash?" Dis continued to back away.

Pierce wrenched the sword, trying to free the weapon.

Nash placed himself between his employer and Dis. "It's at the gatehouse. The keys are in it. I will try to calm her down."

"Don't get yourself killed in the process."

Dis was halfway down the driveway when the headlights of three motorcycles came through the gates.

Bone pulled up to Dis. "30-32, ready for pickup."

Dis laughed and climbed on behind him.

"Where to?" Zade rolled up.

"Pier Alley." Dis rested his cane across his lap. "I'm buying at The Schooner."

"You didn't murder Vicky's aunt, did you?" Otter looked nervously at the mansion.

"Almost the other way around."

Zade waited at the gate for the other couriers. "Frankie, this is 90-32. Package is in hand; you can send everybody home. I'll buy them all beer for their trouble. Thanks for wrangling."

"No problem. You can buy me a beer, too."

Zade grinned as she glided into the curve at the base of the drive. "Deal."

Dis stared at the ocean as they swung around the coast. They rode back through the residential areas of the Hinterlands and into the tunnel. Dis closed his eyes in the underground passage as his estranged lover opened the throttle and they descended under the river.

▽↗◢

As they emerged in Uptown, Bone slowed for the lights at the Straight. Otter dropped alongside and popped up his faceplate.

"Nice to see you on one of those again, dispatch."

"Take a picture. It might be a while before you see it next."

"They make automatics."

Dis's reply was drowned out as the bikes started moving again.

The motorcycles merged into the traffic on Sterling. Zade led them through a maze of narrow streets, flashing her fingers in the air as they came around onto Pierce Street.

Bone glanced over his shoulder. "Hold on, love."

The three motorcycles raced down the street, taking the yellow center strip in front of the Pierce Hotel. Zade zipped into a parking spot at the top of the walkway, the other riders quickly coming up next to her.

"You practicing for the Solstice race?" Otter unhooked his helmet strap.

With his boots on the ground, Bone balanced his motorcycle and waited for Dis to dismount.

"Avery made a bet with me." Zade set her earpiece and gloves into her helmet.

"Ah, can't let your new little brother kick your ass in front of all the girls." Otter shook his fist in mock outrage as he joined her on the sidewalk.

Zade made a dismissive noise. "As if."

Once his passenger was safely on the sidewalk, Bone put his kickstand down and dismounted.

"Thank you." Dis smiled. "If this place doesn't have a table free, we can try the Pierce Hotel … or maybe not." He started down Pier Alley.

"Things didn't go well with Pierce?" Zade glanced at Dis as they walked over the cobblestones.

"I'm hoping her personal assistant isn't dead."

"What did you do to him?"

"It seems I inadvertently declared war on the Pierce family and put his employer in a killing mood."

"What were you hoping to accomplish instead?" Bone put his riding glasses into the inner pocket of his jacket.

Dis looked at him over his shoulder. "To ascertain if she had anything to do with Quail's death."

Otter was the only one who looked surprised. "I thought he was a mugging victim?"

"Generosity Pierce was also one of the Cutter's victims, but her mother is having it covered up to avoid a public scandal." Dis tightened his grip on the handle of his cane. "Pierce thinks the Cutter's boss is still at large and Quail found out who it is. That's why he was killed." Dis stepped down into the entrance of a basement-level restaurant and approached the hostess. "Table for four by the water, if you can."

The woman was about to say something when she caught sight of Bone. "Let me see what I can do." She quickly walked into the main room.

Zade looked approvingly at Bone. "You made her shy!"

Bone shrugged. "Occupational hazard."

A moment later the manager appeared with the hostess in tow. "Right this way, Mr. Bonnrey. We have a table for your party on the deck overlooking the water."

"A deck table." Otter hung his arm over Zade's shoulder.

"Overlooking the water."

Dis watched the two couriers bound out to the elegant open-air dining area. "It's a little bit of magic, isn't it?" Bone indicated the interior of the restaurant. "Fame and wealth making people act like this now when they used to ignore us."

Dis locked eyes with him. "Fortune favors the beautiful." He stepped out onto the deck, leaving Bone staring after him.

❧⊱ɞ⑨❶☙⊰

Outside a private room in the ICU, a uniformed S&P officer yawned. She rubbed her neck, blinked rapidly, and turned another page of her paperback. Glancing up from the pages, she watched a night shift nurse in green scrubs pass by. The man's expression was clouded as he marked a sheet on the clipboard he was poring over.

Her eyes snapped over to the bank of elevator doors as the arrival chime sounded. She jammed her book into the back of her belt. Another officer flipped up his hand to her in greeting as he got off. She relaxed and smiled warmly as the heavy-set man stopped at the nursing station and signed in.

"You're early, Jelly. Your woman kick you out for eating crackers in bed again?"

Both officers pressed against the wall of the hallway as a pair of ICU staff dashed by with a medical cart.

"Hi, Grace. Detective Fuller sent me over. She wants you to head over to the Tank before you're done for the night. You should hustle so you don't miss her. Said she had news for you about that scholarship program." His eyes flickered away from the other officer's.

"Oh, that's a favor for my kid. He's trying to get into a dentistry school out in the Hinterlands after he graduates from St. Anna's High." Grace smiled fondly. "Well, I appreciate you coming over early like this for me."

"Not a problem. Anything I need to know about ..." Jelly jerked his thumb toward the private hospital room. "... that wasn't in the briefing?" His eyes darted to the black hands of the clock above the nursing station.

"I heard him laughing and singing sea songs to himself. Gives me the chills when he starts up. Wish he'd have just stayed in that goddamn coma." She shuddered. "Oh, and the radio doesn't work for shit on this floor, so you can't call in for an unscheduled piss break. Just use the can in the room with the door open if it's an emergency." She locked eyes with her replacement. "But don't let Sergeant Uphimself know I told you to do that."

"I won't." He took up position in front of the open doorway.

"Okay, see you later."

"See you, Gracie." Jelly watched the other officer walk over to the elevators. The vague smile on his face faded as the doors shut behind her. His eyes flickered over to the floor numbers above the next elevator. Sweat beaded on his forehead.

The doors opened. A male nurse in scrubs sneezed into the crook of his elbow as he walked into the ICU. Jelly exhaled sharply, watching the new arrival. He adjusted his collar, tugging at it with two fingers.

"Excuse me, officer. If you could step aside, I need to check on my patient." A quiet female voice spoke over Jelly's shoulder. A surgical mask covered the lower half of her face. She waited with her head down, examining a patient chart.

He started to turn around.

"Please keep your eyes on the elevators, as you were instructed."

Jelly inhaled sharply and stared forward. The woman slipped behind him into the private room.

She walked quickly through the dim space, passing around the monitoring equipment clustered near the bed. The Cutter's eyes opened as she approached. He rotated his head to watch her tug down the neck of her scrubs.

"You're not Maisey, or, or that turd of a boy." His tongue traced his lower lip. The chain cuffing him to the bed rattled as his right hand snapped out from under the covers, reaching for her.

"It's just something for the pain." Her eyes remained cold as she peeled the heart monitor node off his chest and quickly pasted it onto her own. The monitor beeped once and then resumed a normal cardiac pattern.

"I've told you people before, I need to finish my work. I haven't the time for your pills." The old man's voice sounded peevish and tired. "Rot will set in, or they'll stiffen into uselessness. I've made a commitment to my employer."

Without replying, she removed the end of the IV line from the catheter in the crook of his arm. Producing a syringe from the pocket of her uniform, she inserted the needle into the catheter and injected a large quantity of air into his vein. She snapped the IV line back into place and waited a moment, watching him closely.

The Cutter glanced from the back of his hand up to her face. "What are you…"

She jabbed him in the throat with her gloved hand, crushing his trachea. His chest heaved and he gasped, shuddering, his hands thrashing on the bed rails. The pattern on the cardiac monitor's graph blipped upward once and then continued at an even rest rate as she waited, watching him convulse and then lie still. With a clipped nod, she peeled the node off her chest and reapplied it to his. The monitor flatlined, producing a strident alarm. The woman slipped into the dark bathroom.

Jelly pressed against the wall of the ICU corridor as the crash cart team rushed past him into the room.

☙ ❦ ⑨ ❿ ❧

Otter nudged his empty plate to the side of the tablecloth. "So you think there is a killer after the Pierce family?" He slung his arm over the back of his chair. "Or did the Cutter pick Generosity Pierce randomly?"

Dis folded his napkin on the cleared table. "I think Mercy Pierce believes it was intentional. Generosity may have been involved in tampering with our luck, along with her mother."

Zade picked up her crumpled napkin. "Then who killed Quail?"

Dis cast a sideways glance at Bone. "Quail had a premonition that he was going to die soon. Beyond that, I have no evidence it was anything but a mugging."

"You mentioned Pierce thinks this alleged killer is a shared enemy." Bone stared out over the deck railing. "Do you agree?"

"It's on Pierce's orders that S&P is hiding the fact that the Cutter killed her daughter." Dis drummed his fingers on the table. "S&P thinks the Cutter kidnapped Zade because she interrupted him or because of quota instructions, if his alleged employer exists at all. It should be an interesting trial, if he's found mentally fit to testify."

Zade finished folding her napkin. "We've talked about this before but I still don't know how luck can be fucking stolen."

"Thinking ahead for the Solstice race?" Bone looked at her over the rim of his glass.

"Seems having one family member stealing it is enough."

"You're not a member of that deranged family." Dis locked eyes with Zade.

Otter looked uncomfortable. "How can they steal it, anyway?"

"It depends on how you think of luck. Zade mentioned influencing the heart of the coin." Dis produced a silver coin from his pocket and set it on the tablecloth. "If we make bets on the outcome and you influence the result with your luck, are you cheating? If you only win the stakes we agreed on ahead of time, is it stealing?"

"If we both agree we each have some portion of luck, then it's not cheating if mine's better." Zade picked up the coin.

"It's only cheating if the coin is mucked with." Otter held up his own coin next to the first. "If the coin and the toss are fair, then it's a fair contest."

"Then luck is a skill." Bone leaned back in his chair.

"It is more of a talent." Dis kept his eyes on the coins.

Bone looked away.

Zade frowned. "How can you steal a talent or a skill?"

"If they are killing people for it, maybe it can be stolen at the moment of death." Otter overlaid his coin on the one Zade held.

"Then Mercy Pierce really was killing our friends for their luck?" She shook her head. "That's fucked up."

"She thinks it so. But that doesn't make it so. If the deaths were productive to her cause, it was because she was exchanging them, cashing them in, if you will." Dis held his hand out for the coin Zade held. "The gamble is who is holding the Black Cake when it is activated. The stakes are the lives of the participants carrying it. If Pierce played fairly, there would be a risk to her as well, as anyone playing the game could win her life."

"Bear in mind, this is all impossible and quite insane." Bone flipped his hand over.

"We return to the question of how to increase one's luck." Dis tossed the coin. "Call it."

"Heads."

"You use it." Zade watched Dis catch the coin and smack it onto the back of his hand. He lifted his hand, revealing the solemn face of the coin looking up. "Like a skill or a talent, the more you use it, the better it gets."

"Or you could distill it." Bone mused.

"In either case, the person with the best luck would also be the one taking the most risks." Dis looked at Zade. "Intentionally."

▽↗◢

Leaving the restaurant, Bone hung back to walk beside Dis. "Do you want me to run you home?"

"The station isn't very far. Thank you for the ride earlier."

Bone came to a halt in the alley. Dis stopped a pace ahead and watched his couriers put on their riding gear. Resting his hands on the handle of his cane, he looked back at Bone. "If you wish to say something, say it."

"If I say something clever, you will brush it aside. If I say something raw, you will run. If I ask you to stay, you will leave. If I apologize, you will be distant."

"I will stay and hear whatever you need to say and then I am going home."

268

"Why do you always walk out on me when we fight?"

Dis shifted to face him. "I suspect that when we fight, you are seeking to provoke me into physically striking you."

Bone shuddered.

Otter looked at Zade and jerked his head. "Should we wait or bail?"

Zade glanced at the two men in the alley. "Bail." She started her bike up. "See you tomorrow at the Pit."

$$\triangledown \nearrow \blacktriangle$$

Zade parked her bike and removed her helmet. She sat silently, straddling the machine and staring at the entrance to her apartment building. After ten minutes she went inside and got ready for bed. Two hours later, she was still awake and staring up at the ceiling. Her downstairs neighbor's door slammed. She flew out of bed and into a crouched position against the wall.

Ducking her head between her knees, Zade slowed her breathing. She put on her stained gray sweatshirt and cargo pants and headed out the building's back door to Gilbert's Market.

Carrying out two plastic bags of groceries, she tugged her hood up, walked down Pearl to Green, and turned right. She glanced up at the spray-painted tag above a dumpster and went around to the back of the building. She pushed open a fire door, propped it open with a brick, and stepped inside.

In the corridor, she found a fresh tag and continued forward to a stairwell. The cement under her fingertips gave way to brick as she felt her way down into the building's basement. She walked along in the dark until her hand grazed a metal door. Taking a breath, she rapped a knuckle against it.

The door opened and a flashlight shone in her face. Zade held up a grocery bag. The light shifted out of her eyes. She passed the bag through the gap and waited until the door opened enough for her to slip through.

"Stay to the right." A hand shoved her gently to one side as she walked into the room.

She put her hand on the inner wall and kept moving. Flashlights winked on and off as she made her way past groups huddled on mounds of piled cardboard. A swinging light beckoned her.

"Share it." The woman dropped the beam of light from Zade's face.

The members of the group moved aside to let her onto the cardboard. Once she was seated, she began passing out pieces of fruit and packages of food. The scent of orange peels and chocolate cookies mingled with the odors of unwashed bodies and dirty clothing. When the bag was empty, she crawled to the back of the cardboard and lay down. Hands tucked blankets around her and she fell asleep to the sound of the other women talking.

▽↗◢

Two S&P officers walked up behind Dis as he exited Claremont Station the next morning.

"You're coming with us." Officer Low wrenched his arm as the other officer swung open the door of a cruiser. Low pushed Dis's head down and shoved him into the back seat. She said something in a quiet voice to the other officer and he nodded in response.

Dis watched them through the safety glass between the seats. "Good morning, officers."

They ignored him. The lights and siren snapped on. Dis watched the cruiser carve through the morning commuter traffic. After leaving the Straight, the officer behind the wheel shut off the siren. The cruiser drove down Carlisle Lane, under the Midtown Byway, then turned into the Point of Graves.

Gravel crunched under the car's tires as they entered the park near the cemetery. Dis slipped his knife out of his bag and into the front pocket of his jeans as the car bounced over the grass leading to the boat launch. The driver parked the car on the ramp and lifted the parking brake. Both officers got out, leaving their doors wide open.

Fuller approached, pounded on the roof of the car, and leaned in. "You're a stubborn man, Mr. Mthdys." She got in behind the wheel and angled the rearview mirror to look at him. "By the way, are you profoundly stupid or do you actually have a death wish?"

"At the moment, the former."

Fuller smiled. "I wish you had accepted the boss lady's offer. Or at the very least taken my advice to stay away from her family. Why did you bother to go over there last night? Did you think she would get down on her knees and beg you?"

"The possibility had occurred to me."

"Not with *her* pride." The detective leaned forward and looked up through the windshield. "They say people who drown in the sunshine go straight up to heaven. If you believe that sort of thing. You do, don't you?" She sat back, watching him in the mirror.

"It's a corruption of the belief that the Sky-Parent transforms the drowning into seagulls." Dis rolled his left hand away from himself. "The Cutter's supposed heart attack is front page news this morning. You killed him."

"Well, not me personally."

"S&P killed Quail." Dis snuck his hand back into his bag.

"No one on Pierce's payroll would have taken him out. Besides, he was useful to us, too. If the Cutter case went to trial, the truth about her daughter would be made public. The boss lady is tired of scandal. Same reason your misadventure with her daughter fell between the cracks." Fuller offered him a piece of gum through the slot in the safety glass. "She would have made it up to you, you know? Quail thought the world of you and told her what a skilled magician you are. There's a kind of irony in all of you people doing each other in using hands-on methods, just like the rest of us would. Where's the magic in that?"

Taking his hands out of his bag, Dis accepted the gum and unwrapped the foil. "Magic is a matter of perspective. You have to be sitting in the right seat to see the show properly."

"Your view's going to be pretty wet soon enough. By the way, I'd make it quicker if I could, but we've got to make it look like a drowning, for Mother Ida's sake. You understand."

Dis chewed his gum. "You seem like the type who enjoys gambling rather than theater."

"Depends on the game and the stakes." She turned around to look at him through the glass.

"The game appears to be of your making." Dis gestured at the front of the car. "I want to know if you are willing to make a bet with me on it."

The woman narrowed her eyes.

"I'm going to bet I can use magic to win your game. In return, you will leave me and mine alone."

"Why should I gamble on a game I'm already winning?"

"That's the only kind you should ever bet on." Dis grinned wolfishly. "The sure kind."

Fuller unwrapped a fresh piece of gum. "If you did manage it, Pierce would just hire someone else to put you in the ground. She's skittish as hell right now. Which, by the way, is partially your fault."

"I'm only asking if you and I have a deal." He stretched his arms out along the top of the back seat.

"I've always wanted to see real magic. You're on." She shifted the car into neutral and then got out of the vehicle, leaning across the front seat. "Ready?"

Dis brought his hands to his bag. "Ready."

Fuller released the emergency brake and the car rolled toward the harbor. As soon as the front tires slipped into the water, she headed up the slope to join the other two officers. She turned to watch the cruiser submerge. It bobbed once before disappearing. She waited for ten minutes. "Give it another fifteen and then call it in."

"90-32 AT MARKET SQUARE. You got anything?" Zade yawned and leaned over the railing outside of the Dovecot Bakery. Behind her, the patter of conversation ebbed and flowed as office workers and retail clerks ate their breakfast on the bakery's patio. A woman with silver hair pulled back into a severe bun sat at the table directly behind the courier. She opened her newspaper and shook it, glancing disapprovingly at Zade's back.

"Morning, 90-32. I've got a run for you out to the Hinterlands." Iris' voice rang through Zade's headset.

"Where's Dis?"

"He hasn't shown up yet. Before you get worked up, there's a breakdown in the inbound train tunnel from the Point. He's probably stuck in it. You want this run?"

The courier yawned again. "Sorry, yeah. I'll take the milk run."

"Pickup at 19 Grove, Suite 2082. Going to 110 Turtle Drive, out in the Hinterlands. Going to a Doctor Greyer's office."

Zade tossed her coffee in the trash and vaulted over the railing.

The courier wove around a bus and headed for 19 Grove. When she arrived at the law office, the intern behind the reception desk stared at her.

Zade glanced at him as she put her thumb recorder away. "What's your name?"

The teenager's eyes went wide. "Greg. Greg Moxene."

She beckoned to him and walked toward the exit. "You like bikes, Mox?" The intern trailed behind her.

"My grandma does…" The teen swallowed rapidly and nodded as they approached her parked motorcycle. His eyes darted from the machine to the rider and back.

"You know how to ride yet?" She watched him lick his lips and shake his head. "When you do, you come over to Uptown Deliveries and tell them Zade said to give you a chance."

▽↗◢

After finishing her delivery, Zade waited at the traffic light at the corner of Taylor and Greeves. She leaned back and cocked her head at a raggedy man selling flowers outside the gates of Rest and Be Thankful Cemetery. Battered green buckets sat at his feet, containing bunches of yellow and pink flowers wrapped in cellophane. The bouquet he was holding began to slip out of his fingers and he snapped upright, his eyes meeting Zade's. He smiled at her and beckoned.

With a sigh, she flipped on her turn signal and eased out of the line of traffic. "Dispatch, 90-32. Iris, I'm going to take a break at Rest&Be for a bit." She parked her bike against the cracked curb and killed the engine.

"You give 'em my love while you're at it."

"Will do." Zade took off her helmet and gloves. She popped open her hardcase and locked her gear inside before walking over to the flower seller.

"One for five, three for ten." He held out a bouquet tied with a purple ribbon.

"Just one." Zade dug into her hip pocket. "Keep the change."

He hunched down and selected a bunch. "Here, you take these. Best I got.

They'll last. Been keeping them in sugar water mixed with vinegar and bleach."

Swinging her messenger bag around, Zade tucked the flowers inside. The loose white quartz skittered as she walked up the winding drive into the cemetery.

The branches of trees swayed overhead in the breeze. She moved slowly past old fallen monuments covered in moss and crypts barely visible under thick creeping vines.

The trees began to thin and the elaborate marble sculptures gave way to simple granite blocks. The sweet smell of mown hay hung in the air. Seed fluff floated in the wind.

Wiping her hair out of her eyes, Zade branched off the main drive onto a smaller path, stopping next to a newer headstone. She squatted in front of it and ran her fingers along the inscription.

"Sorry I haven't been by more often." Zade reached into her bag, took out the flowers, and placed them beneath the marker. "Otter says Ju's doing better." The courier squinted at the ground. "I still don't know what the fuck is going on … I'll probably be in here next to you any day now. Doubt I'll make it another year at this rate." She stood up and dusted her hands on her thighs. "I got to get back. Iris said to give you her love." She stepped back onto the path. "I miss you, rockstar."

▽ ↗ ◢

The flower seller and his buckets were gone when Zade got back to her motorcycle. She took her gear out of the hardcase and put her headset on. "Dispatch, 90-32 ready for next pickup. Any sign of Dis yet?"

"90-32, I need you to come back to the depot and run a package out to 30-54."

"I'm on the wrong side of the tunnel for it, Iris." Holding her helmet loosely in one hand, Zade watched the traffic on Taylor. "I don't recognize that courier's number. They new?"

"Hold."

Zade put her helmet back on and started up her bike.

$$\triangledown \nearrow \blacktriangle$$

When she arrived back at the depot, the door to the dispatcher's booth was standing open. "Hello?" She left her engine running.

Iris waved her up to the booth. She was toggling the queues when Zade stuck her head in. "He's waiting by the payphone at the Point of Graves." She pressed a heavy paper sack into the courier's arms.

Zade glanced at the bag and then back at Iris. The mechanic had already resumed her post in front of the monitors. The courier lengthened the straps on her bag and stuffed the sack in as she headed down the stairs. With a last look at the booth, she headed out.

She found Dis lying on the top of a picnic table, soaking wet. He had stripped down to his black tank top and jeans. Half of a white brick rested on his stomach. He turned his head as she approached.

She took off her helmet and headset and winced at him. "Iris asked me to bring this to you." She set the package on the bench and looked down into his mismatched eyes. "What have you been doing?"

Dis turned his head away and stared at the sunlight flickering between the clouds. "S&P tried to drown me. Pierce sent them." His voice seethed with repressed fury.

She frowned at him. "You weren't kidding last night about a war?"

Drawing a deep breath, Dis sat up and opened the sack, taking out a pair of boots and dry clothes. "No. I think I've figured it out."

"Figured what out? Are you sure you're okay?"

"I've figured out the Pierce family's curse."

"They really are cursed?" She sat on the picnic table next to him. "By your people?"

"I suspect it's much older." Dis looked over at the colonial-era cemetery.

"Can you undo it?"

Dis held the brick in front of his right eye. "It depends on two things." He handed her the broken chunk.

She held it up, looking at the shattered end. "Are you going to tell me, or do I have to guess?"

"You'll have to win the Solstice race, and I'll have to win the war." He untied his soaked boots. "Do me a favor, run my gear back to the depot, and tell Iris I'll be back in two hours." He glanced over. "Don't say anything over the radio or say anything to anyone else about this. Especially Bone."

□ ♍ ♏ ♋ ■

Dis followed a worn path out of the Point of Graves to the sidewalk. Swinging his sodden messenger bag around, he took out his journal. He used the edge of his thumbnail to separate two damp pages in the center. "There's no sense in it." He read aloud. "It's just a heap of misery up there on Gallows Hill. They should tear it down. It's just blighted ground, full of angry ghosts." Slipping the journal back into his bag, he started across the intersection and crossed the Southern Promenade. His expression was grim.

On the corner of Carlisle Lane and Ginry, he pushed open the cracked door into Ginny's Market. Watching Dis suspiciously, the slovenly woman behind the counter scowled.

"What are you looking for?" The clerk tapped her fingers on the counter as Dis inspected a box of salt.

"Vinegar and lighter fluid." He picked up a single roll of toilet paper, shaking mouse droppings off the wrapper.

"Vinegar's on the other side, by the beer cooler. Fluid's back here."

Nodding, Dis walked over and picked up a glass bottle hazy with a sticky residue. Carrying his selections up to the counter, he looked down into the clerk's rheumy eyes. "Three bottles of lighter fluid and a box of matches, please."

She stared back at him. "What for? You some kind of firebug?"

"I have to curse someone." He turned his face until his blind eye was centered above her.

The clerk took a step back. She quickly reached her hand out over her shoulder, dropped three red and yellow plastic bottles on the counter, and reached for a box of matches.

Dis took his wallet out and extracted three wet bills. "I don't need a bag."

She shrank from him, pressing her back against a display of travel-sized amenities behind the counter.

He laid the bills on the counter, pocketed the matches, and put the rest of his purchases in his messenger bag. "Keep the change."

He headed for the dilapidated houses on Moore Street. A child's tricycle was hung up on a torn fence and a tattered skirt lay in the middle of the road. From behind a high fence, a dog barked, yelped, and fell silent. At the fence corner, Dis opened his telescoping cane and took a left onto a trail leading up the backside of Gallows Hill.

Dis took a side path along the east side of the hill. Empty beer cans on both sides of the secondary path were filled to their brims with rainwater. Ahead, the jagged outline of a ruined three-story building appeared through the trees.

Dis reached down, bracing himself with his cane, and then dropped off the slope. He landed next to a barred ground-floor window. Passing spray-painted tags on the exterior of the battered stone building, he made his way to the third window. He grasped a fist-sized stone in the wall, eased it out, and set it on the ground. He then lifted out a rusted bar and set it alongside the stone. Shoving his bag through first, he squeezed into the historic prison.

Dis slowly made his way to the center of the roofless structure. A trio of crows swooped over the building. From its roost, a pigeon cocked its head, watching.

He nudged a shard of glass with his cane and surveyed the trash-covered floor. He cleared a section, took out the toilet paper, and began to layer a star pattern, adding more strips as it wicked up moisture from the damp ground.

When the roll was empty, he unscrewed the cap of the vinegar bottle and tore the top off the box of salt, setting them at his feet. Staring up through the ruins, Dis knelt slowly, placing one hand on the ground.

"Oldest of the old, hear me. I am the voice of the crow, the keening of the orphan. I am the scream of the murdered and the howl of the dead. I am a ghost shrieking over the graves." He stopped, looking at the weeds growing up out of the cracks. "I give myself, all the life I have left, to you." Raising his voice, he stood up. "I call upon Amrwyn, I call upon Mammor, and I call upon Ournok. I call upon this city, child of the Eldest. I call upon my beloved dead. Hear me. Do not let our enemies, the Pierce family, take any more lives." He clenched his jaw. "Let them be blind and deaf to our joys, let them choke and wither on their own suffering. Let this hallowed ground, let this hallowed water, and let this hallowed sky scald their flesh, sour their luck, and scourge their hearts." Using his left hand, he sifted the salt into a rough circle around the star. "Pierce, all that you have stolen, all those you have murdered, I take from you. I leave you only what wretchedness is yours. May you be burdened and broken by it." He flipped open the tops of the three bottles of lighter fluid and doused the paper star.

Tossing the empty bottles aside, Dis struck a match and flicked it. There was a puff and a quick burst of yellow flame. While black and orange char lines raced over the few remaining sections of the star, he splattered vinegar on its skeletal outline, filling the air with an acrid scent. He upended the bottle, shaking it. The magician stood up as the last traces of the paper design collapsed and the blackened bits dissolved into the dirt.

Standing above the remains of the star, Dis raised the empty vinegar bottle over his head and hurled it violently downwards. It crashed, sending fragments of glass flying out of the circle. Panicked, the pigeon abandoned its roost, flapping wildly out of the old prison and into the open sky.

□♍♏♋■

Kiarna Boyd

In the basement of 62 Moore, a small boy with a bruised face retreated from another boy screaming obscenities at him. The younger child stumbled alongside a table strewn with tools. As the older boy wrapped his hands around the child's throat, the younger one's right hand fumbled onto the worn handle of a screwdriver.

□ ♍ ♏ ♋ ■

A teenager with long hair stuffed under a knit cap hefted a cinder block up the stairs and across the roof of 100 Grant Street. Sweat dripped down the teenager's face as they lugged it toward the edge of the building and heaved it up onto the ledge. They adjusted the cinder block, looking down at the street five stories below. They watched a dark-haired man lock his new sports car and walk toward the entrance directly below. Taking a deep breath, the teenager pushed the cinder block off the ledge.

BONE INSPECTED HIS REFLECTION in the window of a closed fish market, adjusted his collar, glanced down at the bouquet of roses he was carrying, and looked out at the quay. The moorings of the houseboats on the far end clanked and chimed in the incoming evening tide.

A single rock jetty framed the protected expanse of the harbor. Fussing with his shirt collar again, Bone read the numbers affixed to the pilings. The tires strapped to the side of a red and black houseboat bumped up against the granite by his feet. He rang a brass bell on the pier and scrutinized the curtained windows in the boat cabin.

The houseboat's door opened, and Dis stepped out, untying his apron. "Good timing. Come sit down and I'll bring dinner out." He gestured for Bone to come aboard.

Bone maneuvered onto the gently rocking deck. "I thought these might be a pleasant stand-in, as you didn't want me to bring wine." He extended the roses. "Can I help you in the kitchen?"

"Thank you, but no. These are lovely, thank you." Dis's expression softened as he accepted the bouquet. "Only one of us in a kitchen at a time."

"I imagine it's very tight quarters." Bone followed Dis to the deck.

The music from inside was just audible over the lapping of waves against the hull.

"It's surprisingly spacious. I'll give you a tour after dinner. Make yourself comfortable. I'll be back in a moment."

Bone sat down at the table and looked at the containers of vegetables and flowers crowding the deck. Dis returned with a tray of food and set a carafe of water on the table. He arranged several plates of salad and grilled fish.

Bone stared at his plate. "You are planning to poison me and dump my corpse into the sea."

Dis filled their glasses. "I thought you liked sea trout."

"*You're* not eating it." Bone looked askance at his plate.

"I cooked it for you. I bought it at the market this afternoon. The salad is from my garden. The water is from the holy well." Dis picked up his fork. "My plans for tonight do not include murder. By poison or any other means."

Bone picked up his fork and lifted a portion of fish to his mouth. "If you are lying, I will haunt you."

Dis looked down at his glass of water. "We both have enough ghosts to contend with."

Bone tried a bite of fish. "It's very good. Thank you." He sat back, admiring the view. "Did you steal this lovely boat?"

"The owner is a friend of Dr. Gray's. She was kind enough to arrange the loan of it for this evening."

Bone speared another piece of trout. "This evening was your therapist's idea?"

"She's helped me understand my cruelty to you and I wish to apologize properly." Dis set his fork down. "It's important to me that I make amends, now."

Bone wiped his mouth with his napkin and set it down next to his plate. "I fear you and the good doctor intend something far worse than a simple murder."

Dis closed his eyes. "Now that I know what to listen for, I can hear it. The years of never addressing your insecurities, of keeping you always uncertain of my feelings. I have slowly poisoned you until even my anger would be an improvement over my indifference." He opened his eyes. "I'm sorry I've hurt you so badly, for so long. I never meant to hurt you."

Bone stared out over the harbor, into the distant horizon. "I anticipate your next words have been professionally crafted into a merciful, swift strike. You'll forgive me if I don't appreciate the effort you and your therapist have put into them."

Dis watched him. "I want to know if we should stay together. If it's what's best for both of us or if we should it end it now." He turned his head, following Bone's gaze out over the water.

"I suspect that depends largely on if you can stay with me in the first place. Can you stop running from me?"

"It's not you I run from." Dis looked at the stars, then back at Bone. "When I start getting angry, it feels like I'm going to lose control. That's what I run from, not you, Drake. I'm not sure I could stop if I started. I will not allow myself to lose my temper with you ever again. I should never have struck you."

"I'm sorry about that night." Bone shifted to face the table fully. "I've thought about what you said, and you're not wrong about me intentionally provoking you. I shouldn't have picked a fight with you about stealing your Da's body. I knew it was his last request, you were only doing what he had asked you to do." Bone shook his head.

"I'm not just talking about the past." Dis's voice dropped to a whisper. "Even though you are right here, right now, I'm afraid if I say how much you mean to me out loud, you will be taken away, too. Everyone I love has been taken from me. I'm afraid if I say the words, if I say it out loud, you will be taken too."

A slow song played faintly from the radio inside the boat's cabin, mingling with the lapping of waves against the hull and slapping the stones of the quay. "I'm not going anywhere." Bone set his hands on either side of his plate and looked at Dis. "Say what you need to say."

Dis inhaled. "When Jeniel was cutting into me, she told me she believed she could force me to change form by taking just the right amount of my skin. When it didn't work, she got desperate and cut off more. I tried to shut out what was happening, but that only made it worse. I've never felt so alone or powerless in my life. I couldn't change and I couldn't get free. I don't have the talent."

The muscles in Bone's jaw clenched as he watched Dis.

"She kept telling me to use the pain, and the only thing I could do with it was to offer it to the Eldest, hoping they might let me have you. I've missed you so much, but I thought I could never have you. That you were gone for good." Dis hung his head. "If not in this life, maybe I could be with you in the next." He gave a strangled laugh and sat back, looking up at the stars above the harbor. "They who love beauty, I tried to bribe with the only thing I had left. My pain." He blinked away tears.

"That's why you didn't come to the show?" Bone slid his hand across the table to touch Dis's. "You were afraid your gods wouldn't uphold their end of the bargain?"

"No, I was afraid you wouldn't want me now that I'm like this." Dis looked at their touching hands. "Even more damaged, more broken."

"How many times do I have to tell you before you will believe me?" Bone tightened his grip on Dis's hand. "There will never be a day in my life I do not want you, my beautiful, broken-hearted love. Look at me. You are beautiful just as you are. Any damage is merely proof that you are alive, that you survived."

Laughter from the next houseboat brought a fleeting smile to Bone's face. After a few minutes, Bone picked up his fork and resumed eating one-handed. When his plate was clean, he set his fork aside and sat back, rotating his water glass in one hand and holding Dis's with the other. "Since it is to be a night of revelations, I have one of my own to share, if I may."

"If you wish." Dis kept looking at their entwined fingers resting on his knee.

"I know I always give you grief about your beliefs, but …" He gave Dis an apologetic smile. "Since the night I found Zade at the Landing, my dreams have been full of that particular moonrise. Only there is no one else there, no monument, no sewer pipe, no Underground station, and no city. Only the moon and a voice singing. In the dream, I eventually realize it's my own voice. I've woken up with the song looping through my mind for about a month now. It's not so much lyrics as sounds …"

Dis rolled his right hand toward himself and looked out to the right of the rock jetty, at the open ocean.

Bone set his glass down. "I've never tried to sing it out loud, and I'm not even certain if I …" He pushed back his chair and stood. "Of course, before, I could only imagine how it would sound with a full orchestra." His eyes shining, he started to sing, softly at first and then louder, his voice gradually rising until it rang out rich and strong over the water.

□ ♍ ♏ ♋ ■

On the Market Station platform, a girl in a sparkly dress peeked around a pillar at a boy digging through a garbage can. Stiffening, he glanced up, scanned the faces around him and then went back to pawing through sticky newspapers and empty wrappers.

As the train thundered into the station, the girl ran out, placed her lunchbox at the boy's feet and then ran back to her caregiver's side. With a look of awe, he clutched the lunchbox to his chest and watched the girl board the train.

She waved from the window as the train started down the tracks. He shyly waved back, watching the train until it was out of sight.

□ ♍ ♏ ♋ ■

In St. Anna's Home, Mother Ida sat on a couch next to a pregnant teenager. The priestess made a soft clucking sound and gathered the youngster into her arms. The teen sobbed and the priestess rocked them, singing a wordless lullaby.

□ ♍ ♏ ♋ ■

Tears streamed down Dis's face. Bone stepped around the table and knelt down by the side of his chair.

"Was it so badly done?" Bone curled his fingers on Dis's cheek. "You look like I was on the verge of murdering you."

Dis put his hands on either side of Bone's face and drew him close. "I love you, Drake, I have always loved you, and I will always love you." He buried his face into his lover's neck and wrapped his arms around him. "Stay with me, please."

Looking out at the lights in the harbor, Bone kissed the top of Dis's head. "I will never leave you, my love. Never. I cannot be taken or dragged from your side. Even if you order me to go again, I will stay right here. Not in the next life, in this one."

Dis wiped his eyes with the palm of his hand. "We all die."

"Then I will haunt the bedroom and the bathroom, but I promise to stay out of your kitchen."

Dis twined his fingers through the long strands of Bone's hair. "What if I die before you? Would you rather let me go now?"

"No. That I will not allow. I love you too much to ever lose you again, Dulyn." He peered over his shoulder into the cabin. "Is there a tub, or shall I revive you by throwing you over the side?"

Dis kissed him slowly. "Let's go inside."

Bone arched an eyebrow at him and held him away. "I suspect I should be concerned by the sudden shift in your mood, love."

"We have permission to use the bedroom belowdecks and I would very much like to lie down with you." Tightening his grip, Dis pulled Bone closer and kissed him. When he spoke again his voice was rough with emotion. "Please."

Bone nodded and let Dis lead him inside.

Avery stopped, cracked open his faceplate, and waited for the dock workers to lug pallets of freight across the road. He spotted a space between the workers and rolled through the gap. He continued down Black Hawk Wharf, parking outside of the Breakfast Brothers shipping office.

Carrying his recorder in one hand and the delivery packet in the other, Avery shouldered the door open and walked up to the counter. The secretary peered at him with hooded eyes and impatiently waved him toward the office behind the counter.

A grizzled man glanced up, looked at the packet the courier held, and frowned. "I don't like the look of that."

"If you could." Avery held out the recorder. The man angrily pushed his chair back from his desk.

"They can't prove anything." He shook his head and put up his hand, blocking the courier. "You can just turn around and take them right back whence you came, boy."

Avery dropped the packet on the desk and held out the recorder. "Your thumbprint, now, please."

The man got up out of his chair and stood towering over Avery. "Are you threatening me?"

"I'm doing my job. If I could just have your thumbprint …"

"Only way you're getting it is off your own eyeball if you don't get out of here! Now!"

Patty's voice cut over Avery's headset. "We have Mr. Breakfast on camera, 62-91. Confirming delivery without the print. You can bail on this one, dear."

The courier turned around and walked out of the office.

"Take your goddamn lawyers' trash with you!" Breakfast grabbed the packet off his desk and seized Avery by the arm.

Avery shoved the man with both hands. Breakfast stumbled back into the desk. He yelled incoherently and leapt at the courier.

"Run!" Patty's startled voice sounded over the radio. "You're too far from S&P down there if he gets a hold of you."

Avery swung as the man lunged at him. The flat side of the recorder cracked into Breakfast's head above his ear. Avery knotted his hand into the front of the man's shirt and bent him backward over the desk. "Don't fucking touch me."

"You've scared him good and proper, 62-91. Just let him go." Patty's voice was soothing.

Avery backed away, keeping watch as he stepped out of the office and into the main room. Breakfast's secretary busied herself with shuffling papers. She kept her head down as the courier pushed open the door.

"Whew! Why don't you take the rest of the day off?" Patty sounded relieved.

Avery started up his bike. "I can keep running ..."

Patty laughed over the radio. "It's a beautiful day. Use it to practice for the race next month. Go on, there will be plenty for you on Monday."

Avery drove back down the commercial wharf, turning at the end of the line of warehouses toward the marina. Weaving around people on the fishing pier, he made his way to a gated private pier. The security guard at the entrance held up a hand for him to stop.

"It's me, Marn." Avery flipped up his faceplate. The man laughed and waved him through.

"Sorry, Mr. Pierce." Marn nodded to Avery, then spoke into a radio clipped to his vest.

Avery parked his bike alongside a luxury yacht, took off his helmet, gloves, and headset, and walked over to the boarding stairs. A prim man in uniform appeared as Avery reached the main deck.

"Welcome aboard, Mr. Pierce." He offered his hand. "Will you be staying with us long?"

"Thank you, Captain. I just was thinking maybe tonight if it wasn't an inconvenience ..." Avery looked around. "Is my aunt still staying aboard?"

"No, the Chairwoman has gone back to Long Shore. You are currently the only guest of the Pride." The captain lowered his head and directed the young man to the main salon. "If you care to have an early lunch, I can have the second stateroom made ready for you."

"Thanks." Avery stripped off his leather jacket, hung it on the back of a carved wooden chair, and followed the captain over to a long table. A servant in formal attire pushed a cart into the room. He bowed to Avery.

"Welcome aboard, sir." He set a porcelain cup of coffee in front of him. "Would you care for the salmon or the lamb for lunch today?"

"Salmon. Thanks, Reg." Avery relaxed visibly as he picked up the steaming cup.

"Your preference for lunch today, Captain?"

"The lamb for me. Thank you, Reginald." The Captain set his cap on the table.

Avery slouched back in his chair. "Are you staying in port for a while, Captain? My aunt told me she has canceled her summer trip to the Continent."

"For the time being. Until the Chairwoman says otherwise."

▽ ↗ ◢

The sun was dropping behind the city skyline when Avery climbed out of the pool and returned to his stateroom. He dropped his towel on the floor, turned on the faucet, stepped into the marble shower, and let the hot water sluice down his back.

The sounds of furniture being dragged along the floor came from the next room. Avery stepped out of the shower, dressed, and tried the door. It was locked.

On his way back to the main salon, he paused in front of the adjoining room, then continued. One of the lights in the corridor flickered as he passed. He stopped to tap the brass fixture until the light steadied. A crew member inclined her head as she passed him on her way to the bridge.

Arriving in the salon, he walked up to a pair of women setting the table. "Did my aunt come back aboard, Aly?"

"No, sir." The uniformed young woman smiled at him. "Would you care for a cocktail before dinner, sir?"

"Rum and soda, thank you." Avery walked over to the narrow bookcases beside a movie screen.

He ran a finger idly over the spines of the leather-bound books and pulled out an atlas. He carried it over to the tan couch in the center of the room and flipped it open. Aly appeared and set his drink down on the table. She nodded to him as he distractedly lifted the drink. He sat reading until the captain appeared with the senior members of the crew and joined him at the table for dinner.

▽↗◢

After the crew had excused themselves, Avery returned to his book. Aly silently slipped over to replenish Avery's drink. His expression troubled, he closed the book and leaned back against the cushions.

"Would you care to watch a film this evening, sir?" Reg inclined his head, indicating the projector. "We have three of the latest releases onboard."

"Sure. Whatever one you have ready is fine." Avery's voice slurred softly as he set his empty glass down.

Aly drew the drapes around the room while Reginald prepared the projector. As the studio's logo appeared, the speakers set along the bottom of the screen popped with static and the familiar sounds of production sequence music filled the room.

Avery sat on the edge of the couch, enraptured. He released his grip on the tumbler only in exchange for a replacement. He sat back roughly and sighed longingly when the film was over.

"Shall I set up the next movie, sir?" Reginald approached the couch.

Avery shook his head and tried to get up. "I should go to bed …"

Aly came around to Avery's other side and the two servants slowly walked him down the corridor to his room. The older nodded and the younger opened the door and then backed away, leaving her counterpart to escort Avery into his king-sized bed. Avery murmured incoherently as he was undressed.

"Shall I get you a glass of water, sir?" Reginald set a pillow behind his head. Avery pushed him away.

He turned off the lamps in the room and departed, leaving Avery snoring softly. A slight draft moved the sheer curtains and the soft drone of distant engines drifted in from the harbor.

Avery didn't respond to the scratching sound from the lock in the door adjoining the two staterooms. The drapes billowed as a figure entered and moved through the pale evening light to stand over him.

He murmured as the comforter was slipped off his body and he was turned onto his back. The intruder touched Avery lightly, sliding his boxers off his hips until the fabric bunched around his thighs. He moaned as he was stroked erect. As the intruder's weight settled onto him, his eyelids fluttered, but he did not wake.

▽ ↗ ◢

Avery frowned as he pulled up next to Otter's bike. As he opened the front door, Vicky's laughter floated down from the second floor. She started to sing, accompanied by a low male voice. Avery dumped his bag and livery in the hallway and rolled his eyes, groaning. He walked to the kitchen at the back of the ground floor. The copper pots hanging above the granite counter jangled in their iron rack as the ceiling thumped. Taking coffee beans out of the freezer, Avery muttered. A wicked smile crossed his lips as he started grinding the beans, the machine roaring loudly.

The coffee was brewing by the time Vicky appeared on the back staircase. "Avery? I didn't think you were here." She smiled at her brother as she stepped into the kitchen, wearing her nightgown. "Are you okay?" Her smile faded as her brother turned away. "Where were you last night?"

"On the Pride." Avery shrugged and removed the pot of coffee before it had finished brewing. A stream of liquid sizzled on the heating pad as he poured out a mug and replaced the pot.

"How's Aunt Mercy?" Vicky set two blue mugs down on the counter. The coffee machine sputtered and stopped.

Avery shrugged and blew on his coffee as he walked over to the table. "She wasn't there." He eased onto the bench and set his mug down.

"Did something happen?" Vicky walked around and touched Avery's shoulder. "You seem upset."

"I had a weird dream, that's all."

"Do you want to talk about it?"

Avery glanced up at his sister and grimaced. "Don't you need to serve your boyfriend breakfast in bed?"

Vicky swatted at his head. "Fine, I was just trying to be nice."

She walked back over to the counter, grabbed two muffins, and arranged them on a plate. She gathered the two coffee mugs in one hand and the plate in the other and started back toward the stairs.

"Is he staying over tonight, too?"

She sighed and walked upstairs.

"Fine. *I'm going back to the Pride, then.*" He slumped forward around his coffee.

⮞⭑☙⑨⓪⭑⮜

Iris muttered and shifted the lever next to her steering column up two notches. She barely glanced over her shoulder as she swung the end of her pickup truck into the tight parking space in Post Office Square. She snatched a piece of paper off the passenger seat and slammed the door.

She crossed the street and headed into City Hall. The guard at the entrance glanced over as she held up a hand to him on her way in. Sliding her hand up the brass railing, she thundered up the stairs. "I'm going to kick the old bag right in the crotch for doing this to me. Didn't even have the balls to call."

She threw open the City Manager's office door and marched by a confused-looking secretary.

"I'm sorry, do you have an appointment?" The secretary tried to catch up to her.

Iris pulled on the handle of the locked door to the inner office. "Get your ass out here and explain this horseshit to my face, you cowardly bag of piss!" She pounded on the wooden frame until the frosted glass rattled.

"Ma'am, if you wouldn't shout quite so loudly, Mr. Moxene is on the phone." The anguished secretary pawed at her shoulder.

The door was yanked open and a man with rolled-up shirt sleeves glared at Iris. "What, you can't read your own mail now?"

Iris brushed the secretary's hand away and stormed into the office. She turned around with a fist on her hip and held up the letter. "Explain this horseshit."

He waved his secretary away and shut the door. "You've been denied the permit. I'm sorry, but the local businesses don't want your couriers racing in the streets anymore."

"Every year some whining slob tries that horseshit, and every year you've ignored them. Why is this year different?" She slapped the letter on his desk.

"You've lost a lot of kids this year. Too many deaths." Moxene ran his hands over his thinning hair and walked over to the high window. "We can't be seen to endorse such a dangerous profession."

"We haven't had a death in months. Without a spectacle, how am I supposed to recruit replacements?"

"Not my problem."

Stomping over to his side, Iris shook a finger under his nose. "It will be when your people can't run fast enough between the Hinterlands and here. Then what will you do? Carry every piece of paper yourself?"

"There's always new technology coming from the Continent. Eventually, your couriers will be made obsolete, just like the antiquated horse system. Until then, we will have to make do."

"Who bought you this time? It's Pierce, isn't it? She's put you up to this, hasn't she?" Iris poked him in the chest. "Tell her to fuck off."

Moxene threw his hands up in the air. "You're asking me to flush my career down the drain if I do that. Is that what you want? Me homeless out on the streets?"

"No, I want you to give me the goddamn permit for the goddamn Summer Solstice race everyone is expecting."

"I can't."

"You mean you won't." Her chin started to tremble.

"Oh, don't start. I can't have your crazy motorcyclists racing around the streets anymore." He put his hands on her shoulders and tried to pull her into a hug. "If I could, I would …"

"You can just deliver your own legal tirades from now on." She swatted at his hands and turned away. Her shoulders rose and fell as she sobbed quietly.

"Hey, now." He went over to his desk and grabbed a tissue. "What about a race outside the city limits? You've never done that. Come on, Iris. Work with me here. I'll shut down the highway for you, okay?" He pressed it into her hands. "I hate it when you cry."

"You promise I can have my race?" She looked at him over her shoulder and blew her nose.

"I promise. Now stop with the waterworks. I know you do it on purpose."

"I only do it when you're being a shit-poor excuse for a brother. I shouldn't have had to come down here, you could have called."

"I'm sorry, okay? I have to go through the motions. We need to make it look real. I needed you to threaten to strike."

"Should I have yelled more? I could break something …"

Moxene hugged his sister. "I'm just glad you didn't kick me in the balls."

"I considered it." Iris smiled.

▽↗◢

"A new route? What kind of fucking pukedog came up with that?" Kitty grimaced. "I've been practicing on the regular one for months now."

294

Otter patted her on the shoulder. "We've practice laps scheduled."

Clink looked up from a bench in the Pit. "What the hell? Why can't we know the new route now?"

"Same reasons we're all getting our bikes checked: safety, and to make sure everyone has an equal shot at winning." Zade glanced at Otter.

"Scum-sucking fuckjobs." Kitty glared at her. "We all know you already know the route, dispatcher's pet."

Clink gestured at his head and Kitty tore her headset off.

"Dis didn't give me the route, Kitty. I'm getting it tomorrow, same as you." Zade toyed with the strap on her glove.

"Besides, we all know who is going to win." Otter pointed his thumb at Mat.

Mat threw his coffee across the circle at Otter's feet. "You should be more worried about rich boy Avery's top-of-the-line Tiver. None of our bikes can touch it."

"90-32, white hot coming in. You free, Zade?"

"You know it, dispatch." Zade sprinted to her motorcycle. "Where's the pickup?"

"16 Parker, Suite 10. Going to 5 Rose Hill Ave, front desk."

Zade popped the clutch and lunged her bike onto the road.

"Accident on High at Spaulding, recommend you take Manson."

"Got it."

Zade cut down Watt to Pierce and turned onto Carlisle. "Ribbons and curls." She turned onto Parker and dropped her kickstand. Leaving her engine running, the courier pounded up the steps into 16 Parker.

She snagged the package out of the lawyer's hand as the woman jabbed her thumb at the recorder. "Thanks."

"Starting the clock, 90-32. Ten minutes. 5 Rose Hill Ave, front desk."

By the time she got to the bottom of the stairs and jumped onto her idling machine, it had started to pour. Pedestrians opened their umbrellas and the sound of thunder reverberated through the sky. As she took the corner on Fleet, Zade's back tire sent a sheet of water up over the curb.

"Don't go hydroplaning on me, 90-32."

"Shut it, dispatch." Zade dodged a taxi. "Time."

"Seven and a half."

She turned onto the top of Rose Hill in two inches of water and slapped her faceplate up to see through the downpour.

"Four."

She swerved around a taxi door as it opened, hopped her bike up onto the sidewalk, dismounted, and killed her engine. She squinted, looking for an entrance in the metal and glass facade of the building. "I can't see the fucking door."

"To your right, ten feet. One and half minutes."

Zade bolted through the door. Her boots squelched across the wet marble floor. "White hot!" She waved the package at the empty front desk. "Where are they?"

"Time."

"Where …" Zade turned around and staggered back against the desk. "Tell me you fucking see that, Dis."

A faint blue halo shimmered around the building's entrance and lines of light sparked along the ornate metalwork in the interior of the foyer.

"Get on the desk! Now!" Heavy static chattered through the courier's headset.

Zade flung herself on the reception desk. The room crackled as a bright white flash illuminated the space. A loud crashing noise shook the glass in the entranceway.

"Status!"

The courier sat up and looked at the package now lying in the water on the floor. "Shit."

"You're okay. Hold."

Zade retrieved the sopping package and smacked it on the desk. She crossed her arms, waited another minute, and then headed for the door. Overhead, the cloudburst was changing to a light rain as she emerged from the building. She stopped and stared.

"Holy Mother." She walked over to the ruined remains of her motorcycle lying under a chunk of the building shorn off by the lightning strike. "Dispatch, tell Iris to bring the truck with the winch." She took off her helmet and looked up at the structure, shielding her eyes from the rain. "You might want to call S&P and let them know 5 Rose Hill might drop more surprises."

"In that case, I would appreciate it if you removed your head out from under it, 90-32."

"I'M NOT SURE WHAT I've got left for you to ride." Iris surveyed the remaining motorcycles in the garage with her hands on her hips. "Every decent one is out. I can call over and ask Lew if he's got something for you, but I wouldn't trust his machines."

"Kitty and some of the others already think I'm cheating." Zade sat on the bottom step and looked up at the dispatcher's booth. "If I show up on a replacement they'll be pissed."

"You could sit this one out." Iris patted the saddle of one of the bikes. Zade groaned and buried her head in her arms.

The door at the top of the stairs swung open. "I would like to have you both come look at something."

Zade raised her head and sighed as Iris waved her toward the booth.

"I made some calls. The receptionist was trying to find the building manager to deal with the flooding and didn't know a hot was coming in." Dis pointed at one of the monitors. "I want you to keep your eyes on this while I play back 90-32's cam feed."

Iris bent down to look while Zade glanced around the booth uneasily.

"Shut the door." Dis paused as he caught sight of Zade's face. "Yes, we keep the withered heads of bad couriers in here."

The mechanic looked up and grinned. "You afraid to be in here?"

"Seems like I'm breaking a rule." Zade bent down to look at the monitor.

Dis tapped out a command on his keyboard. "Keep your eyes here and tell me what you think you see." He went back to the other monitor and switched his headset channel. "70-22, status."

The monitor screen showed black and white footage of the foyer at 5 Rose Hill Avenue and the outstretched package in Zade's hand as she ran to the reception area. The image panned to the left. They watched static electricity arc off the metal of the entrance.

"11-68, pickup at 63 Market. Going to Jasper 1212, basement office." As the image jostled on the screen, Dis paused it and pointed.

"Who is that?" Iris peered at the screen.

Zade took a step backward.

Dis watched her reaction. "I'll play it again without pausing it." He set the playback to begin when the courier walked into the building and let it run until the totaled motorcycle appeared on the screen.

"They're only there for a split second." The mechanic poked at the image. "Play it again and freeze it. I swear that's a person. What do you think, Zade?" Iris turned. "Zade?"

Zade was staring at the screen, her forehead covered in sweat.

Dis leaned back in his chair. "Iris, please watch the queues for a minute." He stood up and put his hand on Zade's arm. "I'm going to take Zade outside."

Downstairs, Zade paced the line of daylight coming in from the open garage door. Dis traced a finger along the flaking whitewash on the entrance to the garage.

She looked up at the sky outside the depot. "How can a dream be on a cam feed? For what, three seconds?"

"The timing says it's a two-second image. Could have been interference from another cam feed during the lightning strike."

"It was him. The Roadkill King. In person. Can I expect my other nightmares to be showing up?"

"The Earth-Father is not a nightmare." His eyes were troubled. "You didn't let Vicky give you one of the Pierce family names, did you?"

"No, why?"

"Don't let her. Try to focus on winning the race tomorrow. Fairly."

"Iris doesn't have a replacement for me to ride tomorrow. I'm not likely to win the race from the sidelines."

Dis walked back into the depot and eased himself onto the stairs. "Otter's going to be assisting me at the finish line. I'm sure he will lend you his bike."

"What the fuck is going on?" Zade spun around. "You're acting like you expected this to happen."

"My only expectation is that you will win the race tomorrow."

"What happens if I lose?"

"Your birthday present is still valid."

She shook her head. "Kittens. You're trying to distract me with kittens."

"Or a cat. Doesn't have to be a brand-new model. Or we could go to one of your bad movies."

"How is it you're so calm?" She glared at him. "After seeing *that*?" She pointed up at the booth.

"I'll have Otter bring his bike here. You should get a feel for it and have Iris go over it with you. You need to be able to beat Avery's machine. Make sure she checks the chain and the plugs."

"I'm not senile." Iris threw her rag down the stairs at them.

▽ ↗ ◢

Otter picked up Zade at the depot and they rode over to Maddy's. He nodded to Roy while Zade draped her leather jacket over the back of a chair at the bar. Sinking her head into her hands, she sat down in front of the beer taps and stared at the sunbeams streaking through the windows.

Tousling her hair, Otter sat down and grinned at Roy. "A pint each, please."

Zade groaned, cradling her head between her hands. "I need whiskey."

Otter shook his head. "You're not racing with a hangover, so no whiskey." He poked her arm. "I should make you take a vow of sobriety while you've got my bike."

"I don't ride drunk."

Otter snorted. "If that was true, you'd be the first courier in the history of the city to manage it."

Zade looked over Otter's shoulder as the door opened.

Otter glanced over. "Frankie!"

The young woman nodded, keeping her eyes on Zade. "I was checking in with Dis about tomorrow and he mentioned you were on your way over here."

"Hey, I owe you a beer." Zade leaned back in her seat.

Roy set the first two pints down and looked at Frankie.

"A Cygnet, please." Frankie leaned sideways on the bar and looked across Otter at Zade. "I'm glad you're okay. Dis said your bike is totaled?"

Zade groaned and Otter swatted her on the arm.

"She's still upset about it." He shook his head at Frankie's concerned expression.

"You're okay though?" Frankie reached across Otter to touch Zade's arm.

"Mostly." Zade poked at her pint glass as Roy set a beer in front of Frankie. "Put it on my tab, thanks."

"Certainly."

Watching the two women, Otter downed half the contents of his glass. "Keep an eye on 90-32 for me. Make sure she stays out of the whiskey tonight."

"We just got here!" Zade sat up, wailing. "You can't seriously be leaving?"

"I need to clean up before I see Vicky." Otter finished his beer and set the glass down on the bar. "Remember, no riding my bike drunk. Or dumping it, or scratching it, or letting your street friends get dirt on it. I want it back in one piece. Oh, and remember to talk to it like it's alive. Like it's a real horse."

"What?" Zade squinted at her friend as he put a crisp bill next to his glass.

"You'll figure it out." Otter hefted his jacket over his shoulder and waved to the women. "Good luck beating Avery tomorrow."

Zade sighed as he walked out of the bar. She turned to look at Frankie. "I'm glad he's having a good time, but …" She plopped her head into her hand and turned her attention to her beer.

"I'm not sure I understand." Taking Otter's seat, Frankie hung her bag over the back of the chair.

"Boon was like that too." Zade's expression became solemn. She traced a finger through the condensation on the side of her glass. "Suddenly going off to be with her boy when we were out. Crazy fast mood changes."

Frankie's rich laughter echoed in the empty bar. "Dis is worse, you should have heard him on the phone. Zero to sixty when I asked if I could catch a ride with him and Bone in the morning."

"They must have made up. That's why he was so calm after …" Zade raised her glass and took a long draught. "All my friends are in love." She set the glass down. "While I trash another bike."

Frankie dropped her eyes to where Zade's hands were curled on the bar. "Do you want to talk about it?"

"No, it would probably depress both of us."

Staring down at the bar, Frankie sipped her beer.

Zade gave her an apologetic smile. "I'll understand if you don't want to sit in here with me. I'm not very good company right now."

"Oh, no. I'm the boring one. Dis would know what to say to cheer you up."

"He'd tell me to stop whining or start lecturing me about magic. Or both."

Frankie rummaged through her messenger bag. When she turned back around, she placed a bundle of sea-green cloth on the bar. "I need to practice. Can I throw some cards for you?"

"Sure." Zade angled her body to watch the other woman open the silk and shuffle the cards. "Is it like the trick he does with the coin?"

"I'm not sure what you mean." Frankie glanced up. "It's a form of divination."

"Stuff about my future? Vicky did that for me at our birthday party."

"Past, present, and future. If I do it right." Frankie set the deck in front of Zade. "Shuffle and cut the deck however you like and then place three cards face down on the bar in a line for me. Don't look at them."

"You're not going to make one appear from behind my ear or anything?" Zade looked disappointed as she picked up the cards.

"That's an advanced technique." Frankie's eyes twinkled as she picked up her pint.

Zade placed the first three cards down on the bar and handed the deck back. "Now what?"

"Well, this one is your recent past." Frankie reached out and flipped over the card closest to Zade.

"A naked dancing woman. That sounds about right." She grinned.

"Sort of." Frankie flipped over the middle card. "Present."

"Great. A guy with a crown and a stick." Zade leaned in to peer at the card. "Make that a stick on fire."

"Future." She flipped over the last card.

"It's upside down. Should we turn it?"

"No, it's got a different meaning when it is like that." Frankie moved the three cards closer together. "In your recent past, you've achieved a great deal and been given a great deal. Everything has been working out in your favor."

Zade snorted. Frankie frowned.

"Though I can see what you mean. I'm alive, after all. What's the middle one about?"

"Energy to make things happen. Being quick-witted and direct."

"And the upside-down one is the future?"

"Going out into the world to engage directly. Again, taking charge, but this is more personal. Doing something only you can do, something that you've been hesitant to do."

"Huh, I was hoping there would be something about the race." Zade laughed and picked up her pint.

"I'm not very good at this yet." Frankie lifted the deck again. "We can do one more though, to see what's in the next cycle. There might be something new coming up." She flipped the top card off the stack and set it beside the others.

Zade grinned. "It's got a horse on it. I bet Otter would love it." She reached over to pick up the card. "What's with the skeleton? I think Vicky showed me that one too."

"It means a big change is coming." Frankie plucked the card out of Zade's hand, slipped it into the deck, and collected the other cards. "Sorry, I thought this might be fun but I'm not good enough yet."

"I dunno, you seem better at it than Vicky." Zade finished her pint. "Do you feel like going for a ride when you're done with your beer?"

Frankie flipped a braid over her shoulder. "We can go now. I'll leave the rest for the Eldest."

"You haven't even put a dent in it."

Frankie swallowed half the contents of her glass and smiled. "Better?"

"Let me know if you start getting bored and I can run you home." Zade dug a few bills out of her pocket and placed them on the bar before standing up. She grabbed her gear and walked to the exit, holding the door open for Frankie.

The two women rode down to Market, avoiding the water-filled potholes. An updraft from the tidal river hung in the center of the Riverway Bridge. Zade shook her head as they passed through the icy ribbon of air.

The outbound traffic slowed on the other side of the bridge and the exit lane began to back up. Zade glanced into her left mirror, then tapped Frankie's leg. She sat up and shifted her grip to Zade's waist as the bike whipped around the car in front of them.

Zade wove around the orange warning cones restricting access to the right shoulder and dodged a minivan drifting into their lane. She slowed to throw coins into the tollbooth basket.

When the traffic cleared at the boundary of the Hinterlands, Zade changed into the high-speed lane and accelerated, her eyes darting from the gauges to the road markers and back.

A gas station appeared ahead. Zade steered into the right lane and then pulled off the highway.

"Not too shabby with both of us on." She killed the engine and coasted over to the air pump. "Hop off for a minute?"

Frankie dismounted and took off her helmet. She watched Zade swing off the bike and pick up the air hose. There was a hiss and the air compressor started humming as Zade crouched down and uncapped the front tire's air valve.

Holding the helmet by its chinstrap, Frankie looked across the road at the looming mountain. The compressor switched off suddenly and she closed her eyes. "I forget how unnerving the silence is out here."

Dropping the hose back onto the side of the air pump, Zade looked up at the dark mountain. "It's probably too quiet outside of the city for me to sleep."

"You've never stayed out here?" Frankie turned to look at her. "Or on the outer islands?"

"No place to ride on the islands." Zade leaned forward on the bike's saddle. "Besides, in the city, I feel like a little fish swimming next to something bigger. It feels safer that way. Out here everything feels like it is looking at me. Like it wants something from me." She slapped the saddle before settling onto it. "It's getting dark. I ought to run you home. I'm sure Dis will be picking you up early. Where do you live?"

"26 Mason." Frankie put the helmet back on.

"Is it okay if I go a bit faster on the way back?"

Smiling, Frankie took up pillion behind her. "As long as you don't get a ticket, 90-32."

An animal's eyes reflected the motorcycle's headlight as they took a left back onto the highway. Frankie leaned against Zade's back as the gray and black body loped into the forest. In the distance, the lights of the city blazed from the darkened skyline. Zade cracked open the throttle and the motorcycle rumbled as it rushed to join the line of red brake lights moving slowly across the bridge.

The traffic signal at the intersection of Duncan and State flickered from yellow to red just as they made the turn, illegally swinging around the 72 bus.

Zade leveled the bike out by taking the Straight at twice the legal limit and then banked a left onto Mason. A car horn stuttered and blared as the motorcycle cut in front of it. Frankie grinned and tightened her grip.

The smell of grilling meat cut through the stink of car exhaust as they passed the first of the brownstones in the neighborhood. Stopping the bike outside of number 26, she shifted into neutral, leaving the engine running. Frankie dismounted and put the helmet into the cargo net on top of the hardcase. She stood alongside the bike, staring down at the pavement.

"Sorry if that was a bit too fast there. I probably should have taken it slower, carrying a dispatcher." Frowning, Zade killed the engine and peered at Frankie. The leaves overhead rustled in the breeze and the sound blended into the white noise of the air conditioner in a nearby window. She lifted her goggles up. "I'm sorry if I scared you …"

Bending forward, Frankie kissed her. Zade's eyes went wide in surprise, then she reached out and put her hand on Frankie's back. The motorcycle wobbled and the two women separated. Zade snapped the kickstand down, dismounted, and hopped up onto the curb.

Stripping off a glove, Zade slid her palm along the side of Frankie's jaw and caressed her lower lip with the tip of her thumb. "Would it be okay if I did that again?"

With a velvety laugh, Frankie hooked her thumbs on Zade's hips. "I kissed *you*, remember?"

Ducking her head, Zade glanced sideways at her. "Maybe you're just trying to cheer me up?"

"It couldn't be that I like you or anything?"

Zade grinned. "If I could, I'd spend all my luck to make that true." Her smile faltered as she relocated her hand to the back of her own neck. "It might not be a good idea for me to keep company with you right now. I seem to be kind of accident-prone recently. I probably shouldn't have had you with me…"

"Nothing bad happened. Besides, I'm learning how to use magic, so I can keep us both safe."

"If I say that's not enough, I'll have to answer to both you and your teacher, won't I?"

"Mostly me." Frankie tugged on Zade's hips. "Come in and have a drink?"

"One, but then you have to kick me out. Is it safe for me to leave the bike parked here?"

"Yes."

Zade leaned over and took the key out of the ignition.

They climbed the stairs to a tiny studio on the third floor.

Frankie went over and opened the fridge. "Make yourself comfortable, please. I'll be right over."

Zade scrubbed at the elastic strap of her goggles on the back of her head. She glanced at the bed and then eased down onto one of the big floor pillows by a table. She poked at one of the many books on the table and started chewing on her thumb as she read the title. Frankie came over, holding out a beer. Zade accepted it with a shy smile.

"I don't know if I've seen this many books in one room before." She stared up at the overflowing bookshelves and started idly peeling the label off the bottle.

"Most of these belong to Dis." Frankie began to rearrange the books on the table to clear some space. "I have to get them back to him before he gets mad."

Zade locked eyes with her hostess. "If he's a jerk to you, I'll punch him."

Smiling, Frankie glanced down at the shreds of paper falling into Zade's lap. She reached over and put her hand in Zade's. "You're still worrying."

"Huh?" Zade blinked and looked down at the mess she was generating. She fidgeted. "I should …"

Taking the bottle out of her hands, Frankie set it on the table and kissed her. The two women sank onto the floor pillows. Zade rolled Frankie over onto her back and moved her shirt aside to kiss her stomach. The goggles fell off her head and Frankie laughed, hauling them both up onto the bed.

Zade pulled back, looking down at Frankie lying on the violet bedspread. "I've never known anyone as amazing as you, Frankie."

Frankie laughed again. "You ought to look in a mirror sometime." She linked her hands around Zade's waist.

The other woman shook her head. "You're smart, and beautiful, and ought to be spending your time with someone better than me."

"If you think I'm so smart, then listen when I say I want you." Frankie tugged her down and pressed her lips against hers. She slipped her hands under Zade's shirt and drew it up over her shoulders, grinning as Zade wriggled out of it.

Zade pushed up Frankie's shirt and started kissing her way down her stomach, but the other woman stopped her. "You've been doing all the driving today. It's your turn to relax."

Zade looked up with a confused expression. "But …"

"You said one drink and then I had to kick you out. I know you. You'll hog all the fun and then use the race tomorrow as an excuse to leave." Pursing her lips, she slipped her hand under Zade's chin and locked eyes with her. "You are wound too tight. I want you to lie down and enjoy yourself."

Zade blinked and then grinned. "Do you always use your radio voice in bed?"

"Only when I'm dealing with a courier who doesn't know what's good for her." Using her leg for leverage, Frankie rolled Zade over onto the bedspread. Straddling her, she slipped out of her shirt. Her serious expression melted into a grin as she smoothed her hands along Zade's ribs and peeled off the other woman's bra.

Biting her lip, Zade closed her eyes as Frankie's tongue traced circles around her areola, her nipples hardening in response to the touch. Raising her hands, she grasped the top edge of the pillow while Frankie sucked gently. Her braids trailed along the edges of Zade's chest as she worked her way up to her neck. Frankie dropped her hips and used her knee to pry Zade's legs apart.

Zade turned her head, crushing her lips against Frankie's. She moaned as her lover pressed against her. The two women moved together, grinding into each other. Zade unhooked Frankie's bra. The pink straps tumbled down Frankie's shoulders as Zade cupped her breast. Frankie arched her back and threw off the piece of lingerie. It sailed over the edge of the bed and landed on top of the pile of books on the table.

Zade dragged the edge of her thumbnail down Frankie's back and smoothed her hand over the seat of her jeans. Her words came out in a tumbling rush. "I'm going to lose my mind if you keep moving like this."

Frankie's response was another rich laugh. She pulled away long enough to unsnap the buttons on Zade's leathers and slip her fingers under the curve of Zade's pelvic bone. Resuming her sinuous movements, Frankie lowered her hips back down.

Zade's right hand arched up, grabbing the pillow. She covered her eyes with her left. Frankie dipped her head, catching one of Zade's nipples in her mouth, watching as she started to tremble.

Grinding her hips, Zade pressed against Frankie's hand and dragged the pillow over her eyes. A low moan escaped her mouth and she bit her lip, holding the pillow against her face. Lifting her hips back, Frankie kissed her breast. She stroked Zade in long, languorous circles.

Writhing against the mattress, Zade bit her lip harder and her body shuddered. As the fabric under her torso bunched together, her head completely disappeared under the pillow. She drove her hips against Frankie, her muffled moans thick with pleasure. Her body stiffened as Frankie's movements quickened. The women moved in unison and Zade let out a long, wavering cry.

As she relaxed, Frankie grinned and lowered herself against her. Shoving the pillow away, she kissed her.

Zade's eyelids fluttered open and she blinked, smiling slowly. "Holy Mother." As she looked up into Frankie's eyes, her smile broadened. "Your turn." Putting her hand on Frankie's hip, she started to roll them both sideways.

"Oh, no." Frankie smiled wickedly and started moving her hand again. She licked Zade's lips as Zade sank back against the mattress. "Tonight, I've got my heart set on getting a triple." With her free hand, she began tugging Zade's riding leathers off.

▽↗◢

Six S&P cruisers blocked off the highway at the tollbooths behind the starting line. Zade readjusted the pads on her elbows, staring at the line of emergency vehicles on the side of the road.

She stepped out of the starting line, walked over to Kitty, and punched her in the arm. "Good luck."

"Don't cry too hard when I beat the fucking snot out of you." She gave Zade a playful punch back.

Zade grinned and walked back to her bike. She bent over and whispered to it. "Otter said to talk to you. I'm not sure what I should say. Nice bike?" She sighed and straightened up.

Avery was down the line with his bike on its center stand. Zade walked up to him as he was spinning his rear tire and inspecting the chain.

"Good luck." She held out her hand to him.

Their eyes met. Avery flinched and looked back down at the chain. "The bet is still on."

"Anything busted?" She knelt down next to him and eyed the chain.

He stood up and walked around to the other side of the machine. "I'm all set." He checked the throttle cable, keeping his eyes on the motorcycle.

"Okay. Be safe." Zade walked back to her place in line and waited, chewing on her thumbnail.

"I hate this part." The courier next to her tugged at his elbow pads.

"Only a few more minutes." Zade put in her earplugs as Patty and Iris began walking the starting line.

❧ ೞ⑨❶ ☙

Dis sat on the tailgate of a truck, his legs hanging over the edge. He angled the brim of his hat down over his face and spoke into his radio. "All spotters in position and finish line is all set. We're ready when you are, Frankie."

"Ready."

Dis clipped the radio to his belt and gazed down the hill of seagrass to the waves crashing below. A lone gull gliding on the updrafts stared back at the man.

"I've never seen the city from here." Otter leaned against the side of the truck. "It looks like it's rising straight out of the ocean. Pretty."

"Thirty-seven miles allows for plenty of illusions." Dis picked up a pair of binoculars and stood up in the back of the truck. "Starting line, give me your status."

Frankie stared at the sky, sighing as Iris hugged another of her riders. She waited until Patty dragged Iris away. "Starting line here, the babies have all been kissed."

"Go for it." Static crackled through his reply.

She walked out from under the canopy of leaves to the middle of the highway. The long stretch of road curved to the west, following the line of the coast. A half a mile in the distance the first exit cut inland, branching into a secondary road that followed the base of the Ouring Ridge.

Frankie screened her eyes from the afternoon sun and unfurled an orange flag. The sound of the riders' cheers vanished as their engines roared to life. She waited for the racers to fall into position and then swung the flag down.

Three riders shot ahead, spinning off onto the first exit ramp. Two others dumped their bikes on the starting line, knocking over their neighbors. The majority of the pack skimmed out in the leaders' wake, with a few stragglers taking up the rear.

"Three in the front, about twenty in the middle, the rest taking their sweet time." Frankie clicked off the radio after delivering her report.

At the finish line, Otter walked over to where Vicky was sitting on a picnic table. "I wish we could watch the cam feeds out here."

She smiled. "They would probably make me scream. I only hope everyone gets through the race in one piece."

Heading into the first curve, Avery flattened his bike, his knee inches above the pavement. Zade mimicked his movements, bringing her bike back to center as she came through the turn. She tapped her rear brake, keeping the motorcycle's back end down, as she went over a rise seconds after Avery's tires touched the pavement on the other side. Kitty chased behind, the distance between her and Zade increasing on the second curve as they approached the secondary road.

Avery kept the lead into the valley, with Zade right behind him. He switched lanes, blocking her chances at passing him on the last stretch of the highway. They merged onto a narrower roadway lined with whitewashed cottages. A group of people waved and shouted as the three motorcyclists zipped by.

Above the road, Bone watched the riders from the hillside and reported their progress over the radio. "Finish line, this is Spotter One. Leaders are at the quarter mark." He gave a thumbs up to the woman behind the wheel of the truck he was sitting in and she started its engine. "62-91 in first, 90-32 in second, and 11-68 in third."

As the trio of motorcycles disappeared over the next hill, the main group of riders funneled into the country lane. A procession of support vehicles trailed behind. The last car honked at the spotter's truck. Bone waved out the window as his driver turned onto the mountain access road.

Zade lost sight of Kitty in her mirrors as she flew down a series of switchback curves. She grinned when Avery's red and black racing jacket flashed back into her line of sight.

⌖∽☾⑨ ❶ ∾

"Finish, this is cleanup. We've got a rider down on Brayside. Talking, but not walking."

"Start, please notify S&P to send the ambulances over. We should be set with the one we have here." Dis sat with his boots hanging over the side of the cliff face.

"Already on it, finish. We're heading over to join you."

Dis looked thoughtfully at his radio and then back at the incoming tide slapping up onto the rocks. Three cars pulled into the parking lot. The couriers and their friends waved, carrying picnic supplies and lawn chairs over to the others. He watched Otter direct the new arrivals away from the finish line.

"Finish, this is Spotter Two. 62-91 and 90-32 just cleared the halfway mark." Mr. Lew's words crackled.

Dis started walking toward the picnic tables. "Spotter Three, give me your status."

"Spotter Three ready at last quarter." Patty adjusted her binoculars.

Otter adjusted his grip on the load of firewood he was carrying. "Should I..."

"I can take those while you check." Dis tugged the logs out of his friend's arms.

He carried the rest of the firewood to the stack near the fire pit while Otter walked over to the truck. Otter glanced around before pulling out a bundle wrapped in velvet. After another quick look around, he set his divination tool spinning on the vehicle's hood.

☐ ♍ ♏ ♋ ■

Smoke curled up from Kitty's engine as her machine started to vibrate. *"Fuckbag!"* The motorcycle toppled and crashed, sending her tumbling. Her helmet cracked against the pavement. She slid another twenty feet on the road as her bike skidded to a halt against a tree.

Two motorcycles crested the hill as plastic and metal from Kitty's bike skittered down the road. The other riders decelerated to avoid the pieces of shrapnel. One of the competitors pulled to the side of the road and ran over to check on the downed rider.

□ ♏ ♍ ♋ ■

As he careened down the next hillside, Avery slowed down for the hard turn at the bottom. He spotted Zade in his mirror and shifted back into fifth gear, launching into the underpass beneath the highway. His headlight reflected off the concrete walls as the cool shadow of the bridge fell over him.

□ ♏ ♍ ♋ ■

"Finish, this is cleanup. We've got a rider down on Witch's Elbow and another on Deer Hill. The one on the hill is out cold."

"Confirmed, cleanup." Dis kept his back to Otter and waited as the other man intently watched the stone spin.

A few moments passed. "We're good." Otter clapped his hand on his friend's arm and started back to the fire pit.

"Ten minutes." Dis lifted a bullhorn off a picnic table. "Time to take your seats, ladies and gentlemen. Please stay off the road, behind the orange cones."

A truck pulled into the lot and Bone hopped out. "Where do you want me?"

"Fire crew. It's time you learned the proper use for an extinguisher."

Bone grinned and headed over to a group of couriers standing behind the finish line, piling sandbags.

"Camera's all set, Dis." A woman waved a photo over the black and white string of flags that comprised the finish line.

"Let's try it again to be sure." Dis ran a finger along the streamer and tugged it, triggering the camera.

□ ♍ ♏ ♋ ■

Zade's tires reconnected with the ground. She grinned, stretched her shoulder blades back, and leaned sideways, letting the motorcycle's velocity catapult her through the curve. Ahead, at the end of the hedgerow, Avery disappeared into the glare of the full afternoon sun.

Seagulls launched into the sky as the two motorcycles whipped around the coastal road at the base of the Ouring Ridge.

The cool air rushing through Avery's helmet vents dried his sweat to salt. On his right, Zade cranked open her throttle, challenging him on the flat stretch of road. Avery responded by zigzagging across the centerline.

Zade grinned, watching him repeat his defensive maneuver. "Gotcha."

❧☙⑨⓿☙

"Finish, this is Spotter Three. 62-91 and 90-32 are coming up fast and even on White Beach Road. Looks like a dead heat from the final quarter mark."

Dis chirped the bullhorn. "Final quarter has been called. Judges to the finish line, please." He watched as four people in orange safety vests took their positions on both sides of the road near the string of flags. "Emergency crews, please stand by."

The friends and families of the contestants spread out along the road leading into the park. Non-competing couriers waved people off the pavement and onto the grass. Frankie jogged over to the emergency crew area.

"Finish, this is cleanup. S&P taking 11-68 and 22-61 to Mercy. Everybody's awake. Broken wings and a concussion."

Dis winced. "Confirmed."

⌀⁓ℂℬ⑨Ⓞ⁓

Otter found Vicky waiting for him next to the camera. "Bet you a kiss your sister beats your brother."

She laughed. "Either way, I win."

"Hear that? There's only one motorcycle sounds like that." He squeezed her hand.

☐♍♏♌⌣■

Entering Bird's Eye Corner, Zade dropped behind Avery and took the last curve slightly slower. As his wider arc pushed him to the far left of the road, she accelerated, passing him on the inside of the centerline.

"That's it, my bad, beautiful girl." Zade grinned at her motorcycle as Avery slipped in alongside her on the final sprint. "Ribbons and curls."

☐♍♏♌⌣■

Five feet behind the barrier of sandbags, Dis sighted the pair in his binoculars. He consulted the timer on his belt and then resumed watching the race.

"How fast are they going?" The medic next to him shaded her eyes with one hand, holding her first aid kit in the other.

"They appear to be pushing just over a hundred."

The crowds on both sides of the road screamed as the finalists swept down to the finish line. Vicky clapped and shouted as the streamer of flags broke around the two riders. The machines slowed and curved off along the sandbags into the parking lot as the rest of the racing pack entered the last corner.

Dis waited for the two finalists to kill their engines and then carried the bullhorn over to the finish line. Otter brought the photo over to him and they waited for the judges.

"Now that's a photo finish." Mother Ida held her hand out for the bullhorn. "Is this on?" Her laughter rang out over the gathered crowd. "Ladies and gentlemen, if I may have your attention, please. I'm honored to announce the winners of the twenty-first annual Summer Solstice race. Before I name the winners, let us take a moment to pray for the health of those few who have, thankfully, only suffered minor injuries." Ignoring the impatient look Avery threw at her, the priestess bowed her head. The gulls cried overhead and someone groaned. Mother Ida looked up sharply. "I'd like to congratulate everyone who completed the course and the organizers would like to thank S&P for their assistance with making today as safe as possible. Now then, to the results! Third place goes to 80-33, second to 62-91, and first, by a nose, is 90-32."

FOLDING THEIR WINGS into the copper-tinged sea grass, the gulls vacated the sky. Punctuated by the rolling percussion of a hand drum, the surf thundered. Peals of laughter rang out from around the bonfire.

Lying in the grass on the knoll above the beach, Zade rested her head in Frankie's lap. "What constellation is that one?" She pointed to a milky white grouping rising to the east of Ouring Ridge.

"You would have to ask Dis." Frankie plucked a piece of grass out of Zade's hair. "I've only learned the ones he was able to show me from the Riverway."

"I think Ju's starting the drumming circle." She rolled over and sat back on her heels. "Are you done digesting yet?"

Frankie laughed. "You're crazy if you think I'm going to jump around the fire with you after that much food. Go dance if you want to. I'm going to talk to the ocean for a while."

Zade leaned in for a kiss, then stood up and dusted off her clothes. "Promise you'll find me before you leave."

"Oh no, I'm not leaving without you tonight."

On the path to the bonfire, Zade stopped as a backlit figure blocked her way.

"Is that you, Zade?" Vicky waved. "I was just coming to look for you."

Zade continued toward the fire. "What's up?"

The woman fell into step beside her. "I didn't get a chance to congratulate you properly."

"Your brother seemed to need your attention."

"*Our* brother isn't used to losing." Vicky put her hand on Zade's arm. "I'm sorry he carried on like that. He wants to apologize to you."

"It's okay, he doesn't have to."

As the two women approached the ring of firelight, Dis looked up from his place in the drum circle. He watched Vicky guide Zade away from the dancers and passed his instrument to Clink. He tapped Bone on the arm and nodded toward the parking lot.

Vicky waved. "I found her!"

Otter shouted from the tailgate of a truck where he was drinking with Avery. He tossed a can of beer to Zade and hopped down to hand one to Vicky. Avery looked away when Vicky leaned in and kissed Otter.

Zade leaned against the side of the truck and cracked open her beer. She shook the foam off her hand as Avery began staring at her.

"I'm sorry. I should've been more gracious." He shifted his gaze to look at the ground. "You won fairly."

She watched him out of the corner of her eye. "You'll beat me next year."

His laugh was strained as he jumped down next to her. "Not next year and not in all the years after. I will …"

"Bravery." Vicky put her hand on his arm.

He stiffened and then sat heavily on the tailgate.

"Oh, that reminds me. Zade, soon you'll meet our Aunt Mercy. She'll want to give you one of our silly names to be an official member of the family. For now, I think you deserve to borrow my name to celebrate the race. Tonight, you are Victory Pierce …"

"*Avert.*" Dis and Bone walked around the side of the truck. "She is Zade, and you are Victory, and you will not take her luck for your own."

319

Vicky flinched. "You scared me, popping up like that, Dis." She stepped over to Otter's side. "Tell him it's not nice to creep up on people."

"Were you trying to take Zade's luck?" Otter's voice was quiet.

"Don't be ridiculous. I was just trying to …"

"It must be very hard, growing up in your family and hearing the stories of how your relatives die. It's never from old age or even disease." Dis looked from Vicky to Avery. "On your sister's birthday, you told me your family was cursed. I assume you were referring to the Black Cake."

Vicky stepped in front of her brother. "I was just teasing Zade about our names."

"Like you did on your birthday before she ran away. Except that night you were trying to trade her your brother's name, not yours."

"We grew up being overly self-conscious about our names. That's all it is."

Dis leaned against the tailgate. "That's why Generosity preferred Gen."

"Right." Vicky squeezed Otter's arm. "Let's go back to the fire, I'm getting chilled."

"You didn't answer my question." Otter unwound her hands from his arm.

Dis watched the couple. "Gen is perhaps too simple a name for someone used to an old-fashioned one, even if she didn't care for it. That's why when she reinvented herself, she picked Jeniel."

Zade turned and stared at him. "Jeniel was their …"

"Our cousin is not a topic I want to discuss in front of my brother." Vicky's tone was icy.

"You don't want to remind him of her death or why she died. I understand. Perhaps you can tell me about the Black Cake instead. I'm curious how you planned to use Zade's luck against being selected by it."

"I have no idea what you are talking about."

"Your aunt certainly didn't have Jeniel killed. So that leaves either you or Avery."

Vicky slapped Dis. As she drew her hand back again, Avery grabbed it. "How dare you! I loved my cousin!" Vicky yanked her hand out of her brother's.

320

Dis looked at her calmly. "Your aunt loved her brother, your father, but she still maneuvered him to his death by telling Avery's mother about Zade's. That's what happens in your family, each turns on the other in fear of being stabbed in the back. That's how the curse manifests. It drives you insane and you kill each other. Your father wanted to start as many families as possible, hoping some of his children might survive."

"I will not stand here and listen to this one moment more." Vicky yanked on her brother's jacket. "We are leaving right now."

"I want to hear what he has to say." Avery looked at Dis. "I want to hear what he has to say about the Black Cake."

"I'm not certain of the dates. There was a calamity serious enough to require drastic measures for the survival of the community your ancestors belonged to. A catastrophe that motivated them to believe a human sacrifice was required to redress a transgression. Or perhaps it was an annual event to keep the sun running on its rails." Dis glanced at Bone. "Regardless, your ancestors received the mark of the sacrifice lottery in the form of a burnt piece of bread, or maybe it really was a cake. They didn't want to die, so they found a way to cheat the selection." He locked eyes with Avery. "Perhaps it was simply passing on the token, and the result was that another died in their place. Your ancestors' fear and guilt grew in proportion to their sense of relief."

Avery looked away. Dis paused briefly and then looked over at Zade. "The dread of avoiding the sacrifice became the curse, and the elation of surviving it created a fascination with magic and luck. Captain Pierce's obsession with stealing the clans' magic is rooted in the quest to escape the curse."

"I've heard enough." Vicky turned away. "Are you coming with me?" She looked at Otter.

"No, I don't think I am." He turned away and got into the cab of the truck.

She stared at her brother. "Do not challenge me on this."

Avery nodded and walked back toward the bonfire with her.

"Besides home-wrecking, what exactly did story-time accomplish, love?" Bone handed Otter a flask through the truck's open window.

Dis lay down in the bed of the truck. "Neither of them killed Jeniel. Both of them already knew about the curse and are afraid of it. They are hiding something else from one another." He propped himself up on his elbows. "I'm overlooking something vital. There's one missing piece tying everything together."

Bone got in the cab with Otter, and Zade sat down on the tailgate. "How did you find out Mercy Pierce caused her brother's death?"

"I made that part up."

She leaned back and punched him in the arm.

"Ow."

"Move over." She got in and stretched out in the truck bed, putting her head on his shoulder.

He curled his arm around her and they stared up at the night sky.

Zade broke the silence. "How are you doing with the whole Jeniel thing? You okay?"

Dis inhaled and then let his breath out slowly. "Usually I'm fine, but … I'm not sure I'm ever going to feel completely safe again." His voice was heavy with sadness.

"I know what you mean. I keep having to remind myself the Cutter's dead. I still have nightmares about being in that hole."

"They're both dead. We're alive." Dis squeezed her. "We have to learn to live with it."

She curled her head closer to his. "I promise I won't let anyone hurt you ever again."

"You shouldn't make promises you can't keep." Tapping the side of his head against hers, Dis's tone was gently chiding. "Life is about getting hurt. How we deal with the damage is what's important, 90-32."

They fell back into a comfortable silence as Otter and Bone's low-pitched conversation continued in the cab of the truck.

Zade pointed at a cluster of bright stars. "What's the name of that constellation?"

"The Big Net."

She poked him in the ribs.

"Ow, stop that." Dis slapped her hand away. "It sounds more romantic in the original language."

"Teach me how to say it, then. I need to impress a beautiful girl."

$\triangledown \nearrow \blacktriangle$

Otter sat in his swim trunks under a willow tree, watching Mo dive off the dock. He sighed and looked down at the sunlight glinting off the empty beer bottle in his hands.

Zade trotted down the garden path in a tank top and cut-offs. She snagged the bottle out of Otter's hand and replaced it with a fresh one. "You should go in." She dropped onto the grass at his feet and pressed her ice-cold bottle against his bare calf.

"Hey!" Otter swatted at her. "Maybe later. Someone has to make sure none of the drunks stay under too long."

"I can take a shift."

"You've been drinking all day." Otter shot her an amused look. "Can you even swim?"

Grinning, Zade lifted the bottle from her lips. "No, but I can float. I can trade with Bone and he can watch if you want."

"You know how to use a grill?"

"No, but …"

Otter pushed her over into the grass, stood up, took off his glasses, and started toward the river. "Scream if anyone doesn't come up after two minutes."

Zade applauded as he sprang off the end of the dock into the water. She glanced down the river, catching sight of Dis and Frankie on the other side of the garden. She grinned as they put their heads together to look at something in a garden bed.

□♏♏♋⬛

"It's best to harvest under the waxing moon." Dis pointed out a plant with the tip of his cane. "Not full though." He leaned forward to hold back a section of a wild rosebush.

Frankie peered in at the lopsided toad house and smiled up at her mentor. "Did you make that?"

"Maybe." He nodded his head toward the river. "Come on, I want to show you something." She got up and dusted her hands off on her black cut-offs.

He braced himself against the trunk of a tree and stepped onto a hidden set of weathered stairs, following them down into the river. He waited for her to join him in the thigh-deep water. "The source of the Mam is in Awyton, up in the old-growth forest in the center of the island." He turned to face up the river and skimmed his hand over the surface of the water. "Imagine it before the city was built, Frankie. Before all those pieces of brick and metal and all those chunks of glass and concrete were in place. The thick green sprawl, ever-moving and alive with the thousand clans of the three."

She stood next to him in the river, looking past the swimmers to the other shore. "It's so sad that it's gone."

He gave her his half-smile and offered her his arm. "Put your hand on my arm and close your eyes."

Dis guided her carefully under the thick tendrils of a willow, the veil of green leaves trailing over their bodies.

"We need to put our heads under before we open our eyes." He put his hand over Frankie's and lowered them both into the river.

Dis pulled her along as they swam blindly through the currents. Frankie gasped as they surfaced and she opened her eyes. The thick canopy of a ring of ancient trees allowed only a few patches of sunlight to fall on the lichen-covered standing stone at the center of the mossy glade.

Dis turned, tracing a line as he spoke. "This holy one is set on the Winter

Solstice sunset line. There were two more over on the other side of the river before the city was built. The largest stood in the garden behind St. Anna's, in the spot the statue of the Holy Mother now occupies. This one marks the mingling of the waters of the Mam with the waters of the ocean, Mammor. My father's family bought this property to protect it."

"Is it okay for me to be here?" Frankie bit her lip.

"It is where I will teach you about the magic the clans used if you still want to learn." His expression turned solemn. "If anything happens to me, you'll need to know how to protect everyone. We really are at war now."

❧☙⑨❶☙❧

Bone glanced up as a shout rang out from the river. Pushing his sunglasses up onto the top of his head, he surveyed the swimmers and then returned his attention to the grill.

Behind him on the patio, Mother Ida snored in a lounger with Stinky stretched out across her legs. The cat's ears twitched when Patty shouted out the kitchen screen door.

"Do you need me to bring more out yet, handsome?"

"If you wake the priestess, Patchy, I will not be able to protect you from her wrath."

She shoved open the screen door and carried out a platter of steaks, her green metallic dress shimmering. She smacked the seat of his trousers with a dish towel. "Don't call me that, Bone. It took me years to get everyone to stop and I will not have you making it fashionable again."

"If you insist." He grinned. "Did you get all thirty-one candles in the cake?"

"Mr. Myln and Mr. Lew are working on it." She rolled her eyes at the kitchen door, then glanced at Bone's backside. "It seems like only yesterday that you were both barely legal. I'm getting old."

"Imagine how *I* feel." Bone flipped over the grilling vegetables with a set of tongs.

325

"Babies, both of you. We should get everyone up here for a picture before they're too drunk to stand." She smiled as Zade walked up the stone path onto the patio. "Are you getting hungry or just looking for another beer?"

"Both." Zade looked over at Bone. "I thought of something I wanted to ask you, if you're not busy?" She watched Bone transfer grilled vegetables onto a plate and hand it to Patty.

"I always have time for you." Bone smiled.

Patty carried the plate over to the table and fussed with bowls and utensils before going back inside.

Zade watched the door close behind her. "If you get love from distilling the heart of life, what do you get from distilling the heart of death?"

"That's a rather morbid question for such a lovely day, Zee. Besides, it's a metaphor, not one of the birthday boy's formulaic enchantments. Why do you ask?"

"You mentioned distilling when we were talking about luck, and it got me thinking about what you said at the show. Never mind. It's a stupid idea, anyway. What did you get Dis for a present?"

Bone opened his mouth and then closed it. "If anyone asked, I was going to say socks." He turned, locking eyes with her. "Dr. Gray suggested rope from Gloria's."

She stared at him for a moment, then snorted. "No one will believe you got him socks. You're better off telling them to mind their own fucking business."

□ ♍ ♏ ♋ ■

Sweating, Avery pressed his naked body against the cool porcelain of the toilet bowl and gulped air. He shuddered and vomited, dry heaving into the bowl as blood from a fresh cut on his chest dripped onto the floor. He rolled onto his back to stare up at the sliver of sunlight coming in through the curtained window and ran his hands over the long red welts crisscrossing his thighs and upper arms.

"Our Holy Mother who delivers us from villainy, hallowed be thy heaven and hallowed be thy earth. Thy blessings come as ..." He covered his mouth and drew his legs to his chest. He trembled, his head on his knees.

The bathroom doorknob jiggled. Avery scrambled backward into the space between the toilet and tub and held his breath. Something scratched at the door. Avery stared at the door as the scratching continued, steady and rhythmic. He squeezed his eyes shut and screamed.

≈◦☾⑨❶◦≈

On the brick-lined patio behind the brownstone, Vicky put her book down, lifted her sunglasses, and squinted up at her brother's bathroom window. After a moment, she picked her book back up, then set it down again and stared sadly out at the walled-in garden.

WHEN ZADE ARRIVED AT THE PIT, most of the other couriers were congregating in the thin strip of shade down by the public bathrooms. "90-32 at the Pit, dispatch. How hot is it supposed to get today?"

"You don't want to know, 90-32."

Groaning, Zade dismounted and set her helmet on the handlebars. She spotted Otter, topless, lying on one of the granite benches next to the bubbler, using his shirt as a pillow. She scrunched her nose at him and walked over.

"How can you oven-fry yourself like that?"

"Storing up all the heat to get through the winter." He sat up and shook out his T-shirt. "I thought you were going to the night shift for the rest of the summer?"

"Frankie says she doesn't want work to interfere." She accepted the bottle he handed her. A chunk of bottle-shaped ice inside bobbed as she upended the beverage. "She pointed out we only have a month left of this heat."

Otter put his shirt back on. "It usually starts to get cool again by my birthday."

"Speaking of …" Zade touched her headset. "Dispatch, you still haven't told me what you got for Bone? I have to pick something up for him today."

Dis's voice sounded amused over the radio. "You can get him whatever you want. He likes getting presents more than the presents themselves."

"That's not helpful."

"90-32, pickup at the Pierce Hotel, main desk. Going to 15 High."

"On it." She smacked Otter on the shoulder and ran over to her bike.

▽ ↗ ◢

By her third run of the morning, Zade was drenched in sweat. She took a brick out of her bag and wedged it under her kickstand to keep the motorcycle from sinking into the hot pavement. Trotting up the steps to a private practice at 110 High Street, she flipped up her faceplate, tried the doorknob, and then rang the doorbell.

Peering into the glass, she rang the bell again, then knocked. "Dispatch, nobody's home."

"Go around to the back, 90-32. They might be in a meeting."

Grumbling under her breath, she walked down the driveway and went up the back steps of the building. The back door was ajar. She pushed it open and then halted. "Something smells nasty, Dis." She recoiled, putting her hand over her face.

"Garbage left in the heat."

The courier shook her head and went back outside. "Dead-thing-in-the-heat nasty."

"I'll call S&P."

"Give me a minute." Zade took several deep breaths, then went back into the building.

The inner office door was wide open, leading into a remodeled kitchen. Two coffee cups sat on the counter next to a white wax pastry bag. The courier held her nose as she walked into the stiflingly hot back office.

329

"Hello?" Still pinching her nose, she walked around the corner into the executive office. A dead man in a suit lay slumped behind his desk. The wall behind him was splattered with blood. Gasping, Zade turned her head away. "Is that what I think it is, Dis?"

"I'm calling it in to S&P. Go back outside."

"He might need help." Zade walked back into the office. She held her breath as she reached down. Turning him over, she covered her mouth with her other hand as she stared at the gaping wound in the man's throat.

"Go outside, 90-32. You can't help anyone in there. Hold." Dis's line clicked over.

Zade went back outside and ripped her helmet off. Lines of heat wavered up from the driveway as she stared at the weeds withering in the cracks. She walked around to the front of the house and crouched under the shade of a huge maple tree. Sweat dripped from her face onto the narrow strip of grass as the blare of sirens grew closer.

☙ ❦ ⑨ ❶ ❧

Avery sat down at the bar of the Pierce Hotel. He put his hands over his ears and clutched at the sides of his head. The bartender poured a pint of Cygnet and carried it over to him.

"Hot out there today for being on a bike, isn't it, Mr. Pierce?" She smiled as she placed a coaster in front of him and set the pint glass down on it.

Avery glanced up. His eyes were heavily bloodshot. "Single malt, neat. Please."

The bartender nodded, her gaze lingering on the raw pink marks on his wrists. "Shall I call up to Ms. Pierce and let her know you're here?"

"No. Thank you." Avery cradled the stout in his hands. "I don't want to bother her."

The woman nodded and selected one of the bottles from the top shelf. Pouring a small amount of whiskey into a cut crystal tumbler, she glanced over at her customer. "If something's troubling you, Mr. Pierce, I'd be happy to listen." She set the whiskey and a slender glass filled with spring water on the bar. "I might even be able to make a suggestion or two."

"Do you know how to get rid of ghosts?" Avery threw back the whiskey. "I bet you wish you hadn't offered to listen now." He laughed nervously, shaking his head.

"Oh, well, I wouldn't say that." Leaving the water glass, she picked up the empty tumbler and carried it over to the washbasin next to the beer taps. "The house I grew up in was haunted, so I'm a bit familiar with how it can be." She dipped the glass in the tub of blue sanitizer and swirled it before moving it to a tub of soapy hot water. "There's a hundred ways to get rid of ghosts, Mr. Pierce." She smiled reassuringly. "If they're attached to a house, it's easy enough to call in a priestess or a minister to send them off without too much effort."

"Not this kind." Avery dragged his thumb down the side of his pint glass. "It doesn't matter where I am."

"Well, then, what you want is to put water between you and them. Moving water is the best thing for that. You need to confuse them and slip away so they can't find you."

"Like the Mam?" He glanced up at her. "I've been riding over it every day for months now." He hung his head.

"A motorcycle might not do it. These things are funny like that. Have you tried taking a row boat across or walking to the other side of one of the bridges?"

Avery finished his beer. "No. Why would that be any different?"

"Like I said, Mr. Pierce, these things are funny like that. If that doesn't work, I'd suggest stopping by a little shop down near High Street. It's called the Shining Star. Someone there should be able to sort you out."

As Avery started to stand, Vicky entered the hotel lounge. Her expression hardened and she waved him toward a table.

"What is wrong with you? It's not even four." She scowled as she sat down. "Are you still upset about Gen's death?" She twisted the strand of pearls at her throat.

Avery started laughing. She looked at him in alarm as his laughter became choked sobs. Vicky got up and sat in the chair next to him. She put her arm over his shoulder and stroked his hair.

"I know you miss her. I miss her too. But this wild-boy behavior isn't helping anything." Vicky kissed the side of his head. "I'm sorry I've been distracted lately. It's just ever since ..."

"You miss Otter." Avery wiped his eyes. "I know you do."

She looked away. "That's not the issue here. You're the one having a hard time. Do you need me to take you to the Continent? I could arrange to take my vacation earlier and we could go ..."

"No. It doesn't matter where we go, it will always be like this."

"It doesn't have to be. We have Zade now."

"Leave her alone!" He pushed his sister away. "Leave her alone and leave me alone." He bolted out of the lounge.

Vicky stood up and crossed her arms as Avery rushed out into the street. Covering her eyes with one hand, she walked over and leaned heavily on the bar.

"Can I get you something, Ms. Pierce?"

"Soda water with lime, please. Thank you, Mrs. Ollen." Lowering her hand, Vicky smiled weakly. She looked up at the tin ceiling and sighed.

▽↗◢

Otter, Zade, and Mo parked their bikes in front of Bone's loft. A group of people dressed in evening attire ran from their taxi through the evening thunderstorm.

"You think it's going to be wall-to-wall celebrities in there?" She eyed the group as they passed. "We could find you a famous lady-friend."

Lightning cracked and Zade squinted up into the rain, smiling.

"No, thanks." Otter brushed past her and started up the stairs.

Inside the vestibule, the couriers unsealed their rain gear and stowed it as more guests in cocktail dresses and suits pushed by. Zade produced a flask, passed it to Otter and Mo, and then shoved open the heavy fire door that served as an entrance to Bone's home. A mirrored glitter ball spun curtains of light around the darkened loft as nearly 200 people milled around, trying to converse over the dance music.

A pair of industrial steel doors opened out onto the former loading dock. Chocked open, with tarps draped over them to create a sheltered area, they protected a small knot of guests who stood watching the thunderstorm. Lightning ruptured the night sky, and the subsequent thunder rumbled through the building.

Zade jumped as Bone dropped a hand onto her shoulder. "Sorry, I didn't mean to startle you, Zee. Is Dis with you?" Bone nodded to the other couriers.

Otter and Mo shook their heads and Bone sighed.

"We haven't seen him. I signed off early ..." Zade made a face and took a translucent blue-green object out of her pocket. "Happy birthday." She glanced up shyly as the others leaned in to look at the birthday present.

"It's beautiful." Bone cupped his hands to accept the sea glass. "Where did you find it?" He lifted it into the swirling mirrored light.

"I went back to the Landing and fished around near the culvert you found me in."

Camera flashes went off all around them as Bone wrapped his arms around her. "Thank you. I'll always cherish it."

"Was Dis supposed to be here by now?" Zade craned her neck, looking around the loft. "Hey. He's right there, Bone." She pointed to the loading dock as Dis stepped in under the tarps and shook the rain from his brimmed hat.

"He's been making me wait to see him all week. Said he was working on my present."

Otter grinned and rested his hand on Bone's shoulder. "He knows you like surprises, even if you are impatient as all hell. Here." Otter ripped open his messenger bag and handed over an album. "I hope you don't own it already. It's from all of OC. Mo helped me find it." Otter half-turned, pointing his thumb at Mo. "Bikes, bands, and brethren."

Mo smiled nervously and bit his lip as Bone inspected the rare find.

Bone whistled as he slid the record half out of its paper sleeve. "I'm impressed and touched by your efforts. Thank you." Grinning, he reached out to shake Mo's hand. "There's food and beer over in the kitchen. Please help yourselves. I'm going to go show this to Dis."

Zade grinned, watching Bone work his way through the crowd. "Should we stick around to watch or do you want to go get a beer?" She glanced at Otter and Mo as they watched Bone approach his lover.

"Beer. Knowing Dis, he's going to enjoy making him wait all night." Otter dropped his arm around Mo's neck. "See? I told you he would like it."

"Do you think I should have given him my band's tape?" Mo chewed on his lower lip. "I didn't want to seem too pushy."

"I think you are right to wait. I'll remind you when he's out drinking with us." Otter patted his shoulder. "Come on, let's go raid his kitchen."

Standing next to the metal doors, Dis watched his couriers push their way through a group of socialites. He smiled as Zade shoved a party guest who was blocking her and Otter made calming gestures.

"Can I at least have a kiss?" Leaning in, Bone held the album behind his back. He watched Dis straighten his cuffs under the sleeves of his black suit jacket.

Dis's mouth twisted into a half-smile. "Unless you would like me to create a spectacle, you can have your present once your adoring public goes home and we have privacy." Raising his lips to brush Bone's cheek, he spoke softly into the other man's ear. "It's your birthday, so I'll let you to decide."

Furrowing his brow, Bone scrunched up his mouth and glared. "We could leave now …"

A loud boom and a bright white flash cut him off. Shrieks sounded from around the two men as a trio of guests rushed into the loft to avoid the torrential downpour blowing in under the tarps.

Bone narrowed his eyes at Dis. "You called up this shipwrecker to trap us here, I presume?"

"I'm not the one who designed a home without any separate rooms." Dis took a step forward, folding his trench coat over his arm. "You haven't offered me a drink yet."

"You're a wicked, cruel man, my love." Bone dropped his arm around Dis's shoulders and turned to stare at the revelers filling his home. "There is the bedroom or the bathroom …"

Dis walked through the crowd, toward the kitchen. "You are not going to get out of having to choose that easily."

□ ♍ ♏ ♋ ■

A blast of wind buffeted his back as Avery stumbled across the Riverway Bridge. Huddling inside his soaked leather jacket, he staggered into one of the steel girders. He shielded his eyes from the glare of headlights, causing the fresh blood on his hand to streak.

Lightning sliced over the bridge and was reflected from the waters of the Mam beneath it. The thunder vibrated through the metal grating under his feet. Grasping the hand railing, Avery stared into the blackness below. Arching his spine, he threw his head back and screamed. He stared up as the rain fell through the blue lights high up on the bridge supports. "Leave us the fuck alone!" He stumbled, falling to his knees.

The wind whined, twisting through the metal and setting the support cables thrumming. The scent of ozone grew stronger and the sky above burst into crackling brilliance. A roar pummeled the deck of the bridge as lightning struck the eastern support tower, rending the air. The shrilling of car horns blurred into the screech of tires as two cars collided head-on. Another car skidded across the opposite lane, flipped over, and careened against the support beam directly in front of Avery.

The driver crashed through the windshield, spraying him with fragments of safety glass. He watched the blood gush from her crumpled face. She shuddered on the hood of the car and then lay still. A thin wail rushed out of Avery's mouth as rain collected in the coils of the dead woman's long brown hair.

A man threw open the door of his pickup truck and ran toward the wreckage. He glanced at the woman's body and then turned to Avery. "Hey, are you hurt bad? Don't move, okay? S&P will be on their way." He squeezed around the front of the car and approached Avery with his hands out. "Just stay still, okay? Help's coming." Avery shrank from him. "Hey, you should just stay still!"

"Don't touch me!" Getting to his feet, Avery shook off the other man's hands. "I've touched it! Don't you understand?"

"Just sit down, son. S&P will be here any minute to take care of you. It's a miracle you escaped."

"It was just a warning." Avery squeezed his eyes shut. "It can kill us any time it wants." He turned away and ran back toward the city, disappearing into the rain.

∾◌ৎ⑨𝟎◌∾

In the back of a taxi, Frankie wrapped her long braids into a simple crown around her head. She took a hairpin from between her teeth and anchored the end of one braid, then repeated the process for the other. The taxi bounced as it drove through a pothole, splashing water against the passenger window. The vehicle turned into an alley between two warehouses.

"It should be right ..."

"I see it. Thanks." The young woman driving shot her passenger a look in the rearview mirror. "Ten fifty."

Frankie took out a twenty and held it over the seat. "Keep the change."

"Are you sure?" The driver looked startled as her passenger got out.

"I appreciate you taking me all the way out here." She opened her umbrella and shut the car door.

She ran up the steps to the loft in her four-inch heels and hip-checked the door open. Shaking the water off her umbrella, she closed it and straightened the hem of her dress over her thighs. Taking a deep breath, she pushed open the door and walked into the party.

Heads turned as she set the umbrella down and settled her purse over her shoulder. The reflecting lights of the mirror ball danced over her bare arms, and her hips swayed gracefully as she navigated through the crowd.

Standing near the kitchen island, Dis leaned in to murmur to Otter. "This should be interesting." He held up a hand to Frankie in greeting.

Otter grinned as Frankie walked up behind Zade and tapped her on the shoulder. Zade turned around and her beer slipped out of her hand. Otter bent down and picked up the half-full beer as his friend swallowed rapidly.

"You look …" Zade swallowed again and Frankie laughed.

"Stunning is clearly the word you are looking for, Zee." Bone extended his hand to Frankie. "Thank you for coming to my party."

"Thank you for inviting me." She smiled as she shook his hand. "Happy birthday."

Otter poked Frankie in the side of her arm. "You made her shy." They both turned to grin at Zade. Otter handed her back her beer.

"Gorgeous." Zade took Frankie's hand.

༄ৎఠ⑨⑩ৎৎ

Inside the office at 110 High Street, Fuller sat at the kitchen table and pulled a pair of blue paper shoe covers off her loafers. The detective dropped the booties on the floor and peeled off her disposable gloves. Bray walked in the back door and set a cup of coffee in front of his partner before taking the seat opposite.

"Thanks." Fuller dropped the gloves on the floor.

"Did you find what you were looking for?" Bray lifted the plastic lid off his cup and sipped its contents.

"Bet's team in the lab will validate my hunch by morning." Blowing the air out of her cheeks, Fuller leaned back. "Which, by the way, means we're not going to get any sleep, as the Chief will be calling us into the Tank immediately thereafter. The body count has almost reached the magic fucking number, and that means the gore hounds will be here any minute now. If they're not already."

Bray grimaced. "You think this was Mthdys and his friends?"

Fuller stared at Bray and then chuckled as she took the lid off her coffee. "Hell no. There's enough sense in that boy to keep him clear of anything to do with the Pierce family. Now, especially. Besides, I told you before he's not the type to be our killer."

"We've only established the connection to the family." Bray glanced into the office at the other end of the kitchen. "If it's not him, then ..."

"In the morning, Bet will confirm that it's the same left-to-right angle on that knife wound we've found on all the recent victims' necks. As for the Pierce family, they've given many people plenty of reasons." Gulping a mouthful of her black coffee, Fuller winced. "We don't get paid enough to deal with this mess. By anyone. But if we don't take care of this now, the Perlustrate will. Which, by the way, means the end of how we do business in this town. Remember, dogs don't make deals."

A uniformed officer in rain gear stepped into the kitchen and took off his cap. "Sorry to interrupt, detectives, but we've got another one."

Bray smiled over the back of his chair at the man. "It's all right, sergeant. We weren't planning on getting any sleep tonight anyway."

□ ♍ ♏ ♋ ■

Otter handed a cup of beer to Dis and then dropped onto the couch next to him. "He's holding out longer than I thought he could." Otter nodded at their host, who was showing the DJ the album he had received.

"He won't make it another hour." Dis watched his lover. "I give him another half-hour, tops."

The main section of the living room had been converted into a dance floor. Frankie rested her head against the side of Zade's as the two women danced slowly together. Dancers nearby smiled as the couple stopped to kiss.

Zade cupped Frankie's face, inhaled, and started to speak, but was interrupted when the overhead lights brightened and the music faded out. The crowd of dancers looked around in confusion until Bone got up on a coffee table shoved up against the DJ's equipment.

Holding a microphone, he waited until the room quieted. "I'd like to thank you all for coming out to celebrate my birthday with me." His guests started to applaud and whistle. He waved his free hand until the noise quieted. "I have been lucky to receive many amazing and kind gifts this evening. Not the least of which is your company."

Otter poked Dis's knee. "You called it on the nose." Otter stood up and took the cup Dis handed him.

Bone glanced over at them and jumped off the coffee table onto the floor. He slipped the mike cord around his back and walked over to Dis. "Now I would like to ask my boyfriend if he wouldn't mind handing over the birthday present he's been teasing me with all week." Bone laughed as the crowd hooted. He flopped down on the couch next to Dis, holding out the mike.

"I have you all as my witnesses that he's asked for this in public." Dis glanced around as the guests hollered and clapped.

Zade dropped her arm from around Frankie's shoulders. "Do it!"

"Shut up, 90-32." Dis reached into his suit jacket and nodded to the DJ. With an amused smile, the woman set the needle down and a sweet, soft song played through the loft.

"It has three parts. This is the first." Dis offered Bone a blue velvet gift box. "You can open it now."

Bone snapped open the box and then held his breath as he looked down. The articulated scales of the silver fish shimmered as Bone lifted the pendant out of the box.

"It took longer than I thought to hammer the silver and I had a hard time finding the garnets." Dis smiled as the other man admired the gift. "If you don't mind, I need you to stand up with me for the other two parts." He handed the mike to Otter.

Laughing, Bone shook his head in surprise as Dis stood up and took both of his hands in his own. Otter held the mike between the two men, winking at Bone.

"You'll want to listen carefully, as you'll need to modify it for the third part." Dis took a deep breath and Otter patted him reassuringly on the back with his free hand.

Dis's eyes sparkled as began to speak. "I love you, I have always loved you, and I will always love you. I vow this in the presence of the Eldest. Hear me, Amrwyn, Mammor, and Ournok: I claim this man, Drake Bonnrey, and no other, if he will have me."

The assembled guests were absolutely still. Bone's eyes glittered. The sound of the lovers' breathing whispered over the mike.

"There's a question awaiting your answer. Now that we have summoned their attention, it's not wise to leave the Eldest waiting. Will you claim me as your own and no other?" Dis gave Bone a wicked smile.

"I love you, I have always loved you, and I will always love you." Bone blinked back tears, awestruck. "I vow this in the presence of the Eldest. Hear me, Amrwyn, Mammor, and Ournok: I claim this man, Dulyn Mthdys, and no other, if he will have me." As soon as he had spoken, Bone hauled Dis into his arms, kissing him.

Unbridled applause and cheers of delight erupted from the party guests. Camera flashes sparkled around the couple. Bone dragged Dis down onto the couch. The overhead lights were switched off as the DJ switched back to dance music.

"You're such a softie, baby." Frankie wiped a tear from Zade's cheek. Zade gave her a wide grin.

"I know it's probably anticlimactic after that, but …" Biting her lip, Zade cocked her head and took Frankie's hands. "Would you be my girlfriend?"

Otter watched Frankie throw her arms around Zade's neck, jump up and wrap her legs around Zade's waist. Shaking his head, he turned and walked out under the tarps. He sighed, emptied his cup, and stared out at the line of warehouses barely visible in the heavy rain.

"AMEN." FRANKIE POKED ZADE as she started to nod off at the end of Mother Ida's sermon.

Zade opened her eyes as the assembly rose to its feet around them. "Amen."

Otter's grin faltered as he caught sight of Vicky looking at him from the back of the cathedral.

"I'll catch up to you." Otter stepped out of the line of churchgoers heading outside.

"Good luck." Zade nodded to him and walked out.

Otter walked over to the tiered rack of devotional candles. "Did you come with Avery to get his bike blessed for the Autumn Equinox?"

Looking down, Vicky shook her head. "No, he won't ..." She turned away, bringing her hand up to her mouth.

Otter stepped closer. "What's wrong?"

"He's been staying out all night and won't come to church with me. Sometimes he doesn't come home for days, and when he does, he just yells at me to leave him alone." She shook her head and looked up at the stone arches.

"He's scaring me, Will." She looked at him, her lips trembling. "I'm sorry if I'm bothering you, but I don't know what else to do. I miss you."

"I miss you too." Otter glanced away from her face to the candles. "I want to help you, but your family's way of dealing with things is seriously fucked up. You can't go around stealing people's luck."

Vicky's eyes flashed and she turned away. "You don't know what it's like, always wondering if this is it, if this is your last day, how you're going to die."

A sad smile played over his lips. "I've been thinking that every day for ten years, pretty much."

"It's not the same." She sniffed and faced him. "You can quit being a courier any time you want. I can't quit being a Pierce."

He sighed and nodded. "Have you considered other ways of getting luck, besides stealing it?"

She shook her head. "I wouldn't know how. I've never studied the occult like Gen did."

"That's probably for the best." Otter's expression hardened. "Look, just stop trying to steal Zade's luck, and I'll talk to Dis and see if there's another way to improve yours and your brother's."

"Thank you." Her eyes welled up as she looked at him. "Even if you don't want me around, I just wanted you to know how much you mean to me."

Otter pulled her into his arms. "How about if we light a candle for your brother and then go watch Mother Ida do her thing?" He kissed the top of her head.

"I'd like that." She clasped her hands behind his back. "You aren't still mad at me, are you?"

"I'm not mad. I just need you to tell me the truth. We can talk about it after dinner, if you'd like to get some with me later?"

"If you wanted to come over I could cook you dinner? Unless you want to go be with your friends?"

Otter wiped the tears off her face and shook his head. "No, I think I'd like to stay in with you tonight, if you're up for it."

▽↗◢

The next morning, Zade turned her bike's engine off and eyed the gray railings in the hospital parking garage's stairwell. She walked sedately down the stairs to the ground floor and approached the building's main entrance.

Taking the elevator to the third floor, she yawned and checked her reflection in the mirrored wall. Stepping out, she nodded at one of the nurses in the hallway, walked along the beige carpet to a door, and knocked.

"Good morning, Zade. You're right on time. Can I offer you a cup of tea?" The doctor smiled and waved her into the office.

"Good morning, Dr. Gray. Yes, please." Zade tried to stifle another yawn and shot the woman an apologetic smile. She walked over to the couch, dropped her bag and helmet, and sat down.

Zade fidgeted and wedged her fingers under her thighs. Gray set a cup of tea on the coffee table in front of her patient and gave her a reassuring smile. The therapist settled into her chair opposite and blew on the surface of her tea.

"You seem tired. Have you been sleeping?" Gray sipped her beverage.

"Not really. Even going to the nests doesn't help much anymore."

The doctor slid her cup onto the table. "Because of the nightmares?"

Zade nodded and started to lift her hand up to her mouth, only to shove it back under her leg.

"Has anything changed in the dream since you told me about it? The Roadkill King, the Crying Woman, and the Watcher?"

"It changed last night." Zade cradled her cup of tea. "Jeniel had Dis again." She placed the cup back on the table and brought her hand back up to her face.

"Can you remember it well enough to tell me?" Gray watched Zade shove her hand under her leg again.

"I knew the King, the Woman, and the Watcher were there, but it was in Jeniel's apartment, not the subway station. Dis was on the bed and she was sitting next to him with her hand …" Zade dropped her head. "She had her hand *in* his chest." She locked eyes with her therapist. "He was dead."

"What happened next?"

Zade pushed herself into the couch cushions. "We were all dead."

"Who was dead, Zade?"

"Everyone. Everyone in the world was dead. Then the King turned and said something to me. I couldn't see his face, though."

Gray leaned forward. "What did he say?"

Zade shrugged. "The Black Cake is white hot, like stars falling in the river."

"Does that mean anything to you?"

"Not really. It sounds like a line from one of Boon's songs, mashed up with job stuff."

"I see. And how are things with your girlfriend? Have you been able to spend an entire night with her?"

Zade shook her head and poked at the mug. "No, I have to go to a nest if I want to get any sleep now."

"Have you thought about my suggestion?" Gray leaned back in her chair.

"I can't take her down there." Zade made a face at the doctor. "It would freak her out."

"Is there anyone you could bring?"

"Otter wouldn't be able to deal with it." She stared at the floor.

Gray folded her hands over her knee and tilted her head. "Otter isn't the only person you trust."

"Bone's too loud."

"So you need a trustworthy person who can be quiet and respects your secrets."

"I can't ask him."

"Whom can't you ask, and why?"

"Dis." Zade laced her fingers through the handle of her cup.

"Would he freak out too?"

Zade shook her head. "Dis? You know him, he would love it down there."

Gray smiled. "I think he would, too. I also think he would love to have you share it with him." She watched her patient curl back into the couch cushions, her head almost touching her knees. "Do you know why you are afraid right now? Can you tell me why you can't ask him?"

She shook her head.

"I'm going to give you an assignment and I'd like you to try to do it today if you can."

Zade unfolded and sat up. "Like homework?"

Gray smiled. "Yes, it's an art therapy assignment. Do you have time today?"

"I have to stop in and see Kitty upstairs, but then I'm free."

"Good. Here's what I'd like you to do. Purchase a few art supplies. Nothing expensive, just whatever appeals to you. It can be markers or paint, whatever you wish. Can you do that?"

"Yeah."

"Good. Once you have everything, go to a space where you feel relaxed and comfortable. It should be a place where you can be creative. I want you to think of Dis and create a picture of the first thing that comes to mind. Can you do that for me today?"

"Do you want me to bring it in next week?"

"No, this is just for you. You don't need to show me or anyone else. How does that sound?"

"A little silly."

"Silly is good. Let yourself be playful about it. Try not to judge or edit yourself. Remember, no one ever has to see it. It can be your secret." The therapist watched her patient for a moment. "Now, I want you to tell me about the people you've mentioned seeing while you're awake. Do they talk to you? Do you hear their voices telling you to do things?"

"No, they just look at me, but I know they want something."

"Do you know what it is that they want?"

"No."

"Do you know anything else about them?"

"They're dead."

"Do you think there might be a connection between not getting enough sleep and seeing them?"

Zade wrapped her arms under her knees. "Maybe."

"Last week I asked you to think about asking Frankie to watch over you while you took something to help you sleep. Did you think about it for me?"

"Yes." She pressed her face into her knees.

"Could you try that for me?"

Zade shook her head.

Gray leaned forward and placed the tips of her fingers on the back of Zade's hand. "Okay. This week I want you to think about asking Dis. Can you do that for me?"

Zade nodded.

"Are you up for us revisiting our conversation about your anxiety regarding leaving the city? I thought we could talk about your habit of riding out to the city limits when you're having an anxiety reaction."

She sighed and sat up. "Sure."

▽↗◢

Zade knocked on the hospital room door and waited.

"Come in." Kitty turned her head as Zade entered her room. "Oh, shitkittens, it's you."

"Were you expecting someone else?" Zade navigated carefully around the traction equipment suspending Kitty's legs and arm.

"I thought you might be Mat. He's the only other person who ever fucking knocks." Kitty grinned. "I know. It's crazy. He's been stopping in to read to me every day."

"Stalker crazy, or surprisingly thoughtful crazy?"

"Thoughtful crazy." Kitty smiled shyly. "He's been less of a fuckhead since he stopped drinking."

Zade smiled. "Are you doing okay otherwise?"

346

"I'm bored, sober, and not getting laid. After I get out of here I have to go to fucking physical therapy for months before I can ride again. It fucking sucks."

Zade pulled a six-pack of beer out of her messenger bag and set it on the bedside table. "I can only alleviate one of your problems." She cracked open a can and passed it over.

"How the fuck did you know I was dying for one?"

"Bone smuggled them in for me when I was laid up."

The two couriers drank in silence. Zade went over to the window and stared down at the parking garage. A group of teenagers were running on the garage roof in the pouring rain. She watched them clear the side of the building and land on the adjacent rooftop.

"Do you ever think about your last ride?" Kitty asked.

"You mean the last one ever?"

"Yeah."

"All the time." Zade turned back to face her friend. "Every ride, every lay, and every drink. I wonder if there will be a next one or if this is it." She walked over to knock her can against Kitty's. "If this is my last drink, I'm glad it's with you, trash mouth."

□ ♍ ♏ ♋ ■

The rain was letting up by the time Zade arrived at the hardware store. She brought her helmet in and strolled the aisles with a basket over her arm. In the automotive section, she compared the colors of several cans of spray paint and carried her selection to the register.

"You redoing your motorcycle to match your hair?" The sales clerk snapped her gum and rang up Zade's purchases. "I saw you when you parked out front."

"No way. I wouldn't do that to a bike."

She rode Cygnet east to an unmarked side street and turned off in the warehouse section. Leaving the bike parked by the Quayside Market, Zade slung her stuffed messenger bag over her shoulder. Crossing over Grant Street, she wedged herself through a narrow opening alongside a rundown apartment building and began climbing the train trestle. After hauling herself up onto the maintenance walkway above the tracks, she headed back toward the city.

Pigeons and gulls scattered as she trespassed along the rusted metal and climbed the ladder. She fixed her gaze on the Old Port Storage building on the other side of the metal girder. Cinching her bag's shoulder and waist straps tight, she stepped off the walkway and out onto the beam.

She shuffled through a puddle, using a bracing joint for support, and inched her hands along until she made it to the far end. Stretching her arm out, Zade gripped a rail above her head, shifted her weight to her arms, and swung her legs back and forth until she managed to get her boot heels over the edge of the roof. With a jerk, she hauled herself onto the roof of Old Port Storage.

Unclipping her waist belt, Zade pulled her bag around to her hip, took out a can of spray paint, and shook it. The pigeons on the roof fluttered away, alighting on the base of the billboard. Zade stared at the backside of the board and popped off the cap of the first can of paint.

She worked steadily for an hour, stopping only to change cans. She emptied the last of the blue and admired the white star floating on a blue heart. Then she uncapped the black paint. Frowning, Zade started a circling motion around the design.

▽↗◢

"Dispatch, 90-32 here. The inbound tunnel is crawling." Zade shifted into neutral and dropped her boot heels to the pavement.

"Sit tight, 90-32. Hold."

The courier stretched and yawned as the car in front of her moved two inches further into the tunnel.

"There's a tow truck on the way. S&P are clearing the route."

"Are you coming out to the show after the parade tonight, dispatch?" The courier walked her bike forward.

"I don't celebrate Victory Day."

"I know, but Bone put you on the guest list for the after-show at the Pierce."

"He's told me. Several times."

The driver in front of her honked impotently. "Did he talk you into Grava for the honeymoon?"

"Undecided at the moment."

"You should come out tonight. I'm meeting Vicky and Avery for the Parade. Otter mentioned that he's asked you to talk to them about how to make luck."

"I have an errand scheduled after work."

"Oh, come on, when was the last time you saw your future husband's band play?"

"When you get up tomorrow afternoon, you should come with me to the pound. They're having their autumn adoption day."

The courier snorted. "They give you kickbacks on every kitten you find a home for?"

"A cat would help you with your nightmares."

"That the kind of horseshit you spout down at the Shining Star?" She shifted into first as the traffic started to move again.

"I'll come out tonight if you promise to come with me to the pound tomorrow."

"Deal." Zade's eyes tracked to the side of her lane, where an unidentifiable mound of roadkill lay pressed up against the white tiles of the tunnel. "Can I ask you something serious?"

"You know you can." Static cracked through his reply.

Zade bit her lip as she moved another twenty feet into Fisher Tunnel.

"What happens to all the animals killed every day here?" She paused. "I mean the roadkill. All that blood spilled on the pavement every day. Is it all wasted or does it get used by something?"

"Depends on who you ask, though I'd say blood and death are always sacred." His signal broke up as Zade moved further under the river.

□ ♍ ♏ ♋ ■

"Thank you for staying late on a holiday, Dr. Fasu." Nash walked the elderly woman toward the elevator and reached out to push the call button. "The Chairwoman appreciates the extra effort your team has been putting into this project."

"It's rather a strange one, isn't it, Oliver? I do enjoy the puzzle of it, of course." The tiny woman peered over her glasses at him. "There are so few examples of Ornish curses in the literature."

"I can't imagine it would be much of a challenge for you, Doctor." Nash smiled graciously.

"Flatterer." Fasu beamed as she stepped onto the elevator. "You should take some time off and go find some mischief. Life's too short. Don't work yourself to death, Oliver."

"Goodnight." Nash's congenial smile wilted as the elevator door shut.

Closing his eyes, he exhaled and turned on his heel. He walked over to the windows, toying with his cufflinks as he passed the reflecting pool. Humming, he tugged his suit jacket back into place as he watched spectators file out of the Underground and begin to line up in Victory Square. A lost balloon floated past and he watched the blue dot drift out of the square. *"Someday I'll float away."* He hummed quietly to himself.

The elevator chimed. Nash furrowed his brow and started toward it. As the doors opened, he came to an abrupt halt and screamed.

WALKING INTO THE DISPATCHERS' BOOTH, Frankie jerked her head toward the stairs. "Avery is asking for you outside."

Dis started collecting his gear. "Thank you for starting early tonight."

"Not a problem." She sat down, set the headset on, and spun around to face the queues. "Tell Bone and Zade I'll be there in time for the encore."

As Dis came down the stairs, he spotted Avery waiting on the sidewalk outside. Avery stared up at the white symbols painted along the edge of the garage doors.

"Good evening." Dis stepped out of the garage.

"I found it." Avery's gaze moved from the symbols to Dis. His hair was uncombed and his racing jacket hung open over a stained t-shirt.

Settling his bag, Dis watched him carefully. "I'm not sure what you are referring to."

"The Black Cake. I found it in the museum, in my aunt's office. You need to come with me." He stared at Dis desperately.

"Perhaps you should discuss it with your sisters first." Dis narrowed his eyes. "They're expecting you at the Parade starting point soon."

Avery shook his head. "My aunt's left town for the weekend. We need to go while she's gone. You need to come now." His voice dropped to a whisper. "I remember what you said about it."

"If you don't want to go to the parade, go home and get some rest. You look like hell."

Avery grabbed Dis by the arm. "You need to come with me. *Now.*"

Looking down at the man's hand on his arm, Dis shook his head. "I've got an errand to run."

"This is your only chance to destroy it! It has to be now, while she's gone!"

Dis put his hand on Avery's arm and spoke in a soothing tone. "It can wait until your sisters are with us."

"*You made me pick it up!*" The courier trembled. "After it killed Boon, you made me pick it up. Ever since then, I've been seeing things." He spun away. "I don't want either of them near it. I need you to help me get rid of it. Please."

Glancing up at the strip of sky visible over the street, Dis paused. After a moment, he gestured for Avery to lead the way.

□ ♍ ♏ ♋ ■

Zade trilled and hooted as the performance troupe marched down the Straight. Blue silks swirled as a trio of acrobats tumbled behind the musicians. Zade waved and laughed as she flung handfuls of candy from her position on the scarlet and gold float.

Children shouted and held their hands out over the barricades as their parents hoisted them aloft. Cameras flashed and the S&P cruisers at the intersection of Carlisle and Pierce bathed the crowd in red and blue light as the ship rolled by. In her plumes and sequins, Vicky waved regally from behind the ship's wheel. She smiled at Zade. "Next year, you'll have to wear this."

352

Zade laughed. "Hell no."

"Family tradition."

"Make Avery do it." Zade moved over to the treasure chests displayed near the center mast. She scooped a fresh batch of foil-wrapped candy into her bowl.

"He was supposed to this year." Vicky frowned.

Returning to her post, Zade grinned. "Can't blame him for leaving you holding the bag. That thing is ridiculous."

When the parade ended, the floats lined up and the crews descended to join the rest of the performers on the marble floor of Victory Square. Vicky kept her costume on. The others changed and stowed away their blue silks and nautical costumes.

Zade shied away from Vicky's outstretched hand as she tried to smear makeup on Zade's face.

"It washes right off. Or did you want one of the animal masks?"

Zade hesitated. "I don't want either. It doesn't feel right."

"As you wish." Vicky gave her an odd look as she passed the cosmetics over to another performer.

The drummers began pounding out a solid rhythm and the dancers returned, waving scarlet silks. The square filled with people shouting and dancing. A single lane was held open to the monument by the floats' crews. Zade walked alongside Vicky on the red carpet as their crew rolled out ahead of them.

"Avery should be here for this." Vicky surveyed the crowd.

"For what?" Zade looked away from the seething bodies pressed against the line.

A dancer wearing a deer mask tried to grab Zade and a man in a fox mask yanked on her coat. The ship's crew formed a protective circle around her and Vicky. Behind them, the lines collapsed and the crowd surged forward.

"Get the Captain's hat!" A man lunged at them.

Growling as the chant was taken up by the crowd, Vicky grabbed Zade's arm and walked more quickly toward the monument. "Where is he?"

When they reached the white marble steps a performer in red appeared and bowed to Vicky. The woman presented her with a sword wrapped in a garland of flowers. The rest of the crew blocked the passage to the monument as Vicky accepted the weapon.

She turned to Zade. "Follow me." Carrying the sword upright, Vicky ascended the rest of the steps to the seat. "Do you remember last year's parade?"

"I was delivering a package." Zade's expression was troubled. She looked out over the square at the thousands of people screaming and shouting over the drums and pipes.

"It was the anniversary of our mothers' death, mine and Avery's, and of our father's, your father, Honesty Pierce. They died right here." She looked at Zade. "It was at this moment last year that you appeared and took possession of the Seat of Victory. Avery says you shoved him." She offered the sword to her sister. "Next year you will have to be the Captain properly, but for now it's enough for you to sit and hold the sword."

"No." Zade shook her head. "You're wearing the coat and hat."

Laughing, Victory Pierce saluted the square with the sword. Sitting down, she smiled as the crowd's applause roared up to her.

□ ♍ ♏ ♋ ■

In the bathroom nearest to the Pierce Hotel's Grand Ballroom, Zade stared into the mirror, water dripping off her hair and face. People jostled around her on their way to and from the stalls. A pair of performers washed their faces at a sink while another reapplied her makeup. A courier in a blue and yellow jacket slammed open a stall door. Zade flinched.

Drying her hands, Zade left the bathroom and made her way back into the ballroom. Easing her way through the audience, she found Otter by the stage, watching the first band.

He draped his arm over her shoulder. "Thought you drowned in there."

"Where'd Vicky go?"

"One of the staff brought her a message." Her friend shook his head.

"Avery's fighting with their aunt in her office and Vicky went over to break it up. She should be back soon; said she was going to drag him back here. I'm going to the bar, what are you drinking?"

"Nothing yet. My stomach's bothering me."

"You'll be here?"

"Yeah. Keep an eye out for Dis, he said he would come tonight."

Otter pushed his way to the bar and Zade closed her eyes. Strobing colors washed over the dance floor. She stood unmoving, dancers' bodies brushing against her. The opening band's vocalist teetered on the brink of the stage, staring up into the red spotlight.

Opening her eyes, Zade took a step back and bumped into someone. Seeing the mask over her shoulder, she stumbled and fell. When she looked up she was surrounded by a circle of dancers wearing animal masks.

"Are you okay?" A woman pushed up her seal mask and offered her hand.

"Sorry." Zade took it. "Thanks."

"We all go down." The woman smiled. "The important thing is to get back up."

Zade pushed her way off the dance floor. The bathroom door swung shut behind her, cutting off the music. She raced into an open stall and vomited. Tears streamed down her cheeks. She closed the seat, covered her mouth with both hands, and sobbed quietly. "Go away, please, just leave me alone."

When she stood up, Zade wiped her face and flushed the toilet. At the sink, she washed her hands and face and then rinsed her mouth. Inhaling, she looked at her reflection and then exhaled slowly.

As she walked across the hotel lobby, she dug her coat check ticket out and waited in line to present it. The man at the counter smiled as he took it and came back, holding out her bag.

"Where's my leather?" Zade took the bag from him.

He frowned. "This was the only item on the hanger."

"It is a black leather jacket with the numbers nine, zero, three, and two on the back."

The hotel employee went back and looked again. When he returned, he held his empty hands up. "I'm sorry, you will have to come back at the end of the night when the coat check closes."

Zade hung her head. "What's the point of checking it if you're going to lose it on me?"

"I'm sorry. Please come back later." The man indicated the line behind her.

"*Coat check fucking lost my leather!*" Tears sprang into her eyes.

Ju stepped out of line and took off his jacket. "Here, Zade. I'm sure Boon would rather you have it." He gently pushed Boon's blue and yellow jacket into her hands. "Take it. Please."

Staggering back with it in her hands, Zade ran out of the lobby.

"Are you okay, miss?" The doorwoman stepped over to her side. "Would you like a cab?"

"They're all dead." Zade trembled. "Everyone in the whole fucking world's dead."

The woman tried to put her hand on Zade's shoulder but she brushed it off and stumbled away. She started running up Pierce Street. When the Victory Monument came into sight, she sprinted the rest of the way and collapsed halfway up the steps. Curling her arms over her face, Zade started crying into Boon's jacket.

"Is everything okay, miss?" The stranger's voice was warm. "Do you require assistance?"

Dragging the back of her hand over her eyes, Zade looked up. A man in a black suit wearing a dog mask was looking at her from the steps near the Seat of Victory. She recoiled.

The furry muzzle of the mask shifted as the man spoke. "Oh, please pardon me for not removing my mask. It's glued on, you see." The man opened his mouth in an exaggerated manner. The jaw of the black dog opened, displaying white fangs on either side of his mouth. "It seemed like a good idea at the time." He gave her a strange, doubled smile and came down the stairs. "Now then, what seems to be the matter?"

"You wouldn't believe me."

He lowered himself onto the step above her.

"Could be, or it might be that I will. Either way, you have my complete attention and sympathy."

Sniffling, she glanced at him from under her eyelashes. "My friend died."

"They do that, sometimes. I was just leaving a token of remembrance for mine." The man looked over his shoulder at a bundle of white and blue flowers resting at the base of the Seat of Victory. "This is the anniversary of when it happened, you see." He removed the blue square of cloth from the breast of his suit jacket and gave it to her.

"I'm sorry for your loss." Zade wiped her face with a corner of the silk handkerchief.

"Oh, don't be. That's the problem, isn't it, feeling sorry that you've been left on your own? The world isn't falling apart, it's just your corner of it that is. That's the way of things, and it always has been, and always will be." He wrapped his hands around his knee and nodded toward Victory Square. "Did you know a meadow once thrived here? Only 300 years ago, the nights were filled with the perfume of blossoms in the spring and the glow of fireflies courting in the summer. Right where we're sitting, owls used to hunt mice among the autumn leaves and the winter rain. Before the street lamps and the marble, people from the islands to the south rowed their coracles into what was then a natural harbor for yearly festivals at this place." He lightly smacked his hands on the marble step. "Imagine it. The coals of bonfires smoldering in the grass, sparks flying up to join the stars while you listen to songs about love and grief. Relics from a thousand years of annual celebrations still work their way down into the train tunnels." He glanced over. "It's true."

Zade shook her head. "You remind me of one of my friends."

"One of the live ones, I hope?"

She twisted the blue silk. "I'm afraid he might not be for much longer."

Her companion sighed. "I sometimes wonder if they're on the other side, wondering when you're going to catch up. That you're the one who's tarrying too long on this shore, and they're missing you just as badly as you miss them."

"I've never thought of it that way."

The man looked over at the Pierce Tower. "There are some that make a hell out of their lives. Nothing that comes after could rival it, in stupidity or suffering. They let their fear of death get in the way of living. But not you, no. Not you." He rolled his head back toward Zade, and his brown eyes were full of gentle sadness. "You're a motorcycle courier, aren't you?" With a languid motion, he indicated the livery jacket across her knees. "You must be quite familiar with not letting fear get in the way of things."

Staring at him for a minute, she nodded. "What happened to the meadow that was here?" She looked over at the Underground station.

He tilted his head and gazed up at the sky. "The tall ships sailed south and black smoke rose from the smaller islands of the Archipelago for a week. The first wooden hotel, which was built from oaks felled in the meadow, stood right there." He indicated the Pierce Hotel, behind the monument. "Six months after the islands burned, it was set alight in an act of revenge. The fire ran wild, destroying everything on this side of the river, including the meadow, though it was all churned to mud by then anyway. When the oaks were cut … well, that was the end of that particular world."

Zade cocked her head. "Is this supposed to cheer me up?"

"If it was, I've probably made a right mess of it." His laugh echoed over the square. "No, my hope was to illustrate that sometimes our feelings are quite correct, but they only apply to us as we are at this very moment. When our world ends, another begins." Placing both hands on his knees, the man stood up. "I'm afraid that I've stayed longer than I intended. There's an important event at the museum tonight, you see." He offered her his hand.

Zade waved his hand away and climbed to her feet. He curled his fingers slowly, dropping his arm to his side. A breeze snaked across the square. Leaves and pieces of litter from the parade tumbled against the white marble steps below.

"Ah well, allow me to help you put your coat on. The wind is picking up."

Taking the jacket from her, he held it open while she slid her arms through. "Will you go and find your friends now? The living ones, that is." Settling the jacket across her shoulders, the man patted Zade on the back.

"Yeah." She looked at the Pierce Tower. "I should see what's holding them up." Folding the damp handkerchief, she turned and gave it back to him. "Thanks."

"Oh, well, thank you. Your company made my task much more pleasant than I had anticipated." There was the faint sound of metallic jingling as the man slipped the cloth into the front pocket of his trousers. "I hope you find your friends without too much trouble." Looking into her eyes, he gave her his sad, doggish smile again. "Have a good evening, young lady."

"You too." Zade pulled the strap of her messenger bag up over her head and started down the monument steps. Increasing in force, the wind nudged her as she walked across the square.

Taking her thumb recorder out, she hefted it between her hands and glanced up at the building. A determined expression settled across her features as she approached the entrance to the Pierce Tower. The guard opened the door as she came up the steps. "Delivery for the top floor. Chairwoman Pierce's office."

He went over to the long desk and lifted the phone receiver. "Receptionist is done for the night. I'll call up for you."

Zade half-shut her eyes as the man listened to the line ring.

"The lines are busy." The guard looked at her thoughtfully. "I can't leave my post to bring you up. Can you take my print for it?"

"It's a white hot." Zade shook her head. "VIP print only."

The guard tugged up his utility belt. "Mr. Nash usually comes down, but if he's on the phone …" He took out a set of keys and started over to the elevator. "I have to key the floor in, but it will bring you right back down." He leaned into the elevator, turned the access key, and tapped the button for the fifty-eighth floor. He waved the courier in and released the doors behind her.

As the elevator ascended, Zade leaned against the wall, staring at her reflection in the mirrored interior. "Fuck." The arrival chime sounded. She turned and the doors opened. The thumb recorder slipped out of her grip, clattering to the floor.

The smashed glass of a broken display case littered the glossy black marble floor in front of the elevator. Scanning the dark museum, she walked around the fountain toward the center of the exhibit. A body lying half-submerged in the reflecting pool appeared in her line of sight. Mechanically, she reached down and rolled the man over.

Nash's head fell unnaturally to the side as she turned him, his throat slashed to the bone. Grunting, Zade let go, and the man's corpse slipped back into the bloody water. Wiping her hands on her thighs, she glanced over her shoulder. She edged backward to the elevator, then walked quickly into the corridor.

Light spilled into the hallway from the open doorway of Mercy Pierce's office. Zade crept down the corridor and crossed the office's threshold. She looked around the empty room, her gaze lingering on a dense red stain on the carpet. She backed out of the room and slumped against the wall. She looked to her left at the stairwell at the end of the corridor, her ragged breath echoing in the hushed corridor as the wind whispered around the propped-open roof door at the top of the stairs. The light across from her flickered and went out. She continued to stare at the steps leading up to the door until the light next to her head popped and went dark, leaving only the red light emanating from the stairwell.

"*Fuck!*" In the half-light, she slid down and knocked the back of her head against the wall. She covered her face with her hands. Drifting in from the roof, the windblown scent of cut grass filled the hallway. "Why won't you leave me alone?"

Lowering her arms, Zade stared at the sleeves of Boon's yellow and blue jacket. She pressed the heels of her palms into her eye sockets. "Fuck." She pushed herself onto her feet and started toward the stairs.

The metal fire door at the top of the stairs was held ajar with a paperweight in the shape of a miniature sailing ship. The wind whispered around its edges, blowing pink petals over the improvised doorstop's brass hull. Zade pushed the door open and stepped out onto the roof.

The wind tugged her forward through the rooftop garden, showering petals and cut grass onto the path around her.

Near the edge of the building, lamplight winked between the pillars of a small structure. Silhouettes moved on raised platform within it. As Zade walked through the garden, the sigh of the wind through the tall grasses transformed into the sound of sobbing.

Zade stopped as a beam of light began to move toward her.

"Welcome." Jeniel stepped forward, holding an aged lantern and wearing a white fur coat, its front panels saturated with fresh blood. "I laid a spell of summoning to draw you here." Jeniel smiled. "With your arrival, all of the family is present and we can begin the final ritual."

Zade stared at her. "Where's Dis?"

"He's here with us." The long coat swirled around Jeniel's bare feet as she turned back to the platform. "Enter our family's temple to the Black Cake and see for yourself."

Zade followed Jeniel through the garden. The sound of crying intensified. Climbing the temple stairs, her boots pushed into something yielding but heavy.

Jeniel followed the edge of the stage and cut around to the large marble altar in the center. Unwrapping a silver and sable seal skin, she revealed Dis, bound, gagged, and strapped to the top of the marble block. Dis bucked against the stone, his blind left eye staring in Zade's direction. Thick straps of newly tanned skin pinned him to the surface, leaving only his throat and chest exposed.

Jeniel raised the lantern. A cascade of animal pelts spilled from the altar, creating a mosaic of sable, black, gray, and white fur. Zade looked down in horror at the scintillating furs gathered around her feet. She stepped back.

Jeniel addressed the shadows to her right. "Now do you believe in me, Vicky?"

The beam of light swung around, revealing Avery dressed in his hand-painted leather jacket, his eyes distant and haunted. The light highlighted the fresh cuts on his bare chest. Huddled at his feet, his sister wore Zade's missing black leather jacket over her blue cocktail dress. The chiffon fabric shone wetly in the lamplight as Vicky sobbed, cradling Mercy's lifeless body in her arms. The chairwoman's eyes stared vacantly at her niece, her head lolling grotesquely.

"I believe." Avery's voice was hollow.

"He has witnessed my power many times." Jeniel's smile widened as she turned back to Zade. "Since I returned from the dead, I've been keeping him company." She hooked the lantern into a stand and lifted something off the platform. "Now I have taken control of the Black Cake."

Taking a step forward, Zade bent down and caressed the pelts pressing against her shins. Her eyes followed the straps over Dis's body, pausing as she examined the slots where the leather looped through the stone altar. With a frown, she dropped her eyes to the sleeves of Boon's jacket and then back down at the furs. She stood upright slowly, her expression thoughtful.

"No one in our family ever has to die because of the curse again. Not even you." Jeniel raised the red delivery packet in the air. "Though I did doubt you were a Pierce until you escaped the Cutter." She set the packet on Dis's chest. "Then it became clear how you were able to take him from me."

Jeniel picked up a bundle from the side of the altar and unwrapped it, removing an ancient piece of tanned brown leather. She walked around the perimeter of the altar toward Zade. "For generations, our family's magic lay hidden in stories. We grew up thinking that the key to escaping the curse was in taking skins."

As Jeniel gently unfolded the object, Avery made a low keening noise in his throat. Vicky glanced up at him and pulled Zade's leather jacket closed across her chest. Zade recoiled as Jeniel unfurled a weathered human skin.

She took measured steps toward Zade. "The furs at our feet are trophies our ancestors took from every kind of animal on this island. Each is imbued with everything the Ornish believed to be sacred. The thousand clans had the ability to change from human to animal and back again. In addition to all of the islands in the Archipelago, our revered ancestor claimed all but the very last trace of that magic." She raised the human skin, brushing it against her lips as she stepped beside Zade.

"Until recently I thought, like Vicky does, the power was only in a name or in a skin. Only after I tried to help Dis change did I begin to understand it was a riddle. The skins are symbols of the Ornish magic, like our names. Symbols of our power to conquer everything we desire, even death. The spirits are the gatekeepers, and if we listen, truly listen, they'll teach us what we must do, directly." Jeniel raised the skin up and paused as Zade backed away from her. "Vicky thought trading names would give her your luck, but it is by taking one of our names that you will share in ours. Don't you see? You *must* become a Pierce. That's why you are here." Jeniel smiled reassuringly as the coppery smell of blood billowed from her matted fur coat. "Only then can we finish this."

Zade glanced at Dis and hesitated. She took a step forward and Jeniel set the scalp on the top of Zade's head. Thin strands of black hair still clung to the leather as the ancient length of flayed skin trailed down Zade's back, the lowest strips falling to rest behind her calves.

"Lost daughter of Honesty Pierce, I bestow on you the greatest name of our family, Sincerity. You are now and forever more Sincerity Pierce." Jeniel kissed Zade on both cheeks. "I forgive you for taking him from me, Sin. It is, after all, our family's nature."

Zade reached out, clamping her right hand around Jeniel's throat. She laid her thumb across the other woman's windpipe and began to squeeze. "I won't let you hurt him."

"Avery is too afraid of the dead to kill anyone, but he knows what will happen if we don't finish the ritual." Jeniel's voice was choked with the pressure Zade applied to her throat. "I've told him to jump off the roof with Vicky if anything happens to me. You will do it, won't you, baby?"

Avery yanked Vicky to her feet, sending their aunt's body tumbling down the steps of the dais.

Vicky struggled in his grip. "Stop it! Stop listening to her!"

Zade dropped her hand.

Jeniel glared and walked around to the far side of the altar, rubbing her neck. "If you attack me, Avery and Vicky will die. Avery was picked to be this generation's sacrifice, but I will save him." She lifted a curved knife from the corner of the altar. "I will remove our family's curse from you as well, Sin. It tries to bleed you to death every month." Looking at Zade, Jeniel stroked Dis's chest. He shuddered under her touch. "Vicky was so excited to find you. You were the way out of losing her dear brother. You could die instead, just like your father died to save my mother. You should all be thanking me. I died to learn how to save all of us. No one in the family has to die for the Black Cake anymore."

"Liar." Zade took the tanned skin off her head and lowered it onto the pile of furs. Wading into the soft, warm weight, she moved closer to the altar. "You never died. The Cutter was yours, and now that he's dead, you're the one killing people. S&P lied about your death because your mother paid them to. She tried to protect you and now you've murdered her."

"*I died in that room!*" Trembling, Jeniel pointed the tip of the knife at Zade and then lowered it. "She had people kidnap me off the street. She tried to lock me up! Her own child! She doesn't even know how to feed ..." Jeniel bared her teeth as Zade took another step toward the altar. "Avery." Blood welled up where Jeniel set the tip of the blade against Dis's throat.

Avery stepped up onto the ledge at the edge of the building, hauling Vicky up with him. She cried out and then froze, staring down the side of the building to Trellis Street below.

"Stop using Avery." Zade watched Jeniel. "You don't have to kill anyone else."

"I alone am willing to make the sacrifice demanded. Only I have the strength to give the Black Cake to the person most precious to me. Not even Vicky is willing to do that much." Jeniel leaned over her captive. "Dis will deliver the Black Cake back to the land of the dead and into the hands of Amrwyn himself." She locked eyes with Zade. "He will join his ancestors and be reborn whole.

Surely you want to see him saved? I know what you feel for him."

"He doesn't need to be saved by you or anyone else. And you don't fucking know shit about how I feel."

"You think you can do better? I will give the Black Cake to the last magician of the clans. As the inheritor of all their magic, he has the finest luck of all. All doors will be opened for him by his ancestors. What do you have to offer the dead? Nothing. You have nothing, you know nothing, and you can do nothing." Jeniel looked at her with contempt.

"Liar." Zade stretched her fingers, digging into the seal pelt bunched against her knees. "I can do something. The Roadkill King told me." She looked into Dis's blind eye. "I just don't want to do it."

The wind whipped through the garden, muting the other sounds on the rooftop. Zade suddenly sat down on the stacked pelts. She untied her boots, kicked them off, and then removed her socks. The pile shifted and she sank down further with each movement. She stepped up onto its slippery surface and walked barefoot to the altar, the fur pressing between her toes.

Jeniel brandished the blade at her. "If you touch him, I will tell Avery to jump. Only I …"

"Liar." Zade stared up at the stars visible over the garden, then looked over at Avery. "This is all horseshit. She's a murderer, a rapist, and a fucking bad liar. The dead don't speak to her and she doesn't see them. If she did, she couldn't do this. They don't come to her. Not like they come to us."

"They speak to *me!*" Jeniel grew livid. "I …"

"You've touched it too." Avery's eyes focused on Zade's as Jeniel stared slack-jawed between them.

Zade nodded. "They do want a life from us. But it has to be ours to give. We can't keep stealing them from other people."

Making strangled noises, Dis arched against the straps. His eyes were pleading as the gag muffled his cries.

"Any time I'm about to do something stupid, I hear your voice telling me not to do it." Zade put her hands on either side of his head and gazed down into her friend's eyes. "If you said not to, I might not be able to … but I've been practicing this route for a while now, dispatch." She touched a fingertip to the buckle on his gag. "It's white hot, like stars falling in the river."

Tears streamed out of the corners of Dis's eyes as he looked up at her. The leather straps binding him creaked as he strained against the surface of the altar.

"It's okay. I'll make it on time." Leaning down, Zade rested her cheek against his. "I figured it out. I make my luck by distilling the heart of death." Standing up, she brushed her lips against his forehead. "Please, Dulyn, don't be mad."

She locked eyes with Avery. "When I return the Black Cake …" She set her messenger bag down next to the altar, then stripped off Boon's leather. "None of you will have any reason to kill anymore. It will be over." Reaching out, she grasped the corner of the red packet in Jeniel's hand. Meeting no resistance, she slid it free of the other woman's fingers. Zade's feet sank into the furs as she walked in the direction of the rooftop's edge. "Can you keep everyone out of my way, Avery?"

With a curt nod, he restrained Vicky against his chest. His eyes blazed as he silently watched his other sister walk away.

Vicky struggled against his grip. "You don't have to do this!"

Zade tossed Boon's yellow and blue jacket aside.

"Tell Otter and Frankie …" She climbed up onto the four-foot-high metal ledge of the Pierce Tower. "… I'm sorry I had to leave early."

"No!" Vicky thrashed in Avery's grip. "This is crazy! Zade! There's no reason to do this!"

"Don't let him come after me." She jerked her chin toward Dis.

Sagging against the altar, Jeniel stared at her in awe. "You're actually going to do it. Why?"

"I made a promise." Zade walked away, heading along the ledge away from the temple. She kept walking until she reached the northeast corner of the building. In the garden behind her, the wind spun up tiny whirlwinds on the gravel pathways. Far below on Trellis, the nighttime traffic continued along in red and white streams. The clouds began to clear and break apart over the city.

The courier looked down the east side of the building at the Pierce Hotel. Behind the fluted marble columns, electric lights shone from a hundred windows and balconies. The flags of the Archipelago and the Continent snapped and danced above the brass-framed entranceway.

As she turned to the northwest, Zade's gaze swept over the Mam River to the lights of the Point. Taking another step, she looked down the length of the building. The clouds shifted and the black outline of Ouring Ridge was visible behind the Hinterlands against a smattering of stars.

She began to run, her bare feet lightly striking the metal surface of the ledge. Her arms pumped, the red packet swinging at her side. Nearing the temple, Zade averted her eyes from the altar and increased her speed. Reaching the northwest corner, she swung to the left, turning toward the distant harbor. With her eyes fixed on the southern constellations above the city skyline, Zade began to sprint, pumping her legs and arms. "Ribbons and curls, everything for the girls." She clutched the packet to her chest. Her feet pushed off the edge and she launched herself into the night sky above Victory Square.

□ ♍ ♏ ♋ ■

On stage, Bone's right hand blurred over his electric guitar's strings. His music rumbled out of the speakers and over the writhing audience. Behind him, the rest of the band redoubled their efforts to match the intensity of his playing. His head fell back as the song peaked to a crescendo.

□ ♍ ♏ ♋ ■

In the dispatcher booth, Frankie removed a note from her bag. As she read it, she smiled and put her fingers to her lips. Rotating her chair to look at a screen, she bumped into a glass of water. It spilled over her fingers, causing the inked lines of the note to feather.

Kiarna Boyd

□ ♍ ♏ ♋ ■

Otter brought a beer over to Ju. He laughed as his roommate yelled in his ear. "To Boon and Zade!" He paused with the glass on his lips, staring at something on the stage.

❧ ☙ ⑨ ❶ ❧

Vicky removed Dis's gag. His long, anguished cry echoed through the garden. He struggled against the altar, his limbs contorting from the strain. Shoving the rest of the furs off him, she fumbled at the grisly straps.

Avery gripped the ledge and stared at the river. Jeniel lifted her mother from the steps of the temple. The sound of sirens filled the streets below and she began to wail.

UNDER A WINTERY SKY, Dis locked the door to the Shining Star and walked to Market Square Underground, then got on a train to Victory Square. When it arrived at the station, he exited and walked down Appleton Lane to the Pit.

Descending the granite steps, Dis opened his bag and took out a bottle of Black Dog. He poured out the contents around the candles and flowers at the makeshift shrine. He sat on a bench drinking a second bottle and smiled at the collection of notes and cards plastered to the inactive fountain. The cart workers waved to him as they closed down their carts for the night.

He stood up, took out a silver coin, flipped it, and started walking. Repeating the process, he walked until it brought him back to the Underground entrance of Victory Station. He got on the first train that pulled up to the outbound platform and rode it, flipping the coin until he was directed to get off at Market Station.

When Dis arrived at the Dovecot Bakery, a miniature whirlwind spun up. It rustled through the flowers and notes tacked to the railing of the outdoor patio while he sat and drank a cup of coffee. Watching the wind leaf through the faded flowers left around the shrine, he finished his beverage and took out the coin.

Looking at the offerings fluttering on the patio, he put it away.

He followed the meandering breeze down High Street Extension toward the harbor. The sun sank beneath the downtown skyline as he walked to the edge of the warehouse district. The leaves and trash settled into the street as the wind dispersed in front of Mimi's. The pink neon sign flickered on and Dis went inside. He sat at the bar, ordered a bowl of soup, and ate in the company of the restaurant's calico cat.

After he finished, he stepped out of the restaurant and examined the darkening sky. The sound of rats squeaking led him into an alley where he found a spray-painted tag on the bricks. Outside the restaurant's back door, he examined the narrow patch of sky again. He piled crates under the fire escape ladder and stowed his telescoping cane. Keeping his weight on his right leg, he climbed between the shadow of the warehouses. A cold drizzle of rain started. He paused, peered up at the landings above, set his jaw, and resumed climbing.

He hauled his upper body over the rooftop, swinging his right leg up and over onto the wet surface. He walked across the tarred surface to the western side of the building and stepped up onto the ledge. Fat raindrops splattered against the bricks at his feet and the wind buffeted his legs. A truck horn blared, followed by the sound of distant shouting.

Dis swayed, the cold winter rain dripping from his hair. Closing his eyes, he turned his face up into the rainfall. Rumbling along the tracks, a northbound train made the turn for the tunnel beneath midtown. The wind shrieked through the metal girders, slamming through the trestle to snatch at his coat.

Opening his eyes, he brought his head down as the headlight of the engine struck the rooftop of Old Port Storage on the opposite side of the trestle. As the train swept by, a patch of graffiti on a billboard blazed blue and white in a ring of black. The wind whipping up from the tracks forced him to step back onto the roof.

Dis stared across the darkened tracks at the billboard's silhouette. He swung his bag around, took out his journal, flipped to a blank page, and began sketching. Finishing a ragged black circle around the symbol, he grabbed a creased piece of paper from his bag's inner pocket. Unfolding the large square of paper, his expression changed as he compared the crumpled sheet to the page in his journal. Looking up from the images, he stared across the trestle. Tipping his head back, the magician laughed into the rain.

Star River City

They told me you were trouble
full of whiskey and pain
so I ordered a double
and rode in the rain

They told me you were cursed
full of decadence and shame
so I dove headfirst
a moth to the flame

They told me you were wrong
full of drunks and insane
so I wrote you a song
and caught the last train

I told them you were blessed
full of bright lights and fame
so I shunned the rest
and asked for your name

I never dreamed I'd be your lover
filled with sorrow and the sea
so I'll never recover
and I'll never be free

Chorus:

Clouds kiss the sky and the heavens shiver
Your lips burn cold
Like stars falling in the river

www.ingramcontent.com/pod-product-compliance
Lightning Source LLC
Chambersburg PA
CBHW020258030726
47499CB00001B/253